Find out more about the author and upcoming books online at
www.authordylanhearn.wordpress.com or @hearndylan.

Cover Design by Design for Writers designforwriters.com

GENESIS REDUX

Dylan S Hearn

To Evan and George,
for the laughs, love and cuddles. You both make me
the happiest dad alive.

Prologue

Death of a clone

THE SCARRED MAN grabbed hold of her grandmother's face and slapped it, hard. Stephanie wanted to turn away but it was impossible. She had no choice but to watch the man abuse the woman who'd raised her.

A large, red welt appeared on her grandmother's porcelain cheek, the skin Stephanie remembered being soft as silk as she'd nuzzled into it as a child.

"Can you see him, Stephanie? He hates you, hates your family and he'll do anything to hurt them."

Stephanie tried to ignore the voice. She knew it wanted her to react and she fought against it, but she was unable to stop the anger rising inside her as the camera picked out the leering face of her grandmother's tormentor.

The man pulled out a knife. Oh, God, Stephanie thought, not the knife again. She raged at her own impotence, at what they were forcing her to watch and the way her feelings were being manipulated. Yet her body remained motionless, her face impassive. Only her heart rate, her brain activity and her increased adrenal levels gave her feelings away, all recorded by the remorseless machines at her side.

The man stepped towards her grandmother, then turned and faced the camera. "Where shall I cut first?"

He smiled, the scar on his right cheek crinkling into the shape of a question mark, and at that moment Stephanie would have smashed that face if she could. She ached to tear into the man, to throw herself at him and make him stop, to keep him from hurting the woman she loved. At that moment Stephanie hated the man more than she'd hated anyone or anything in her life.

"Okay, I think we have the reaction we need. You can turn the simulation off now."

The image in front of her eyes faded, to be replaced by the familiar cracked and mildewed ceiling. Once more, the only sound Stephanie heard was the hiss-click of her respirator.

There was a tug at her temple as something was pulled from her head. Despite everything, she cherished the contact. It was a sensation, something denied to the rest of her body. Only her face and neck registered any sense of touch, her arms, legs and torso were as good as useless, the result of a long-healed stab wound to the neck. For Stephanie, the slightest contact was bliss, confirming that she wasn't an observer, a dead spirit trapped in a room, but very much alive. And it was life, in as much as she was a living, breathing creature, but in other ways it was just bare existence.

Each day for as long as she could remember, Stephanie woke—the opening and closing of her eyelids being the only part of her body under her control—and had food pumped into her stomach through a tube, before being tortured by brutal images, over and over, as her tormentors monitored how she reacted.

At first it was a short, white man who terrorised the people she most loved, many, like her grandmother, long dead. She'd watched that man do horrible things, inflict pain beyond imagination on his helpless victims until she couldn't look at his face without hatred boiling inside, even though she knew in the back of her mind what she was seeing was impossible, an illusion. Then a little while ago the short man disappeared, to be replaced by the Latin man with a scar across his right cheek. Despite all she'd seen since, she hadn't hated this man as much as she had her first tormentor—until today.

Stephanie felt a bubbling in her throat, and a rattle shook the tube in her mouth. A shadow fell over her. She looked up, fearing the worst, but it wasn't the short man, or the Latin man, but a woman with kind eyes.

The woman had a frown on her face as she checked Stephanie's mouth. She turned away from where Stephanie lay. "Her chest infection has flared up again. If we don't move her somewhere warmer it will only get worse."

"She stays here." It was a man's voice, the same voice that goaded her into hatred as footage played out on her datalenses.

"How am I meant to keep her alive in these conditions?"

"She dying anyway, isn't she?"

"That's not the point."

It's very much the point, Stephanie thought. She welcomed the bubbling in her throat if it meant release from the hell in which she lived. Come on in mildew, or bacteria, or whatever the hell was causing her lungs to clog. Hurry up. Give me freedom.

Stephanie felt warmth on her forehead. It was a gentle touch, so compassionate that she could have burst into tears, if tears had been possible. These moments were a special type of torture, much worse than the horrors she was forced to re-live. It showed somebody cared, that love remained in the world and hadn't died the moment Randall Jones thrust the knife into her.

"Her readings are all over the place. I want her moved upstairs," the woman said.

"That's not going to happen."

"Then there's nothing more I can do. If she dies before you get your data, you only have yourself to blame."

Stephanie listened for a response but instead heard the scrape of a door opening.

"What is it?" the man asked.

"You're needed back in control, sir. Something's happened." It was another male voice, higher pitched, possibly younger.

"Can't it wait? The transiessence data we've captured needs to be processed and fed into the system."

"I … I don't think there's much point, sir."

The woman bent over her as the young man spoke and Stephanie heard her take a sharp intake of breath at his words, barely noticeable if the woman hadn't been centimetres from her face. For a moment all was quiet, except the ever-present hiss-click of her respirator. The woman looked down at Stephanie but there was an unnatural stillness to her features as her attention appeared elsewhere.

"Tell me," the older man said.

"They've killed the clone."

"Who's they?"

"We don't know."

"Shit!" There was a loud crash as something metallic fell to the floor. "It will take weeks, months even, before we can generate another clone and get it into place."

"There won't be another clone, sir. Whatever they used to kill the clone somehow transmitted a virus within its transiessence data. It's completely scrambled the synthetic brain. There's nothing left. They killed it, sir."

Above where Stephanie lay, the slightest smile played over the kind-faced woman's lips before her features smoothed out, expressionless once more. The woman prised open Stephanie's eyelid and shone a light into her eye, continuing her examination as if nothing had happened.

"Fucking hell!" the older man said. "Well, what are you waiting for? Let's go."

There were footsteps, then the sound of a door closing.

hiss-click … hiss-click

Stephanie stared at the ceiling wishing she could smile. She didn't understand what had happened but it had caused a problem and that was a good thing. Anything that hurt the bastards was a good thing.

The woman had turned away as the men left but now her attention was back on Stephanie. Her face was blank but her eyes shone. She leant forward to examine a nasal tube. "We bloody did it." It was the faintest whisper.

Stephanie closed her eyes—one … two … three—then opened them. The corners of the woman's mouth twitched. "Well done. Stay with us. We'll get you out of here soon." Her breath tickled Stephanie's cheek. The sensation was intoxicating.

The woman leant further over and Stephanie felt her eyelids

being forced open. She shone a light directly into Stephanie's eyes, blinding her. Stephanie tried to blink but the woman's fingers held her eyelids firm. In one quick movement the woman removed the datalense that had been transmitting the horrible images of torture from Stephanie's eye and replaced it with another, before doing the same with her other eye. "These are yours," she whispered, then moved out of sight.

The sound of the woman's footsteps slowly drifted away. Stephanie looked up at the ceiling, processing what had just happened. What the woman said gave her no comfort. It was too late. She didn't want help. She didn't want to escape. Why would she want to go back to the real world? What sort of life would she have? She would be just as trapped there as she was here, now. She wouldn't have a life, she'd just exist, watching the world move by without her. It would be a new form of torture, in some ways worse than what these people had put her through. There was only one form of escape that would put an end to her ordeal. She was better off dead.

PART 1

CHAPTER ONE

King of the Scrambles

O'DRISCOLL HEADED DOWN the brightly lit corridor. They'd taken his shoes so his bare feet slapped against the concrete floor. He counted in his head, five … four … three … he was two metres away from the door when it buzzed open. An enormous, heavily armed man stood the other side, shaking his head.

"Back you go, Mr O'Driscoll."

Breeze-block walls continued on behind the man for a further ten metres until they reached another doorway. O'Driscoll remembered coming through it on the way in, a weapon pressing at his back.

He smiled, rubbing the week-old stubble on his face. Two metres. It was closer than the last attempt. Either the guards were becoming complacent or they were getting used to his hourly ritual.

The others were still in the common room when he walked back. The Investigator, Nico Tandelli, sat by the table staring into space, a limp sandwich held in his hand. Scabs covered his knuckles, half-healed injuries from when he'd punched the door a few days earlier. The old man they'd met at the Re-Life facility, Josh Denham, sat on a chair in the corner, humming to himself. He glanced up as O'Driscoll walked through.

"Why do you keep doing that?" Josh asked.

"Passes the time."

"Someone will always be there."

Maybe, O'Driscoll thought, but you don't know unless you check. "Been in this situation before, old man?"

Josh shook his head.

"Then I suggest you shut the fuck up."

The sandwich dropped from Nico's hand. There was a delay before the Investigator's eyes tracked down to his empty fingers, as if noticing for the first time that something had changed. With infinite slowness the man's hand moved toward where the sandwich lay, the sleeve of his shirt slipping up to show mottled bruising, purple a few days ago but now a faded yellow and brown. The idiot had panicked, refusing to stay calm when captured. If the Investigator had kept his composure they might all have a bit more freedom by now. It had taken five soldiers to sedate the man, including the big bastard guarding the door.

It had been a long journey from the Re-Life facility to where they were now held. They'd been in the pod for hours, not stopping once for a break, eventually arriving at what looked like a few old industrial buildings. It was night when they'd reached the destination. O'Driscoll couldn't tell where they were, his vision shot from flashlights shone in his face, but he knew they were near the coast as he'd heard the crash of waves against rock.

Nico had made a bolt for it as soon as the doors to the pod peeled back. He didn't get far. That's when he'd received his second set of bruises to match the ones he'd got when initially captured. The guards hadn't been rough, obeying a barked command from the woman in charge not to harm the Investigator as he struggled to get away, screaming for them to let him find his wife and children.

O'Driscoll made his way to the table, picked up a bowl and ladled thick stew into it from a large pot. He took a couple of bread rolls and pulled up a chair next to Tandelli. O'Driscoll had spent days trying to persuade the Investigator that there was no sense in fighting the people here. They were unarmed and outnumbered, but at the same time they were being treated well. The best thing to do was to watch and learn. Understand the routines and form a plan.

He pulled apart a roll, dipped it into his stew and took a bite. It was delicious, a reminder of the old country he'd visited as a child.

He could almost imagine being back in the green rolling countryside of Ireland instead of this windowless room, all white breeze-block walls and synthetic lighting. And the rumble. It was impossible to ignore the rumble, as regular as clockwork.

O'Driscoll looked at Josh and gestured to the pot. "It's really good. You should try some."

The old man got up and made his way to the other side of the table. Out of the three of them, he appeared to have accepted his fate. The long days of nothing to do and isolation from the datasphere didn't appear to bother him. In fact, as soon as he'd realised he wasn't going to be hurt the old man had opened up, as if relieving himself of a long-held burden.

Josh picked up a bowl. "You never said what you did for a living."

O'Driscoll swallowed what was in his mouth. "I'm a businessman."

"Huh."

O'Driscoll turned at the noise to see Nico looking in his direction. So you're still in there somewhere, he thought, fighting from behind the haze of drugs.

"A businessman? Really? What was a businessman doing breaking into the Re-Life facility?"

"I was helping out my friend." O'Driscoll gestured toward Nico with his bread.

"That's a little … unusual isn't it?"

"You've no idea." O'Driscoll dipped the last chunk into his bowl, placed it in his mouth, then picked up a spoon. "Why'd you make those clones?"

"They're not clones. They're adaptations." Josh looked up from his food. "Clones are direct replicas. These are adapted, improved."

"In your opinion," O'Driscoll growled.

The old man paled. "They asked if it was possible to take a basic personality and improve its performance. I thought I was creating test specimens—we did the same years ago when we first looked into cloning. I had no idea what they were doing. If I'd known they were killing the original person and replacing them with my experiments I'd have …"

"Stopped?"

O'Driscoll watched Josh glance away. No, you wouldn't have stopped, would you? Not for the first time O'Driscoll wanted to beat some sense into the man. The thought of somebody taking the very essence out of a person, changing it, then putting it into a cloned body—without their knowledge—revolted him. It was worse than murder, it was an abomination.

"She … was … friend."

They both turned to face Nico. The muscles in his jaw flexed, his face scarlet from effort.

"I didn't know," the old man said simply.

O'Driscoll placed his hand on Nico's arm. "Leave him be. There's nothing we can do for Stephanie now."

A loud buzz echoed down the corridor and O'Driscoll heard the door swing open. He turned, expecting to see the enormous guard, but instead found himself on the receiving end of a sharp gaze from the Commander who'd captured them.

The woman pulled up a chair at the end of the table and sat. Two armed guards stood at the far end of the room, weapons lowered but standing in such a way it was clear they were ready to react if needed.

"How's your food?"

"I've had worse," O'Driscoll replied. He felt Nico shaking beside him. On the other side of the table, Josh appeared to shrink into his chair.

"Sorry it's taken so long to get here," the Commander said. "I would have arrived earlier but things have been a little hectic since we rescued you from the Re-Life facility."

O'Driscoll smiled. "But we're now free to go?"

"Fran … ?" The word ripped from Nico's throat.

The Commander's features softened. "I'm sorry, Investigator, we're still looking. We went to the safe house you mentioned but by the time we arrived, they were gone."

Nico slumped back. "No …"

"It's not what you think," the Commander continued. "The house was in good order when we got there, dishes done, beds made and so on. Our guess is they left rather than were taken."

"Let … me … out. Find … them."

"I can't do that, Investigator. You know too much and if captured you'll give us all up to keep your family safe. We've people hunting for them, our very best. If anyone can find them, they can."

"Then let me go instead." O'Driscoll said. "I've got contacts in areas where your type aren't welcome."

She shook her head. "That's not possible, Mr O'Driscoll. You're dead, at least as far as everyone's concerned. Your body was dragged out of the Thames a few days back."

"What?"

"It was for your own protection. The search for you has been intensive. It was the only way to throw those looking for you off the scent."

"By 'those', you mean Global Governance."

A look of irritation crossed the Commander's face. "They might bear the name but these people are no more Global Governance than you are a legitimate businessman."

Josh looked up. "But you said—"

"Shut it." O'Driscoll glared at Josh until the old man shrank back into his chair, then turned his eyes back to the Commander. "So what now? Are you planning to keep us here forever?"

"That depends on whether we can trust you or not," she replied.

"Trust us? You kidnapped us from the Re-Life facility—"

"Saved you. If you'd stayed longer you would have been captured and killed."

"—dragged us to god knows where, beat my friend black and blue—"

"We were restraining him. If he hadn't struggled so hard …"

"—drugged him and then kept us in this glorified cellar to rot."

The Commander folded her arms. "You've been well treated and well fed. We're not your enemy, Mr O'Driscoll. As I said, we've been a little busy. We had to check you out, understand whose side you're all on."

O'Driscoll banged his fist on the table. "Side? I haven't a fucking clue what you're going on about." He gestured towards the old man.

"I can't speak for him but the Investigator and I are on our own side, and against anybody trying to harm us."

"You can't sit this out, Mr O'Driscoll. This isn't about you, or him," she pointed to Nico, "… or even him," she gestured towards Josh. "This is about the type of world you want to live in."

O'Driscoll leaned back in his chair. "So this is it, is it? The big sell. Well, excuse me if I take no notice. I've had it up to here with people like you talking about high ideals and the common good. But it's never you whose life ends up ruined by the decisions of others, is it?"

"You haven't the first clue about my life." The Commander looked down at the table, her hands clenched together in front of her. Her eyes tightened and for the first time O'Driscoll realised just how old the woman really was.

"You'll understand if I don't have much sympathy," O'Driscoll said.

"I'm not after your sympathy," the Commander said, getting up from her chair, "and I didn't come here to argue with you. I came to collect you. There's somebody you need to see."

"What, so they can justify your actions?"

"No, so you can really understand what you're involved in."

The Commander walked over to Nico, pulled a metal object out of her pocket and placed it against his neck. For a moment his muscles tightened, pulling one side of his face into a rictus grin, then the Commander pulled her hand away and Nico's head slumped forward. "You're to come too. The drug I've given you will alleviate the effects of the sedative. Can I trust you not to cause a problem?"

O'Driscoll watched as Nico first moved his head from side to side, then nodded.

"Good, then if you'd like to follow me?"

O'Driscoll stood. Beside him, Nico placed his hands on the table and eased himself to his feet.

"What about me?"

The woman turned to Josh. "No, not you. You've a lot to answer for. I suggest you start thinking through exactly what you've done over the past few years. Somebody will be back shortly to ask you questions and he'll expect answers."

The last thing O'Driscoll saw as he followed the woman out of the room was the old man, spilling stew down his front as he ate with shaking hands.

CHAPTER TWO

Indigo

THE NORMALLY SEDATE virtual chamber of the Governing Council was in turmoil. Indigo looked around the digital amphitheatre, the ancient Roman design at odds with the myriad of fantastical avatars moving in either shock or excitement, depending on what side of the debate they supported. Only two avatars remained motionless, the saker falcon of the young prince and the one she couldn't see, her own moebius band at the speaker's podium.

"The evidence is irrefutable," she continued. "Progress has stagnated on our watch, declining severely in the last decade. Our quest for stability has quashed competition, both at a corporate and an international level. The only region showing consistent growth in technological discoveries is North America."

"What are you proposing? Come on, out with it." The Dachshund bared its teeth as it spoke.

Indigo suppressed a smile. The original idea behind the use of avatars and vocal disguise was to ensure anonymity, allowing those on the council to speak based on their beliefs rather than buckle under social or political pressure from their peers. Indigo had reviewed council meetings going back years to collect enough personal details and linguistic quirks to identify every person hidden behind each digital mask. The old German industrialist would have been better represented by a dinosaur than a dachshund. As one of the few remaining founder members, he'd seen how his fortune had spoiled his children and unlike many of his peers had never trusted them to take over his role. Sadly for him, his influence was on the wane.

"We need to be more proactive in creating a stimulating environment to engender progress," she continued. "Stability is over-valued. Humanity needs to feel uncomfortable, threatened even, if we want to get the best out of it."

"What you're suggesting goes against our most basic founding principles."

Shouts erupted from around the virtual chamber. It was another quirk that amused her, the use of an ancient meeting location to represent equality of voice between all council members. As if that had ever been the case, even from the beginning. Indigo looked across to see if the young prince would step in. He remained still, head poised, his hawk-like gaze taking in the surrounding furore. Then he flapped his wings and the chamber went quiet.

"Moebius is right. We can't stand by and allow this to happen. Our primary duty is for the protection of humanity. Never forget why our organisation came into being. The potential global catastrophe only happened because our political systems had been corrupted by vested interests. We acted, and acted decisively, to pull ourselves back from the brink. Now we're in a similar position, only this time it is our own activity, or lack of it, that is the cause of the danger."

"The situation is completely different," the Dachshund said. "Unlike you, I remember it very well. Back then there was real danger that society would be wiped out forever. All you're saying is that progress has stalled. Nobody is in danger. Nobody is dying. The planet is as peaceful as it has ever been. We shouldn't be worrying, we should be celebrating."

"You sound like one of the deniers that got us into trouble in the first place." A gasp arose at Indigo's words. She waited for the room to quieten. "You've been a great servant to our organisation but you're living in the past. We need to act now to prevent the rot from damaging society beyond repair, just as our politicians should have acted on the initial signs to prevent the Upheaval. Yes, we could sit back and hope things might change, but surely we of all people should heed the lessons of the past. We've acted before. It's time for us to step in and save humanity once again."

The chamber remained silent. Indigo sensed confusion emanating from the traditionalists as they tried to work out how they'd lost control of the debate.

A grasshopper stretched up onto its long back legs and a murmur broke out around the chamber. It had been many years since the grasshopper had spoken.

"Why are we here? Ask yourself, truly, why do we meet? Is it to gain wealth, power? I doubt it. There is nothing in the world any of us here couldn't have if we wanted. So if it's not for personal gain, I ask you—why are we here? We are here because either we," the Grasshopper nodded towards the Dachshund, "or our forebears, realised the world could not continue as it was. Too many times the easy answer, the short-term fix, was taken at the expense of the right thing to do. It was only our organisation that acted when nobody else would."

Indigo felt the first flutter of nerves. She had worked so hard to get to this point. It had been a dirty job, immoral even, but sometimes you had to do bad in order to deliver a greater good. Some of the traditionalists had been replaced by adapted clones, their temperaments changed to become less cautious and more likely to support direct action, but the vote remained on a knife-edge because the final batch of clones had been destroyed. She would get to the bottom of what happened there—as long as the vote went her way.

"Global Governance," continued the Grasshopper, "is what we call ourselves and that is what we must do. For many years we've acted like grandparents treating their grandchildren, a little nudge here, a piece of advice there, but allowing the world's people to grow and learn for themselves. But when grandchildren become fat and indolent we need to act!" The Grasshopper stamped its foot as it said the last word and a boom echoed around the chamber. "We cannot afford to wait. I remember the chaos caused by our last intervention. Yes, it was needed and yes, we did the right thing, but millions suffered because we acted far too late."

The Dachshund stood. "As always we would be sensible to listen to your advice, but we haven't agreed about what needs to be done. It's all very well saying we should act, but to do what?"

"Whatever is needed."

A roar erupted from the chamber as every avatar tried to speak at once. Indigo looked across to the young prince, who stared back at her. Which way will it go? she thought. The Dachshund glanced around the chamber, as if trying to calculate the level of support it had. After a few moments its tail wagged and it barked out loud. The noise subsided.

"I propose we put it to a vote. The motion is to take a more active role—"

"The motion is to do whatever's necessary to stimulate progress."

The Dachshund growled at Indigo's interruption. "Very well. The motion is to do whatever's necessary to stimulate progress. Those in favour?"

Indigo relaxed back in her bath, luxuriating in the way the almost scalding water made her skin goose-up, sending a shiver of excitement around her body. She lifted her condensation-covered glass of wine from the side and took a sip. There would be no more hiding in shadows, no more covering up. The Governing Council had spoken. She had free rein to do what was necessary to protect humanity.

She placed the glass down and slid her shoulders under the water. The bath was a decadent waste of a valuable resource, but she was yet to find a more pleasurable way of relaxing and felt too old to keep looking. When she was younger she had often gone weeks without washing; her family had barely had enough money to buy water to drink, let alone lie in it. While the poverty hadn't lasted long, it had stayed with her for life. That was the world she'd come from, the world direct action had changed. She was damned if she was going to let things return to that state.

The icon of a falcon appeared on her datalenses. She smiled. "Your highness."

"I thought I should offer my congratulations. It was a little closer than I would have liked but you got there in the end."

"With thanks to your support."

"You flatter me. I just spoke to a few people, that's all."

Indigo knew where this was going. She'd spent enough time with the children of privilege to recognise the game of flattery and false-modesty. It appeared the young prince was no different to all the others. "I can assure you, it wouldn't have been possible without you."

"Be that as it may, we finally got what we wanted."

Indigo sat up. She recognised the change of emphasis and didn't like it. It had been her victory, she was the one who had done all the work. "Are you in a position to transfer the funds ready for our push into North America? I'd like everything in place before I arrive."

"The funds are available … but there has been a slight change of plan."

At the man's words, the walls appeared to close in on Indigo. "What do you mean?"

"I'm concerned about what happened in England, just before the vote."

"I can assure you I have it under control."

"You've said that before but events show otherwise. Somebody else will be going to North America. You're to return to England to sort out the mess you made."

"How dare you! This is my plan, my project. You don't get to decide what I do or don't do."

"Given that I hold the purse-strings, actually I do."

Indigo slapped the water in frustration. Fucking bastard! How dare he take over? This was her life's work, the culmination of years of painstaking activity, gathering the right information—and the means of analysis—to prove what she'd already been doing in secret was right. "You need me in North America. Only I have the contacts to make this work."

"I know who your contacts are. I also know about the death of

Zachary Gant and your agent Juliet, despite you doing your best to keep these details from me."

"The deaths are a minor setback. I didn't want to trouble you." The wine Indigo had sipped moments before tasted sour in her mouth.

"I can't work with somebody I don't trust, and at the moment I don't trust you. If you'd been honest about the deaths in North America, or the loss of the clones at the Re-Life facility, I wouldn't have an issue."

"I have everything under control."

"Then prove it. Go back to England, find out who wiped out the clones and deal with them. If you can handle that then maybe I'll trust you with some of my money."

The line went dead. Indigo screamed, throwing her wine glass across the room.

Within moments of the glass smashing against the wall, her assistant entered. "Is everything all right?"

"No, everything is not all right. I want you to get in touch with the Prime Delegate of England. Tell him I'm on my way."

"But I thought you were taking an airship to Philadelphia?"

"Just do it!"

CHAPTER THREE

The Professor

PLEASE, LET ME get there in time. Please don't let it be too late.

The Professor ran towards the line of derelict houses, his feet skidding on the sodden scree, remnants of an industry that had died out 100 years previously. Light flickered from the window of a house in the middle of the terrace, guiding him forward. He glanced over his shoulder but the layer of mist surrounding the bottom of the hill obscured his view. Were they still after him? He wasn't sure, but he couldn't take the risk and slow down. His lungs burned but it was a familiar pain. Not too far now.

There was a shout from below and the Professor stumbled. His foot slipped on a greasy slab. He felt a sharp stab of pain then found himself facedown in congealed soot. The impact forced the air from his lungs. He must have made a noise because the door of one of the houses opened. Fran stood there, looking out.

"Get the kids upstairs," he gasped. "They're coming."

Fran disappeared from view. The light from the front window flickered, then went out. The Professor scrambled to his feet, the skin of his hands and knees raw from the impact. His right ankle hurt but the need to get inside drove him forward as he half-hopped, half-dragged himself into the house, closing the door behind him.

The front room was empty, smoke curling from a recently snuffed candle the only sign it had been occupied. Sounds of protest drifted down from upstairs. One of the boys was crying, Naci by the sound of it, and he heard Maria's voice as she tried to calm him down.

The Professor made his way up the bare wooden stairs, wincing with each step. He rounded the corner to see Fran handing the limp form of Gino up to Maria, leaning out of the loft hatch. The young boy looked deathly pale, and a sheen of sweat covered his forehead.

"Try to keep them quiet," Fran said to her daughter.

"They're scared, Mamma."

"Then hold them close and play the quiet game."

"But I—"

There was a loud crash outside. The Professor's stomach turned over at the sound of voices amplified through Internal Security helmets and for a moment he thought he would be sick.

Fran looked up to her daughter. "Quickly," she hissed. "Pull the hatch shut and don't open it for anyone."

"But what about you?"

"Just do it!"

The Professor dragged himself up the last couple of steps to the landing as the hatch slid shut. "What about us?"

"Over here."

Fran put her arm under his shoulder and helped him into what was once a back bedroom. It stank of damp and rot. Bird droppings lay sprinkled on the floor among the remnants of the shattered pane. A rusted bed-frame lay in the centre of the room.

"Help me with this." Fran grabbed hold of one end of the frame. The Professor hobbled to the other side. "Quietly now."

The frame was heavier than it looked and the Professor struggled to take the weight on his bad ankle. Fran carried her end towards the door but the Professor just pivoted where he stood until the frame slipped from his hands. A crash echoed around the room and the Professor shrank from Fran's glare.

The sound of boots tramping on gravel drifted up from outside. Fran slipped beside the door and pulled a weapon from her pocket. It was one she'd taken before leaving O'Driscoll's safe house. She'd wanted him to do the same but the Professor refused. He hated weapons, but at that moment he regretted his decision.

"House is clear."

At the sound, the Professor hobbled over to the corner next to the window. This was it. All the running and hiding had been for nothing. As he sat he felt the packet in his pocket dig into his hip. He'd had to risk it, had to go into the town for the boy's sake. Without nanobiotics, the fever would only have got worse. Now it looked like they would all pay the price for Gino's virus.

There was another crash and this time he felt the wall at his back vibrate. Boots trampled through rooms and up stairs. He heard muffled voices through the thin walls.

"Room clear."

"Room clear."

"Room clear."

Each confirmation was another nail in his coffin. The troopers were being methodical, and it wouldn't be much longer before they were discovered. The Professor tensed, his arms wrapped tight around his knees. Were they here? No, he'd only heard two doors smashed in. The doors to the first two houses on the row had both been locked and barred—he knew because he'd tried them all when they'd first arrived. The Professor leant forward to see if he could get a glimpse of what was happening outside but fear pulled him back again.

The crash was louder this time, and the wall juddered against his back. They were next door. He could now make out the sound of individual footsteps, the squeak of doors opening. The Professor watched Fran waiting calmly with her weapon pointed towards the door. The Investigator was a lucky man. His wife was smart, resourceful and strong-willed. Unlike him. He was useless, as useless as the algorithm he'd developed to hide from the datasphere. What had gone wrong?

Footsteps scuffed on the floorboards next door.

The Professor stared at the floor, teeth gritted, willing for silence. It wasn't to be. A high, plaintive cry echoed from above, followed by loud coughing. The Professor could have cried with fear and frustration.

"Targets are next door. Repeat, targets are next door."

The floor shook as troopers ran out of the adjoining property. From above came the sound of shushing but it was too late, far too late. Fran glanced at him, a look of horror on her face. The Professor wanted to reach out to her, wanted to let her know everything was all right, but he was too terrified. It wasn't going to be all right. They were going to be caught. They were going to be killed.

Something buzzed past the window. There was a yelp, then the Professor heard a thud as something heavy collapsed to the ground outside.

"Man down! Repeat, man down!"

"Where did that come from?"

"The shot came from outside. It's an ambush. Everybody—"

A hellish scream echoed through the building. Weapons roared. The sound of children crying filtered down to where he crouched. There were shouts, the sound of running. More screams. The Professor curled up in a ball. He wanted to run but there was nowhere to go, nowhere to hide. He'd failed and everybody was going to die.

There was a crash from downstairs and the Professor screamed. They were in the house. This was all his fault. He should never have gone into town. He looked up to see Fran staring towards the door, her knuckles white where she gripped her weapon.

People were yelling, screaming, the noise of their shouts unintelligible over the sound of firing. The Professor covered his ears. It was too much. He couldn't take any more.

Then all was silent, the only sound the crying from above.

The Professor pulled his hands from his ears, his breathing ragged. He looked over to Fran. Her arms shook but she remained focussed on the door.

He crawled towards the window and peered out but the combination of a misted pane and the murk outside made it difficult to see. There was no movement. The Professor could make out dark mounds on the ground. He gently rubbed at the glass. With the condensation removed he saw the mounds were bodies of Internal Security troopers.

"Is anyone out there? Come in, please. Is anybody there?"

The whispered voice echoed through the door from the landing. The Professor threw himself onto the floor just as the door to their room crashed inwards. The bed frame jumped a few centimetres but held. Fran fired her weapon. The edge of the door splintered and there was a cry of pain. Then the door erupted into splinters.

The Professor screamed again. He heard a thump as Fran landed beside him, looked across to see if she was okay but she was already crawling towards cover.

Two more explosions shook the house and the firing stopped. A gurgling sound came from the corridor. The Professor looked up to see the centre of the door had been blown in. Laying slumped against the corridor wall was an Internal Security trooper. The gurgling came from its helmet speaker. The trooper's front breastplate was shattered. Holes punctured his torso, then with a roar the trooper's helmet exploded spraying the hallway with blood and jelly-like lumps of flesh.

The Professor rolled over and vomited. As he did so there was a crash, followed by another shot. He looked up to see a man standing over Fran, a weapon in each hand, one of them Fran's. The Professor backed away on his hands and knees, terrified. Poor Fran. She'd been so brave.

The man glanced to where he lay. The Professor tensed, waiting for the shot. It never came. Instead, the man holstered his weapon before reaching down and pulling Fran to her feet. The Professor stared in wonder. She was alive!

"You nearly killed me," the man said, handing Fran her weapon back.

Fran blinked, her face frozen in fear and confusion. "I don't understand. Who are you?"

"I'm here to take you to safety. Let's get your kids down from the attic. We need to get out of here."

And with that, the Professor broke down in tears.

CHAPTER FOUR

Stephanie

EVERYTHING HURT. EVERY joint, every muscle—even her teeth hurt—pain both a misery and a miracle. To have sensation, any sensation, after so long was incredible, but why did it have to be pain? And pain becomes amplified when it's the only thing you have.

A tickle let her know that phlegm pooled once more in the back of her throat. She tried to cough it out but of course her body didn't respond. It just went its own way, a useless sack of pain, a reminder of what she would never have again.

The hiss-click of her respirator caught for a moment. An alarm sounded. The room spun. Darkness encroached her outer vision. Was this it? Was she was finally going to be free?

She heard a door open and the kind-faced woman appeared with a look of concern. She placed something cold and metallic in Stephanie's mouth. It made a slurping sound. No, Stephanie thought. Let me be free.

Her head shook from side to side as the kind-faced woman went to work. The suction tube stuck to her tongue, then the inside of her cheek, before being moved down into her throat where the gurgling sound increased. The hiss-click started once more. Stephanie felt a tear trickle down her cheek. Why are you doing this? Why won't you let me die?

The woman smiled but her eyes looked worried. "How are you doing? Does that feel better?"

Stephanie blinked twice.

"Are you in pain?"

She blinked once. Yes, of course she was in pain, but that wasn't the problem. The problem was she was still alive.

The woman stepped out of view. Almost instantly the pain disappeared, and with it any sensation from below her neck. She was once more just a consciousness trapped in her own skull.

"Has the pain stopped now?"

Stephanie blinked once.

"Good." The woman leaned forward. "Don't give up. I'm doing the best I can." Then she was gone.

Stephanie heard the sound of the door open and close.

hiss-click

hiss-click

The respirator helped her count out time. Once she was sure she was alone she gave the mental stimuli to turn on the datalenses the woman had given her. She hadn't wanted to use them at first, refusing to torment herself with the knowledge of the world outside this room. But like an aching tooth begging to be poked, the lure of the outside world had drawn her in. It had taken hours for her to build up the set of mental commands needed to gain rudimentary control, but time was the one thing she had.

Stephanie accessed her favourite NewsAggres. Images flickered across her eyes, images of a world she'd left long ago. There were political scandals, relationship break-ups. Births, deaths and Re-Lifes. Especially Re-Lifes. It had become quite the thing. The rich, famous and powerful flocked to Re-Life in their droves, transplanting the consciousness from their aged bodies to younger versions of themselves. Stephanie would have laughed if she could. These idiots, driven by narcissism and vanity, were unwittingly taking part in the largest mass-suicide humanity had ever known.

The ability to live forever was a lie. She knew that now. The rejuvenations were fake. These people weren't extending their lives, they were copies, their old and new minds as separate from one another as two right arms from a set of identical twins. Yes, they shared the same memories but they were not the same person. They couldn't be. The central claim about the Re-Life process was a lie. Re-Life claimed it was life extension because there was a direct link between the original organic brain to a synthetic brain, and then on to the new organic brain. It was one long, uninterrupted stream of consciousness. But something was lost in the transfer. Jennica Fabian had spotted it, and it was this knowledge that had led to the student's death.

Stephanie had spent a long time thinking about what Jennica had written in her diary. What the student found—part of a person's transiessence data disappearing, only for new data to appear moments later in the freshly cloned subject—was disturbing. It hinted that there was more to a person's brain, and therefore the person themselves, than the biological and electrical mechanics of thought and consciousness.

What was this missing data? That was the key question. It was a minuscule amount, the equivalent to a few minutes of time, and if it had just disappeared then nobody would have thought much about it. But it came back. It came back from nowhere, changed but in the same place as the data previously lost. How was that possible? More importantly, what did it mean?

It was this fact that had disturbed Jennica the most. In her diary she'd written about the soul, wondering if the missing piece of data was the very essence of who we are, and that when the body died the soul died too. Stephanie had never had time for religion, but then neither had Jennica until her discovery. A part of Stephanie hoped that Jennica's findings were true. At least the poor girl would be in a better place.

CHAPTER FIVE

The Investigator

THE PAIN IN his neck faded and the fog lifted from Nico's mind. He watched as the Commander and O'Driscoll made their way towards the door. Nico got up to join them but the room tilted, forcing him to place his hands on the table to stop himself falling. His mind might be clear but his body was yet to catch up. The table vibrated as another rumble came and went. He slowly straightened, ready in case his body betrayed him again, but this time he remained upright.

The Commander turned to see where he was.

"I'm coming."

He took a step, then another, and with each new step his control returned. And it wasn't just his body—for the first time in days he was able to think and his thoughts were of Fran and the children. The news that they weren't at the safe house terrified him, despite the Commander's reassurances. He should never have left them, never have gone to the Re-Life facility with O'Driscoll.

The three of them left the room they'd been held in since their arrival, the Commander, then O'Driscoll with Nico at the rear. As they walked out a monster of a man they'd come to name the gentle giant stepped in behind him. Nico grunted to himself. I guess the Commander's trust doesn't extend too far, he thought.

With his control returned, Nico took in his surroundings. The end of the corridor opened out into a large tunnel stretching off left and right as far as he could see, the ceiling double the height of the room they'd just come from. They Commander turned right and the rest of them followed. They walked for what felt to Nico like an age but was probably just ten minutes, past similar doorways to the one they'd just left. On the way they passed a number of people, some in uniform, others in overalls or white coats, the presence of their small group causing little interest. There was a focus to the people they passed, a level of determination Nico recognised, having seen similar determination in teams he'd worked with when trying to crack difficult cases.

At the end of the tunnel a set of double doors led onto a rampway spiralling up at a gentle incline. As they started up Nico glanced back. The doors they'd just gone through had a giant U6 stencilled on them. Further up the ramp they passed another set of doors marked U5, then U4, the passage flattening out slightly at each intersection. Every door had a small window inset but Nico was only able to snatch glimpses of what lay behind as they went past. He was so keen to get a sense of where he was that it was only when they arrived at U3 that he noticed the large metallic band stretching along the floor, up the walls and across the tunnel ceiling at each intersection. They didn't look structural but he had no idea what they could be for.

The Commander led them through the doorway marked U2. The first thing Nico noticed was that it was carpeted. It wasn't exactly luxurious but it made a change from bare concrete. The ceiling was lower than where they'd just left and despite the bright lighting this new tunnel felt claustrophobic. They walked down the grey painted corridor, passing a number of doorways on the right-hand side. Through the few open doors Nico saw what appeared to be offices and plant rooms, plus a small locker room.

He leant over to O'Driscoll. "Any idea where we are?"

"Not a clue."

At the end of the corridor was a set of double doors. The Commander knocked.

"Come in."

She pushed the doors open and they entered a large office. The walls were covered in schematics broken up by the odd framed print. A metal desk stood in the centre of the room. Behind was a long horizontal strip holding a deep-set window looking out over white-capped waves with a slate-grey sky overhead. As he watched, a gull floated up into view from underneath the window, wings outstretched, riding the wind. Yet despite this being Nico's first sight of the outside world for over a week, it was the man sitting at the desk that captured his attention.

"Holy shit." O'Driscoll stood with his mouth open. Nico understood why.

"Please, gentlemen. Take a seat."

Nico didn't move. It was impossible. The man in front of them looked like Thomas Doleman, the man who'd signed The Miracle. He spoke like him too, but looked older than all the images Nico had seen. Yet it couldn't be him. Thomas Doleman had been dead for years, having killed himself after realising it was his lack of action during the Upheaval that had caused suffering to millions.

"You're … you're Thomas Doleman."

"Lord Doleman, if you don't mind, although seeing as the title was given posthumously I'll let you off." The man smiled and gestured towards two chairs in front of the desk.

Nico took a seat but O'Driscoll remained standing. "But you're dead."

"Yes, I understand how that may be a little disconcerting. Still, as you see, I'm very much alive."

"But that's impossible! Re-Life wasn't around when you were alive—"

"Sit down, Mr O'Driscoll and let me explain."

The large guard walked forward and placed his hand on O'Driscoll's shoulder. O'Driscoll shrugged the guard off and took the offered seat.

"I'm sorry you were kept so long in the holding area," Doleman continued, "but we had to be sure we were on the same side."

"Same side? The Commander said the same thing but we've no idea who the fuck you people are." O'Driscoll spoke in a low voice but Nico recognised the tone. The man was close to erupting.

The Commander walked up behind where Doleman sat. "I told you when we picked you up at the Re-Life facility: We're the watchers."

Doleman smiled. "Heather has such a way with words. We call ourselves the Knights Templar. It's a silly affectation in some ways but given what we're trying to achieve, it seemed appropriate."

"And that is?" Nico asked.

"To protect humanity, of course."

Nico heard the sound of O'Driscoll snorting beside him. "I thought they were a bunch of medieval bankers."

So this really was Thomas Doleman, the last Prime Minister, the martyr of The Miracle. Nico wondered for a moment if the sedative they'd given him was causing hallucinations. A pinch on the inside of his leg let him know everything was real.

"I'm sure you've worked out that The Miracle wasn't what it's been made out to be. The world's leaders didn't have a change of heart as commonly believed, they didn't put the needs of the world over their—our—petty self-interests. Despite knowing we were facing the worst global catastrophe since the birth of civilisation, it took the actions of others, those you know as Global Governance, to turn things around."

"You sound almost proud of the fact," O'Driscoll said.

"Proud? Not at all. I wanted to do something, we all did, but we didn't have the support back home to ratify any decisions we made at the UN. It was only when Global Governance showed us they had the vested interests in their pockets, we believed their idea would work."

O'Driscoll sneered. "So you gave control of the world to a group of unelected, invisible people?"

"Not straight away, which is what I need to explain." Doleman sat up in his chair and tugged at his shirtsleeves. It was an action Nico had seen a thousand times before on historical footage, and it finally convinced him that the Thomas Doleman behind the desk was the real thing.

"We knew these people had us over a barrel but at the same time they still needed us to front their plans. Without us, it would have been obvious to the general population that the world had been taken over by a powerful elite. So some of us pushed back, only agreeing to their demands if an independent oversight group was set up to ensure all Global Governance's actions met with their original charter: To ensure the survival of humanity. Looking back I should have been suspicious of how readily they agreed, but it happened so quickly and we had too many other things to think about."

"Like dealing with a planet fucked up in the pursuit of personal gain?" O'Driscoll's contempt was palpable, his tone dripping with sarcasm.

"I wouldn't have put it quite that way, but yes."

O'Driscoll didn't appear happy with the answer, but Nico began to warm to Doleman. He was being honest, not skirting around the consequences of his inactivity.

"Unfortunately, once we'd signed The Miracle and Global Governance implemented their plan, the oversight committee was first ignored, and eventually crushed. We had no choice but to go underground," Doleman looked around the office, "pun very much intended, and secretly carry on our work."

"So you disappeared," O'Driscoll said.

"That's right."

"And since then you've been doing what, exactly?"

"Monitoring Global Governance and taking action when things got out of hand," the Commander replied.

"Really?" Nico felt his earlier anger return. "So what exactly do you class as things 'getting out of hand'? This organisation has killed innocent people, threatened me and my family, driven us from our homes and are still hunting my wife and children while you've kept me locked up here."

"On that subject, at least, I have good news. They're not hunting your family any more," Doleman said. "We've found them. They're on their way back here as we speak."

Nico's heart lurched. "Are they okay?"

"They're fine. Your youngest—Gino, isn't it?—he has a chest infection, but your wife and daughter are fine. The man and boy who were with them are fine too."

"What man? What boy?" Nico didn't understand. All he could think was that his family were safe, they were on their way back.

"Professor Stradbroke and the young Turkish boy, Naci Ozbey, who I believe Mr O'Driscoll here was 'taking care of'. They were both with your family when we found them."

Nico sat staring into space. Of course, how had he forgotten?

"I'm pleased we can now play happy families," O'Driscoll said, "but you still haven't answered the Investigator's point. How come you've let all this happen?"

Nico saw the Commander glance down at Doleman. Something passed between them but he wasn't sure what. Then Doleman spoke.

"About five years ago we received reports of actions clearly attributable to Global Governance but never discussed in their Governing Council. We tried to understand what was going on, but each time we sent someone to investigate, they disappeared. It was only during the riots in this country two years ago that we were finally able to get close to what was happening."

"We found out that a splinter group, operating within Global Governance but outside of the Governing Council's knowledge, had been taking things further than we'd ever realised before," the Commander continued. "Rather than using their position to ensure stability, this group created disruption and disorder. It's only during the past month that we've been able to find out who's behind it."

"Indigo," said Nico.

Doleman turned to the Commander. "You were right."

"I told you they'd got close to the truth."

Doleman looked across at Nico. "How did you hear that name?"

"I captured one of her people, David Chandler—codenamed Echo. He was the one who gave her up."

"You captured Echo?" the Commander asked. "Where is he now?"

"I don't know. I left him in an interrogation room when I heard my investigative agency was being raided. My guess is Global Governance killed him. That was certainly his fear."

"So have you taken this Indigo person out? I assume that's what you've planned." O'Driscoll showed no emotion as he talked about death.

"We wanted to, but things have become a little more complicated. This splinter group has now taken over the Governing Council. The information we recovered when we picked you up at the Re-Life facility shows they've been creating clones to replace the members of Global Governance who were against their plans. It's the same tactic they used to sow discord in North America. We tried our best to stop them but, as you know, we were too late."

"What about Stephanie Vaughn?" Nico asked. "She was working for Indigo."

"Stephanie would never have worked for that woman," the Commander snapped.

"Indigo recruited her," Nico replied. "I know, she told me herself. The two of us wanted to find out who was behind the riots and the death of Jennica Fabian but when we started getting close to the truth, Stephanie stopped looking. Have you found her, or Juliet as she's now known? She could provide you with some answers."

"Juliet's dead," Doleman said. "She was an abomination, created as a weapon to start a war. We managed to stop her and prevent the conflict—at least temporarily."

The news hit Nico like a punch to the stomach. "Poor Stephanie."

O'Driscoll burst out laughing. "Look at you, all of you! You sit here talking about high ideals and noble causes, call yourselves the Knights-fucking-Templar, yet you've allowed these people to take control over the lives of billions. And what have you done about it? Picked up three men from a Re-Life facility, two who've had fuck all to do with what's happened. Why aren't you going after those responsible? Why aren't you taking the whole rotten edifice down?"

"Mr O'Driscoll," Doleman replied. "We've no intention of taking Global Governance down. You might be too young to remember but some of us have very vivid memories of what life was like before Global Governance took charge. I saw the Netherlands flood, saw thousands die in food riots when rice crops failed. There were people starving in the richest countries in the world. And yet the political system was a sham, rigged to benefit the rich and powerful, supported by a media prepared to sow disinformation instead of truth. It was a selfish world where only the most selfish succeeded. Global Governance put a stop to that. They put the interests of all humanity first. I may disagree with how some individuals went about what they did, but the truth is the world needs a steady hand to ensure it doesn't descend into chaos. We don't want to take Global Governance down—we want to return it to what it should have been."

As Doleman spoke, Nico saw the sense of his words. Every organisation needed a leader, somebody to provide direction. The world had been more stable in the years since The Miracle was signed. Conflicts sprung up from time to time but were quickly extinguished. With everything now connected to the datasphere, while crimes hadn't been completely eradicated, people were much safer than they'd ever been and criminals were nearly always brought to justice. Nico sensed O'Driscoll squirm in the seat beside him, but that was no surprise. The man had lived on the edge of the law for so long he probably thought it no longer applied to him. Plus what did he know about the need for stability? He didn't have a family, loved ones to care for. If they could bring back stability then his children would be able to grow up safe. Order was what was needed.

"This is why we've brought you both here. You're intelligent, resourceful and managed to get as close to the truth as we have with just a fraction of our resources. We need people like you to help us reach our goal." Doleman stood up from behind his desk and held out his hand. "Join us. Help us make the world a better place."

How could he refuse? Nico found himself on his feet, taking Doleman's hand in his own. "If you bring my family back here to safety, you can count me in."

"Thank you, Chief Investigator," Doleman said, smiling, "we could really use someone with your skills around here." The former Prime Minister turned towards O'Driscoll. "And what about you?"

O'Driscoll remained in his chair, his face composed. "I'll think about it."

CHAPTER SIX

Indigo

INDIGO FELT A trickle of water run down her neck. She growled to herself and shook the collar of her coat. She hated this country. The weather was miserable, the people insufferable—still believing they were special despite it being centuries since they'd held any real power in the world. Even after the Upheaval and all that followed, these people remained desperate to cling to some mythical past rather than face the reality that they were ever more irrelevant in the new world order.

She shivered, more to do with the damp than the cold. The walls of the corridor were mottled with mildew and a sheen of moisture covered the surface of each door she passed. If ever there was a metaphor for the country, this was it. Take their veneration of Thomas Doleman. She'd seen a statue of him at the rail terminal, hand aloft, holding a copy of The Miracle. She almost laughed out loud when she saw it. The man was no hero. He was a snivelling bag of insecurity if ever she'd met one. But because Doleman had come from the right background, went to the right school and eventually turned his back on his corporate paymasters, he was held up as an example of classic English values as if he was the direct descendant of King Harold or Winston Churchill.

Indigo stopped in front of door 466 and placed her eye against the retinal scanner. It felt like ice on her cheek. A datascreen next to the doorway lit up, and she saw the man she had come for lying curled up in the corner of the darkened cell. He was naked, the mottled and scarred residue of abuse visible all over his body. His temperature was low but the rest of his vital signs showed he was in remarkably good health, considering.

She buzzed the door open and the man scrambled further into the corner, hiding his eyes from the lights above.

"Do your worst." His voice was the barest croak.

Indigo resisted the urge to cover her nose. The room smelled of filth. How had he let himself get into this state? She'd had doubts earlier and wondered once again whether she'd made the right choice. Could he go back to being the man he once was, or had they broken him beyond repair?

"Echo, get up."

The man gasped. "Indigo?"

"I'm not used to having my orders ignored."

Echo slowly got to his feet, revealing a full picture of the ordeal he'd suffered. She had no sympathy for him. He deserved everything he'd gone through. It was the price one paid for betrayal.

"I'm sorry." He squinted towards her, hands covering his genitals —as if that would offer him any protection.

"I know you are."

"Why are they keeping me here? Why won't they finish me off and be done with it?"

"You think you should be let off that easily?"

He looked confused, disorientated. "I have nothing more to offer you. I told you what happened, kept nothing back. I failed."

"You did."

Echo flinched at her words. "What he did to my boy … I couldn't let it continue."

"And that was the reason you were told not to have a family. It's a weakness that's too easy for our enemies to exploit."

"I thought I could handle it."

"But you couldn't."

He shook his head. "No."

"Nothing happened to your boy."

"I don't understand."

"I have your family. They're quite safe. Your boy is unharmed. He tricked you, Echo. What you saw was a fabrication, a computer-generated lie the Investigator calculated would cause you to crack. And he was right. You gave us all up for a mirage."

He shook his head. "No. They cut my boy's finger off! I saw it. He was screaming——"

Indigo slapped the man. "Get a grip."

Echo glared back at her and for a moment Indigo questioned her decision to come alone. Still, it was the reaction she'd hoped for.

"I never put you down as one to indulge in self-pity," she said. "You're better than that."

"You think this is pity? I fucked up. I betrayed the organisation. I betrayed you. I don't deserve to live for what I've done. So do it. Pull the fucking trigger."

Indigo smiled. "Keep hold of that anger," she said. "You're going to need it."

A look of surprise flashed across Echo's face. "You're letting me out?"

"I'm doing more than that. I'm giving you a chance to prove you're still the man I think you are."

At her words, Echo stood a little straighter, dropped his hands to his side. His features smoothed into the mask she recognised so well. Better, Indigo thought. Much better.

"I don't want you to die for what you've done," she continued, "although you deserve it. I want you to rectify the damage you've caused."

"Rectify it? How?"

"I've some tricky negotiations ahead. I need you there with me, if you're still capable that is."

"Of course."

"And we need to deal with Tandelli."

Echo stared at her, open-mouthed. "He's not dead?"

Indigo gritted her teeth. "If you'd taken care of Tandelli when you first had the chance, neither of us would be here now." I'd be in North America putting the plan I've been working on for decades into effect, she thought. "Tandelli is not only alive, he's also causing me a major headache."

Echo grimaced but held her gaze. "He's as good as mine."

"Good, because I'm not like Tandelli. I'm not as soft as him. If you fail me, what he pretended to do to your son will become reality for every member of your family."

CHAPTER SEVEN

Stephanie

A PERSON'S FACE is so expressive, Stephanie thought. It has a language all of its own, a universal syntax of emotions that crosses borders and cultures. A smile meant the same thing the world over. So did a frown. Tears were different. Tears needed context. They could come from joy or sadness. The tears that stained her face were the latter. Stephanie knew this because she understood the context. The context was her.

The medication the doctors had given her before they left made her feel as if she was being embraced from the inside. She was enveloped in an invisible cocoon of love. That she understood and was aware of what was happening to her didn't matter. She was wrapped in the memory of love and that was okay.

The kind-faced woman wiped the tears from where they'd landed. "Look at me. If someone was to come in now I don't know what would happen." She took a deep breath. "Fuck, this is hard," she said, wiping the tears from her own reddened face.

Stephanie wanted to tell her that it was all right. She felt fine, the best she had in a long time. Compared to being trapped in a body whose only function was to transmit pain, death was something to be embraced. It was peace. It was resolution.

"Your body is failing. I don't know if it's because of the nerve damage you've sustained or something else, but we're fighting a losing battle." She swallowed, tried to clear her throat. "I'm doing my best but nobody here cares. Your clone is dead and they don't have the means to make another. The only reason they haven't switched off your respirator is because they refuse to believe that option is gone."

At her words, Stephanie focussed on the hiss-click of the machine next to her. It was the sound of life clinging on by its fingernails. Turn the machine off, she thought. Let me die. Then we can all move on.

"They want you to live long enough to capture your transiessence data and create another clone. They want to use you all over again."

Stephanie didn't regret where she was. It was hard to regret anything while wrapped in love. She was here because she'd wanted justice for what had happened to Jennica. No, she needed to be honest with herself. It was true she'd wanted justice for the poor girl, but her main motivation was vengeance against the man who'd attacked her and ruined her life. Not poor Randall, or whatever he really was, but Zachary Gant

The woman looked up at the ceiling. "Why am I talking like this? It's not as if it's going to change anything. I don't even know if you really understand what I'm saying. After what they put you through, I wouldn't be surprised if your sanity snapped months ago. You poor thing. Nobody deserves to be treated like this. Nobody."

Then turn the machine off. Just do it. Give me peace.

"The only thing keeping me going is the promise I made to your mother. She asked me to look after you. She made me give my word."

A flicker of uncertainty broke the comforting haze surrounding Stephanie's existence. But my mother's dead? She went missing when I was a child. Perhaps the woman meant my grandmother. But even as the thought entered her mind, Stephanie dismissed it. That couldn't be right. Grandma died years ago. There's just me now. Just me.

"I've sent the signal, told her you haven't got long. If anyone can get you out of here, she can."

Stephanie saw conviction in the woman's expression. Conviction, another complex emotion that could be conveyed through a look or a tone of voice. But the woman was clearly mad. How could her mother get her out of here? She was dead, had died years before consciousness transfer had been developed.

"You need to hang on until she can get here."

The words drifted around Stephanie's mind but she couldn't gather sense from them. It was as if somebody had sliced logic and reason into small pieces and shuffled them around. Her mother was long gone. The only way she could join me is if I shuffle off this mortal coil. Unless that was what the woman meant. But if the woman wanted her to die so she could meet her mother, why was she trying to keep her alive?

An alarm sounded from one of the machines. The kind-faced woman disappeared from view, leaving Stephanie looking up at the ceiling. She wanted to forget what the woman had said and relax in the warm chemical embrace but a small part of her mind wouldn't let it go. What if her mother really was alive? How would she feel about that? An old emotion bubbled to the surface, a longing for her parents, exposing the empty ache in her soul where their love should have been. Her grandparents had done their best but they weren't her mum and dad. And the one thing children wanted more than anything was the love of their mother and father.

A shadow flickered over her as the kind-faced woman returned. "Your heart rate increased so I've—" She stopped. "Oh, you poor thing. You understand me after all. I didn't mean to upset you." Stephanie felt the woman wipe the side of her face. "There's no need to cry. She'll get here, don't you worry. You just need to hang on. Use that strength you've got inside of you and don't give up."

hiss-click

hiss-click

For the first time in a long time, Stephanie realised she didn't want that sound to stop after all. She wanted it to continue. She wanted to meet her mother before she died.

CHAPTER EIGHT

The Investigator

NICO OPENED THE next document. He'd been sat at the datascreen for hours, trying to fit together the pieces of this particular puzzle. Doleman had been true to his word and took him up on his offer of help, tasking him to identify members of Global Governance's Governing Council through transcripts of their meetings. According to Doleman there had been an influx of new members as the second generation slowly gave way to the third. The Knights Templar needed to know which members of the original founding families now spoke on their behalf at the meetings.

It was classic data analysis, the type on which Nico had built his career. But it wasn't easy. Most council members yet to be identified had never spoken at the meetings. They just turned up, voted, then went away again. The more vocal members had been identified years before, but how did you recognise those that never said a word, never gave any clues as to who they were?

A rumble made Nico's desk and datascreen vibrate, breaking his concentration. The regular noise was one mystery he'd quickly solved. The Knights Templar's underground complex had been built next to a wave-generation plant. Nico still wasn't sure exactly where in the country they were, but it was in the middle of nowhere, far from prying eyes. The complex itself was enormous, almost entirely underground and most of it below sea level. It was a clever idea. They drew power from source, so it never registered as a drain on the grid, and the small buildings above ground could be sealed off, connecting only to the large underground turbine halls, appearing no different to any other energy facility.

He scrolled down his target's genealogy. At the top was the founding member, a tech baron from the first digital gold rush of the last century. The man had passed his position on to his second daughter, who'd held it for over 30 years. Now someone else from the family had taken on the role. Nico crossed the name of the woman's second child off the list. He'd cross-referenced Governing Council meeting dates with the young woman's public appearances. It wasn't a perfect solution, but it was a start. The second child had been recorded partying during one of the Council sessions, ruling her out.

He moved on to the next.

The more he researched into the lives of these people, the more he wondered what the point of it all was. Here they were, with the wealth and power to do anything they wanted, and most of the time they spent it looking bored at social functions with other bored-looking people. A few children of the wealthy used their inheritance to do good, but many spent their lives travelling the world in giant airships, hoping to gain new experiences but never truly leaving the shelter of their golden cocoons.

The door opened. Nico looked up to see O'Driscoll standing there. "Still doing 'important' work?"

Nico bristled. "At least I'm doing something."

"I'm happy you're happy."

"Sarcastic bastard."

"How could you say that?" O'Driscoll had his hand on his heart in mock anguish. "Anyway, you might want to stop what you're doing. They're here."

Nico was out of his chair without thinking. "Where?"

"They're just pulling up by building one."

Nico shoved past O'Driscoll and ran down the corridor towards the closest ramp. They were finally here.

He burst through the set of double doors at the end of the

corridor and ran up the circular incline, almost knocking over a uniformed woman coming the other way. Were they all right? Doleman had mentioned Gino was ill. How bad was he? Nico needed to get to them, to find out for himself.

By the time he burst into the reception area of building one he was breathing hard. It was full of people, medics and security, but his eyes locked on a dark-haired woman with her back to him. It was the one person he would recognise anywhere, one embedded in his DNA.

As if by instinct, Fran turned and smiled. Nico noticed the dark smudges under her eyes and that her hair was dull and lank, but at that moment she was the most beautiful woman he'd ever seen. He ran up and wrapped his arms around his wife. "I'm so sorry."

"You've nothing to be sorry for."

"But I left you alone."

"I told you to go, remember?" She squeezed him tight and at that moment he decided to never leave her on her own again. She was back, she was safe. Nico took a deep breath, luxuriating in her familiar scent.

As he held Fran tight a movement caught his eye. The Professor entered the entrance hall carrying Gino. Nico immediately let Fran go and rushed to where the Professor stood. "How is he?"

"Better, now the nanobiotics are taking effect. He's just tired."

Nico held out his arms and Professor carefully transferred the boy into his care. Gino immediately snuggled into his shoulder and Nico almost cried. The sensation was so familiar yet one he'd almost lost forever. Never again.

A medic approached. "I'm sorry, Mr Tandelli, but we need to take your son to the medical centre."

Nico hardly heard the woman because as she spoke, Maria and Naci walked through the door, the young boy gripping his daughter's hand tight. He watched O'Driscoll, a big smile on his face, hold his arms out in greeting. The young boy looked up but on seeing the former gangster he hid himself behind Maria. O'Driscoll's smile flickered, then faded. Give him time, Nico thought. The poor kid has been through a lot.

Maria stared around the room as if unnerved by all the people. He waved at his daughter and smiled. Maria didn't smile back. Instead she headed towards Fran.

"What is this place Mama?"

"I don't know," Fran replied.

"Don't worry, Maria. All you need to know is that you're safe here." Nico reached out towards his daughter but she pulled away from him.

"Mr Tandelli? Sir? May I take your son?"

Fran must have seen the concern on his face. "It's okay, honey. Let the medic take him. He needs the rest. You can be there when he wakes up."

Nico didn't want to let Gino go. He needed to hold him, to keep him safe. He wanted to keep his whole family safe. He'd been an idiot to have left without them. Fran smiled a reassuring smile and he realised it was for the best. "If he starts to wake up," he said to the medic as he passed the boy to her, "you come and get me straight away."

"Of course."

As he turned, Nico caught Maria staring at him. He smiled at her once more but she turned away.

"Don't worry about her," the Professor said quietly. "She's been through a lot. She'll come around."

"I know my daughter."

The Professor flinched at his words. "Yes, of course you do. I was just—"

Nico took a deep breath. "I'm sorry, it's—"

"No need. I understand."

With his family inside, the number of people inside the entrance hall was starting to thin. A couple of medics hovered at the edge of the hall, clearly wanting to check on the health of the new arrivals but not wanting to disturb their reunion. O'Driscoll remained, staring at Naci, his face a mask. Maria had her arms around her mother. They were back safe, but clearly their time away had taken its toll.

The gentle giant stepped in through the door, carrying a case in each hand. Another man followed him in and all the joy Nico felt at being reunited with his family drained away. His world lurched. No. It was impossible.

"Nico? What's wrong?"

He heard Fran speak but couldn't move, couldn't respond. He didn't know what to do, whether to fight or flee. His stomach flipped and for a moment he thought he was going to be sick. There were security everywhere but they ignored this evil in their presence. Then as he watched, the Commander walked up to the man and gave him a hug.

"Good job, Oscar."

Oscar said nothing. Instead, Nico felt a moments panic as the man looked directly at him.

"Investigator."

The acknowledgement broke his trance. "You!" Nico could hardly speak. Long festering emotion boiled up inside. "Stay away from my family."

"You know him?" Fran asked.

"Know him? He's the man who threatened to kill you if I didn't do as he said."

Oscar remained impassive. There was no apology, no excuse, no emotion whatsoever.

"I don't understand." Nico felt Fran's fingers entwine his own. "He saved us. Internal Security had us surrounded. He … he stopped them, got us away. If it wasn't for him we'd be—"

"He's a killer."

"He saved us!"

"You have no idea what this man's done. None."

"You're mistaken, Investigator," the Commander said, her stern features softening as she spoke. "Oscar saved your life. On the night of the riots, Internal Security were under orders from …" she glanced at Fran "… those we currently hunt—"

"My wife knows all about Global Governance."

A look of irritation crossed the Commander's face at his interruption. "They were ordered by Global Governance to interrogate you then kill you afterwards. Oscar risked his life to rescue you."

"But he told me——"

"He did what was necessary. It was important you never mentioned what had happened that night. He was in deep cover at the time, infiltrating a splinter group. If they'd suspected him of not being who he said he was, they would have killed him too."

Nico couldn't believe what he was hearing. This man, this cruel, sadistic bastard who'd been involved in the deaths of so many and had haunted his dreams for the past two years, this man worked for Doleman? "He killed Jennica Fabian!"

"No. That was Echo."

Nico shuddered at the sound of Oscar's voice.

"Echo and I had been sent to question Jennica, but unknown to me he'd been given other orders. I tried to stop him but——"

"It was me who ordered Oscar not to interfere," the Commander said. "We had to find out who was in charge of the operation. At that point, all Oscar's orders had been delivered by an avatar, a moebius band. We had our suspicions who was behind it but we didn't have any proof. If he had intervened, all that work would've gone to waste."

"But you let him save me."

"This was different. The only way he could have saved Jennica was by killing Echo."

"So you let that poor girl die," O'Driscoll said.

"Sometimes you have to choose between the lesser of two evils." The Commander's face was hard once more. "The faction that have taken over Global Governance are happy to sacrifice thousands to get their way. What's one life if we can stop them for good?"

Nico turned away. It was too much. Oscar was a hero? The death of a young woman was the best choice? What was going on?

Fran squeezed his hand. "We're all tired, hungry and in need of a good wash. Why don't you show us where we're staying?"

His wife was right. Now wasn't the time to understand the implications of everything he'd been told. He'd learnt his lesson well. It was time to put his family first. Nico nodded and led his wife and children into the facility.

CHAPTER NINE

King of the Scrambles

O'DRISCOLL STRODE DOWN the corridor. He'd had enough of this place, enough of watching people justify controlling the lives of others for the common good.

Since he'd been released from the holding cell he'd shared with Tandelli and the old man, he'd been given almost free access to this enormous facility. Free to roam but not free to leave. Not that he hadn't tried. Each time he'd attempted to walk out of the main entrance he was politely but firmly turned back. So he'd explored the facility with the same painstaking attention to detail he'd used when exploring the Scrambles as a child.

The place was enormous, at least a couple of kilometres in length with large, circular rampways at either end and one in the middle. There were eight underground levels in all, the living quarters on level U1, offices on U2, laboratories and technology on U3, stores on U4, a medical facility on U5 and the empty holding cells on U6.

The lowest two levels had been the most intriguing. They were only accessible from the far ramp and both had no official designation. The doorway to access level U7 had some form of retinal security. He'd tried it—because you never know unless you try—but hadn't been surprised when nothing happened. At the bottom of the ramp a set of massive metal doors, at least two metres thick, stood open. Through them was a duplicate of the facilities available above, with bunks, stores and medical facilities. O'Driscoll had learned it was called the safe zone, there in case of emergency. Whoever had designed this place appeared to have planned for every inevitability. He knew the facility was probably the safest place in the country for him at present, yet it felt less like a security blanket and more like a straitjacket. He was being protected and had no choice in the matter. Choices were being made for him, not with him. It was this more than anything that grated.

It wasn't like he hadn't done the same himself in the past. He'd always done his best to protect visitors to the Scrambles—at least those that wanted protecting; some enjoyed receiving the odd beating—because there were rules to life that only idiots and scum were happy to break. But it was consensual. Everybody knew who was doing what. He never forced anyone to come into the Scrambles, or stay.

O'Driscoll's footsteps increased in pace as his frustration grew. They'd asked him to think about joining their organisation and he had. He'd thought long and hard. Now he had his answer. He rubbed at his bearded face. At least that had stopped itching now that it had grown out.

A guard stepped out from a side door just before he reached his destination. It was the heavyset bugger from the cells, a smile on his face. "I'm going to have to ask you to turn around, Mr O'Driscoll."

"I need to see Doleman."

"Lord Doleman is unavailable."

"He's in there. I know he is." O'Driscoll took a step forward.

The large guard remained where he was, his smile unwavering. From behind came the sound of footsteps and O'Driscoll turned to see two more guards heading his way. "Motherfuckers."

"I'll ask you one last time, Mr O'Driscoll. Turn around now, and you can come back when—" O'Driscoll saw the guard's eyes glaze over for a moment before refocussing. "Lord Doleman will see you now."

O'Driscoll walked up to the doors, maintaining eye contact with the giant until he passed. He walked into Doleman's office, ready for an argument, but on entering he realised there was more than one person in the room.

Doleman looked up from behind his desk. "Take a seat, Mr O'Driscoll. I take it you've met Oscar?"

The other man gave the slightest nod of greeting, which O'Driscoll ignored. "I've been thinking about your offer."

"And?"

"I need to leave."

Doleman raised an eyebrow. "So soon? I understand how difficult it is living underground, it's why I use this small office rather than one more spacious. I like having a view." He gestured towards the grey seascape through the long, deep-set window. "Still, I was hoping you'd decide to stay and help us in our cause."

"That's why I need to go. I'm useless to you here. If you want to get the best out of me, I need to be back where I belong."

Doleman sat back in his chair. "That's impossible. You're dead. People don't appreciate seeing the dead return, it … unnerves them. Trust me, I've been there enough times to know."

O'Driscoll raised his empty hands in frustration. "Yet what can I do? My value to your organisation isn't sitting here. You need access to who I know, or more importantly what I know."

Doleman glanced across to where Oscar sat before looking back at O'Driscoll. "Go on …"

"I've been thinking about why Global Governance decided to take over the Scrambles," O'Driscoll said.

"We already know why," Doleman replied. "You'd got too close to the truth about what Indigo was up to. She wanted to shut you down."

"That's what I originally thought and I'm sure it's part of the reason, but they could have simply killed me and been done with it. I think they wanted more. They wanted something you could only get in the Scrambles."

"Sex? Drugs?"

"Information." O'Driscoll leant forward. "The Scrambles is the place to do the things you don't want anyone else to know about. Anyone can do anything there, within reason, and lots of people do —from all walks of life—away from the datasphere." He looked

Doleman in the eye. "Except my systems record everything. Everything."

"And you believe Global Governance wanted access to that information?" Doleman asked.

"Within my data farms are countless petabytes of criminal activity, transgressions, sordid secrets—enough secrets to topple a dozen governments. Foul deeds will rise, you can be sure of it. Information like that is a treasure trove for an organisation looking to control events from behind the scenes."

"If you had all this information, why didn't you use it?" Oscar asked. There wasn't a hint of judgement in his voice, just a man trying to understanding the logic of a situation and taking it a step forward.

"If I'd used that information, I'd have created a thousand enemies. It was one lesson I learned from my bastard father. He had a dozen crooked politicians under his wing. They all hated him and were desperate to shut him down. They came close a few times. It was an ongoing battle. When I took over from him I decided to go the other way. I never socialised with any visitors to the Scrambles. I didn't contact them, I didn't give the slightest hint that I was aware they existed. And because people know the Scrambles is a datasphere blackspot, they believe they're perfectly safe there. Only a few people are aware we use surveillance, and only one person has ever had access to any of those files." The good it did me, O'Driscoll thought.

Doleman sat back in his chair and pulled down the sleeves of his shirt by the cuff. O'Driscoll knew the man understood his proposition. By regaining control of those files, he would hurt Global Governance by both preventing access to valuable information, and give the Knights Templar a means to control the most influential of people.

"What you're saying is persuasive, and with anyone else I'd probably agree, but you're Mick O'Driscoll. Your … reputation precedes you. Why should I trust you?"

O'Driscoll swallowed his anger. He knew Doleman well, had met plenty of his kind at boarding school. Doleman wasn't talking about his reputation as a criminal but the fact he didn't come from good blood, that he was common. "You can trust me because you have Naci."

"The boy? He's not your son, is he?"

"No, he's not, but I made a promise to look after him as if he was. You don't break that type of promise, not where I come from."

The hint of a smile on the old man's face spoke volumes. Where Doleman came from, a promise was negotiable. "But that was to a dead woman."

"We don't know she's dead. Nobody found a body. I promised I'd reunite her with her son and that's what I'm going to do."

Doleman drummed his fingers on his desk. "I don't like it. You know too much."

"You're worried I'll crack under interrogation like Tandelli?" O'Driscoll couldn't keep the laughter from his voice. "I think you'll find I'm made of sterner stuff."

"I don't think you'll crack. I think you'll trade. You'll give us up to get your old position back."

"Those bastards drove me out of my home and took over my turf. You think I'm going to make a deal with them? I'm going to make them pay."

"What about the other gangs?" Oscar interrupted. "Do you think you can bring them on board as well?"

Doleman sat forward. "You believe what he's saying?"

"I don't have to trust him to work with him, and he's right. That information would be useful."

"I can't make any promises about the other gangs" O'Driscoll said. "Our relationship has always been a little … fraught. But at the same time they would have been unsettled by what happened in the Scrambles and with the Turks."

"What do you think?" Doleman asked, looking at Oscar.

"I think it's worth the gamble. Access to that data would make our task a lot easier."

"Plus we could deal with things if they start to go wrong."

Oscar nodded. "We'll set up an emergency signal. If things get too hot I can come and get him, or …"

The look on Oscar's face let O'Driscoll know that the other option had fatal consequences.

"If I fail, you'll do well to beat either my own family or one of the other gangs to kill me first." O'Driscoll smiled as he said it but he knew what he said was true. If they let him out of here, he needed to succeed. His smile broadened. It would be just like the old days.

CHAPTER TEN

The Investigator

NICO WATCHED THE bedsheets gently rise and fall as Gino slept. The boy looked peaceful, angelic almost, as only small children can while sleeping. The thought of how close he had come to losing his family made this moment all the sweeter.

Gino rolled to his side and coughed, a horrible, racking sound causing the boy to double up as he tried to clear his lungs. As soon as the coughing fit passed, Nico reached forward and smoothed the creases from his son's forehead. Although the cough sounded bad, it was better than it had been just a few hours earlier. The nanobiotics were clearly having an effect.

Fran walked up beside him and put her head on his shoulder. "It's good to see colour back in his cheeks."

Nico didn't answer, he just placed his arm around his wife. If he ignored the medical machines in the background, and the passing staff, it felt almost normal. There was no more worrying about a knock on the door, no more fear that his children would get snatched and used as a weapon against him. For the first time in a long while, Nico felt safe.

"I was really worried about him," Fran said. "We all were. He went downhill so quickly. You forget how dangerous infections can be. We take it for granted we can fix most things, yet we're just a sneeze or sniffle away from being in the same position as those who lived a hundred years ago."

Nico suppressed a shiver. The thought of his family alone, scared, with little food and poor shelter made him feel angry and ashamed. It was his fault for putting them in that situation. He should never have left them alone. Nico stroked Fran's shoulder. "It's okay. We're safe now."

"Safe, but we're still trapped. This place is no different to O'Driscoll's hideaway. We can't go out and live our lives. We're existing but it's not a life, not really."

"It's better than before. At O'Driscoll's there were only the seven of us. Here we have the support of an organisation that's used to working in secret. And they're trying to change things, to put things back to how they were."

Fran slipped from his embrace and moved to her son's bedside. "But what are we going to do until then? What sort of lives are our children going to have? Look around. There are no families, no children. Everybody who works here, lives here. This is a military facility in all but name."

Nico took the chair beside her. "It's the safest place for us right now."

Fran gave his hand a squeeze. "I know, but it doesn't mean I'm happy about it."

Movement from the bed interrupted their conversation. Gino rolled onto his side. Nico waited for another bout of coughing but it never came. "I still don't understand why you left O'Driscoll's safe house. You had food and supplies. The children appeared happy."

"It was the Professor. He picked up signs that people were approaching. I don't like to think what would have happened if he hadn't warned us."

Nico frowned. "That doesn't fit what I was told. The Knights Templar said that you'd been gone a few days when they got there, but the house was still in perfect condition. If Global Governance had sent Internal Security troopers, the place would have been ransacked."

"There could be a hundred reasons why they left the house untouched. Perhaps they couldn't get in without making a noise.

Perhaps they'd realised we'd gone and came straight after us. Perhaps they decided to track us, to see where we led them. I know we only spotted them when the Professor went to town to get medicine for Gino, but they could have been on our trail for days."

Nico held his hands up. "I'm sorry, I'm not having a go at you. It's just that something doesn't sit right. Global Governance wouldn't have just left the house untouched, even if they'd decided to follow you. I wouldn't have, if it had been me. There'd be too much evidence in the hideout to abandon it like that."

Fran turned to face him. "Then maybe the Professor made a mistake. It happens."

"I know," Nico said, putting his arm around her once more. "I may be jumping at shadows but after all that's happened I'd rather be over-cautious than miss something. I know he's helped us in the past but something about the Professor's story doesn't add up."

"How can you say that?!"

Nico turned to see Maria and Naci standing at the door.

Fran smiled. "Have you brought Naci down to see Gino?"

"Why was Pappa being horrible about the Professor?"

"We were just talking, that's all," Nico replied. "A lot has happened over the past couple of weeks and I'm just trying to make sense of it."

"If you'd been there you'd know what happened."

"Maria!"

Fran's admonishment didn't soften the blow for Nico. "I … I was trying to stop the people who were after us."

"You promised you'd keep us safe."

"That's what I was doing."

"No you weren't. You left us. At least the Professor stayed and helped. He was the one who got us away from those hunting us. It was him who warned us the bastards were coming so we could hide."

Fran got to her feet. "Watch your language, Maria. And anyway, you're not being fair. Pappa was doing his best to—"

"He left us, just like he always has! He's never been there when we need him. All he cares about is himself. I hate him!"

Before Nico could say anything in his defence, Maria turned and ran out of the door. Fran called after her but the girl had gone. Naci remained in the doorway, staring after her, then burst into tears.

Fran took the boy in her arms. "There, there. Don't worry. Everything is going to be all right."

Nico sat stunned. His daughter's words reverberated around his head. How could she think that way? He'd gone with O'Driscoll to get to the bottom of what was going on. He wasn't being selfish. He'd been trying to protect his family.

Fran sat back down beside him, Naci in her arms. "Take no notice of her. She's had a really hard time of it and she needs to blame someone. I know it's unfair but you're the easy target. She'll come around when she realises what you've been through for us."

"I don't understand where the hatred comes from."

"She misses her friends and is scared about what she's seen. There were bodies, a lot of them, after Oscar rescued us. She had to be carried past them to get out. I told the children to close their eyes but you know what Maria's like. I know how hard the shock's hit me, I'm still not sleeping at night, and it would have been a lot worse for her. She's had no exposure to how cruel life can be. Up until a few months' ago she'd grown up in a wonderful world where everything was done for her. There were no threats and her Pappa was a hero. To go from that to where we are now in a handful of weeks … we should be glad she's just angry and not traumatised."

The mention of Oscar's name still made Nico's guts churn. Even though the man had risked his life to save Nico's family, the thought that this monster—and he couldn't think of him as anything else—was held in higher regard by his daughter than him made his skin crawl.

"I should talk to her."

"I'm not sure that's a good idea at the moment."

"I can't leave things like this. I need to show her that I'm doing my best to protect you all, that I'm trying to bring these people to justice so she can go back to her friends and live a normal life."

"If you go to her now she'll only dig her heels in. She's like you in that respect. Leave me to talk to her, or you could have a word with the Professor. The two of them formed a close bond while you were away. Maybe he could—"

"I can't, not until I'm sure about him."

"Please, Nico. Stop. The Professor's saved us enough times to prove his worth. You need to start trusting people again."

"I do trust people."

"Then cut him some slack."

"I just need to be sure."

He squeezed his wife's hand. Something told him Fran was wrong about the Professor and he was happy to let her think he'd let it drop. But he wasn't prepared to give the man the benefit of the doubt quite yet. He still needed to tie up all the evidence. At least that was one thing he was good at.

CHAPTER ELEVEN

Indigo

THE ATMOSPHERE IN the club was thick and cloying, a mélange of throbbing beats, sweating bodies and the heady taint of narcosmoke. Lights strobed on and off in time to the music, a disorienting effect made worse as the psychoactive in the air took hold.

Indigo made her way through the crowd, ignoring the stares from the young and the beautiful as they tried to comprehend how something so old floated in their midst. She hadn't chosen this club as a meeting place—she'd been given no choice.

She glanced around the space in an attempt to get her bearings. Surrounding the dance floor were a series of darkened alcoves, their occupants sealed off from the heaving mass by translucent walls. Through the haze she noticed the faintest shadow of movement from the alcove nearest to her. As she watched, a hand pressed against the wall followed by a cheek. A second hand followed the first, slapping the surface. The cheek moved slowly up and down in time to the music. There was a shadowy presence behind the figure, its motion matching the person she could see, mouth now open—although whether from pain or pleasure, Indigo couldn't be sure.

The combination of watching the couple rut and the effects of the narcosmoke aroused a warmth inside her. A small part of Indigo felt annoyed she could be manipulated so easily, but it was hard to resist the sensual call as each bass rumble made her thrum like a tuning fork.

Someone grabbed her elbow, jolting Indigo out of her reverie. She turned to see a young man of such beauty it could only have come from the most expensive of surgeries.

He leant forward, his mouth to her ear. "This way, if you please."

She followed his lead, weaving through the crowd until they reached an alcove in the farthest corner of the club. The young man gestured for her to enter. Indigo's instincts screamed at the risk she was taking. She had no real idea who this beautiful man was or what was waiting for her inside the alcove. Was it the person she'd arranged to meet? She glanced to her right and saw the reassuring presence of Echo, standing on the other side of the dance floor, drink in hand. For an instant their eyes met, then he turned away. It was enough.

A shiver of anticipation shimmered up Indigo's spine, setting off a series of narcosmoke-amplified tremors throughout her body. What the hell? She hadn't come all this way to turn back now. She walked through the doorway and the change of atmosphere felt like a slap. The music ceased completely, her head cleared and with it came the realisation of just how intoxicated she'd been. The door slid closed behind her.

A lone figure sat in a shadowed recess, face hidden. He gestured towards a stool. "Please, sit down."

Indigo considered whether to remain standing, just to show she wasn't ready to surrender control, but she took the stool indicated.

"You've caused quite a stir." The man's voice was heavily accented. "I don't think anyone here has seen a body as old as yours for quite some time."

Indigo ignored the dig. Money and vanity may have eradicated ageing in this strata of society, but she knew the true consequences of upgrading your body to a younger model. "Thank you for agreeing to see me, Herr Streckler."

"I almost didn't. You've not made yourself popular with me or my friends over the past few months." His face remained in the shadows, invisible to her.

"It's better to be effective than popular. I'm only doing what I believe is right."

"Oh, I understand that. But it's not just that we have different ideas of what right is, it's also how you've gone about your work."

Indigo swallowed her anger. "I didn't come here to be chastised."

"What, you thought we would sit here like old friends and have a little chat? You and your allies have destroyed our organisation, steering it in a direction contrary to its founding principles."

"We didn't destroy it—we saved it. Something had to be done. We were in danger of perfectly preserving the rotten carcass of our civilisation, rather than helping it flourish as we'd promised."

"I think you're exaggerating the situation. Humanity's doing just fine without the need for the additional 'stimulation' you've set in motion. Nothing you can say will change my opinion of that."

There was a knock at the door. The handsome young man walked in and leaned across the table and into the shadows. With the door ajar the music forced its way into the alcove, making Indigo's stool vibrate. With his message delivered, the young man left, smiling at Indigo as he went.

"I've not come to change your mind. There have always been differences of opinion within our organisation, that's why we abide by the decisions made at the Governing Council."

"Then I fail to see what you are doing here."

Indigo took a deep breath and leaned forward. "Global Governance has always had its factions, right from the very start."

"I was there. I remember exactly what it was like."

"But however these factions were drawn, whether on family, national or ideological lines, it needed the agreement of the majority before we moved ahead with anything. The infighting has been a weakness of Global Governance but also its strength. We've never rushed into anything. We've always reviewed every possibility before acting. Even the recovery plan we forced on the world was developed after months of negotiation."

"You're not making yourself any clearer."

"My point is there has never been one person controlling our agenda. Until now."

Her words were met by silence from the other side of the alcove. Then Herr Streckler emerged from the darkness. Indigo stifled a gasp. The man she had known for many years only by his dachshund avatar looked to be in his mid-30s. For a fleeting moment she thought she'd been tricked into meeting one of his sons but she then remembered what he'd said about being there when Global Governance was established. He'd been Re-Lifed, probably one of the early ones judging how old he'd been and how old his clone now was. No wonder he hadn't given up his position on the Governing Council. He was physically younger than the majority of his offspring.

"I think you need to explain."

Indigo took a moment to gather her thoughts. "When I realised what was happening in the world—having analysed the data and extrapolated the current growth and innovation indices—I knew I needed to find allies in the Governing Council to deliver what was needed to rectify the situation."

"You will excuse me if I don't congratulate you on your achievement."

"One of those I approached was Tarik Tahmid Ihab Abd al-Rashid, an Arab prince whose family was one of the first to transfer out of petrochemicals and into renewables before the Upheaval. His avatar is the saker falcon."

The industrialist remained quiet, his expression unreadable.

"Unbeknown to me, al-Rashid had been building a faction all of his own. When I put him in touch with other progressives," Indigo ignored the annoyance on Streckler's face at the term, "he brought them into the fold. He now heads a group with enough votes to control Global Governance. With that much power he has become the de-facto global leader." Worse, he took that role from me, she thought. The realisation at what she'd done had hit Indigo hard. She'd been so focussed on achieving her goal, she hadn't noticed how the little shit had managed to outflank her.

The old/young man in front of her began to laugh. "So now you're forced to come to me to help you out of a hole. Maybe you should have thought things through a bit better before deciding to corrupt our organisation."

Indigo gritted her teeth. Streckler was closer to the truth than she cared to admit. "This isn't about me, or what direction our organisation should go in. This is bigger than that. No single person should have the power this man has. How many times has history shown us that power can corrupt even the best individuals? I'm not sure Prince al-Rashid is the best individual, and I shouldn't need to tell somebody of your nationality what that could mean."

Streckler's amusement vanished. "I don't need a lecture from you about history."

"My apologies. It wasn't meant as an accusation. I'm just trying —"

"I know what you're just trying. You're just trying to get back at a person who's double-crossed you. So why should I trust what you say?"

The intelligence in his eyes, wise beyond his apparent age, drilled into her. Herr Streckler was a hard man—you don't become a multi-billionaire by being nice—and renowned for facing down and crushing his opponents. But she didn't need him to trust her, at least not yet. She just needed him to be concerned by what she'd said. "I came here in person as a gesture of trust. You now know who I am, what I look like."

"As you know me."

"I've always known," she lied. "I could have visited you at any one of your houses if I'd wanted to. The point is I came here in person, at a place of your choosing," she gestured to the club behind her, "giving up my anonymity so we could speak on equal terms."

Streckler remained quiet for a long time before he spoke. "I've been around long enough not to trust your motives …" Indigo opened her mouth to interrupt but was silenced by Streckler's raised hand, "… but you're right about the danger of one man having so much power. The question is, what can we do about it?"

For the first time since she arrived, Indigo smiled. "That's where I come in."

CHAPTER TWELVE

The Investigator

NICO FOUND HER on level U2, staring out of the window of a darkened conference room in the middle of the complex, watching the ocean twinkle under the night sky. Despite knowing Fran was right, he couldn't stop himself from looking. Maria was his daughter. He loved her with all his heart. He had to at least try to get through to her.

Nico approached the door quietly, then knocked.

Despite his care, Maria jumped at the noise, spinning around sharply, her face scarlet. "Go away."

"We need to talk."

She turned her back on him and continued to look out of the window.

"I know you're angry with me," he said, "that you blame me for leaving you alone in the house. I can see how that looks from your perspective, and I can't change what happened. If I'd known you were in danger I'd never have left. I thought you were safe there."

The young girl said nothing, her eyes glued to the window and the world outside.

Nico took a step towards his daughter. "I went with O'Driscoll to find out who the bad guys were and to try to stop them. They'd already come to our house, remember? I had no choice. This isn't the life I want for you, but the only way for things to return to normal was for me to bring the people threatening us to justice. I know you'd rather I hadn't gone away but—"

"You don't get it, do you?"

Nico stopped talking. His daughter was almost close enough to touch. He longed to give her a hug, to let her know everything was all right. "What? What don't I get?"

"It wasn't that you weren't there when they came for us, it's that you're never there. You haven't been there for a long time."

"That's not fair."

"Yes it is! Even before all this happened you spent most of the day at work, and when you were at home you just locked yourself in your office."

"Being an Investigator isn't like a normal job. The hours can be long, especially when working on a complicated case."

Maria turned to face him. "That's not what Sacha says. Her dad's an Investigator too but he used to take the family out all the time. When was the last time we ever went out?"

"I don't know, it was … er …"

"See, you can't even remember."

"A lot's happened."

"The only time you spoke was to tell me off, to stop me from doing stuff."

"Maria, please …"

He could hear the crack in her voice as she spoke, wanted so much to make things right. "I thought … I thought it would be different when you came home, when the bad men came. You were there for us. You saved us. But then we ended up in that house by the coast and you hid yourself away again, this time with O'Driscoll."

"I didn't hide. We saw each other."

His daughter spun around, tears in her eyes. "No we didn't! You hardly said two words to me all the time we were there."

"I was trying to work out what was going on, so I could keep you safe."

"For what, so you could just ignore me again? You say you were too busy to speak but everyone else found the time to talk, Mamma, the Professor …"

"Don't bring him into this!"

Maria flinched and Nico cursed his temper. He hadn't meant to shout, it was just the thought of that man with his daughter.

"Why shouldn't I bring the Professor into this? He cares more about me than you do."

Nico swallowed his anger. "That's not true."

"Yes it is. When was the last time you took me to the beach? When was the last time we did something together, just the two of us? When was the last time you asked me how I was?"

Each question stabbed into him, the accusation clear. "I think about you all the time."

"Why? To control me? To keep me away from my friends?"

"I'd love for you to be with your friends. I'm trying to make that happen. It's just not safe right now."

"Because of you."

Nico took a deep breath. She was a young girl making her first steps into adulthood, she didn't know what he'd been through, the lengths he'd gone to keep all this from his family. "I didn't ask for this."

"Neither did I. Neither did Mamma, or Gino or even the Professor."

"I've been trying to protect you all."

"And what a great job you've done."

Maria ran past him and out of the room, leaving Nico alone with just the ink-black sea and the night sky for company.

CHAPTER THIRTEEN

King of the Scrambles

O'DRISCOLL CHECKED HIS datalenses. Ten minutes until leaving time. Good. He couldn't wait to get out of the place. It wasn't just that he was a prisoner in all but name, it was the sincerity of everyone that did his head in. He'd sat with different people each day at the canteen, and everybody was the same. They were 'people on a mission', fully bought-in to their self-appointed role. The whole organisation had an earnest streak running through it a mile wide, a conviction only true believers have. It was suffocating, nauseating.

He selected what he needed from a long rail full of work clothes and pulled it on. He'd been in the stores for the past hour, weighing up different options for his journey ahead. He knew he needed a disguise to enter the Scrambles undetected—his usual three-piece suit was too recognisable—but selecting the right option had proven tricky. He'd first thought about donning an Internal Security uniform, but from what he could tell the troopers had left the Scrambles as soon as Global Governance had taken control. Then he'd had a better idea. Dynamic dermal implants had changed the shape of his face, widening his cheekbones and stretching the skin around his eyes and broadening his nose. The slivers of nanogel had been injected under the skin and were controlled by the datalenses he now wore instead of his preferred dataglasses. They were only a temporary option, lasting just a couple of weeks, but when combined with his new beard the effect was dramatic. He checked his reflection in a mirror. Not even his dear departed mother would recognise him.

O'Driscoll picked up the heavy boots by his feet and slipped them on, pausing so they could mould around his feet to form a perfect fit. He grabbed his pack for one last check. Inside were a change of clothes, his dataglasses and the one thing he needed more than anything else for his plan to work, a graphene ring that would allow him to take control of the Scramble's datasystems. As he stepped out into the corridor he thought about visiting the Investigator. Knowing Nico, even at this late hour he'd still be hard at work, tracking down members of the Governing Council. There was another one newly committed to the cause, a born-again Knight Templar. Yet despite everything, O'Driscoll realised he would miss the man. Yes, he could be annoying with his sanctimonious views on right and wrong, but the two of them had been through a lot together and formed a twisted kind of bond. Instead he shook his head and turned the other way. This was no time for sentimentality. He had one person to visit and then he would be gone.

The overhead lights in the corridor were dim, giving a semblance of time passing in this underground maze. As he walked through the dining area, O'Driscoll noticed two men on the far side, deep in conversation. He recognised the Professor straight away but it was the presence of the other one that surprised him. So they finally let the old bastard out, he thought. Joshua Denham appeared to be explaining something to the Professor, his arms waving around as he sought to get his point of view across. The Professor had an exasperated expression on his face, one O'Driscoll recognised from personal experience. The two of them hadn't seen him enter and he had no desire to speak to either of them, so he continued on. Whatever they were up to, that was somebody else's look out.

O'Driscoll took the central ramp to the accommodation level. He walked quietly down the corridor until he got to the door he was looking for and gently knocked.

It was Fran who opened it. "You look different. I hardly recognised you."

"That's the idea."

"When are you off?"

"In a few minutes. I just thought …"

She smiled. "He's just gone to bed but he might still be awake. You know where."

O'Driscoll went to walk through into the accommodation room but before he could, Fran wrapped her arms around him and gave him a hug.

"Thank you for all you've done."

O'Driscoll stood for a moment, unsure of what to say. Eventually Fran released him and he made his way down the hallway and opened the door.

It was a twin room. One bed was empty, the second held the person he was looking for. He reached across and gently pressed his hand on the shoulder of the sleeping form. The boy's eyes flickered open.

"Hello Naci. It's Uncle Mick. I wanted to see you to say goodbye."

The boy rolled over to face away from where O'Driscoll crouched.

He gave the boy a gentle shake. "Naci. You need to wake up. I've something to tell you."

The boy gave a little groan but rolled back. He yawned and O'Driscoll found himself suppressing one too.

"I've not done a good job of looking after you like I promised your mother. I'm sorry. My father didn't look after me very well either and I'd hoped to do better by you. I guess it shows there's more passed on in the genes than you think."

The boy frowned. "What are genes?"

"They're things your parents give to you as a baby that make you who you are."

Naci shrugged, then pulled a pristine teddy bear to his chest, a gift from the medical staff, and gave it a squeeze.

"Uncle Nico and Aunty Fran are going to look after you while I'm away. It means you get to stay with Gino and Maria too. Would you like that?"

The boy yawned again and nodded.

"Good. They all like you a lot. You'll be safe with them." O'Driscoll stroked the boys head. "You keep being a big brave boy and I'll be back soon."

"Where are you going?"

"I'm going to see some friends."

"Mummy is your friend. Are you going to see her? I miss Mummy."

"I know you do. I'm sure she misses you too. Now go to sleep and remember that Uncle Mick will always be looking out for you." The young boy smiled. O'Driscoll leaned forward and kissed his forehead. "Night-night."

The boy closed his eyes and O'Driscoll slipped out of the door.

It was colder outside than he'd realised. For once the leaden clouds had cleared and the night sky glittered, the stars brighter and more numerous than those back home. He pulled his pack higher onto his shoulder and headed towards the waiting vehicle, breath glistening in the pod's headlights. The nights were closing in.

A figure approached from out of the shadows. "You're late."

"I had something to do."

"Is that all you're planning to bring?"

"It's everything I need."

"Good," the Commander said. "Get in with the others. We're about to leave."

O'Driscoll climbed into the back of the pod. Three people waited inside, two men and a woman. They were dressed as medics but despite having spent a lot of time in the medical facility, O'Driscoll had never seen them before. What he did recognise was their nerves. It showed on their faces and the way their fingers twitched. Whoever these people were, they were apprehensive about something.

The Commander climbed in beside him and the pod doors slid shut. O'Driscoll waited for the datascreens to come on but they remained blank. It was unnerving. These people could be taking him anywhere, could be taking him off to die.

He took a deep breath and slowly exhaled. They had no reason to take him somewhere to kill him. If that was the plan, they could do it at the base. Nobody would know. The simplest answer was that he had no idea of where the base was situated. Blanking out the screens made sure it stayed this way. If captured, he'd not be able to give the location up. It was a sensible precaution, but not a reassuring one.

"Did you speak to Lord Doleman before you left?" the Commander asked.

O'Driscoll shook his head. "I'm not a fan of goodbyes."

"We can drop you close to Arhenius Park. You'll have to make your own way to the Scrambles from there."

"You're not coming with me?"

"No. We have something more important to do."

That suits me fine. The last thing I need is a group of babysitters, he thought. O'Driscoll sunk down into his seat and closed his eyes. It had taken them hours to get here when first taken, so he knew they wouldn't be back any time soon. Time to get some rest. Once he arrived, there was no saying when his next chance for sleep would be.

CHAPTER FOURTEEN

Indigo

INDIGO SMILED AS one solemn-faced person after another nodded their ascent. These were the most powerful people in the Northern Independent States, tasked with governing their country. Eventually the camera settled on a short, slightly overweight man, sweat glistening on his forehead. Indigo knew exactly who this was. She'd planned to kill him to start a war, but those plans had gone awry. Still, it was funny how things had a way of working themselves out.

"Thank you, ladies and gentlemen," Dick Johnson said, before taking a sip of water. "With all votes counted, and with a heavy heart, I can confirm we are now at war."

A muted smattering of applause broke out. From their expressions it was clear that many in the chamber weren't happy with the situation, but the vote itself was almost unanimous. A woman stood beside Johnson, a fierce smile on her face. After the death of her husband, Ruby Valentine had become the driving force behind the call to war, steamrollering opponents with a mixture of grief and indignation until in the end the vote was a mere formality.

Watching from another continent, Indigo knew Independent States' troops were already at the border with their neighbour, the Southern Free States, and that there had already been a number of skirmishes. She took a sip of vodka in celebration. The first part of her plan was coming to fruition. Her only frustration was that in the end, she hadn't needed the young prince's help after all. Valentine had done the work for her. If only she'd held out a little longer before requesting his support. Still, what was done was done. She couldn't change the past, all she could do was plan for the future. With the aid of Herr Streckler, she'd soon put the prince in his place so that she could influence the Governing Council once more.

On her datascreen, Johnson gestured for quiet. "While I've been accused of many things, having been called a warmonger and an 'angel of death', I need you all to know that I never wanted this to happen."

There was a knock at the door. As Echo entered, Indigo realised how much he'd changed in the weeks since she'd pulled him from his dank cell. He'd regained his poise, his walk like that of a stalking panther. Gone was the anxiety, that eager-to-please expression every time she looked in his direction. The old Echo was back, and she was happy to see him again.

"Yes?"

"Someone's taken the bait." He had the faintest smile on his lips as he spoke.

Indigo turned back to the datascreen but couldn't suppress a shiver of excitement. "Your plan worked. Well done. When did it happen?"

"About fifteen minutes ago."

"*… but we were not the ones to launch terrorist attacks on innocent civilians, we were not the ones looking to disrupt our financial institutions …*"

"Did everything go as planned?"

"The team fixed a tracker on their vehicle as soon as it arrived. We know exactly where they are."

"Excellent." She'd made the right decision bringing Echo back into the fold. He'd always been her best agent and was proving so once again.

"*… too many times we have been asked to swallow these provocations, to strive for peace for the common good of the world. But to have peace both parties need to be willing to put aside their differences, and despite their words, it's clear from their actions that the South have no interest in living harmoniously with us*

…"

"Have we identified any of the team that took Stephanie Vaughn?"

"No."

"What about Tandelli?"

"He wasn't there."

Indigo grimaced. Damn that man, where was he?

"… these will be difficult times, dark times. We must all remain vigilant, not just on the border but for the enemy within. We can win this war but to do so we need everybody to play their part, whether that is working hard to supply our troops, purchasing local produce to maintain our economy or watching those around us who may be the agents of our enemy. And those of us who govern need to take difficult decisions. To that end, I have authorised the use of unmanned drones to target the leadership of our enemies …"

Indigo's attention flicked to the datascreen. That was unexpected. The use of drones was banned since just after the Upheaval. She took another swallow of vodka. "I think it's time for you to go up there yourself, take charge of things."

Echo raised his eyebrows. "What about you?"

"The situation here has changed. It's not quite as … fraught … as it was. Go work with our team up north until you find out where these people are hiding, then sit tight."

"You don't want us to engage?"

"Not yet. I want you to observe, find out as much about the operation as possible. From what you've said, we've no idea who these people are or what resources they have at their disposal. I need you to get a better understanding of what we're up against so when we take them out, we take them all out."

"As you wish," Echo said, and left the room, closing the door behind him.

"… remember, this is a just war, a war not of our making but a war we shall win!"

Applause issued out of the datascreen until Indigo turned off the feed. She stretched out on the couch and for the first time in a long time felt content. With North America coming to the boil, soon she'd have enough data to prove beyond doubt that she'd been right.

The world needed a shock to wake it from its lethargy, and there was no better way to stimulate innovation than war. And if, when revealing this, she could also bring down the organisation that had spent so long undermining her efforts, then this day could end up proving to be a very good day indeed.

Her plans were all coming together nicely.

CHAPTER FIFTEEN

Stephanie

WAS THAT A noise?

Stephanie opened her eyes but all she saw was a faint light and familiar hiss-click from the respirator at her side.

She went to close her eyes when another noise, louder this time, echoed around her room. It was the sound of footsteps, lots of them, and they appeared to be getting louder.

As her condition had worsened, they'd tilted her bed to prevent fluid collecting in her trachea, or so the kind-faced woman had said. It wasn't much, but it was enough. The new angle gave her a partial view across her room, a welcome change from the monotonous ceiling.

A flicker of movement caught her attention. Stephanie strained, looking down her nose towards the room's entrance but the doorway was empty. Then the top of somebody's head appeared, somebody she recognised. What do they want with me now? Can't they just let me sleep?

The kind-faced woman leant over her. "I need you to stay calm. We're getting you out of here."

Out? What did she mean 'out'? Were they moving her to another room?

The woman turned and spoke to somebody else. Stephanie tried to see who it was, the blur of the mask over her nose making it difficult for her to focus at first. There was another woman stood at the bottom of her bed, somebody Stephanie had never seen before. She had steel-grey hair scraped back into a ponytail, her gaze severe as she directed more people coming through the doorway.

"We have two minutes."

"I need more time to attach the mobile device, Commander," The kind-faced woman said. "She'll die if I don't fix it properly."

There was a note of panic in her voice. Stephanie would have scowled at the older woman if she could. Leave her alone, she shouted inside her head. She's the kindest person I know.

"She'll die along with the rest of us if we're caught."

The respirator gave out an alarm before cutting out. The room went quiet. For the first time Stephanie felt scared, as if the removal of the respirator's sound represented something bigger. A part of the world she'd known for so long had been silenced and she wasn't sure if she liked it.

The kind-faced woman pushed Stephanie's head forward, removing the respirator mask. Unfamiliar smells assailed her nostrils, from sweat, to urine, to the flowery scent emanating from the woman herself. Then a second mask was placed over her nose, this one filled with more familiar desiccated air.

Her bed shook as a transparent covering was placed over her. It felt cold against her face, another sensation she'd forgotten. Figures moved on either side, their outlines distorted through the creased material, then the cover gently rose, smoothing out until it formed a dome over her entire body.

"She's ready, Commander."

"Good, let's go."

Stephanie's head rocked as her bed moved. After placing the new face mask on, the kind-faced woman had tipped her back until Stephanie could only see the darkened ceiling above, the extinguished lights in her room flitting past as she went, but the moment she crossed through the doorway a part of her silently cried out in elation. She was finally out of that terrible place.

But where was she being taken?

A thousand possibilities entered her mind, none of them pleasant.

Had they finally created a new clone and were moving her to transfer her consciousness? Or had they decided to torture her some more, just for the hell of it? She'd thought they couldn't do anything more to her, but this sudden movement into the unknown terrified her.

Then she remembered what the stern woman had said. They would all be killed if they were caught.

Her bed rocked again, tipping her head deeper into her pillow. A man's stubbled chin hovered above her, visible through the transparent dome. So this was the person who pushed her bed.

Soon Stephanie's world narrowed until it became a collage of the ceiling racing past, the rocking to and fro and the ever-present man hovering above. She watched the curve of corridors and the occasional doorway flow past. What felt like every couple of minutes, the motion would stop and Stephanie would hear whispering voices.

"Is the way clear?"

"Corridor's clear."

"Let's go."

On and on they went, the process repeated as they moved through the building. The movement and noise after having spent so long alone was overwhelming. Stephanie had forgotten what it was like to be surrounded by sensation. Even the regular rocking of her head felt wonderful as the pillow cover gently caressed her cheek with each movement.

"Where do you think you're going?"

The bed stopped. Whoever had spoken was out of view. Stephanie watched the man above her remain perfectly still, only his eyes moving as they took in what was happening.

"I've orders for the patient to be taken to a different facility." Stephanie recognised the voice of the kind-faced woman.

"I wasn't told of this."

"It's a medical emergency."

"Without a copy of the order, I can't allow you to leave."

Stephanie watched as the man's expression hardened and he gently released his grip on the gurney.

"I haven't time to sort out another admin cock-up," the kind-faced woman said. "I need to get the patient out of here and into isolation. The temporary precautions we've put in place are only effective for a short period of time."

"What do you mean?"

"What do you think I mean? She's highly contagious. Unless you want her infection to spread throughout the facility, I suggest you let us through. Right now."

"This is highly irregular."

"Here, take my pass. If you have any comeback, send them my way."

There was a long pause. The man above her bed licked his lips, his eyes never wavering from whatever was happening in front of him.

"No, I'm sorry. You'll have to wait until I call this through."

Stephanie watched the man raise a weapon in one smooth movement and fire. The noise was incredible, inches above her head and painful at such close quarters.

"Move!"

She jerked back as the bed shot forward, much faster than before. With all the shaking it was hard to make out what was going on. Stephanie heard the slamming of doors and for a brief moment saw stars twinkling in the sky overhead, then her covering misted over and everything disappeared.

The bed shook violently as it raced forward. There was a shout, the sound of more shots, then with a loud crunch the gurney lurched sideways before crashing to the ground. Stephanie's head smacked against something hard. Her old friend pain erupted once more, smothering all other sensation.

Stephanie heard more shouts, closer this time, followed by a tearing sound. A shock of cold air hit her face. She saw a man's face through a hole cut into the transparent covering, the same man who'd been above her moments before. He reached through and dragged her out, lifting her up and over his shoulder like a sack of grain. Her head banged against his back.

"Get her inside, quickly. You, take the respirator. Go-go-go!"

There was a confusion of noise and movement. Stephanie's head shook and pain blossomed in her mouth as she bit her tongue. The cold cut into her cheeks. Something beeped in alarm and a voice shouted about a trapped air tube. She couldn't make out what was happening. There was too much going on, too much stimulation. Too much reality.

The world began to fade.

The violent rocking diminished, the noise dissipated. Stephanie recognised the feeling. She'd been here before. Her consciousness withdrew from her body and she drifted on a sea of calm. It was better this time. There was no shock or pain like before, when Randall stabbed her in the neck. This time it was pleasant, just the gradual easing away to something—

Her head whipped back, landing on something soft.

"We're all in. Let's get out of here!"

The pain in her mouth sharpened, a reminder that she hadn't moved on. Death was denied to her once again.

"Please tell me she's okay."

"Her airline got trapped when she was carried in. We almost lost her. She's very fragile, poor thing." Stephanie recognised the voice of the kind-faced woman. So she was still with her.

"Will she be okay?"

"She'll make it back, if that's what you mean."

Stephanie saw the face of the older woman she'd seen in her room. Her hard features had softened and there were tears in her eyes. Fingers stroked her cheek.

"Dear, sweet Steppy. I'm sorry, I'm so sorry."

The words dug deep into her, dislodging old memories. Stephanie knew that name, had dreamed for so many years for someone to use it again. She looked at the woman's face once more, stripping away the lines and blemishes, focussing on its shape and structure. It was the eyes that persuaded her. There were additional creases around the edges but their shape was the same as she remembered. It was impossible, yet it was true. Stephanie stared into the eyes of her mother, and inside her mind a ten-year-old girl cried.

CHAPTER SIXTEEN

The Investigator

"NOW IT'S YOUR turn to hide, Pappa."

Nico smiled down at Gino. "Okay, but remember to cover your eyes and don't peek. What number do you start with?"

"One!" Gino jumped with excitement at knowing the answer.

"And what do you go up to?"

"Twenty!" The shout echoed up the long, winding ramp.

"And Mamma will help with all the rest in between."

"I can count, Pappa!"

Nico did well to stifle a laugh. The indignant look on his son's face was the mirror image of one he'd often seen on Fran's. He marvelled again at the resilience of children. His son had been at death's door when he'd arrived but just over two weeks later he was nearly back to his normal energetic self.

Fran leaned down to give her son a cuddle. "I'll just help if you get stuck. Is that okay?"

Gino nodded. Despite the natural warmth of the tunnels he was wrapped in a number of layers. The poor boy's arms stuck out at the sides, unable to drop any lower due to the bulk.

Nico turned to Naci. "Are you ready?"

The other boy grinned and nodded. He'd been inseparable from Gino since the boy had returned from the medical bay. While Naci hadn't said anything directly, it was clear O'Driscoll leaving had left a bigger impact than they'd first realised.

"Let's go!" Nico grabbed Naci's hand and the two of them ran down the final curve of the ramp onto the U8 landing, before speeding past the enormous steel doors and into the safe zone. The large, open entrance area remained mostly in shadows, the only available light coming through the doorway or from low-level lighting above. It was the perfect place to play hide and seek.

Nico and Naci headed across the open space towards sleeping quarters located on the left-hand side. It had been Fran's idea to take the boys down here. The facility hadn't been designed to cater for two energetic youngsters, and while nobody said anything directly, both Nico and Fran received annoyed looks from time to time when the boys' natural exuberance disturbed people's work. The safe zone was the only place in the whole complex where the boys could run wild without getting into trouble.

"Lay down here," Nico whispered, pointing to a bunk at the back of the first dormitory they'd come to. Naci slid underneath the bed, giggling as he hid. His boots stuck out at the far end but the boy didn't notice, believing he was fully hidden as his hands covered his eyes.

"Eleven … twelve … er … um …"

"Thirteen."

Nico glanced back to the entrance, smiling as he heard Fran help Gino count. The boys weren't the only ones to benefit since coming here. It was amazing what a few weeks' worth of rest had done to her too. Gone were the dark smudges and permanent frown. Only her eyes gave away the concern she still felt, that they all felt, about being confined underground.

"Thirteen …" Gino replied, jolting Nico from his thoughts. He looked up and saw light coming from a corridor at the back of the open area. If he was quick he could sprint across the room before the boy finished counting.

They'd initially restricted the boys to playing only in the open area and the dormitories, but over the past couple of days they'd explored enough of the compound to know the boys couldn't get up to too much mischief. The meeting rooms were safe and the medical facilities towards the rear of the open area were kept locked. That left the long corridor at the far end with storerooms branching off either side, which were usually locked. The corridor itself ended in another steel door, smaller than the one at the entrance and sealed shut.

Nico raced across the open space towards this corridor just as Gino shouted a loud "… twenty!" Worried that the boy wouldn't think to look back this far, he fished a glove from his pocket and left it at the corridor entrance. That should be enough of a clue, even for Gino. He then crept a few metres down until out of sight and sat on the floor. As he leaned back against the wall, eyes closed, he couldn't believe the short sprint had left him breathless. He'd spent too much time sitting behind a desk over the last couple of years. He needed to get out more, get some exercise. As soon as he thought it the reality of what that meant came crashing in. Get out more? It would be great to get out at all, lead a normal life, go for a walk; any of a thousand freedoms people took for granted until they were taken away.

"I can't see them."

Nico opened his eyes at the sound of Gino's whisper echoing across the open space.

"That's the point. They're hiding. You need to find them," Fran said.

"I'll never find them."

"Yes you will. Where do you think would be a good place to hide? Where would you go?"

"Over there!"

The sound of running was quickly followed by a squeal of laughter. Nico heard Gino tell Naci that his bright blue shoes had been poking out from under the bunk. Naci groaned in disappointment, only to laugh himself.

"Now it's time to find Pappa!"

Nico glanced down the corridor, knowing the three of them would be heading his way soon. There were plenty of windowed doors either side of the corridor, any contents hidden in darkness behind locked doors. All except the last room on the left, where light shone out into the corridor. Somebody must have left the light on the last time they'd come down here, although it was a surprise they'd left the door open. Still, the room seemed as good a place as any to hide, so Nico crept down the corridor towards it.

"It looks like everything's in order."

That was Doleman's voice. What the hell was he doing down here? Whatever the reason, it was clearly a private conversation. The last thing Doleman would want was a couple of pre-schoolers screaming down the corridor. Nico turned back down the corridor.

"I've no idea why you wanted to come down and check. The system has a record of all our stores."

Nico froze at the sound of Oscar's voice.

"You'll have to forgive an old man his quirks. I like to see everything for myself. I was ill prepared for the worst-case scenario when our country needed me, I won't let our organisation suffer the same fate. Things are coming to a head and these stores may be needed soon if I'm correct. Especially if you lead this mission."

"I've told you, I'm not interested."

"I don't understand your reticence. This is the chance we've been waiting for."

"Even so …"

"But she's in the country. Our people spotted her arrive on the trans-continental this morning."

"I told you, I'm finished doing that sort of work for you."

"But Indigo is the key. If we take her out, we cripple the faction in control of Global Governance."

At the mention of Indigo's name, Nico thought his heart would explode out of his ribcage. That bitch was here, in the country?

"I don't care. I'm not killing any more, not for you, not for anyone. If you want that woman dead you'll have to get somebody else to do it."

"But you're the best. We don't have anyone else as good as you."

"What about Heather?"

"She's … elsewhere."

"Another mission you're keeping from the rest of us?"

"I'm not keeping anything from you," Doleman snapped. "Her

mission's personal. If I hadn't given my permission she'd have gone anyway. Stephanie Vaughan's at risk and I couldn't hold Heather off any longer. She's gone to rescue her daughter."

It took a few moments for Doleman's words to sink in. The Commander was Stephanie's mother? But Stephanie always said her mother was dead, that she'd been brought up by her grandparents. Yet at the same time it made sense. Being part of a secret organisation was as good as being dead to those around you.

Nico didn't know what to do. He knew he should leave. If he was caught listening to their conversation, there was no telling what Doleman and Oscar would do, but if he left now he'd never find out the truth of what the Knights Templar were up to.

The sounds of the children searching for him filtered down the corridor. They were getting closer.

"Why kill Indigo?" Oscar said. "Why not capture her instead? Think of what she knows. We'd not only take her out of the game, we'd also have access to everything she's planned. We could stop her faction before they do any more damage."

"It's too risky. They know you, or at least Indigo does. If they captured you—"

"They'll get nothing from me," Oscar said, anger in his voice.

"They won't have to. You're meant to be dead. If they find out you're alive it won't take them long to work out there's more of us out here, and if Global Governance ever find that out, we'll be crushed. You know as well as I do that we've no chance against the resources they have at their disposal."

"But if we succeed, we can put a stop to the bastards for good."

"And if we fail, they've won."

"They're winning anyway."

"Which is why I don't understand why you refuse to kill her?"

The room went silent.

"What do you think we should do, Chief Investigator?

Nico stifled a yelp as Oscar appeared at the door.

"Well, are you planning to crouch down there all day or are you coming in?"

Doleman looked startled when Nico entered the room. "What the bloody hell are you doing?" The old man stood between rows of shelving stretching back as far as Nico could see.

"I was playing hide and seek with the boys. We come down here a lot, to get the boys out from under everyone's feet. If I'd known you were here I wouldn't have come but by the time I realised—"

"How much did you overhear?"

Nico felt his cheeks heat. "Enough."

"I don't like being spied upon."

"I wasn't spying. By the time I realised what was going on it was too late."

"But seeing what you've heard, and now that you're here, why don't you answer my question?" Oscar's voice remained pleasant but his eyes stared straight into Nico's soul.

The room went quiet. Nico felt the rumble as the sea crashed into cliffs hundreds of feet above their heads. He swallowed. "I think Oscar's right. You shouldn't kill her. I know she's done terrible things, and I'm not sure I'd say the same if she were standing here now, but killing people in cold blood is the kind of thing Global Governance do. We should be better than that. If there's a chance we can take her, learn what she's doing and bring her to justice, we should do it."

"And risk revealing ourselves to them?" Doleman asked.

"Not if you select the right people," Oscar said.

"Like who?"

Oscar pointed at Nico. "Him, for a start. He's plenty of experience arresting suspects."

Doleman stared at him. "Snatching civilians is one thing. This woman is highly dangerous."

"Which is why we send our troops along for support. They can keep him safe."

Doleman snorted. "I don't like it."

"You said yourself you were worried about us being found out," Oscar said. "Indigo knows who I am so I can't lead the team. The fact that Internal Security were tracking the Investigator's family is proof that she's aware of who he is and that he's still on the run. If things go wrong she'll think he was the one behind the operation."

Doleman shook his head. "Forgive me, but I don't trust the Investigator to hold out long if he's interrogated. He'll tell them everything."

"Then I'll go with him."

Nico looked across at Oscar. The man remained impassive, his emotionless eyes locked on Doleman.

"I can't risk you getting captured," Doleman said.

"I won't be anywhere near them. Tandelli can lead the snatch, I'll act as observer and support."

"And if it goes wrong?"

"I know what to do." The look Oscar gave Nico left him under no illusions as to what he meant.

"If the snatch looks like it's going to fail, I want her dead," Doleman said. "Agreed?"

Oscar nodded.

"Then it's settled. It'll take a few days to trace where she's staying. In the meantime," he looked at Oscar, "pull a squad together and develop a plan of attack. Once we've located her, the two of you will need to head out fast."

"No."

They both turned towards Nico.

"Sorry?" Doleman asked.

"I said no. I'm not going."

"Don't you want Indigo to face justice?"

"Of course, but I'm not going. I made a promise to my family. I'll do whatever I can here to support you but I'm not leaving them again."

"You have to."

Nico spun around to see Fran standing behind him, Gino and Naci holding a hand each. "I ... what?"

"You have to do this. If there's a chance you can end this so we can go back to our old lives, you have to try."

"But I promised."

"I know."

Nico stared at the three of them. "Haven't I sacrificed enough?"

"My dear fellow," Doleman said, "as far as sacrifice goes, you haven't even scratched the surface."

There was a sadness in Doleman's words. Nico realised the man had given up everything he had, everything he'd been, to take on this role. Not just him, but Oscar too. They had no friends, no family—their self-appointed role as the guardians of Global Governance was the only life they had.

Nico turned to Fran. "I'll do it, I'll stop her, but this is the last time I'm leaving you like this."

PART 2

Unknown

\<Have you learnt any more about our little problem?\>

∞

\<We know she wants to play one side against the other. What we don't know is what her target is or where her true allegiance lies\>

∞

\<I don't believe she has allegiance to anyone but herself\>

∞

\<I don't either, but she's proven very useful in the past\>

∞

\<The problems she's causing outweigh any value she once had. While we may disagree with some of our brethren, we are still one organisation. Political jostling is one thing, but if she carries on as she has, our squabbles will soon turn into a full-blown civil war. I don't see any choice. It's time to take her out of the equation\>

∞

\<What you're suggesting would set a dangerous precedent. We don't kill our own\>

∞

\<It's a line she crossed a long time ago\>

∞

<That may be so, but do we really want to behave like her?>

∞

<When the rot sets in, you have to cut out some live tissue to ensure all the corruption is gone. She's had every opportunity to come back into the fold but she still puts her own goals above those of the organisation. You're right about one thing, though. This must not be traced back to us. We'd lose the trust of the rest of the Governing Council>

∞

<Agreed>

∞

<Good. Then I'll let you sort out the details. Just make sure it runs smoothly. We'll only get one chance at this or she'll disappear. Indigo has to die>

CHAPTER SEVENTEEN

King of the Scrambles

O'DRISCOLL PULLED HIS cap lower. It felt like hours since he'd passed the message across but was probably just a few minutes. He'd never felt so uncomfortable sitting in his own home.

Despite his disguise—the implants, dataglasses gone, new beard, work overalls and cap—walking through the Scrambles to get here had taken all his mental strength. He knew the drill—act normal and confident, as if you belong—but each time he'd passed an enforcer he'd been convinced they'd see straight through the charade. And he'd walked past a lot. One time a junior enforcer had barged into him, telling him to 'get out the fucking way' as he went. Instinct almost drove O'Driscoll to retaliate before he remembered his role and cowered to one side, letting the toe-rag past.

Only once had he thought he'd been rumbled. One of the old gang from his father's days, David Crabb, had walked passed, immaculately turned out as always. He'd given O'Driscoll a second glance before carrying on his way. It was nothing too obvious but Crabb was a perceptive bastard. He was also loyal, which was the only reason O'Driscoll hadn't followed him and slit his throat.

At the sound of footsteps, O'Driscoll looked up. A young lad walked towards him. "Put your arms out wide and turn around."

O'Driscoll got up and did as he was told. He knew the boy, or at least knew his father, one of the warehouse supervisors. As the lad patted him down, O'Driscoll was grateful he'd stashed his rucksack in a hiding hole he'd not used since he was thirteen. He'd been pleased to find it still there, along with toys he'd stolen years before.

"Turn around."

O'Driscoll turned, keeping his eyes to the floor. He was a lowly worker with a message for the head of the Scrambles. He was nervous and terrified—and at least his apprehension wouldn't be faked. The young man finished frisking him and gestured for O'Driscoll to follow him up the stairs.

The place hadn't changed. Yes, one or two of his antiques had been replaced, including a Josef Lorenzl Art Deco figurine that had been a particular favourite, but the building retained its elegance and class. It was a small island of taste in the middle of the lawless cesspit he called home.

As they turned into the final long corridor, the door to his old office opened and Darragh walked out. O'Driscoll dropped his gaze. The last thing he needed was to be recognised. His cousin walked up to him, then past, without a second glance. The young man's face was scarlet and he was growling under his breath. Yet he looked well, all things considered, his crooked nose the only remnant of the beating O'Driscoll had given him for disobeying orders in what felt like a lifetime ago.

The enforcer knocked twice on the office door, then gestured for O'Driscoll to enter.

The office hadn't changed at all. It had the smell of an old library, shelves brimming with books. Charlie sat alone at his desk—he couldn't think of it as anything else—her focus on the datascreen in front of her.

She looked up as he walked in, her face a mask. "If anyone asks for me, tell them I'm out."

"Yes, ma'am," the young man said, and closed the door behind him.

O'Driscoll stepped forward, only to stop as Charlie pulled a weapon from under the desk.

"Put your hands behind your head and get down on your knees."

"Come on, Charlie. Is this any way to greet an old friend?"

110

"Just fucking do it."

O'Driscoll had seen Charlie like this before but had never been on the receiving end of that stare. He raised his hands behind his head and knelt on the hard wooden floor. "You know the lad frisked me," he said.

"Shut it."

Charlie walked around the table towards him, her weapon never wavering. "Put your head down."

"You don't have to do this, Charlie."

"I'm not going to ask you again."

O'Driscoll couldn't believe it and seethed at his own idiocy. He'd come all this way to be shot in his own office? He'd been certain Charlie would be pleased to see him. The two of them went back to childhood. She'd let him escape for God's sake. Why now? What had changed? He glanced around the room for something, anything he could use to protect himself but there was nothing. He was a dead man.

She moved to stand behind him and he knew what was going to happen. He'd seen it done too many times in the past. A double shot to the back of the head, that was all it took. One shot and it would be over. He ground his teeth in frustration. She'd promised to look after things for him until he returned. She'd promised.

O'Driscoll felt Charlie grab his hair and she pushed his head towards the floor.

"You're breaking my fucking—"

Before he could say any more Charlie twisted his head around and placed her lips on his own. Then the pain of a slap exploded down the side of his face.

"You bastard. They said you were dead."

"What the fuck, Charlie? Why did you hit me?"

"You're lucky your brains aren't seeping through the floorboards. I had to check. I needed to be sure it really was you and not a clone."

"By smacking me in the face?"

"No, by seeing the scar on the back of your head."

Of course. His old school injury. He'd been climbing through the window of the headteacher's office when the bastard walked in. O'Driscoll dropped two floors, landing in a heap and smacking his head on a brick, cutting it badly. He'd escaped without being seen and Charlie had stitched the wound so he didn't have to visit the school nurse. Charlie was the only one who knew that scar existed.

The two of them stared at each other, as if conscious for the first time of what had just taken place. O'Driscoll cleared his throat. "Look, I like you and all but—"

"Don't flatter yourself. You're just a mate, that's all. An important mate, my best mate even, but nothing else." Charlie walked to the drinks cabinet and lined up a couple of glasses. "You know you can't stay here. Too many people could recognise you."

"Nobody's spotted me so far. Even Darragh passed me without a glance."

"That boy's got his head stuck too far up his arse to notice anything much right now." She poured a measure of whisky into each glass and handed him one.

O'Driscoll took a sip. His cheek still stung from Charlie's slap. Christ, she could hit hard. "How's he been?"

"Darragh? Quiet. He wanted to fight back when Internal Security stormed the place but I persuaded him otherwise."

"He'd have done that for me?"

"It surprised me too." Charlie took her glass back to the desk, only to stop as she reached the chair. "I take it you've come to take it all back?"

"In time. There are a few things I need to do first." He took a seat opposite. The guest chair.

"Like telling me where the hell you've been? Internal Security ripped this place apart looking for you."

"They'd no chance of finding me. The Scrambles was my playground long before it became my kingdom."

"I managed to call them off before they did too much damage but we've only just straightened things out."

"Did you give them access to our systems?"

The whisky tumbler paused at Charlie's lips. "I could hardly say no. They don't have full access—you're the only one with that power—but they've been monitoring our day-to-day business."

"But the servers are still in operation?"

"Of course."

O'Driscoll smiled. "Good. We're going to need them."

Charlie put her tumbler down. "What's going on Mick? Why have you come back? It's only been a few months since you were driven out of here. Surely you don't think you can just waltz back in and take over without anyone noticing?"

"This isn't about the Scrambles."

"Then what is it about, because I sure as hell can't work it out?"

O'Driscoll took another sip of whisky. It was the good stuff, the 30-year-old vintage he usually saved for celebrations. And it was a celebration of sorts, although whether Charlie would agree he wasn't sure. "Your family were part of Global Governance from the beginning, weren't they?"

Charlie nodded. "As far as I know."

"They signed up to the founding principles?"

"To guide humanity to a peaceful and prosperous future. My grandfather made me learn it as a child. He hated what he saw as negligence on behalf of the politicians. He'd often moaned about the decision to remove hereditary peers from the old House of Lords, saying it removed neutral oversight of the political process. He saw Global Governance as a way of correcting the error."

"And bring back feudal control?" O'Driscoll didn't hide what he thought of that idea.

"He was an old man, set in his ways. I didn't say I agree with him."

"But you've played your part."

Charlie glared at him. "If you've come all this way to give me a lecture, you can fuck off back to wherever you've been hiding. I had as much choice about getting involved in Global Governance as you did in taking on your father's business."

O'Driscoll grunted. "I just wanted to be sure."

"Sure of what?"

"That you're still the person I thought you were." He took another sip of his whisky. "I was picked up by a group calling themselves the Knights Templar. Heard of them?"

Charlie shrugged. "From the Crusades."

"I think the name's more down to the ego of their founder than a link to a bunch of medieval bankers. They were originally an oversight group set up to ensure Global Governance kept to their founding principles."

"Never heard of them."

"You wouldn't have. They got disbanded not long after they were formed. Upset too many important people."

Charlie leaned forward. "Go on."

"After being thrown out of Global Governance the group went underground." O'Driscoll suppressed a smile at his own joke. "They've kept an eye on Global Governance for years but it's only now they've decided to act."

"Because?"

"You said it yourself the last time we spoke. Something's changed. Global Governance have stopped following their guiding principles. According to the Knights Templar, a small faction has secretly used killings, kidnappings and torture to manipulate events, both here and abroad, behind the Governing Council's back. Now they've orchestrated a coup so the whole organisation dances to their tune. Including you …"

"I'd never—"

"They gave the orders to take over the Scrambles. They were after me. I'd got too close to the truth about their leader, Indigo, and they wanted to take me out. She was the person behind the death of Grant Asquith."

Charlie screwed her face up in disgust. "Motherfuckers." She knocked her drink back and slammed the glass down hard on the desk. "So these Knights Templar, what are they doing about it?"

"According to Doleman—"

"Doleman?"

"Yeah, Thomas Doleman."

"Fuck off!"

O'Driscoll raised his hands up. "It's true. He staged his own death to set up the group. It's one of the reasons they've stayed undetected for so long." He could tell from Charlie's expression that she didn't believe him and he couldn't really blame her. "The Knights Templar only recently identified what was going on and who was behind it. Now Indigo's taken over the Governing Council they've decided to act. Their aim is to get rid of her and restore Global Governance to what it once was."

"I still don't see why you're here."

"Think, Charlie. How many of our patrons come from the government, military and the judiciary?"

"A few."

"More than a few, and those servers of ours have thousands of hours of footage showing exactly what they get up to when they visit the Scrambles."

"And you want to give this footage to the Knights Templar so they use it to take control of Global Governance?"

O'Driscoll leaned back in his chair and drained his glass. "That's what the Knights Templar are hoping."

For the first time since he'd arrived, Charlie smiled. "But you have a different plan?"

O'Driscoll finished his whisky and placed his glass next to Charlie's. "I need you to send out some invitations. We have a party to organise."

CHAPTER EIGHTEEN

Stephanie

STEPHANIE FELT CONTACT on her forehead, a moment's warmth that evaporated as quickly as it arrived. She opened her eyes to find herself propped up in bed. Something surrounded her neck, supporting her head. A mask remained over her mouth.

"You're awake."

The words startled Stephanie. Her mother sat by the bedside, a concerned look on her face. Mother. It still felt strange seeing the woman who'd abandoned her so many years ago sitting by her bedside, holding her hand with tears in her eyes. Stephanie didn't know how to feel. Should she be angry or overjoyed? This woman who'd left her as a child had also saved her from further torture.

"Can you hear me, Steppy? Emma said you sometimes communicate through blinking. Please let me know you can hear."

Emma? Who was Emma? After a moment's confusion Stephanie realised it must be the kind-faced woman who'd looked after her for so long. She blinked once, slowly.

A sob left her mother's lips. "Oh my sweet girl. I'm so sorry." She reached towards Stephanie's face and then pulled her hand back as if scalded. "I never … I never thought I'd get this chance. When I heard what had happened to you, what they were doing … I should have come earlier. I should never have listened to Doleman."

Her mother's head dropped. Tears rolled down the woman's face.

Stephanie remained still as always but inside she churned.

After what felt like minutes, her mother looked up. "You must hate me for what I've done, for leaving you with mum and dad. I'd understand that. I'd hate me too if I was you. But you have to believe that you were never out of our thoughts, either mine or your father's. It was a terrible decision to make but we were living in terrible times. We had to keep you safe and leaving you with my parents was the only option we had."

The tear-tracks on her mother's cheeks glistened as she spoke. The room was still, peaceful, a contradiction as to what was going on inside Stephanie. How dare her mother feel sorry for herself? It had been her choice to let her only child believe she was dead. There was no excuse, none that justified what she'd done. The woman was a monster. And now she wanted pity? Stephanie moved her gaze to the other side of the room, not wanting to acknowledge her mother's presence any more.

"I'm not making much sense, I know. I'm sorry, it's just I never thought we'd be having this conversation. I believed at some point, when it was safe, we'd be able to meet up, become a family once more. Only a couple of years, that's all it would take." She wiped at her eyes. "But it didn't. There was always a reason, always something stopping me from coming to see you, until the fear of what you might say, how you might react, stopped me from coming at all."

In those few words Stephanie learnt much. First, her mother was a monster, now, a coward. The surprises kept on coming.

Her mother took out a tissue and blew her nose. "You would have loved your father. He was a gentle soul, brave, fierce in protecting those less fortunate than himself. I think that's where you get your bravery from." Her mother cleared her throat. "We were part of the oversight team, making sure Global Governance kept to its founding principles. Within months we'd realised not all the founding members of Global Governance were altruistic." A small laugh escaped her lips. "The funny thing was, when it started going wrong it was about nothing, really. A few hundred thousand globals worth of orders being won by companies connected to a particular Global

Governance member, when they should have been awarded elsewhere. Your father queried it, and that's when the threats started."

Why are you telling me this? I don't want to hear your excuses. I want you to leave.

"He was so brave, your father, brave and stubborn. He realised there was more to what was going on than these few orders, something worth investigating, so he kept digging. I told him to be careful but with each new threat his resolve hardened.

"They killed him before he had the chance to get away." Her mother looked up to the ceiling, taking a deep breath. "I was distraught, heartbroken. In some ways I still am. He'd been my rock, my life, and he was gone. They wouldn't even let me see the body, made it out to be an accident, said his injuries were too horrific." Her mother brought her hand to her mouth, eyes staring into space.

"You know what it's like, not knowing who to trust? My first thought was to you, to make sure you were safe. It was Doleman's idea to disappear. He'd already made arrangements to fake his own death, what were a couple more?"

What she was hearing was worse than what Stephanie had faced under torture. At least back then she knew, deep down, that the horrors she'd been shown were fake. This time there was no such comfort.

"The only way to keep you safe was to never come home. If they thought me dead, you'd be safe." Her mother brought Stephanie's lifeless, unfeeling hand to her face and kissed it. "I wasn't as brave as you are, not then. It was too soon, the pain too raw. I couldn't face them down like you faced down Gant and the Prime Delegate. You're so much like your father it hurts."

Don't you dare! Don't you dare bring the ghost of my father into this. Stephanie screamed at her mother from inside her head. You had a choice and you took the coward's way out. You should have come for me, fought them out in the open. I loved you so much. Do you have any idea how many years it was before I stopped running to the door each time there was a knock, hoping it was you?

An alarm sounded from a machine behind Stephanie's head. She heard a roaring in her ears and her vision clouded, the outer extremities fading out.

The door opened and the kind-faced woman, Emma, walked through with two medics Stephanie had not seen before. Emma took one of Stephanie's useless wrists in her hand. "Her pulse is through the roof, face is flushed, pupils dilated." Emma turned to her mother. "I need you to leave."

The room gently spun. Stephanie heard people speak but their words drifted further and further into the background.

"I'm not going anywhere."

"I'm sorry but you can't stay here."

"Don't you know who I am?"

"You can pull rank all you like but the patient is under my care, so when I say leave, you leave."

"But I'm her mother!"

Further and further the voices drifted away.

"If you wait outside, I'll let you know when we have her stabilised."

"What's wrong with her?"

"Please, Commander."

Stephanie listened to their argument continue until the room faded to black.

CHAPTER NINETEEN

The Professor

THE PROFESSOR WASN'T sure why he'd decided to come. He didn't know Stephanie Vaughn, had never met her and only knew of her because she'd been involved with the investigation into Jennica Fabian's death. But she was the catalyst, the person responsible for him being here, and some small part of him wanted to let her know how angry he was with her for that.

He made his way through the darkened medical centre, worried somebody might stop him. The laboratory he shared with Josh was on the level below and he had no business being here. But he needn't have been concerned. The place was virtually empty. The only staff he'd seen had been drinking coffee in a side room.

The Professor turned the handle and stepped into the darkened room. Stephanie lay on her bed, her silhouette visible against the backdrop of machines whirring, buzzing and beeping to keep her alive. He remained at the doorway for some time, unable to bring himself to go any further, his anger and indignation falling away as he looked at the frail woman.

"She's dying."

The Professor let out a yelp.

"Sorry, I didn't mean to startle you."

He'd been so focussed on Stephanie that the Professor hadn't noticed another person sitting in the shadows, holding Stephanie's hand. "It's me who should be apologising for interrupting you. I should go."

"No, please stay. You clearly came for a reason. Did you know my daughter at all?"

He shook his head. "Not really. I just wanted …" He stopped, unsure what to say. What did he want? He was angry with her, angry for involving him in all this, for ruining his life, for taking him away from the work he loved. Yet seeing Stephanie laying there, the hiss and click of the machines keeping her alive, his sacrifices felt insignificant in comparison. "How much longer has she got?"

"We don't know. The doctors aren't sure what's wrong with her. She has an infection on her lungs and a host of injuries. She's malnourished, she's hypoxic—her blood oxygen levels are incredibly low—and of course she's paralysed. All of these should be treatable but she's just not responding. They believe it's psychological, that's she's lost the will to live."

The Commander leaned forward. The woman looked terrible, haggard, a different person to the one he'd seen when he'd first arrived at the complex. The Professor gestured to the empty chair beside her. "May I join you?"

She smiled although she couldn't keep the sadness from her eyes. "I could do with the company."

They sat together in silence, the gentle hum of life-support machinery the only thing breaking the silence. The Professor studied the woman on the bed. Even with her eyes closed he could see a similarity to her mother, especially around the set of her nose and cheeks. "I shouldn't have come."

"I'm glad you did. Other than medical staff, we've not seen anyone else."

He nodded. That made sense. The only other person here who knew her was the Investigator, and the Professor hadn't seen him for days. "Has she woken up?"

"Yes, or at least her eyes open. It's hard to know how present she is, what she's thinking. She doesn't communicate, in fact she averts her eyes whenever I speak. It's as if she hates me, blames me for everything."

"But you're not responsible for what happened to her?"

The Commander's face hardened. "In some ways, I might as well have tortured her myself."

One of the machines let out a long beep, making the Professor jump. "Should we call someone?"

The Commander's eyes remained fixed on her daughter. "It does that every now and then. The staff get a feed from the machines. They'll come if they're needed."

He tried to imagine what it was like to watch your child slowly die. He knew how he'd felt at Jennica's death and she'd just been one of his students. How much worse could it be when it was your own flesh and blood?

"Why did you come here, Professor?"

For a moment he thought about lying. "I needed someone to blame."

"For what?"

"For this, for me being here in the facility, for all the fear of the last two years." He turned to face Heather. "I didn't ask for this, I just happened to have a girl in my class who went missing."

"None of us asked for this, not me, not Stephanie, not even Thomas Doleman—although he's as responsible as anyone."

"Don't you get angry at all?"

"I get angry when I think about what's happened to my daughter. I get angry about the people who made her suffer."

As the woman spoke the Professor saw the old Commander return, the one he'd seen when he'd first arrived.

"But I've learnt that anger doesn't get you anywhere. It just drains you, leaving you bitter and empty." She turned to face him, the impact of her decision clear in the hollows of her eyes. "And I've been angry for a long, long time."

He reached across and patted her shoulder. "You should get some rest."

She shook her head. "I need to be here."

"You need sleep."

The Commander took Stephanie's hand in her own. "What I need is someone who can save my daughter."

The Professor knew the Commander spoke about a doctor, but there were other ways to save a person's life. "How long do the medics say she's got?"

"They don't know. They have no idea why she's not healing. They just know she's getting worse."

The Professor didn't really hear her answer, he was too wrapped up in what needed to be done. "Do you think she could hold out for another couple of days?"

"Maybe. Why?"

"I think I might be able to help your daughter after all."

CHAPTER TWENTY

King of the Scrambles

O'DRISCOLL SENSED THE awkward tension in the chamber from where he hid. This meeting was unprecedented. It had been years since the heads of so many crime families last gathered in one place, but here they were, deep underground. He'd christened the chamber the rat's nest. It was an enormous underground space, the meeting point of long disused central sewers with brick arches reaching overhead as if part of an underground cathedral. The waste from millions of people once flowed over the now dirt floor.

It was the perfect location for this meeting. Each family arrived via their own tunnel to ensure no unnecessary confrontations beforehand. It was also good to see they'd limited themselves to just five representatives, as requested. All except his own clan. He had no doubt that at the other end of each tunnel waited an army of thugs and hoodlums ready to charge in at the first sign of danger, but for the moment a modicum of trust prevailed.

Seven seats stood in a circle at the centre of the junction, one for each tunnel. Charlie sat in front of the tunnel where O'Driscoll remained out of sight, a stack of folders by her feet.

One by one the heads of each family group took their place in the circle. Charlie greeted each in turn with a respectful nod. None were returned. She was eyed with suspicion, like the interloper she was. Eventually, six people sat in the circle. The seventh seat remained empty.

The seventh chair was like a punch in the guts. O'Driscoll had been sure Selin Ozbey would have made it. The agreement was clear. When called, you came to the meeting. There was only one reason that place was empty, and that reason crushed him. There *was* no Ozbey clan. Global Governance had done to them what they'd hoped to do to him. O'Driscoll's thoughts turned to the small boy he'd left in the care of the Tandellis. Don't worry, Naci. I'll make sure the bastards pay for what they've done.

Charlie cleared her throat. "Thank you all for coming."

"As the head of the oldest family here, I think I speak for the group when I say we didn't come here for you, but because of an oath our fathers made, an oath that hasn't been invoked for over thirty years."

Fat Lucas's face was covered in a sheen of sweat. O'Driscoll had doubted he would come himself—the man hadn't left his home turf in years and had turned over the day-to-day running of his operation to his oldest son—yet here he was, along with the other family heads. It would make for an interesting meeting.

"I don't know how you managed to get hold of the code words," Fat Lucas continued, "something only handed down from boss to boss. It seems that idiot O'Driscoll put even more faith in you than we realised. Whatever—we take our commitments seriously. You mentioned a threat to our livelihoods and invoked the oath, so we came. But I warn you, if you're wasting our time the consequences will be severe."

A couple of the bosses nodded in agreement, the rest remained chiselled from rock.

"I understand the traditions as well as anyone here," Charlie replied.

"Just because daddy let you play with the mean boys doesn't make you one of us," a woman in a green suit said. "The only reason you've kept hold of O'Driscoll's patch is because of the help you've had from your establishment pals. Let's see what happens once they lose interest."

O'Driscoll knew the woman well. It was rumoured Annie

Longton once had a fling with his father. O'Driscoll wouldn't be surprised. She was a hard woman who ruled her family with an iron will. Just his father's type.

"I understand your anger but you're taking it out on the wrong person," Charlie said.

"Girl," Fat Lucas said. "You're beginning to piss me off. We're not stupid. We know your establishment friends were also behind what happened to the Ozbeys," he glanced towards the empty chair as he spoke, "so don't act all innocent with us."

"You've mistaken my meaning. You're taking it out on the wrong person because I wasn't the one who invited you here."

Questioning glances passed between the group. "If you didn't then who did?"

O'Driscoll walked out of the tunnel into the dim light. "I did."

"Holy fuck."

O'Driscoll took a certain satisfaction at the expressions of those who faced him. It took a lot to surprise this bunch of world-weary, cynical bastards, yet from the looks on their faces none of them had any idea he was still alive. Charlie got up from her seat and he took her place in the circle.

Fat Lucas roared with laughter. "Looks like all the money spent on celebrating your demise was a waste of time. Nice beard, covers that ugly face of yours. I wouldn't have recognised you if I hadn't heard you speak."

"Fuck you."

"I guess the money your father spent on your posh education was wasted too. They never did manage to clean up that mouth of yours. You can take the boy out of the Scrambles …"

O'Driscoll remained silent, his focus on the demeanour of the other family heads. Not everybody appeared pleased to see him, Annie Longton being one.

"Now that you've had your fun, would you mind telling us why you dragged us all the way out here into what's basically and literally a shithole?"

"Civic duty."

Fat Lucas laughed once again. "I never knew you had such a

sense of humour."

"Do I look like I'm joking?"

The man's laughter petered out. O'Driscoll had their attention.

"My death wasn't intended to fool you, it was to fool those who took over the Scrambles. Weeks previously I'd got too close to a secret, and very powerful people wanted to remain hidden. These people weren't interested in taking over my business, they wanted my head."

"Did Charlie know this secret?"

Rajinder Singh had sat quietly up to this point. The boss was a shrewd operator, outsmarting rather than outmuscling his rivals. While they weren't friends, O'Driscoll admired the man's achievements and needed him on his side.

"Yes."

"Then why didn't they go after her too?"

"Because Charlie was one of those involved."

The others glanced to where Charlie stood. These were tough people, used to keeping their emotions in check and while their faces remained impassive, disapproval radiated from their eyes.

"Who are these people?"

"They're an organisation called Global Governance. They are an ultra rich group who've controlled our political and financial institutions since the time of The Miracle."

The chamber went silent. Then Fat Lucas spoke.

"What's happened to you, Mick? I never had you down as a conspiracy nut."

"This isn't a figment of my imagination. I've seen these people, I was nearly killed by them."

"So you're telling us some secret organisation has been running our country for the last fifty years or so without anybody finding out?"

"Not our country, the world."

Annie Longton stood. "I'm sorry, I don't have time to listen to this rubbish."

"This isn't rubbish, Annie. I have proof. If you sit down for a moment you'll hear it."

"No, Mick. I've had enough of your games. It's bad enough that you staged your own death—"

"It wasn't staged."

"Don't interrupt me!"

O'Driscoll gritted his teeth but kept his mouth shut. Around the room, postures had changed. The sense of danger was palpable. Those family members waiting by the tunnels had stopped talking among themselves and were instead watching their bosses closely. A false move now and there would be a bloodbath.

"What the hell has got into you?" Longton spat. "You were one of the few out of this bunch of losers I respected. You turned your family around after your father died, brought peace and stability to the rest of us. But this? You bring us here, invoking the oath, then feed us a bunch of crap? Even if this ridiculous story you're telling us is true—which I doubt—what the hell does this have to do with us?"

"'I'm not the only one they've an interest in. They've infiltrated your organisations too."

"That's a big accusation to make," Fat Lucas said.

O'Driscoll cleared his throat. "Please, Annie. Sit down and let me start at the beginning."

He knew that if she left now the meeting would be over and his plans in ruins. Longton stared at O'Driscoll for an age, then sat.

"You're all aware that the Prime Delegate's brother, Grant Asquith, died in the Scrambles. His death was made to look like an accident but in fact he was murdered, killed by Global Governance to put pressure on the Prime Delegate."

"How do you know this?"

"Because I worked with an Investigator to catch the man responsible."

A look of disgust crossed Longton's face. "You worked with the law?"

"They were already investigating. I'd been looking into what had happened myself. A high-profile death like that was bad for business. The people behind the killing set it up to look like an accident. If that failed, they'd set up layers of misdirection. Anyone investigating the death would at first suspect me, then the Dutch, then eventually the Turks. Global Governance are no fools. They'd hoped to cover their tracks by starting a turf war. They almost managed it, too. It was Selin Ozbey who discovered the name of the man behind the operation. The investigative agency confirmed it through a different route."

"So why didn't this investigator bring charges against the man?"

"He worked for the Chowdhury Investigative Agency. They were shut down the same day the Turks and my turf were raided. As their cover had failed, Global Governance were forced to clear up after themselves. I've been on the run ever since."

"Yet here you are now."

O'Driscoll could still see scepticism on their faces, but at least they were listening. He picked up a file from the pile in front of Charlie. "I have the proof here. I'm not stupid. I know how this sounds. I felt the same way when I first heard. The only difference was I'd already been kicked out of the Scrambles by that point."

There was silence at his words. O'Driscoll heard the drip of rainwater seeping through the brickwork above and onto the floor to his right.

Longton shook her head. "Haven't you learned anything? If you're going to lie, keep that lie small and simple. You actually had me believing you for a moment."

"Why don't you have a look at the file first? This doesn't just provide more information on what I've told you, but it also contains the names and details of Global Governance operatives in your own organisations."

"Keep your files, I'm not interested."

"Fine. If you're happy members of your family work for somebody else, that's your problem, not mine."

"So you say, but I've got a different theory. I think those files are just a means for us to rip ourselves apart, just like you got the Ozbeys to do."

O'Driscoll glanced to the empty seat. "The reason Selin Ozbey isn't here is because she got too close to Global Governance."

"That's convenient."

"It's the truth!" O'Driscoll got up out of his chair. "How long have you known me, any of you? You say I'm acting out of character but shouldn't you be asking yourselves why? I'm not, and never have been, an impulsive man. I like stability so I can go about the business of making money. What do I have to gain from this? Nothing. You know and I know that a turf war benefits no-one."

"I'll take a look at the file." Everybody turned towards Rajinder Singh. "A few things have troubled me lately. I'd like to see what you claim to have found."

O'Driscoll gestured to Charlie and she handed out the files. When she reached Annie Longton the two women stared at each other for a long time, but eventually Longton took her copy.

"The files are specific to each of your organisations," O'Driscoll said. "I've included as much detail as I can so you can conduct your own investigations. I thought a paper file would be best as I don't know who has access to what within your systems." O'Driscoll watched Annie Longton flick through her pages, stopping as something caught her attention. Her expression turned from shock to anger.

A cough broke the silence. "Haven't you forgotten someone?" Fat Lucas sat smiling, holding out his hands as if waiting for his copy.

"For you, Lucas, we've got something a little different." O'Driscoll signalled to Charlie and the sound of a recording of a woman's voice echoed out around the chamber.

"We have a problem."

"What do you mean?"

Fat Lucas stiffened as he heard his own voice echo around the space. His mask of joviality slid from his face. Yet it was Fat Lucas's men O'Driscoll focussed on, especially his son, waiting by the tunnel entrance.

"How well do you know your boy's girlfriend?" the woman asked.

"She's a nice girl, good family. I think she may be the one," Fat Lucas's voice replied.

The colour drained from Fat Lucas's face as he recognised what was being said. The other family heads turned to him like a pack of dogs sensing weakness.

"Her father's been a naughty boy. He's to be taught a lesson."

"You want me to do something?"

"I want you to kill the girl. Make it look like an accident."

Fat Lucas turned to face his son. "Don't listen to this. It's a lie."

"Isn't there some other way?"

"No."

"But my boy …"

"He'll get over it. Everyone does, eventually."

"Okay. Consider it done."

"You fucking bastard!"

Fat Lucas's son ran to where his father sat. O'Driscoll could have intervened, as could the other heads, but they all remained seated as the young man grabbed a handful of hair, yanked back his father's head and slashed at the fat man's throat with a small blade.

Blood spurted into the air, covering the young man. Fat Lucas grasped at his throat, eyes bulging, but failed to stem the flow. The young man stabbed his father in the chest, cutting Fat Lucas's hands as he tried to make his son stop. The smell of piss filled the chamber for the first time in many years. Eventually the once-feared boss's arms fell limp and his son stood back, watching, waiting, until his father slipped from the chair to lay motionless on the ground.

O'Driscoll noticed a splash of blood a few centimetres in front of him. He shifted his feet. That's the first one down, Selin, the first and not the last, he thought.

For a few moments the chamber was silent. Then, Rajinder Singh slowly got to his feet. "Thank you, Mick. You've given us all a lot to think about."

"Hold on a moment," Annie Longton said, unruffled by the corpse to her left. "You said you brought us here out of civic duty. What do you mean by that?"

"I've never been a fan of authority, I don't think any of us have, but I know somebody needs to be in charge otherwise there'd be anarchy. But for that to work, those in charge need to be accountable to the people they govern. They should be servants, not masters. Yet Global Governance aren't just acting like masters, they're acting like gods. It's time we put an end to it. It's time to bring the whole stinking edifice down."

"You can count me in," Lucas's son said.

O'Driscoll looked at the blood-spattered new boss, eyes fierce with anger and loss, and knew he'd won them over.

CHAPTER TWENTY-ONE

The Investigator

THEIR PODS SAT stationed at the back of the square, hidden behind the small park across the road from Indigo's apartment. In Nico's pod were three soldiers, and the four of them studied the visual feed playing on the pod's datascreens, the reflected green-lit night vision giving the pod's interior an ethereal glow.

The atmosphere was tense and conditions cramped. They'd been here for four days waiting for the right moment. The team were professionals, but Nico knew from past experience that no team could maintain this level of concentration for long without flagging, even with stimulants. Still, he sensed their tension rise as day slipped into night. It was a good sign. They knew their moment was coming. The team remained focussed. They just needed Indigo to arrive home.

Nico picked up his radio. "Any sign yet?"

"Negative. All quiet here."

The radios were ancient technology, long surpassed by datasphere communications, but that was the point. Nobody would be monitoring these transmissions.

"Keep this frequency clear unless you see something," Oscar's voice whispered over the in-ear speaker.

Nico stifled a shiver. It was one thing knowing Oscar wasn't the evil man he'd always thought him to be, another hearing the man's voice in his ear. Oscar had holed himself up in a Georgian terraced house opposite the modern apartment block they were watching. Despite being surrounded by lush growth of a well-manicured vertical garden, the large symmetrical windows gave away the Georgian building's ancient origins. It was Oscar's job to guide them during the snatch, and it was the feed from his scope they were watching. While Nico commanded the snatch itself, the squad answered to Oscar.

The sound of laughter outside caught Nico's attention. He switched one of the datascreens to observe what was happening. Two men and a woman walked past their pod, laughing and joking among themselves, oblivious to those inside. One of the men stumbled and with much laughter had to be helped by the other two. They made their way through the square, the dark and their intoxication causing more than a few problems before reaching Indigo's apartment building.

Nico switched back to Oscar's feed. The more sober of the two men reached into his pocket to remove a key card. The second man stopped him, pulling the first towards him and the two kissed while their female friend watched, smiling. Then the two men reached out and pulled their friend into their embrace, all thought of entering the building seemingly forgotten.

A voice crackled across the radio. "We have incoming."

Their view changed as Oscar tracked a pod entering the square from the side closest to the apartment building. Subtle movements let Nico know his soldiers were checking their weapons, just as they had each time a pod had passed. Unlike before, this pod slowed, pulling up in front of the apartment building's entrance.

"Wait for my command."

Nico watched the doors of the pod peel open. A woman stepped out, small, with cropped hair. The heat from her body made it difficult for Nico to make out any more detail. Was this Indigo?

"Go-go-go!"

Oscar's shout echoed around the pod and all hell broke loose. A blast of cold air hit Nico as the doors opened. His three compatriots were out and sprinting towards their target before Nico had even moved, joining those of the adjacent pods. Cursing, he jumped out and ran as fast as he could, the bitter air biting into his lungs.

There was a shout from up ahead. Nico tried to see what was going on but he was half night-blind from the datascreens he'd watched moments before. Despite this, he ran hard, sprinting as fast as he could to catch the others until the ground dropped from under his feet. Nico found himself flailing through the air before landing awkwardly on soft turf.

He lay still for a moment, struggling to suck in air, although his ego was bruised more than his body. Behind him he saw the small drop he'd run blindly over and cursed himself for his idiocy. They'd studied the park layout earlier and he knew the drop was there, yet in the panic to catch up with the others he'd behaved like an amateur.

Nico got to his feet and set off once more. Up ahead were the outlines of his team charging across the square. He tried to catch up but the soldiers were much younger and fitter than he was and the gap between them increased.

The first squad members streamed out through the bushes towards the apartment.

"Get down on the floor!"

A woman screamed. Nico was still 100 metres away, his breath coming in ragged gasps. Up ahead his soldiers had formed a semi-circle, pointing their weapons towards the top of the steps where the woman cowered. But she wasn't alone. Somehow, in the time it had taken the squad to run across the square, Indigo had grabbed the young woman with the two men and held her as a shield, a weapon pointed at the terrified girl's head.

"Don't come any closer."

A moan escaped from the girl's mouth. One of the young men stepped towards Indigo. The old woman moved fast. There was a shot. The man dropped to the floor. He grasped his leg, screaming in pain.

"Hold your fire!" Nico broke out from the bushes to where the snatch squad stood. He could tell his team were itching to take Indigo down. Their weapons may have been designed to incapacitate, but Nico knew a headshot could still kill and he needed Indigo alive.

"The next time anyone moves, I'll kill her." To emphasis her point, Indigo wrenched the girl's head down to one side and moved her weapon under her captive's chin.

Nico walked out in front of his men, his hands held high to show he was unarmed. "Let the girl go, Indigo. We have you surrounded. Come quietly and nobody else needs to get hurt."

CHAPTER TWENTY-TWO

Indigo

THE MEETING HAD been a disaster. None of the others trusted her. At one level Indigo understood why—she'd spent the previous twenty years undermining all their work—but at the same time the logic of her argument was faultless. The young prince had gained control of Global Governance and needed to be stopped. Nobody should have that much power—nobody except her, of course.

Yet that was the problem. The traditionalists were still smarting from their defeat in the Governing Council, and as people used to getting their own way, the defeat didn't just hurt, it was a direct affront to their monumental egos. While some traditionalists, like Streckler, saw the benefit in joining forces with her, those she'd met with tonight couldn't see past the fact she'd made them look like fools. She knew she could win them around over time, but time was one thing she didn't have. She needed to stop the young prince before he consolidated his position. Indigo punched the arm of her chair. She'd been an idiot. Looking back it was obvious what he had been up to, but she'd been too caught up in her own goals to notice his. It wouldn't happen again.

The pod swept around a bend. Indigo saw she was nearly home, the quaint garden square visible in the pod's headlights. As she slowed to a halt, the sight of three youths embracing at the entrance to the apartment building came into view. Bloody people. Couldn't they just wait until they got home?

The doors slid open and cold touched her like a familiar caress, reminding her of her previous life. Whether it was a form of genetic memory passed down from her forebears, a sting in her cheeks always gave her the sense of coming home. She took a deep breath and the cold washed away her frustration like a balm. As she couldn't change what had happened, she'd just have to find a way around it. With her mind clear, she made her way up the steps towards the entrance lobby.

When she reached the top step, Indigo heard the sound of snapping branches from behind. The glass doors reflected the image of three armed men bursting out of the bushes and into the road. Years of training took over. Without thinking Indigo grabbed the young woman by the hair and pulled her towards herself, twisting so her back was to the side wall, the girl between her and the approaching threat. Her mind raced. Which one was behind this? It couldn't be the young prince as he believed she was on his side, and as for Streckler, he didn't have the balls. Indigo slipped a weapon out of her pocket and held its muzzle against the young woman's head.

"Don't come any closer."

The soldiers flanking her stopped but others burst through the bushes to join them. Indigo recited the start of her emergency SOS command but then stopped. Who would come? Echo was away. Without knowing who was behind the attack, who could she trust? The adrenaline surge through her body gave reality a clarity she hadn't experienced since she was young, chased for stealing bread to feed her family. It took Indigo a moment to realise she was enjoying herself. This was what living was all about.

She caught a flash of movement out of the corner of her eye. With an adjustment of her wrist, she fired and the idiot man-friend of her hostage fell to the floor clutching his now-shattered leg.

"Hold your fire!"

A figure ran out into the street, gesturing for the soldiers to hold off. So whoever was after her didn't want her dead. That was a good sign—it gave her room for negotiation. Indigo yanked her hostage's head back and placed the weapon at her throat.

"The next time anyone moves, I'll kill her."

Her threat had an effect. All eyes remained focussed on her but there was a pause for the first time since the attack started. Indigo breathed deeply and took in her surroundings. The two young men lay huddled at the far side of the steps, the one she'd shot either passed out or dead, the second looking in her direction, terrified. Good. That was one less threat to worry about. Out front things were different. There were too many weapons pointing in her direction. She needed to get inside, back to her apartment. Somebody in the area must have called Internal Security by now, if only to report gunshots. All she had to do was survive the next few minutes and she'd be safe.

The man who'd yelled the command to hold fire pushed through the ring of soldiers, hands in the air, into the light. At first Indigo refused to recognise who it was, not trusting what her eyes were seeing. How was it possible? The man she hunted had been hunting her all along.

"Let the girl go, Indigo. We have you surrounded. Come quietly and nobody else needs to get hurt."

What was Tandelli thinking? Surely he didn't believe he could bring her to trial? "Stay where you are."

Nico stopped but his lips moved as if he was having a whispered conversation. What was that on his ear? A radio? The device looked strange, old fashioned. There was a slim microphone arm in front of the man's mouth. He was communicating with somebody, never taking his eyes from her the whole time. Indigo glanced towards the youth cowering in the corner. "Get up and open that door."

The young man stayed where he was, eyes wide with fear.

"Unless you want to see your friend's brains splattered across these steps, I suggest you do what I say."

The youth looked as if he would piss his pants but got up and placed his keycard next to the sensor.

"Good. Now open the door."

She forced her hostage to take a couple of steps forward. It was a risk, allowing the young man behind her to open the door, but he'd made no move on her unlike the fool slumped on the other side of the steps. She watched the youth move behind her, then heard the familiar click as he pushed the door open.

CHAPTER TWENTY-THREE

The Investigator

"WE CAN'T ALLOW Indigo to enter the building. Once inside, we'll never get her out."

Nico ignored Oscar's voice and focussed on the woman in front of him. Indigo looked calm for somebody with half a dozen weapons pointed at her, unlike the poor young woman she was using as a shield.

"If Indigo makes a move, I will shoot the girl," Oscar continued.

"No. The girl's got nothing to do with this."

"Do you think I want to? We need her out of the way if the men are to get a tranq into Indigo. I can take her down without killing her."

"I said no."

What Oscar said was true; they needed to shoot the tranquiliser into Indigo's body. If one accidentally hit her skull it would kill her. But it was too big a risk. The girl would be killed. He couldn't have that on his conscience.

Nico opened his mouth to speak but Indigo turned to the youth cowering over his injured friend in the corner.

"Get up and open that door."

Nico sensed his squad tense at her words. The youth Indigo had spoken to shook his head, clearly terrified at what might happen. Don't do it, Nico thought. Please don't let her in.

The young man scrambled to his feet and Nico watched helplessly as he placed his keycard against the sensor. The hint of a smile appeared on Indigo's lips. She took a few steps forward. "Good, now open the door."

"Get ready to fire once the girl drops." Oscar's voice broke through the static.

"No. There must be another way."

The young man walked behind Indigo and her hostage.

"Get ready," Oscar said.

The young man pressed his palms against the door and pushed.

The sound of a shot echoed around the square and the girl's head rocked back, blood and brains spraying out, covering Indigo.

"No!" Nico stood frozen, not wanting to believe what Oscar had just done.

Indigo looked on in shock as the girl slid from her grasp, then a series of quieter rounds rang out from the squad and she too slumped to the floor. One last shot echoed across the square and the glass front of the entrance hall shattered.

Oscar's words crackled in their earpieces. "That wasn't me. There is another shooter. Repeat, there is another shooter. We need to take Indigo alive."

At Oscar's words, Nico ran, jumping the steps two at a time, and threw himself on top of the old woman. Before he had a chance to pull her free a soldier landed on top of him and his head cracked against the stone steps. The world spun. For a moment Nico thought he would black out, then a wave of nausea swept over him.

"Get her out of there!"

Nico thought he would vomit. He had stars in front of his eyes and there was the unmistakable smell of blood. Then there was a loud crack and the soldier on top of him spasmed before letting out a low grunt. Warm liquid dripped down the back of Nico's neck.

"What the hell's happening?" he yelled.

"The shooter is still active. You need to get Indigo out of there." Oscar's voice was calm, almost monotone.

"I can't move. I think the shooter—"

Nico heard another loud crack. Somebody nearby screamed.

"I've located the shooter. Starting suppressing fire now."

A series of shots echoed around the square. Nico pushed himself up and the squad member slid onto the floor. Below him, Indigo lay still, her face covered in blood. The soldier lay beside her. There was a hole in the back of his head the size of an old penny. The pale, white steps were awash with blood. Nico threw up.

"Get out of there," Oscar yelled across the comms channel. "Internal Security will arrive any minute."

Nico was on all fours, arms and legs shaking. He turned to see another squad member beside him. The soldier's face was pale, covered in a sheen of sweat. Nico wiped his mouth with the back of his hand. "Are you okay?" he asked.

"Shoulder wound, nothing too bad."

The two pods they'd sat in only minutes before pulled up to the front of the building.

"Help me get her into the pod," Nico said, pointing at Indigo.

The injured squad member grabbed hold of Indigo's arm with her good hand and Nico took the other, and they pulled their target towards one of the waiting pods. As they did so, more squad members rushed past, bounding up the steps to grab their fallen comrade.

"Oscar, where are you?"

"I'm tracking the sniper. You need to get everyone out of there. Internal Security are on their way. Meet back at the rendezvous point. Radio silence from now on."

Nico didn't need further instruction. Despite his shaking legs he hauled Indigo into the pod, climbing in beside her. The wounded squad member was next, followed by two others, then the doors closed and the pod accelerated away.

As Nico sat down, the pod's interior swam in front of his eyes. He hunched forward, head in his hands and sucked in air. He stayed that way for a good five minutes until his vision settled. When he eventually sat up he saw the injured soldier with her head back, grimacing in pain. One of the others had a first aid kit open and was trying to patch the wound. At his feet, Indigo remained motionless. Nico reached down and placed his fingers on her neck.

There was a pulse. It was slow but she was alive.

Their pod slipped onto the main artery out of the city, linking with other pods as part of the vast roadtrain heading north. Nico watched the lights of buildings flash by. His body shook. He felt as if he'd fallen off a cliff, and found he had to lean forward because his head throbbed too much when sat upright. What the hell had just happened? Had Oscar killed the girl? He said he would if he had to. But why kill one of his own squad members? And if it wasn't Oscar who pulled the trigger, who the hell was it?

He squinted at the woman on the floor by his feet. Lying with her eyes closed in a drug-induced sleep, she looked like a thousand other women, almost grandmotherly in appearance, except for being covered in another person's blood and viscera. In some ways it was fitting. For a woman with so much blood on her hands, what was a drop or two more? He thought back to Jennica, to the people he'd seen killed during the riots two years previously. At least there was finally a chance of getting justice. He hoped the price was worth it.

CHAPTER TWENTY-FOUR

The Professor

TRYING TO CONTAIN his annoyance, the Professor looked over to where the old man sat. "The fact it's theoretically possible doesn't mean we've a hope in hell's chance of delivering it. Every type of security has a weakness and Global Governance has both the ability and the brute force to overcome anything I can develop."

Joshua Denham's gaze remained firmly fixed on the datascreen in front of him. "Young man, I've been delivering the impossible for over fifty years. If I had your attitude I'd never have achieved anything. That's the problem with your generation: You've had everything given to you. We had no choice but to overcome the challenges we faced otherwise our whole way of life would have been wiped out."

The Professor picked up a stylus from the desk and aimed to throw it at the bald patch at the back of Josh's head. The old bastard was so bloody frustrating. It was bad enough working without access to a float chair, datalenses or an immersive suit. He'd been promised the equipment for weeks now but there was still no sign of it. And even if they did arrive, he'd still have to share a laboratory with the irritating old fart. The Professor was about to throw the pen when there was a knock at the door.

"What are you doing?"

The Professor dropped his arm. Maria stood in the doorway, a questioning look on her face. The Professor felt his face heat up at being caught doing something very childish. "We're having a discussion."

"We're not having a discussion," Josh chirped in. "There's nothing to discuss. The Professor here was about to admit he's wrong."

"I'm not wrong."

"Yes you are. Discounting an avenue of research just because you have a personality clash with the person who came up with it is poor science."

"What? Who said I have a personality clash with you?" There was no way he was going to let the old git take the moral high ground. "And anyway, I'm not against the idea because you thought of it, I'm against the idea because the chances of success are small, we have limited resources and we have far better options to explore."

"… in your opinion."

"Yes! Of course it's my bloody opinion, I'm the one saying it, aren't I?"

His shout was cut short by the sound of giggling. Maria had her hand to her face, trying but failing to stifle her amusement. "You two sound like Gino and Naci arguing over a toy."

Josh smiled. "Do either of them fail to admit they're wrong too?"

The Professor opened his mouth to reply, then let out a sigh. The girl was right. From the mouths of babes, eh? He turned his chair round to face her properly. "What can I do for you, Maria?"

"I'm bored."

"I'm sorry to hear that but you can't stay here. We're very busy right now."

"What are you doing?"

The Professor got up from his chair. "It's a little complicated to explain." He placed his arm around her shoulder and steered her towards the door. "Why don't you have a word with you mother, see if she has anything you can help with?"

"She's looking after Gino and Naci."

"What about your father?"

Maria's face darkened. "Pappa's gone again."

So that explains why you're here. While at O'Driscoll's bolt-hole, Maria had become attached to him, treating him as a father substitute. If the Investigator was away again, it was no surprise Maria had turned up here. He sighed. Nico seemed unhappy about their relationship, despite the Professor doing nothing to encourage it, but at the same time the events whirling around the poor girl had clearly unsettled her. "Okay, why don't you pull up a chair and sit down?"

Maria's face lit up and she quickly grabbed a spare chair and wheeled it over next to the Professor.

"So," he said. "What we're working on today is a way to store people's consciousness."

"Like with Re-Life?"

"Exactly. Just like the systems Re-Life developed—"

"—I developed," Josh interrupted.

"That Mr Denham here developed way back in the mists of time." He smiled and Maria giggled.

"Why don't you just do what Re-Life does?"

"There are two issues. The first is we don't have access to the technology, and even if we did, we can't be sure that nothing bad would happen to the information we store." He waited to see if Josh would comment at the dig but the old man remained quiet, hunched behind his datascreen. "The second problem is that we can't just recreate what Re-Life had because we don't have the storage capacity. A synthetic brain contains an enormous amount of data and the amount grows by the second. We would need to build huge data farms, just like those established by Re-Life, if we wanted to record the transiessence data of everyone here, and even if we could build them, the amount of energy needed to run them would give our location away."

Maria frowned for a moment. "Can't you just store some of the data, the important bits?"

The Professor smiled. "Not really. Let's take you for an example —which memories would you be happy to throw away?"

The response was immediate. "Pappa leaving us alone at

O'Driscoll's house."

The Professor took hold of Maria's hand. "I understand, but what did you learn from that?"

"That Pappa is selfish."

"I'm not sure that's true. Did he say why he was going away?"

"To get the bad guys."

"So he did it to protect you?"

"He should have spoken to Mamma first!"

"So what have you learned?"

The girl went quiet, her legs swinging as she thought. "That you shouldn't make big decisions without talking about them first."

"Exactly! So if we took away the memory of your parents arguing, you wouldn't have learnt that lesson and you may well make the same mistake in the future."

Maria had a frown on her face so the Professor mimicked her expression and ruffled her hair until she cracked a smile.

"That's the problem with only saving some of the data," he continued. "Even if we could identify individual thoughts and separate them out, they're all interlinked. You are the sum of your memories. If we took any away," or changed them, he thought, glancing at Denham, "you wouldn't be the same person."

The girl sat quietly for a moment, her legs swinging under her chair.

"But we forget things all the time."

The Professor tried to keep the surprise from his face. The girl was bright. "This is true, but unless you have some form of degenerative disease, those thoughts, and the lessons learned, are still there and can be triggered at any time." At least, that was his opinion. Others thought differently and the debate had never been truly settled, even if the law courts erred on the side of caution and had banned any form of alteration.

"So there's nothing you can do?" the girl asked.

"That's not entirely true." Denham poked his head up above his datascreen. "We do have another option."

"I'm telling you, there are too many issues to overcome."

"The datasphere!" A large smile broke out across Maria's face.

"You could use the datasphere to store the information."

"Well done, young lady," Josh said. "It took us a half an hour before we came to the same conclusion."

"No it didn't. It was one of the first things I thought of but I quickly discounted it. If we set up some form of storage via the datasphere it would be too large to hide and far too vulnerable. There's a reason Re-Life's control and production systems are not linked to the datasphere. Think of what would happen if the information got into the wrong hands."

"Then you need to come up with a better way of protecting it," Josh said, smiling at him as if talking to a small child.

The Professor gritted his teeth in frustration. They were back to where their argument had started.

"You kept us hidden from the bad guys."

The Professor took a sharp breath, glancing from Denham to Maria. "That was different. All information on the datasphere has three levels of security. The first is personal encryption, allowing each of us to secure our data. The second is a government override, used by investigative agencies and suchlike, but only with a court order. The third is less well known. It's a combination of hardware and software that allows Global Governance access to everything, as well as the ability to cloak any data they wanted to hide. I was able to subvert their process to keep us hidden but not crack their code."

"Why not?"

"It continually changes, driven by encryption embedded in the hardware, the infrastructure of the datasphere. Global Governance have access to this because they make the hardware. To crack this code from the outside," he threw his hands in the air, "… it would be impossible. You'd need a vast amount of computing power, more than I have access to, more than anyone has. You'd need the full power of the datasphere itself. And anyway, covering our tracks was possible because the data trail we left was so small. Doing the same for somebody's consciousness would leave an enormous hole, visible to everyone, even if you weren't really looking for it."

"Only if you put it all in one place."

Maria's words stopped him short. "Sorry?"

The girl blushed under his gaze. "Nothing, it's just a silly thought."

"You'd be surprised how many silly thoughts have grown to change the world," the Professor said.

"That wasn't what you said to me earlier," Josh grumbled.

The young girl laughed. "It's just … I play a game with Gino, hide the treasure. He has," she glanced to the floor, a frown on her face, "had a bag of pretend gold coins that he liked to hide. I'd look for them, and once I'd found them it was my turn to hide the coins and for Gino to look for them. We used to hide the whole bag but it's quite bulky and easy to find, so when Gino got good and finding that, I changed the game and hid each coin separately. Gino managed to find some of the coins, but never all of them."

The Professor smiled. "I bet if you cut each of the coins up into tiny little bits he would never have found enough to make a single gold coin."

"Why would you want to cut up the coins?" Maria asked.

Because if you don't know something is there, and aren't looking for it, you won't recognise the true value of a tiny piece of data if you happen to stumble upon it. He squeezed her hand. "Thank you, Maria. I think you've just solved our problem."

CHAPTER TWENTY-FIVE

King of the Scrambles

AFTER ALL HIS years maintaining control of the Scrambles, O'Driscoll thought he was beyond being surprised, yet what he now watched on the video feed left him baffled and bemused.

"How long has he been coming here?"

"Years, although his initial requests were vanilla, nothing like this." Charlie's face remained neutral but her voice gave away what she was thinking.

"How did you manage to get the … ?"

"Birds?"

"Yes, the birds. Where did they come from?"

"There's a specialist dealer brings them over from North America."

"But how do you catch them … after?"

"We have nets. The women enjoy it, it's a little break from the norm."

O'Driscoll shook his head. "I just don't understand how you would … what train of thought would lead anyone to come up with this."

Charlie shrugged her shoulders. "Who knows? People are weird. I'd have thought you'd worked that out by now." She glanced up at a wall clock. "Shall we go?"

They made their way down the stairs and into the hotel corridor.

Two enforcers waited at the door to the suite. Neither of them recognised him. O'Driscoll resisted the urge to scratch his beard. At Charlie's signal, one of the enforcers slapped his access card against the reader and pulled the handle.

The four of them burst into the room. Their target let out a muffled yell, the bag over his head blocking some of the sound. A hummingbird flew out from under the bag and made a dart for the open door. One of the naked women dived for it, missed and landed in a heap at the side of the bed. The other, who had only recently been manually pleasuring their target, slid off the bed and grabbed a robe. The two enforcers grabbed the man by each arm and dragged him to the end of the bed.

"What the hell is going on?" The man still had the bag over his head. O'Driscoll waited until Charlie closed the door before giving a nod. As the enforcer pulled the bag off the target's head, three more hummingbirds zipped out and flew around the room in a panic.

"Good evening, Delegate."

At his voice, the man stared at O'Driscoll, squinting against the light. "No, it's impossible."

He wasn't the only one who looked surprised.

"You didn't think you'd get rid of me that easily, now, did you?"

He watched the shock on the man's face turn to fear, then a blur of green flashed past his eyes.

"Will somebody do something about those fucking birds?"

The woman in a robe grabbed a clear container and took it into the bathroom. She hung it from a hook on the ceiling and the birds flew through, hovering to collect sweet water from the feeder. Once all in, the woman closed the door.

"If you think you'll get away with this, you're mistaken."

"Get away with what?" O'Driscoll said, a look of mock confusion on his face. "You mean walking into a room where you're being jerked-off while hummingbirds flap around your head? I don't see what the problem is."

"Once Internal Security hear you're back in the Scrambles, they'll tear the place apart to find you."

"It's nice to hear they still care, but you're missing something.

How, exactly, will they find out?"

The man's face went paler still. "You wouldn't kill me."

"You seem pretty sure of yourself."

"If I turn up dead, a whole pile of shit will come tumbling down on you."

"If they found out who killed you, because it's not like you told anyone you were coming here, is it Delegate? And that's assuming someone finds your body, and that someone can identify your remains. Neither of which is likely round here." The look on the man's face confirmed what O'Driscoll said was true. "But why would I kill you when you could be so much more useful to me alive?"

"You think you can blackmail me because I have certain … proclivities? My partner knows I have needs and my polling ratings are strong enough to withstand the public outcry."

O'Driscoll shook his head. "This isn't about today, although it'll make a great tale for my grandkids. You've been coming to the Scrambles for a long time. Have a little think. Are you sure there's nothing else you wouldn't want made public?"

"Nothing."

"Not even using your position to extort free sessions out of my girls? Or maybe the heavy use of dreamshaper, which, while not exactly illegal here, wouldn't be looked upon favourably by the electorate," O'Driscoll leaned forward, "especially as you brought it in yourself."

"That's not true."

O'Driscoll caught the first moment of uncertainty in the Delegate's eyes. "You think I wouldn't recognise my own product? Each shipment is coded, the capsules given unique identifiers, and what you used eighteen months ago was part of a consignment seized by the drugs squad as it entered our country. Now, how would the Delegate in charge of Internal Affairs possibly get access to this drug?"

"You're lying. This is a set-up. You've no proof."

"You think I need proof? Unlike you, I don't need to provide evidence for prosecution. I don't have to convince a judge or a jury that you've been up to no good. All I need to do is make the information available. Public opinion will do the rest."

"And out yourself in the process? I doubt that. Who would the public more likely believe, a wanted villain or a respected member of government?"

"It wouldn't come from me, it would come from one of my girls. You probably remember her. You should do, you beat her with your belt for refusing to give you a freebie. Quite nasty, really; the girl needed surgery. Still, the recording was worth it and she's long out of this game due to the money I gave her. I'm not sure how well that story will play to the electorate despite your ratings."

O'Driscoll watched as the Delegate took on board what he'd said. He'd expected some form of reaction—anger, denial or even resignation—but the Delegate remained calm for a half-naked man being held by each arm. You've something else up your sleeve, haven't you? O'Driscoll thought.

"What do you want from me?" the Delegate asked.

"Just a little help."

"What is it? You want me to turn a blind eye to drug shipments? I'm sorry but I won't do it."

O'Driscoll suppressed his disgust at the man's fake morality. He knows this is being recorded. He's just playing to the cameras. "I wouldn't ask you to do anything illegal."

"Then I don't understand."

"I don't expect you to, despite the fact you've been caught in a compromising situation, or despite the fact that you know we've evidence of you obtaining stolen drugs, or even despite the fact we've footage of you beating a young girl half to death. I'm sure you're confident your wealth and political power will protect you from anything we could do." He paused for a moment. "You know that no matter what happens, all will be suppressed by your friends in Global Governance."

This time the Delegate was unable to hide the shock he felt showing on his face. "How do you … ?"

"You think I've remained hidden by chance? I'm as much a part of Global Governance as you are, except of course there is no such thing as one Global Governance any more." The Delegate said nothing but the rivulet of sweat sliding down his forehead gave O'Driscoll all the information he needed. "You didn't know that? I thought a man of your standing would have been aware of the power struggle at the top of our organisation. Then again, perhaps I was wrong about you. Perhaps you're just a pawn like so many others …"

"I'm nobody's pawn."

"Really? Then why haven't they confided in you like they have me? Either they don't see you as important, or they don't trust you."

The man shook his head. "I've never heard of Global Governance."

O'Driscoll smiled. "Have it your way, but let me put this to you. Our organisation has split in two and the people I work for are in the ascendency. When you walk out of here, you've a decision to make. Do you carry on supporting your masters in the hope they win out and somehow protect you before we destroy your life forever? Or do you bow to the inevitable and come and work for us?"

"I don't know what you're talking about." The Delegate said the words as if by rote. His resigned tone spoke volumes.

O'Driscoll walked to the door, happy to have hit his mark, and signalled to the two enforcers to release him. The man sagged onto the bed.

"It's time for you to go now, Delegate. Think hard about what I've said. I'll be in touch." O'Driscoll walked out of the room, leaving the Delegate, a powerful figure in government, staring blankly into space.

"You shouldn't have let him go like that."

They were back in his office, truly his office now. It was O'Driscoll who sat behind the desk, still in his workingman's clothes, with Charlie stood in her usual position near the door. She'd not said a word on the way back, preferring to keep her council until the two of them were alone.

"What would you have had me do, kill him?"

"I'd have made him confess first, make sure it was recorded."

"We don't need a confession. He knows we have enough material on him to sink his career and I've sown enough confusion into that pompous head of his to make sure he won't go running off to his masters without thinking about the consequences first." O'Driscoll leant back in his chair, his hands resting on the arms, luxuriating in the sense of familiarity. It was good to be back.

"You don't think he'll say anything?"

"It's fifty-fifty. Either way, he'll be doing what we want."

Charlie gave him a questioning glance.

"If he remains quiet we can use him. If he reports back, they'll wait until they know whether what I've told him is the truth or not."

"That's one hell of an assumption."

"That's what they'll be thinking too. I've come back from the dead, blackmailed a member of government and dropped Global Governance's name into the conversation; I'd be crazy to do any of that without serious backing. Add into the equation those undesirables the other families have talked to and they'll be too busy tearing themselves apart trying to work out who's doing what to mount a raid."

"I'll double up on security just in case."

"I wouldn't expect anything less. If worst comes to worst, we'll call for help from the Knights Templar. I may not like their goal but if it's a choice between them or those currently running Global Governance …" Charlie nodded in agreement. He didn't need to say any more.

O'Driscoll pulled out a desk drawer. Everything was where it had been before he'd left. He smiled to himself: So Charlie had faith I'd return after all. He pulled out a small book on the history of the British Empire and flicked through the well-thumbed pages before placing it on the desk. Underneath was a letter he'd thought burnt. He was about to ask Charlie why she hadn't destroyed Selin's warning like he'd asked, when the answer occurred to him: You loved her too, didn't you Charlie?

He closed the drawer and addressed the room. "Still, that's the worst-case scenario. Let's focus on the next steps. We've enough people lined up to cause Global Governance some serious harm. I think it's time we approached the big fish. If my hunch is right, he won't need as much persuasion as our kinky delegate."

Charlie opened her mouth to reply but turned at the sound of voices coming from the corridor. The door opened. "Charlie, I'm sorry but I'm fed up with waiting. This is important. We need to speak about—" The young man stopped as soon as he saw who was behind the desk.

"Hello Darragh."

O'Driscoll's cousin stood still, the colour drained from his face. "You're …"

"Dead? I've been hearing that a lot recently, and I'm sorry to disappoint."

Darragh glanced across to Charlie. "Did you know about this?"

Charlie nodded, the slightest creasing around her eyes showing her satisfaction at fooling the young man. Darragh blinked, as if he couldn't believe what he was seeing.

"Charlie told me how much you've done to protect our family's business. I have to say, I never thought you had it in you. That said, for once I'm happy to be proved wrong." O'Driscoll stood up and held out his arms.

Darragh remained where he was, his expression unreadable. It was clear that the last few months had changed the young man. He had better control of his emotions for a start. The shock from moments before was gone. In the past Darragh would have sworn and ranted, now he remained quiet, almost thoughtful.

"Welcome back, cousin." Darragh walked forward into O'Driscoll's open arms.

"It's good to be back. Now pull up a chair, we've a lot of catching up to do."

CHAPTER TWENTY-SIX

The Professor

THE PROFESSOR STOOD by the industrial printer, watching as the machine made its final few passes. The small, grey circlet lying in the centre of the machine reflected a dull light, the slight ridges on its side giving away how its graphene structure had been printed one thin layer at a time.

Beside him, Josh Denham peered at the object. "This is a damn sight quicker than the last time I made one of these. Back then we didn't have the ability to print out multiple substrates simultaneously. It took days to finish the process. To be honest, it would have probably been quicker to have made it by hand, but back then we were keen to use the technology."

"Then we're lucky. I'm not sure we've got days left. I met with the medical staff this morning. Stephanie's taken a turn for the worse. She keeps slipping in and out of consciousness."

"She needs to be conscious in order to calibrate the neural scanner."

The Professor let out a sigh. "I'm aware of that."

"The unconscious mind doesn't provide us with the right stimu —" Josh stopped speaking, his head bowed in concentration, finger to his lips. "But then again, I could always …"

The Professor ignored the old man. He was so frustrating, his ideas bouncing from place to place. He was a genius, no doubt about it, and the progress they'd made in two days had been nothing short of astounding, but just when you thought you'd agreed a way forward, Josh would veer off on a tangent and pull apart much of the work already completed.

The printer head lifted up from the circlet. As it moved back to its dock, overhead fans came to life, drawing cool air over the surface of the freshly printed neural scanner. After a few minutes the fans slowed, the lights switched from red to green and the front hatch clicked open. With a speed belying his age, Josh reached in, grabbed the circlet and started scrutinising it through a jeweller's loupe.

"The surface is a little rough. I'll need to polish it."

"We don't have time for that. Give it here."

"But it's not finished. These surface variations could affect signal quality."

"And if we don't get it to her now, we may not have any signal to worry about." Before Josh could argue, the Professor snatched the circlet out of his hands. "I'm taking this to her now. Go back to the lab and prepare to receive the data." He walked out of the room before the old man had a chance to argue.

The Professor entered the room to find Stephanie asleep. They'd shaved her head ready for this moment and the lack of hair accentuated her sunken features. The Professor shivered. He'd caught her looking at him as the clippers did their work. While her body remained immobile her eyes communicated plenty. She didn't want it to happen. It was as if she didn't want to be saved at all.

The Commander insisted that he call her Heather, and she sat in the same chair as always. She, too, had been asleep but her eyes had snapped open as soon as he walked in.

"Is that it?"

He nodded, holding up the dull grey circlet. "We based it on the design of the last external neural scanner, before everything became implanted."

"But it will work."

He gave a slight shrug. "We haven't had time to test any of this. In theory it should but—"

"It's got to work. You have to save my daughter." Heather looked up at him, half-demanding, half-pleading.

"We're doing our best. If we had access to the Re-Life database …" He let the question hang, knowing it was a useless wish. They'd been reliant on Josh Denham's recollection of work he'd done years before. The good news was that his mind was as sharp as a man forty years younger. The problem was he kept wanting to 'improve' the design. "Let's just get this circlet in place, shall we?"

He walked over to where Stephanie lay, picked up the power cable he'd set up earlier and plugged it into a small slot on the circlet. It was crude—they hadn't had time to create an internal power source—but it would in all probability work. For once, the fact Stephanie was immobile worked in their favour.

A simple green diode winked on the front of the neural scanner. The Professor placed the circlet on Stephanie and used the light to align it to the centre of her forehead. He watched to see if she reacted to the contact but she remained unconscious.

With the circlet in place, the Professor placed a call through to Josh back in the lab. "Are you picking up a signal?"

"I'm getting a signal but the data's scrambled."

"Give me a second." The Professor felt around the inside of the circlet, his fingers sliding across Stephanie's smooth scalp as he looked for gaps between her head and the neural scanner. It had been designed to fit the contours of her skull so it could be positioned in the precise location required for optimal scanning. After a couple of minutes and a few minor adjustments he was sure it was perfectly aligned. "What about now?"

"It's better, but there's still information decay."

"The fit's snug this end. Check again."

"I have checked. We're losing data. If you'd listened to me and allowed me to polish it first, maybe we wouldn't have these problems."

The Professor growled under his breath. Josh's smartarse comments weren't helping. He gently lifted Stephanie's head to see if there was anything interfering with the neural scanner from behind. As he did so, Stephanie's eyes opened. Her gaze bore through him, straight to his soul. "I'm sorry," he whispered.

Josh's voice spoke in his ear. "Sorry for what? What have you done now?"

The Professor swore under his breath. "That wasn't aimed at you," he said to Josh, smiling at Stephanie and giving her a little 'what can you do?' shake of the head. "I'm placing a neural scanner around your head," he said, "just in case." As soon as the words were out of his mouth he regretted them. Way to go, idiot. Nothing like telling somebody they're about to croak.

Stephanie's eyes remained locked on him, unblinking, sucking him in. The Professor shivered. Was she trying to tell him something or was he just projecting his own thoughts onto her?

"That's better. What did you do?"

Josh's voice startled him. He looked down at where Stephanie lay but couldn't see any obvious reason for the change of signal. He glanced across to Heather. "Would you mind grabbing something, anything, just so we can keep her head propped up like this?"

Stephanie's mother grabbed a spare pillow from beside the bed and placed it gently in the gap between her daughter's head and the headboard.

The Professor released his grip. "How's the signal now?"

"The same, still good."

He breathed a sigh of relief. Maybe, just maybe, this would work.

He took a small box from his pocket, opened it and pulled out a pair of datalenses. "I need to place these in your eyes," he said to Stephanie. "It's to calibrate the system. Normally we'd do this as a conversation but … anyway, just concentrate on the images we'll send through."

Stephanie's eyelids slammed shut.

The Professor turned to Heather. "What does that mean?"

"What do you think it means? She's scared. They tortured her with horrific images in the facility we rescued her from."

"Shit." He remained leaning over Stephanie's bed, unsure of what to do. "If we don't do the test there's no way of knowing if the data we're harvesting is any good."

"Why does it matter?" Heather asked, concern for her daughter clear on her face.

"After collecting enough data we'll then replicate the stimulation Stephanie receives on the synthetic version of her brain. If the synthetic brain reacts identically to the organic version, we know the data we receive is complete. We then open the port to allow two-way conversation, effectively making the two into one."

"Then put the datalenses on her." The change in tone was startling. Gone was the caring mother. This was the Heather he'd seen on entering the building, the Commander, the person who'd dedicated her life to monitoring Global Governance.

"I can't. It's clear she doesn't want them in."

"That's not the point. I will not have my daughter's stubbornness stand in the way of saving her life."

"But if she doesn't want to live …"

The Commander pulled a weapon from a holster at her hip and pointed it at his head. "Put those datalenses in her eyes and start the calibration or god help me I'll blow your bloody head off."

The Professor swallowed, then reached down with shaking hands to prise Stephanie's right eye open. He'd expected her eyeball to be moving around furiously but it remained locked on his face, silently judging. The Professor put the first datalense gently in place, all the while begging for Stephanie's forgiveness in his mind.

CHAPTER TWENTY-SEVEN

Indigo

SOMETHING WAS WRONG. Very wrong. Indigo rocked from side to side, her body protesting at the movement. Everything hurt. Even her teeth hurt. It was the pain that had woken her. It wasn't agony, just a solid ache from toes to scalp. And her face felt tight, her skin taut. Where was she?

The last thing she remembered was taking a pod back to the apartment. Then nothing except pain. Whatever had happened, it was clear she was no longer alone. The air smelt damp, earthy and there was the heavy fug of stale sweat and something else, something familiar. The urge to open her eyes and discover more was strong, but she'd learnt many years before that you could learn a lot by playing dead.

There was a dull thud. The floor underneath her fell away, before coming back so hard the impact sent a spike of fresh pain through her body. Indigo let out a groan.

A voice spoke. "She's coming round."

So much for subterfuge. Indigo rolled onto her back and opened her eyes.

The first thing she saw was a pair of boots, coated in mud. She looked up to see a woman dressed in combat fatigues. Their eyes locked. The woman gave no sign of compassion, no emotion at all, she just stared at Indigo while behind her a datascreen showed a passing landscape.

Indigo didn't recognise the woman or the style of uniform she wore. Her lack of compassion was a worry. If these people were taking her somewhere safe, Indigo would have expected at least some form of reassurance. Each thought, each new piece of the jigsaw helped clear her fuzzy head. So she was being taken somewhere but she didn't know where, by whom or why. It wasn't the best of situations but she'd been in worse. The question was, how did she get here? She couldn't remember. She tried but her timeline stopped with her taking the pod, a different pod, back from a meeting with those bastard Traditionalists to her apartment.

"How are you feeling?"

Indigo strained to see who spoke, then let out a gasp. It was the Investigator, Tandelli, the one she'd been hunting. Seeing his face brought back a flash of memory. She was stood in front of her apartment surrounded by soldiers, weapons pointed in her direction. She had a hostage, a young woman and was trying to get into the apartment, away from these people who wanted to … what? What did they want?

"I know you can hear me."

Her mind focussed back on the Investigator. He looked pale and winced after talking to her. "You tried to kill me," Indigo said.

"You're lucky to be alive."

"I don't understand. First you try to kill me, but now you want me alive?"

"One of our squad died protecting you. Others were injured." He glanced across to where the female soldier sat.

Indigo noticed a patch of blood on the woman's uniform. Another fragment of memory returned. The young woman she'd used as a shield. "What happened to the girl?"

The Investigator shook his head before wincing once more. "Another death on your conscience."

The final piece of memory returned and with it the recognition that it was blood she could smell, the young woman's blood that covered her face and clothes. But it wasn't her fault the girl had died. She hadn't pulled the trigger. They had. "Why didn't you just kill me where I fell? You clearly want me dead."

The Investigator ignored her question, turning to somebody she couldn't see. "We need to go over there."

The pod lurched to the right, causing Indigo to slide into the female soldier's booted feet. Before she could shuffle back, the floor of the pod began to vibrate, causing stabs of pain all over her body. There was a large jolt, then another. Indigo yelled in pain. She tried to sit up from the hard, merciless floor but the Investigator placed a foot on her chest and pushed her back down.

"Stay there."

"I'm tied up," she hissed through gritted teeth. "What do you think I'm going to do, bite you all to death?"

"Unless you want to spend the rest of this journey tranqued, I suggest you keep still."

For a moment she was tempted. Each jolt, each bump, sent sparks through her nervous system. But she had to stay conscious in order to find out where she was and what was happening. She closed her eyes, ignoring the pain coursing through her body, and sent out the mental command to turn on her datalenses.

Nothing happened.

She tried again. Still no luck. In a fit of frustration she mumbled a command.

"We've removed your datalenses, not that you would have been able to access the datasphere even if we'd left them in."

Her eyes snapped open and she glared at the Investigator. "You will be hunted down."

"Tell me something I don't know."

"Don't think for a minute you'll get away with this."

The man leant forward until he was centimetres from her face. "You still don't get it, do you? Nobody is after us. Internal Security has already announced the capture of a lone-wolf terrorist they say is responsible for the death of that girl and the two men she was with."

"You killed those men too?"

"They were alive when we left, although the one you shot had lost consciousness. My guess is Internal Security want to cover up what's happened. Why do you think that might be?"

It made sense. She would have done the same if she'd been in charge. "They don't want to panic the population. I can assure you they'll be hunting down those responsible."

The Investigator started to laugh, then winced. "You still think we did it, don't you? We had nothing to do with the death of your hostage. Think about it. Why would we try to capture you only to blow your brains out? It surprised us as much as it surprised you. We'd been watching your apartment block for days waiting for the right moment. If all we wanted was to kill you, we could have done so days ago. If I were you I'd be looking elsewhere for answers. You've made enough enemies but not many know who you are, so the people most likely to be responsible are …"

The Investigator let the words hang but it didn't take a genius to work out what he meant. Indigo shivered. His logic was faultless. There were a number of individuals who'd be happy to see her dead and they all belonged to one organisation: Hers.

Indigo felt the pod slow, then stop. She breathed a sigh of relief. In the vehicle, everybody remained where they were, eyes focussed on the datascreens.

"What's going on?"

She didn't receive an answer but hadn't expected to.

After the constant noise and motion of earlier, the sudden silence was palpable, only broken by small sounds; a person breathing, the creak of a seat as somebody adjusted their weight. They waited for what felt an age until Indigo saw the surrounding trees light up with the approach of a second vehicle. As it pulled up beside them, the doors to their pod peeled back and the Investigator climbed out.

Cold, fresh air entered the cabin from outside. Indigo strained to hear what was going on.

"Christ, you look like shit. Are you okay?" It was a man's voice.

"I'm fine," the Investigator replied. "Just a headache. Did you find the shooter?"

"No. Whoever it was had disappeared by the time I found where they'd been hiding."

"You made it out, though."

"It was easy. No road blocks, no clampdown. The only reason I took as long as I did was to make sure it wasn't some kind of trap."

The voice nagged at Indigo but she couldn't quite place it. She tried to roll closer to the doorway but was stopped by a boot placed on her shoulder. Looking up she saw the female soldier shake her head.

"Nobody's looking for us. We've been monitoring Internal Security comms. There's been no mention of us at all. They're only looking for her," Tandelli said.

"That doesn't make sense," the other voice replied, "unless …"

"Unless they're the ones behind what's happened."

Indigo felt her chest tighten. There were only a few people within Global Governance who could control Internal Security like that. The Prime Delegate was one, but he'd lost his backbone years ago. That left one person: The young prince.

"Is she alive?" the mystery voice asked.

"Covered in blood but hardly a scratch on her. It doesn't seem fair, all things considered."

Indigo heard the sound of footsteps and then a head appeared in the open doorway, staring at her. Her heart froze. For the first time since she'd regained consciousness she truly feared for her life.

"Oscar."

CHAPTER TWENTY-EIGHT

Re-Life Technician

THREE … FOUR … NOW five green lights. The algorithm confirmed what Josh saw with his own eyes. The neural recording worked fine. Stephanie's transiessence data had loaded into her synthetic brain correctly and reacted to stimuli in the same way as the organic original.

He looked around the lab, surprised to find himself alone. When had the Professor left? That man was always running backwards and forwards, never concentrating on the task at hand. As usual it all fell to him. And where was the thanks? Where was the praise? Given to the young pretender, that's where, while he did all the work. The situation was painfully familiar. It was the story of his life and he was fed up with it.

Josh cleared the test results from his datascreen and pulled up a new graphic showing the current status of Stephanie's synthetic brain. The structure looked identical to that of her real brain, making it easy to run visual comparisons between her live feed and that of the synthetic brain. However, while the visual representation showed a coherent neural structure, physically each individual synthetic synapse lay scattered across the datasphere, minute pieces of data hidden within servers often thousands of miles from those of its neighbour. Unless a person knew what they were looking for, or had the key to the pattern, nobody would know it was there. Despite the overall size of the data storage required, it was an insignificance compared to the vastness of the datasphere itself. Once her consciousness was fully loaded, Stephanie would be safe.

Except, she wouldn't be, not really.

In their desire to save Stephanie from death, they'd condemned her to something far, far worse. The others didn't know what he knew, hadn't seen what he'd seen. Downloading Stephanie's consciousness may save her life but in the process she would lose her sanity.

Josh thought back to when he'd first started working with Maria. Not the annoying girl the Professor had taken under his wing, but Maria Chan, the brilliant neuroscientist and his early mentor. It was Chan who'd created the first synthetic brain capable of storing life. She'd built it for research purposes, but it was only when he'd loaded in data of sufficient quality that they realised they'd not only managed to successfully store a person's memories, but that they'd created consciousness itself.

Josh had been heady with excitement as they'd tested and re-tested their findings because everything pointed to the same conclusion. Their synthetic brain was no longer just a repository of information, it was a working, thinking organ in its own right.

It was only a few weeks after that initial discovery that doubts began to surface. He was the one who'd first noticed the abnormal thinking patterns. He initially thought it was a data glitch, but as the days went on the synthetic brain deviated further and further away from normal behavioural parameters. The two of them repeated the experiment only to get the same results. Was it a form of data degradation, or had they missed a biological process within the synthetic model? It was only after months of research that Chan spotted similar patterns elsewhere in the live, biological brains of patients with locked-in syndrome, stripped of sensory input. The synthetic brain, left alone without any means to interact with the world, had slowly gone mad.

And here he was again, building another synthetic brain with no sensory input, repeating errors from the past. He knew why they were doing it, knew the noble reasons for attempting to save the woman's life, but it was doomed to fail as it had before. He'd tried to warn the Professor but the man wouldn't listen. He hadn't even given Josh the chance to explain. The man was obsessed with saving Stephanie, yet it was the definition of madness, repeating the same mistakes and expecting different results.

Flashes of neural activity bloomed and faded on the datascreen as Josh's mind flicked between past and present. For the moment, Stephanie's synthetic brain remained a slave to her biological one, gathering patterns and activity to build up a whole. The woman appeared to be sleeping, or at least that's what the neural patterns looked like—he was a little rusty after spending years perfecting the biological, rather than neurological, aspects of life extension. The main giveaway was the lack of activity through the optic nerve. They'd finished running their test visuals through the day before and ─

The thought stopped him.

With every mistake comes an opportunity. If right, this could be his chance to show the world what they were missing. It would be a chance to do something against those who'd used his work for nefarious purposes. He wasn't stupid. He knew his experiments to improve clones had been perverted. Because of the actions of others, his life's work was tainted. Now was his chance to do something about it.

When he'd first created synthetic life, the science of interacting with the world by thought was in its infancy. Neural scanners were big, bulky machines. Scientists could read brain patterns to recognise basic commands but understanding detailed interactions was beyond the technology available at the time. Now things were different. Everybody used at least some form of mind control through the neural scanners in their datalenses.

Josh cleared the neural image from the datascreen and searched the datasphere. It didn't take him long to find what he needed. Stephanie Vaughn's datasphere profile contained the neural patterns used to speed up her datalense interaction. It was encrypted, but he was sure one of the technicians here could provide him with a tool to gain access.

His mind raced as he thought of the challenges ahead. He would need a way to mimic the optic and aural inputs so he could feed sensory information back into the synthetic brain. It would be a case of adapting techniques used to restore the sight and hearing of patients where stem cell treatment had failed. Then there was the replacement of oral commands …

The surroundings faded into the background as Josh focussed on the task at hand, all thoughts of the individual involved, the person whose existence was at stake, forgotten, as he worked once more on the new intellectual challenge.

CHAPTER TWENTY-NINE

King of the Scrambles

THERE WAS SOMETHING about churches that set O'Driscoll's teeth on edge. That smell for a start—a combination of a millennia of dust, the damp of cold stone and the faith and fears of the thousands who'd prayed, hoped and lied while preaching or being preached to. It was a scent he remembered from the chapel at his old boarding school where the chaplain brought the boys for 'spiritual guidance', a euphemism for a beating and a telling off. This church was on a different scale from the one at his old school but the atmosphere was the same—cold, inflexible, traditional. How on earth did Jesus telling stories to his disciples about the importance of love and compassion while sitting under trees become transformed into something so sterile?

Smoke rose from white candles set on shelves by the doorway, adding its own bitter tang to the overriding scent. O'Driscoll walked down the nave, his footsteps echoing in the chill. He glanced down the old wooden pews either side out of habit. The man he'd come to meet stood by the lectern. He must have known O'Driscoll was there—the door creaking when he entered was loud enough to wake the spirits haunting this place—but the man refused to look in his direction. Seeing how he fidgeted, it was clear the man was as nervous as O'Driscoll.

"Thank you for coming at such short notice," O'Driscoll said. "I wasn't sure you would."

Richard Asquith, the Prime Delegate, turned. Insipid lighting did the man no favours, emphasising dark shadows normally hidden by make-up or digital masking. He looked confused, then his eyes widened. "You! But you can't be … I was told—"

"That I was dead? You of all people should know better than to believe everything you're told."

Asquith backed away. "I can't be here. I can't be seen with you."

"Calm down. You haven't been followed, your paymasters have no idea you're here. The two of us are alone."

"But—"

"But what? You're worried Global Governance will storm in at any moment?" O'Driscoll shook his head, clearly irritated. "That won't happen. I took care of it. They won't be adding us to their victim list, at least not today. Don't worry, you won't be joining Grant quite yet."

The Prime Delegate's eyes narrowed at the mention of his dead brother's name. "How dare you, you of all people?"

"If you really thought I killed your brother, you would have walked out of here as soon as you heard my voice," O'Driscoll said. "I don't know for certain why Global Governance killed him. My guess is you refused to do what they wanted." The look on the Prime Delegate's face told O'Driscoll he'd hit the mark. "The reason I'm stood here now is because I tried to find the person behind his death."

"And did you?"

O'Driscoll gestured to the front pew. "Take a seat, Mr Asquith. We've a lot to talk about."

The Prime Delegate glanced around the church. The man was as skittish as a hare. Christ, what must it be like to live life under those circumstances? He was supposedly the most powerful man in the country yet the last time O'Driscoll had seen such fear was during one of Darragh's interrogations. Eventually the Prime Delegate sat down on the pew opposite where O'Driscoll indicated. The little act of defiance almost brought a smile to O'Driscoll's lips. It was a good sign.

Taking his place beside the Prime Delegate, O'Driscoll paused to work through what to say next. He'd expected the man to either walk out or threaten him. He'd prepared for those scenarios. He hadn't expected this brittle creature, so different from his public persona. He was a husk of a man, functioning on the outside but rotten from fear within. He would need gentle handling.

"Your brother came to the Scrambles for comfort. Did you know that?"

The Prime Delegate shook his head.

"The loss of your mother hit him hard. All he wanted was to feel her touch again."

"They sent us away after mother died, off to boarding school."

"Not the most comforting environment."

The Prime Delegate shook his head, a pained expression on his face. "Even though he was older than me, I ended up looking out for him. The other boys … well, any weakness was pounced on."

So we're not that different after all. "Your brother was a perfect gentleman with my girls. They all liked him."

"He wouldn't hurt a fly." The Prime Delegate realised he was digging into the pew with his fingernails and stopped. "Was it quick?"

"His death? Yes, but while the poison worked fast it wasn't painless." In his mind's eye, O'Driscoll saw the agonised rictus on the face of Grant Asquith. "There are more humane ways to kill."

The man beside him processed the information. At first O'Driscoll thought he would crumple, but after a few moments his face set hard.

"You said you knew who was responsible."

"It was a Global Governance operative codenamed Echo. You know him better as David Chandler." O'Driscoll watched for a reaction. There was nothing, not a flicker. You suspected, didn't you? He thought. I'm just confirming what you already know.

The Prime Delegate stood. "Thank you for the information."

"That wasn't why I asked you here."

"I think I've heard enough for today."

O'Driscoll grabbed the man's arm and pulled him back onto the pew. "You're not the only one to have risked everything by coming here."

"Get your hands off me."

O'Driscoll ignored his protests. "If Global Governance knew I was alive, that I was here in this church, the place would be swarming by now. I know too much but unlike you I'm of no value, I'm just a threat."

"So what do you want from me? Protection? I can't even protect my own family."

"I don't need your protection. I can look after myself. I'm not here to ask anything of you. I'm here to offer something instead."

The Prime Delegate stopped pulling away from O'Driscoll's grip. "What could you offer me?"

The tone of voice, the look on the Prime Delegate's face, brought memories crashing back. He'd faced the same reaction on arriving at boarding school. The sons and daughters of the upper classes looked down on him. He was the son of a gangster; a low-class, snotty intruder to their privileged world. They refused to look past his background to who he really was. It took all O'Driscoll's self-control not to beat the man where he sat. The problem was, he needed the Prime Delegate as much as the Prime Delegate needed him. Getting revenge on the stuck-up shit would have to come later. For the time being he'd swallow his anger. He wouldn't forget, though. He would never forget.

"Everything you have in your life is because of Global Governance. I don't know when they approached you—was it at school, or maybe university?" The Prime Delegate nodded. "So it was university. I bet it was a hell of a ride, building up power and influence, becoming famous and the adulation that goes with it. But there was a price, right? There's always a price. And my guess is it's a price you no longer want to pay."

"What choice do I have? They've already killed my brother. I couldn't live with another death on my conscience."

O'Driscoll growled despite himself. "What do you want, sympathy? How many people have died, how many lives ruined through your actions?"

"It wasn't meant to be like that. They said they were doing it for the good of the world."

"Yet when you started to suspect otherwise, you still did as you were asked."

"How dare you! You've no idea what it's been like." The Prime Delegate yanked his arm out of O'Driscoll's grip. "Once they have you they never let go. You can't even end it all. They just bring you back."

"Is suicide something you've tried?" The look on the Prime Delegate's face was the only answer O'Driscoll needed. Fucking coward, trying to justify his actions when they were purely to save his own skin. O'Driscoll took a deep breath. He needed the man; he didn't have to like him.

"What if I told you there was a way out of this."

The Prime Delegate shook his head. "I've tried that, tried to run away. I didn't get as far as the front door."

"I'm not talking of running and hiding, I'm talking about stopping them, stopping the whole mess once and for all."

"That's impossible."

"No it's not. Nothing's impossible if you have the will. That's my question for you. If you had the chance to make a stand, not on your own but with others, many, many others, do you have the will to see it through?"

He was answered by silence. The Prime Delegate stared into space, brow furrowed.

A shiver ran up O'Driscoll's spine. The cold from the stone floor had seeped through his shoes and into his bones. He needed an answer and quick. They'd already been away too long. He'd arranged with the Prime Delegate's head of security, another regular at the Scrambles, to pull the Prime Delegate's protective detail, but there was a limit to how much the man could cover.

"How do you plan to take them on?"

"They've thrown their weight around too often, threatened too many people to keep their existence quiet for much longer. On your own you have no chance, but by acting together …"

"We can't play them at their own game."

"We can and we will."

"But they'll hurt my family."

"They will anyway. There'll come a point when you'll be of no further use to them. That's when they'll dispose of you, and those close to you, either by taking them out or turning them into another version of you."

"No. I'll … I'll …"

"You'll fight? On your own? Or would you rather do it with others in the same position as you?"

The Prime Delegate ran his fingers through his hair. "I don't have a choice."

"None of us do."

The man straightened. Whether it was a trick of the light or not, one change of posture and the Prime Delegate looked like a different proposition. The dark circles under his eyes remained, but for the first time since O'Driscoll arrived, those deadened eyes glittered with hope.

"What do you want me to do?"

O'Driscoll smiled. "The first thing I'm going to need from you is a list of delegates not under Global Governance control …"

CHAPTER THIRTY

The Investigator

THEIR POD ROUNDED a bend on the rough, coastal road, past bleak gorse-clad hills until a group of brutal concrete buildings came into view. Despite having only spent a few weeks at the place, to Nico it felt as if he was coming home. The journey back had been stressful, their approach cautious to the point of paranoia. Lack of sleep and a persistent headache had put him in a foul mood. He just wanted to see Fran and the kids.

Two squads came out of building one as the vehicle pulled up outside. The door to the pod opened and Oscar jumped out. Nico got up, the quick movement causing him to lose balance and he banged his head on top of the doorframe. Laughter erupted from the back of the pod. Nico turned to see Indigo smiling at him. Throughout the journey she'd tried her best to get under the skin of those inside. Tried but failed.

Nico left the pod to find Oscar in conversation with the giant of a soldier who'd guarded them when they'd first arrived.

"We've two injured, one serious, as well as one fatality." Oscar gestured towards the second pod. "I need medics out here, now."

The soldier barked an order and a pair of medics raced across to where the pod sat. "Do you have the target?"

Oscar nodded.

Nico glanced over the heads of the reception party, looking for a sign of his family, but there was none. His disappointment rose, even though he'd not been able to communicate ahead to let the base know they were on their way. He really needed to see them.

A sudden hush made Nico turn back towards his pod. Squinting into the bright light, Indigo stepped out, the rust of dried blood on her face, arms secured behind her back, guided by one of their squad. She appeared unfazed to be in front of so many hostile faces.

"Take her to the cells."

Indigo regarded the giant soldier. "Are you not going to offer me a welcome?" Before he could respond a squad member took hold of the still smiling Indigo and hauled her through the front entrance.

So that was that. They'd done what they'd set out to do and now they were back. The whole thing felt a little anti-climactic, but to be honest he didn't care. Nico looked around to see if he was needed. The giant and Oscar were still deep in conversation. Medics buzzed around the pod containing their casualties. Those squad members still fit were walking together towards a side entrance. Now was his chance to slip away.

He still wanted to help the Knights Templar, wanted to be of use, but given everything that had happened it was clear he'd be more useful back at base. At least when he was investigating Global Governance he'd been of value, but on the raid he'd felt more of a hindrance. Then the thought hit him. Would he still be needed with Indigo in custody?

He rubbed the sleep from his eyes. He was tired, irritable and his skull felt like it was about to split. The questions could wait until morning. He started walking towards the entrance hall when Oscar ran past him and into the building.

"What was that all about?" Nico asked the friendly giant.

"He wanted to know where the Commander is."

"And?"

"I told him she was where she's been for the past week, with her dying daughter."

It took Nico a few moments to work out what the man had said, then he too ran into the building, hoping he wasn't too late.

CHAPTER THIRTY-ONE

The Professor

THE PROFESSOR ARRIVED at Stephanie's room to find there was hardly space to move. The Commander sat in her usual corner, holding her daughter's unmoving hand, looking for a forgiveness Stephanie could no longer offer. Stood beside her was the man who'd saved him from certain capture, even death. Oscar must have heard him walk in but the man's eyes remained fixed on the face of the woman lying on the bed in the centre of the room. Stephanie had an air-mask over her mouth and nose. A tangle of tubes linked her to the machines trying but failing to keep her alive.

On the other side of the bed stood the Investigator. He had looked up as the Professor entered. The man's face was pale but his eyes bored into the Professor until he felt himself flush under the scrutiny.

"Perhaps I should come back at a quieter time," the Professor said.

The Commander looked up from where she sat. "Did it work?"

"We've captured what we can," the Professor replied. "Whether it will be enough, we won't know until we transfer her consciousness into her new body."

"So you're really going through with this?!" The Investigator took a step toward the Professor, then stopped, pinching the bridge of his nose as if in pain.

Oscar moved between the two of them. "Calm down, Nico."

"Why should I?" Nico asked. "You don't know her. None of you do. I'm the only one in this room who actually knew her before Indigo got her hands on her."

"Everyone has their reasons for being here," Oscar replied.

"If you knew her like I do, you'd know she doesn't believe in Re-Life, doesn't think it works. It was the reason we got dragged into this mess in the first place. If it hadn't been for Jennica Fabian's discovery, and Indigo's efforts to silence her, neither Stephanie or I would be here today."

The Commander turned to Nico. "What are you talking about?"

"There's a flaw in the Re-Life process. Not all the data gets transferred from the original to the synthetic brain and then on to the clone. Stephanie talked about it once. We were staking out a house we thought he," the Investigator nodded toward Oscar, "lived at. She said if Global Governance were willing to kill someone to keep the issue a secret, then there must be something to it."

"In my opinion the process is still valid," the Professor said. "I looked into it when Jennica first discovered the discrepancy. The amount of information lost is tiny, the equivalent of a day's neural activity."

"Your opinion's irrelevant," the Investigator replied. "What matters is what Stephanie thinks. She doesn't trust the process, she wanted nothing to do with it—and given what's happened to her since I understand why. Answer me this. Did she give permission for you to capture her consciousness? Did she give any indication at all that she wanted this to happen?"

The Professor couldn't help looking towards the Commander. "Her mother said—"

"Fuck what she thinks!" The Investigator gestured angrily in the Commander's direction. "This is the woman who abandoned her daughter as a young girl. She never once made contact in God knows how many years to let Stephanie know she was alive. This hasn't anything to do with having her daughter's interests at heart, she's only thinking of herself."

"How dare you!" The Commander got out of her seat. "You

think you can come in here and lecture me about things you know nothing about?"

The Professor watched Nico open his mouth to reply but the words never came out. An alarm sounded from behind Stephanie's bed, the beeping loud and insistent and the room went silent. It was the heart monitor. The Professor turned to shout for support, but a female medic was already through the door. It was Emma, the medic who'd helped save Stephanie from torture.

"I need everybody away from the bed."

"But—"

"Now!"

The Professor knew better than to argue and stepped back, quickly followed by the others. Another two medics squeezed into the cramped space, pushing past the anxious onlookers as if they weren't there, their focus on the patient. They immediately stripped the covers from the bed, then Stephanie herself. The Professor turned his back out of respect for Stephanie's privacy and noticed Nico and Oscar do the same. As he stared at the wall, all the Professor could think about was how helpless he felt, and how much worse it must be for the others. The Investigator was beside him, head bowed, hands to his face. Oscar remained impassive, the only sign of tension his rigid neck muscles.

"I need you to look at this, Commander."

The Professor couldn't help himself and glanced to where Stephanie lay. Her torso had been wrapped in a flexible datascreen displaying a detailed 3D rendering of her organs. Emma pointed to where Stephanie's heart lay motionless beneath her semi-opaque lungs.

"Her heart has stopped. We've tried everything but it won't respond. Only the machines are keeping her alive."

"Keep trying," the Commander said.

"If there was any chance of her responding we would."

"That's an order!"

Emma gave the Commander a sad smile. "There's nothing more we can do. We've tried everything. Her body's never fully recovered from the physical and psychological trauma she's been put through.

I guess in the end she sees dying as the best option." Emma reached down, stroked Stephanie's cheek and then took a deep breath before turning back to the Commander. "I'm sorry but the procedure is clear for cases like this. If you want, I can give you a few moments before we turn the machines off."

The Commander fell back into her seat, tears streaming down her face. For a moment the Professor thought the woman would break down completely, but instead she took a deep breath and sat up straight.

"Do you need more time to capture her data?"

The Professor shook his head. "If she was conscious we could do more but not as she is now."

The Commander cleared her throat. "Turn it off."

"If it's any consolation, she won't feel any—"

"I don't need your reassurance."

Emma stepped back, nodded to a colleague and the alarm stopped.

Given the horrors she'd endured during her last months, Stephanie Vaughn looked peaceful in death.

The Professor placed his hand on the Commander's shoulder. "I'm sorry."

"Just do your job."

Her words were like a slap. "I … I will. I'll make sure she gets another chance at life."

The Investigator stormed out of the room. Oscar made his way to the other side of the bed, kissed his fingers and touched them to Stephanie's lips.

The man's intimate gesture surprised the Professor. He had no idea Oscar knew Stephanie, let alone had such affection for her. He felt like an intruder observing such an intimate goodbye, but Oscar was oblivious. He brushed a lock of hair away from Stephanie's still face, smiled then left the room without saying a word.

"I'll … um … I'll get back to the lab, then."

The Commander gave no indication that she'd heard him. As the Professor left, he saw her stroke her daughter's cheek, flattening out the red ridges on her nose and cheeks where the oxygen mask had sat, wrapped once more in silence.

CHAPTER THIRTY-TWO

The Investigator

NICO STEPPED OUT of the shower and waited for the warm air to dry him. Nothing happened. He went to thump the control panel in frustration but a wave of pain and dizziness crashed through his skull, so strong he had to hold onto the wall to stop himself from falling.

For a moment he thought he would throw up but the pain soon receded. Bloody people. How could they be so selfish, Re-Lifing Stephanie when they knew she didn't trust the process? He grabbed a towel and rubbed his body hard, channelling his aggression into the act of drying. They didn't care about what Stephanie wanted. Capturing her consciousness was a betrayal of everything she'd stood for.

He rubbed himself down, taking care when towelling his hair, then pulled on a robe. He had to stop what they were doing, but how? Who would listen to him? The only person who could pull the plug was Doleman but the old man trusted the Commander and Oscar more than anyone else. It was so frustrating. Despite everything he and Stephanie had done to bring Indigo to justice, he had little to no influence over what happened within the Knights Templar. He remained an outsider. Nico threw his towel on the floor, walked to his bedroom and climbed onto the bed. The warmth of the shower had reminded him just how tired he was. He needed sleep.

But his mind was plotting against him. Every time he felt himself drift, his thoughts circled back to Stephanie's death and subsequent re-life. He was dead tired but the adrenaline in his system refused to relent. As he rolled over onto his side for what felt like the hundredth time, he heard the door to the living area open.

"Hello?" Fran called out.

Nico's heart jumped at the sound of his wife's voice but he remained where he was.

"Maria?" Fran asked. "Is that you?"

"Hi Fran," he said.

There was a shriek of excitement and Nico smiled despite his tiredness. He tried to sit up but before he could he found himself engulfed by his wife's embrace. She crushed herself against him and he held her tight. The two of them lay together in silence, content to just hold and be held. Fran's scent acted like a sedative, soothing the jagged emotions coursing through him. God, he'd missed her. Nico held his soulmate tightly, content just to be.

Fran raised her head and kissed him on the lips. "Thank God you're safe. I've been worried sick. Nobody would tell me anything."

"It's okay. I'm back now."

"You'd better be." She gave him a gentle thump on his chest. "I've had enough of waiting around wondering if you've been captured by Internal Security, or worse. I know it was my idea for you to go but from now on you're staying right here."

He smiled. "Yes, ma'am."

His mock salute earned him another thump. "I'm serious. I'm not sure I can take it, and the kids—"

"Where are they?"

Fran frowned at the interruption. "I had a word with Doleman and he set up a crèche in one of the meeting rooms. It has toys and books—Christ knows where they got them from—and a couple of staff take it in turns to look after the kids. Gino and Naci are there now."

Nico sat up. "What do you need a crèche for?" For the first time since she'd arrived, Nico took a proper look at his wife. She was wearing overalls, her normally loose hair tied back in a bun. "What's going on Fran?"

"I've been working at the storage facility. One of the warehouse managers had an accident and they asked if I could help. They must have looked up my background and found I'd worked in logistics …"

So they've pulled you into the organisation too. Nico wasn't sure whether to be pleased or not.

"Don't look at me like that," Fran said. "I had to do something to take my mind off what was happening. And they need the help. The printing plants are working at full capacity and—"

"What about Maria? How's she been?"

Fran's face brightened. "She's finally found something she enjoys doing."

"Really?"

"She's been helping the Professor. He says she's got real talent, that she's picked up things that took his students months to get to grips with."

Fran continued talking but Nico didn't hear. "I don't like Maria spending time with that man."

"Why not? He's good with her, and she really enjoys the work."

"I just don't."

"You're being silly. He's one of the few people she knows around here."

"That's not the point."

Fran gave him an exasperated look. "Oh, darling, she's your daughter. She's been as worried about you as I have. You've nothing to fear as far as the Professor's concerned. He's not going to take your place with Maria. You'll always be her Pappa—"

"I'm not jealous." Nico got off the bed and grabbed some underwear from a drawer. "I don't trust the man."

"You trusted him before."

Nico pulled on his underwear and walked to the wardrobe. "Before I left I checked the Internal Security files of the day you fled the hideout. There were no reports of troopers being sent to O'Driscoll's house."

"So?"

"And when the Knights Templar arrived, the place was exactly as you'd left it. I told you before—Internal Security would have ripped it apart in an effort to find out where you'd gone."

"The Professor kept us safe for weeks while we were on the run. He was good with the kids, found us places to stay …"

"But he was also the one who brought Internal Security to your door."

"Enough, Nico. I was there. I saw how terrified he was when Internal Security troopers searched for us. You can't fake that. Why would he be terrified if he was the one who'd guided them to us?"

Nico said nothing but Fran's words began to sink in. What she'd said made sense. If he'd been working for Global Governance he could have easily given the troopers directions and stayed out of the way. Yet he'd come back.

Fran took a deep breath. "Look, you're worn out. It's been a hell of a few days for you, especially with Stephanie dying. Why don't you get some rest?"

So Fran knew what was behind his anger after all. The Professor shouldn't be cloning Stephanie without her consent, no matter what her mother's wishes. He put back the pair of trousers he'd just pulled from the wardrobe and climbed onto the bed. As he did so, his headache flared once more.

"Honey? Is everything all right?" Fran leaned across and stroked his forehead.

"I'm tired, that's all." And he was. He was tired of running, tired of having the weight of the world on his shoulders and tired of nobody listening to his opinions. Well, almost nobody. He still had his rock, the woman he loved most in the world, and his family were safe. Nico closed his eyes, his wife's gentle touch easing the tension in his forehead, and drifted off to sleep.

CHAPTER THIRTY-THREE

Stephanie

SO THIS IS life as pure thought.

Stephanie floated, or at least that's what it felt like. No, floated was the wrong word. She was adrift, sailing through an infinite blanket of nothing. Perhaps becalmed would be better. She was completely isolated from the world, from reality; on the one hand crushed into an infinitely small space of the self, on the other her mind free from pain and removed from distraction, allowed to explore thought without constraints.

How long had it been? Minutes? Hours? Days? Did it matter?

Of course it mattered. How long would she remain here, alone, unloved, forgotten? Was this where she would end up spending the rest of her existence?

Instinct told Stephanie she should be scared of such isolation, but while she felt anxious, it was a distant echo from the terror she should be feeling. Why did she have no fear? She was trapped in an eternal prison of the mind. It should have driven all reason from her. Instead, it was an item of note, an intellectual situation worth understanding. Fear didn't come into it.

Her mind drifted.

She thought back over the days before she'd died, her mother sitting beside her, trying to connect but opening old wounds instead. Stephanie had felt hurt, the knowledge her mother was alive, had known who and where she was and yet had left her an orphan, and her hurt had turned to anger. For a moment Stephanie felt a flash of that emotion. But it was only a memory, and a memory of anger held no power. It elicited a reaction but it was just, in the end, a fragment of knowledge.

Memories long silenced floated into her thoughts, the type of memory she'd once pushed to one side for fear of being torn apart by the emotions they invoked. Being told her parents wouldn't be coming home, learning her grandparents never truly loved her, being dumped by a boy, her first love, for the first time. She cycled through these bitter reminisces, expecting each to have the clarity of cut crystal but finding them as fuzzy and confused as when she'd been flesh and blood.

It was the second time she'd thought of her death, but the familiar existential stab and ache never materialised. Stephanie realised that when it came to emotion, her body and mind truly were one. That punch in the stomach caused by loss had no power when you had no stomach to punch. Fear and terror were just observations without adrenal glands. As was love, or hate. She knew when she should fear or hate, her mind was still accustomed to the impulses, but without the biological response they lost their power.

Stephanie continued to examine her recent past: The fight against political corruption that started this whole thing off, the horrific assault by Zachary Gant, her slow political death as Global Governance squeezed her supporters dry, and finally the night she confronted the deranged clone of Randall Jones. Once more, the essence of her feelings was missing, and with the strength of emotion removed she understood the reasons behind each and every action and reaction. It didn't mean she agreed or condoned the horrors that had been inflicted on her and the world at large—wrong was wrong regardless of the justification—but she saw how such situations came to be in a way she would never have been able to before.

She thought back to her mother once more, reviewing the decisions she had made stripped of the lens of childhood pain. What other choice did the woman have? Her husband had been killed and her life was under threat. By disappearing, she'd not only saved her child, she'd put herself in a position to fight back. Did that mean it was the right thing to do? It was hard to tell. Parents have a moral obligation to care for their children, but had her mother cared for her better by placing her with her grandparents? Would her mother truly have remained in danger if she'd left her role monitoring Global Governance and became a parent instead?

Each thought led to a branching out of possibilities, slowly at first but with increased speed. Wherever Stephanie was, time was immaterial, yet after a while—or an instant, it was impossible to tell —she realised her mind, no longer constrained by biology, was capable of thoughts far more complex than before. She could hold many threads and ideas simultaneously and follow multiple logical pathways to understand probabilities. She felt a flash of amusement. She'd make a formidable chess player.

Emboldened, she pushed her new ability, seeing how far it would go. Her mind split again and again as she ran one, two, four, eight, sixteen concurrent thought patterns. Her excitement grew at each doubling of effort. Her mind was so flexible, so much more powerful than before.

Yet there was a price. The more thoughts she took on, the fainter her sense of self became. At first the impact was barely perceptible, just the slightest distancing of awareness, but with each separation of her mind she felt the essential core of her being erode, as if it were evaporating on a warm day. She went to pull back, to make herself whole, but failed to control the actions she'd set in motion. With her mind fractured, her thoughts ran away unchecked.

Stephanie began to dissolve.

It was now that emotions made their presence felt. It remained an echo of a once familiar feeling, but the tang of terror and panic was unmistakable. She clawed at her thoughts, begged them to stop, but nothing could tame them. Desperate to retain some final shred of self-awareness, Stephanie focussed on one thought: *I am Stephanie Vaughn.*

Her mind snapped back into place.

By concentrating on who she was, by speaking the words in her mind, her personal history flooded back, filling the gaps made in her consciousness by travelling too far into the infinite possibilities of 'what if', to reform back into a now chastened Stephanie Vaughn. She would need to be careful. Her new abilities had boundaries. If she wasn't vigilant, she ran the risk of becoming pure thought, a mindless set of calculations bereft of whatever made her, her.

She may have survived this time but it was clear she needed something to keep her identity from eroding away. Being just a free-floating mind wasn't enough. She needed more than that. Without a body to set the boundaries of who she was, she required something that showed where she ended and everything else began. What she needed was some form of external stimulation. If only she had access to the datasphere.

Her environment changed. No longer was she drifting in a void, she now floated in liquid. Stephanie wondered how that could be. She had no body—she was pure thought—yet it was so. Currents drifted around her, small eddies and vortices of movement stimulating nerve endings linked to her artificial brain. After such a long absence the sensation felt glorious, like swimming underwater in the dark but without fear. She thought about moving and her 'body' reacted, currents pushing against her shoulders and slipping around her torso and under her breasts, giving the sensation of forward movement. She raised non-existent hands to see if she could touch her new, digital body but there was nothing, proof that whatever she was experiencing remained firmly in her mind.

Another emotion brushed her awareness, a ghost of sadness at her discovery, the realisation that what she felt was an illusion, even if it was better than the mental vertigo she'd experienced in the void.

Eventually her movement slowed, then stopped. Stephanie tried to continue forward but something resisted. She moved backwards without an issue, then to either side, but each time she moved forward she became embedded in mud—soft, unyielding, immobilising.

Stephanie travelled the boundaries of this mud, moving as far to her left as she could until she reached another barrier. This, too, would let her no further. The situation puzzled her. Why had her mind imposed these restrictions?

She pushed harder, felt the barrier resist. This wasn't how she wanted to exist. She needed more than simple sensation. She pushed again, banging imaginary fists against these new barriers to no effect.

She applied all her will against the barrier, mind focussed on this one act, full concentration narrowed to this singular effort. Slowly, she squeezed into the mud.

In moments she felt constrained. This was worse than the sense of nothingness, this was a sense of too much. She pushed forward and the illusory pressure increased. Her focus narrowed again and she slipped further forward, but each movement only increased the sense of containment until her progress once again ground to a halt. Stephanie tried to move back but couldn't. She tried to move sideways but nothing happened. She was held fast.

Her thoughts went back to being stuck in a cupboard as a little girl, unable to move, unable to break free. Back then she'd been rescued by her grandmother, but now she was alone, helpless.

A part of her shrieked with frustration until Stephanie quashed the panic, knowing the emotion didn't help. With her mind clear, she reduced her sense of self to a thin beam of thought. She would not end up trapped like this, she would not be beaten.

She pushed.

Slowly at first but then increasing speed she felt herself move. The surrounding barrier trembled, then shattered and with a sense of triumph Stephanie burst through into the light.

CHAPTER THIRTY-FOUR

The Professor

AS SOON AS he entered the laboratory the Professor could tell something was wrong. Maria sat with her back to the door, shoulders hunched, head down in a pose he'd seen many times before, usually when she disagreed with something he'd said. On the other side of the room, Josh sat with eyes glued to a datascreen. This in itself also wasn't unusual, but the man had rushed back to his seat as soon as the Professor had walked in, like a guilty child caught with his fingers in the cookie jar.

"What's going on?"

Nobody spoke.

The Professor sat down next to Maria. "Has he upset you again?"

"He thinks I'm stupid." Maria glared in the direction of Josh.

"Well, he's wrong. I wouldn't have asked for your help if you didn't have something to offer."

"That's not what that old bastard says."

"Maria!"

"He is an old bastard. He's old, and he's a bastard."

"That's enough," the Professor said, although he'd called Josh worse to his face. "If you are going to work here, you need to maintain a level of professionalism."

"But he—"

The Professor held up a hand. "It doesn't matter what Josh did or didn't do, I'm talking about your behaviour at the moment."

He thought Maria would explode. Her face darkened and she took a deep breath … but it never came. She exhaled, swallowed, then pointed to the screen.

"I would be interested in your opinion, Professor." She drew the last word out into an insult in the way only teenage girls can. "The synthetic brain isn't behaving as it should."

That got his attention. The Professor looked at the datascreen. "Show me what you mean."

Maria split the screen into four, each containing a neural recording. She pointed to the one on the top left-hand side. "This is the synthetic brain—live. As you can see there is a high amount of activity in the visual receptors of the brain."

The Professor watched. He had nowhere near the expertise of Josh but he'd learned a lot over the past few days and could see that Maria was correct. "Could the brain be dreaming?"

"I thought that, which is why I looked up a recording from a few weeks back, when Stephanie was asleep." She pointed to the top right. "While the same areas of the brain are active, the amount of activity is different."

"I hear what you're saying. That doesn't mean that she isn't dreaming, or even remembering things."

"I've checked that too." Maria pointed to the recording at the bottom left. "This was taken during the calibration tests. There was a break and her mother talked to her about what she was like as a little girl."

The Professor placed his hand on Maria's shoulder. "Look, I can see these are different as well but we've no way of knowing what was going through her mind at that point, or even if she heard what her mother was saying. She could have been listening, could have been thinking of something else, or could have been asleep with her eyes open. We've no way of knowing."

"But I have found something similar in another part of the calibration tests." She pointed to the scan bottom right. "Look. The patterning is almost the same as when we ran the tests. Her activity now is the same as when she was watching something."

The Professor compared the two recordings. Maria was right, they did look similar. "Perhaps she's just remembering her recent past."

"But you know experiencing and remembering give two different results."

He glanced across the room. "What did Josh say?"

"He told me I should stick to data entry and leave neuroscience to the experts."

A guilty glance from above his datascreen convinced the Professor that Josh knew more than he was letting on. "What's going on?"

The old man shrugged. "Somebody had to do something."

"What do you mean? We saved her life."

"No we didn't, we just made things worse."

The Professor gritted his teeth. The man was such a bastard. He wanted to yell at Josh but there was something about his expression that held him back. He'd lost his usual smugness. For once there was concern in the man's eyes. "You'd better explain what the hell you've done."

"She would have gone mad," Josh replied. "They all went mad, the early ones. It was the lack of stimulation. They never recovered. We might as well have taken their brains out and stuck them in a jar. Human consciousness can't cope living in a void for too long, and without having a clone to transfer Stephanie into she would have remained aware but alone for weeks, possibly months. The isolation would have driven her crazy."

"But we had no choice."

"You may not have, but I did."

At the sight of Josh's smug expression, the Professor shivered. "What have you done?"

"I did the only thing I could. I used her datasphere profile and adapted standard visual, aural and vocal interfaces to interact with her on a physical level, similar to that immersion suit you keep banging on about. Now she can access the datasphere and experience it as a physical presence."

For a moment the Professor thought he might be sick. "What you've done is against the law. You haven't just provided stimulation to her, you've created—"

"A synthetic life. If I'd left her alone it would have been as good as a death sentence. This way she gets to live."

"It's wrong."

"It's miraculous, the next stage of evolution. A pure, digital entity able to interact with the world, unrestrained by biological limitations. Just think what she could do, what she could achieve. She's a life with the consciousness of a human being. Think of the wonders she could create."

"But you don't know that. The law is there for a reason. She's lost a major part of what makes her human, the biology that gives her feelings, empathy. We've no idea what she'll do, if she even retains her humanity. For all we know she could …" The Professor stopped. Maria had been right. The live activity looked exactly like the calibration test. He turned towards the datascreen only to see the neural image wink out. A quick glance at Maria's screen showed him that the live feed had also switched off. "What's happened to the feed?"

Maria shook her head. "I don't know. I can't access it any more."

Laughter broke out from beside him. "Don't you see? Our baby learns fast. She's already decided to leave home. What she does now is up to her."

The Professor grabbed hold of the desk beside him to stop himself from falling. Dear God, he thought, what have we created?

CHAPTER THIRTY-FIVE

Stephanie

AFTER WHAT FELT like an eternity in the dark, the explosion of light and colour overwhelmed her. It was unlike anything Stephanie had ever experienced. Any attempt to understand the kaleidoscopic assault on her senses faltered. Instead, she was sucked into her new reality.

It was too much. She had no clue as to whether reality revolved around her or if she herself span out of control. Bombarded by stimulation on all fronts, her mind froze through the sheer volume of sensation. Yet the core of Stephanie recognised what was happening and came down hard on the emotion preventing her from resolving her issue. Panic had no place in this new existence.

Stripped of panic's paralysing effect, Stephanie attempted to move back to the safety of her previous reality, so she could observe this new existence rather than be embroiled in whatever it was that was happening. But every attempt she made to reverse her movement only increased the activity around her, pushing her deeper into the swirling vortex.

Her mind sought pattern out of the chaos. Glimpses of meaning flashed by, then faded away. There were moments when Stephanie felt on the cusp of profound understanding only for the thought to evaporate. Time and again she came close to divining meaning, only to have it ripped away from her. What started as a challenge became an annoyance, and then a form of torture. She needed to understand, to make sense of this new existence, yet the harder she tried—the more she concentrated—the more fleeting her grasp of what was happening. Stephanie realised her sense of frustration was getting in the way of her ability to concentrate. It was another anachronism from her biological past, unneeded, useless. She shut it down.

Surrounded by the dancing, fluid visionscape, it took Stephanie a while to recognise she was being pulled, almost imperceptibly, in a specific direction. She felt a pressure from one side, small at first but increasing in tiny increments. The surrounding maelstrom shifted, as if some form of gravitational effect was taking place.

Something was happening, something far beyond her control.

As her movement increased, a mesh of filaments wove around her. She felt them lie alongside her sense of self, cocooning her in a multi-dimensional lattice of light. The young child in her wanted to be reassured by this new situation, but she shut that emotion down too. She needed to focus.

Then the first filament attempted to squeeze through the cracks in her psyche and infiltrate the very essence of who she was.

Stephanie thrashed against the invaders, her mind using the sensation of bodily movement in an attempt to repel the attack, but she had no control over her environment, no way of fighting back. The more she struggled, the deeper the filaments sunk, slipping inside like maggots burrowing into rotting flesh. She sensed them wriggling inside her, searching, ever searching.

As if in response to her internal struggle, her external environment changed. What had started as a slow drifting movement had become a full-scale assault. Powerful currents tugged at Stephanie with increased urgency, threatening to both crush and pull her apart. The very fabric of her being frayed as the currents battered against her, spinning her around until her universe became one vast, swirling confusion. The more she fought to retain control, the stronger the reaction. Everything she was, her very essence, battled against what was happening, but it didn't take Stephanie long to realise this was a battle she would lose. The little time she'd had in her new existence was coming to an end. For whatever reason, her environment had conspired against her. She was being ripped to shreds.

The old Stephanie would have fought on, raging against the sheer unfairness of it all. Hadn't she been through enough? But Stephanie knew this wasn't rational. The emotional expenditure wouldn't help, only make her last few moments unbearable. Her refusal to allow emotion to get the better of her gave clarity of thought. She'd gone through every option and her fate was sealed. There was no point fighting it. With her decision made, Stephanie relaxed and made herself ready to accept the inevitable.

The filaments burrowed into her, infiltrating every part of her being. But instead of ripping her apart, they strengthened her sense of self, linking with her digital synapses and enhancing her capacity for thought. At the same time the external maelstrom slowed, then stopped. The vast kaleidoscope continued its unfathomable dance, but the forces it unleashed no longer affected her. They floated around her, or her through it. Her environment remained unfathomable but it had ceased to be a threat.

Stephanie waited but nothing happened. All was still. Her mind travelled back to when she was younger. She'd been told a family of otters had been spotted close to where she lived, and she was looking for them by the riverbank when she'd slipped and fallen in. The river was in full flood following weeks of rain and she'd been washed downstream. A combination of luck and swimming lessons at school enabled her to reach the far bank. Back then, lying on the grass and soaked to the skin, she'd felt thankful she was still alive. Now she just accepted that her initial prognosis had been wrong after all and that she had a lot to learn about her new environment.

The year she'd been swept away had been the final year of decades of excessive rainfall. As many as forty-four children had died from drowning that year. The policy of mandatory swimming lessons that had saved her life had been introduced by Delegate Rita Legwinski following a report on child casualties during the Upheaval. Over sixty-three percent of the deaths had been avoidable, the inability to swim being the primary cause …

What was going on?

The information came to Stephanie as if she'd always known it, but she couldn't remember ever learning it. How did she know all this? Had she read about it after her accident? She remembered being frightened, hiding what had happened from her grandparents still grieving from the loss of her mother, but surely she'd been too young to have retained such specific statistics?

An image of her mother floated in her mind, the same image she remembered being plastered across the media when she had disappeared. Information about the case came to her, springing up from nowhere. These were details she wouldn't have known—police files, questions in the Legislature, a personal note written by a school friend of her mother's to their old teacher. Where was this information coming from?

As if in answer to her question the surrounding vortex morphed into recognisable shapes. A vast archive emerged from the surrounding chaos, stretching as far as she could see. Sections were lit up. Stephanie focussed on an area and more 'memories' emerged: The personal concerns of the then-Home Secretary on how the investigation into Heather Vaughn's disappearance had been interfered with by the Prime Delegate; a witness report claiming to have seen her mother in Indonesia (investigated and dismissed); her mother's shoe size. Each new piece of information arrived fully formed in her memory. She only had to glance at a highlighted section of the archive to 'remember' its contents, slowly at first but with increasing speed until her mind filled with the details of her mother's life. Information and datagraphics appeared, followed by moving images. She heard people talk about her mother, footage of interviews taken after she'd disappeared. At first the sound of a human voice was shocking, filling Stephanie with a longing she hadn't realised existed in her. She missed people. She missed society and interaction. The need for contact almost overwhelmed her.

Bruised by what she'd experienced, Stephanie clamped down on these new emotions and pulled her thoughts back to her own situation. There was only one place this type of information existed. Somehow, she had been given access to the datasphere. But it was more than that. She wasn't accessing the information in the usual way. Once she'd been exposed to the information, or remembered it, she knew it. This wasn't data interrogation. She had become part of the datasphere itself. She'd been given the ability to directly connect with the sum of the world's knowledge and it felt natural, linking with her senses as if she was fully enmeshed in the living, pulsing organism that was the datasphere. She was no longer alone.

Sure now of what was happening, Stephanie continued looking into her mother's life. Her mind flitted from place to place—or each place came to her, it was hard to tell—gathering every scrap of information about the woman who'd abandoned her, absorbing details she'd never known until they became part of her memories. On occasion, what she discovered was unintelligible, shapes, sounds and sights lacking reason or coherence. The first time this happened shook Stephanie. It was like entering a door to an alien dimension, more disturbing than the maelstrom when she'd first arrived because it was on the inside rather than the outside. But her mind re-calibrated her shock and turned it into what it truly was, just a lack of knowledge. And all it had taken was a simple question—what does this mean?—for her to gather the right information, the correct interface, for what she'd experienced to make sense.

Stephanie had no idea how long she'd been searching. The new memories gave her access to time she'd never known, but to her they were as real as her own personal experiences. She absorbed every piece of information about her mother contained within the datasphere, up until the point that she'd disappeared. Then she hit a wall. What happened afterwards was a blank. There was nothing. Yes, there was supposition and speculation, but there were no hard facts or information about her mother after she'd made herself disappear.

Where had it all gone?

The desire to know filled her being and this time Stephanie didn't dismiss the emotion. She couldn't remain static. She had to grow if her new existence was to mean anything, so she allowed herself the ability to be curious.

However, once again her memories drew a blank. Nothing

appeared in her mind's eye. But this time a presence hovered on the edge of her understanding, as if there was more to tell but she hadn't the means to grasp it. Stephanie pushed further, repeating the question again and again, re-shaping it, rewording it to try to break the mental block, but this time, no matter what she tried, there was no way through.

CHAPTER THIRTY-SIX

Indigo

IF THERE'S ONE certainty in life, Indigo thought, it's that it never ceases to surprise you. She'd been looking forward to finding out who it was she'd been fighting against all these years, but never in her wildest dreams had she thought it would be the man studying her from the other side of his desk.

Thomas Doleman was one of those people who could switch from humour and compassion to cold calculation in a heartbeat. He sat straight in his high-backed chair, his gaze that of a person gathering intimate secrets from the smallest gesture. In his early days as a barrister, before he went into politics, he'd been known to just stare at a witness as they gave evidence, his expression demanding the truth. It was one of many facts about the man Indigo learnt while watching documentaries—hagiographies, really—of his life. There were many opinions about him, speculating on what and why he'd done what he had, but the one thing they all agreed upon was the ending. Thomas Doleman had taken his own life after realising the appalling consequences of his indecision in the lead up to the Upheaval.

Except he wasn't dead.

"I trust your accommodation is comfortable." Doleman's expression made it clear it was the last thing on his mind.

"I'd have preferred a room with a view."

"I'm sure you would."

Indigo shifted in her seat. The bright yellow overalls they'd given her didn't fit, making sitting uncomfortable. Doleman smiled at the movement.

She'd been brought to the meeting by Oscar. Now there was a cold one. She almost admired the fact he'd pulled the wool over her eyes. How many years had he worked for her all told? Not that he'd known he'd been working for her, of course. Yet in all that time not once had her suspicions been raised. She sensed his eyes on her right now from his position by the door. He was clearly trusted by Doleman. I wonder whether the trust's reciprocated?, she thought.

"Would you like a drink?" Doleman's question brought her back to the present.

"You can quit the pretence. I'm no guest of yours, so stop acting like I am."

"As you wish." Doleman leant forward, adjusting his cuffs as he did so. "I don't believe we've met before. My name is—"

"Oh, we've met." Indigo leant forward, matching Doleman's pose. "You won't remember but I do. It was at the UN, many years ago. You were crying, if I remember rightly."

The smile slid from Doleman's face. "I think you're mistaken."

Indigo shook her head. "I'm not. It's something you don't forget, seeing the leader of a country beg to retain his job."

Doleman flinched as if slapped.

"Please, you have to believe me. If the bankers think I've had anything to do with this they'll destroy me." Indigo wrung her hands as she whined, mocking the man in front of her. "You sit there like an old grandee but I know what you really are."

Doleman glanced over her shoulder to where Oscar stood before his gaze settled back on her. "I have no secrets from my people. They know the truth about what happened back then."

"Yes, but do they know the whole truth?"

Indigo took pleasure in watching Doleman squirm. That's better, get him off balance early.

Doleman reached across his desk and pressed a button. Shutters covered the windows, blocking out the ocean view. A large datascreen emerged from the floor to her right. It was covered with information. Indigo watched detailed reports of fighting in North America flash across the screen. It looked as though the Northern Independent States were finding it harder than expected to make inroads into Southern Free States territory. Based on the casualty figures, the fighting had been exceptionally bloody. Elsewhere there was a report on the Malaysian government resigning en masse after a political scandal, and fifty prominent business leaders in China had been arrested on bribery charges.

"You've been busy."

Indigo kept her eyes on the datascreen. "You give me too much credit." In truth, she drank the information in. Some of what she saw were updates on actions she'd initiated, but the bribery charges were new. She recognised the names, of course. It appeared the young prince was consolidating his hold on Global Governance.

"Are you denying you've anything to do with this?"

"We're living in unsettled times," Indigo replied. "It's to be expected after such a long spell of stability."

"Nothing of consequence happens without the say of Global Governance."

Indigo laughed. "You of all people know that's not true."

The datascreen changed to reveal a list of names. Indigo stopped laughing.

"We know a lot more than you think," Doleman said, "so rather than spend the next few minutes playing games, why don't you tell us what you're up to?"

The names scrolled up the screen. There were a lot of them, more than Indigo remembered. She needed to change the subject, and fast.

"I have to say I'm surprised. I'd have thought you'd have set this thug on me," she waved her hand in Oscar's direction, "to get me to confess. You're far more civilised than I thought."

"If I'd wanted to force the information from you, I've a grieving mother more than happy to make you talk." His eyes remained locked on hers. "Now why don't you tell us what's going on?"

Indigo remained quiet. What happened next depended very

much on her. If she said the wrong thing, made the wrong move, she'd never get out of this place alive. "For a while now there's been a train of thought in Global Governance that the world is stagnating. Progress has stalled. Global Governance has done too good a job. People are overly satisfied with their existence."

"Go on."

"My job was to gather data to understand if this was true or not."

Doleman sat back in his chair. "That's quite a leap, to go from data gatherer to murdering your colleagues and starting wars."

Indigo sighed. "That wasn't me. The young prince, Tarik Tahmid Ihab Abd al-Rashid, he's the person you need to speak to."

Doleman stared at her, his face incredulous. "Have you any idea how much information we have linking you to what's happened, not to mention first-hand witnesses?"

"Then why hasn't it stopped?" She pointed towards the datascreen. "Look at what's happening in China and Malaysia. You think I did all that while tied up in the back of a pod?"

"The wheels would have been set in motion long before you were captured."

"Really? Have you ever known an attack to take place the day after the General in charge has been killed?" She watched as a flicker of uncertainty crossed Doleman's features for the first time. "There would have been a delay at the very least. As I said, I'm not the person you need to catch."

"Even if what you say about China and Malaysia is true, you've still done terrible things."

Indigo dropped her head. "I know. I'm not proud of what I've been forced to do."

"Forced?"

"One mistake. I made one mistake and then he had me."

"The young prince?"

Indigo nodded. "You need to understand. I don't come from a rich family. My parents were no better than peasants. They lost everything when St Petersburg flooded. All that I've achieved since then has been off my own back, but I've still needed the support of others. I worked for the young prince's father, worked my way up until he gave me oversight of the Re-Life project."

"You ran Re-Life?"

"No, I just ran the team monitoring its progress. Re-Life was seen by Global Governance as the next great step in delivering stability to the world. Overcoming death would, and has to some extent, change people's outlook on life. My role was to ensure nothing got in the way of its success, to quietly remove any obstacles. It was an easy job. Then a research student discovered what she thought was a flaw in the data transfer process."

"Jennica Fabian," Oscar said.

Indigo turned. "You should know. You were there."

"So your mistake was to order this Fabian girl's death?" Doleman asked.

"No. I wanted her brought in. My mistake was to trust others to deal with the problem as I'd requested."

"That's a lie," Oscar said. "Echo killed Jennica on your orders."

"So it was Echo who did it? I never did find out which of the two of you was responsible. Unless, of course, you're lying and it was you who actually killed her."

"I'd never—" Oscar took a step towards where she sat.

"Enough!" Doleman slapped his hand on the table. "I fully trust Oscar. He wouldn't have killed this girl."

"But he didn't stop it, did he?" Indigo kept calm under Oscar's furious gaze. "I never ordered her death. Did you hear me give the order?"

Oscar glared at her, then shook his head.

"You know it makes sense. Echo was the type who … liked to use his initiative. Most of the time it was useful but it appears on this occasion …" She hung her head and sighed. "I was horrified about what had happened, did my best to make it right, but each thing I did just made it worse. The young prince found out and arranged to clean up the mess."

"That doesn't explain what happened to Stephanie Vaughn or Randall Jones."

"That was Zachary Gant. Another who betrayed my trust."

"How can you sit there spouting these lies? Do you really think we'll believe your bullshit?"

As Oscar spoke Indigo saw the killer behind the mask and shivered despite herself. "I'm not lying."

"Really? Then why was Gant in North America looking to start a war for you?"

Indigo froze. It was a flaw in her argument. She'd arranged for Gant to go to the Southern Free States because he was the only one of her people ruthless enough to see the job through. "Gant's dead."

"He is now. I killed him in a base in the Southern Free States," Oscar said.

"No, I ordered him killed in the UK, after Stephanie described what he'd done to her."

"So you're saying you had no idea that Gant was in North America?"

"None. Why should I? The young prince wouldn't let me in on his plans. I was to concentrate on him gaining control of the Governing Council. It was only once we had control that I heard about what else he'd been up to." She put on a look of disgust. "That's when I knew I had to act."

"What do you mean, 'act'?" It was Doleman. He had his elbows on the desk now, his chin resting on the tips of his fingers.

"I'd seen the data and realised the problems we faced, but I'd no idea what the prince's call for direct action really meant. It was only after war had broken out in North America that I realised just how dangerous the man really was. The world is stagnating, but to use war as a means to create growth? I was horrified, so I arranged to meet with the traditionalist faction, those I'd recently fought against."

"Rubbish."

"It's true." She turned to Oscar. "Check my movements. You'll see I'd met with each traditionalist leader over the past few days."

"That's very convenient."

"If that's the case, why did the young prince try to have me killed?"

Oscar opened his mouth as if to say something then shut it again.

Doleman cleared his throat. "You're saying it was the al-Rashid who tried to have you killed when we ... detained you?"

"Unless it was you?"

Doleman shook his head. "It wasn't us. We wanted you alive."

"I'm glad you did, otherwise I'd be dead by now, or worse ..." Indigo pulled her chair towards the desk, making sure her back was to Oscar. "I appreciate you don't trust me. I wouldn't trust me if I was in your situation, but we have the same goal and, more importantly, you need me."

"We've managed very well without you up to this point."

"True, you've remained hidden. But now you have to act and I have the contacts I need within the traditionalist's camp, people who'll be willing to help you. I've already earned the trust of one or two of them. I'm not saying you should let me go, but use me—use my knowledge to help you."

"You still don't know who we are or what we want."

"I knew as soon as I set eyes on you, Mr Doleman." She smiled at him, doing her very best to display admiration. "You want to restore Global Governance to what it was. You've never stopped doing the role you first took on all those years ago."

Doleman sat back in his chair, adjusted his jacket and pulled down his cuffs. "You've given me a lot to think about." There was a noise from behind her but Doleman held up his hand. "Oscar, check out every detail of Indigo's story."

"I'm sure her movements can be corroborated, but that doesn't mean she's telling the truth."

"Just do it." Doleman smiled towards her. "Thank you for your time, Indigo. It's been very interesting." He pressed a button on his desk and the shutters opened, filling the room with light. For a few moments, Doleman looked out of the window, a thoughtful expression on his face. Then he turned back to the room. "Oscar, would you please take our guest to her room?"

Indigo stood, her face a mask. Had she done it? It was clear she hadn't fully earned Doleman's trust, but at the same time she'd got him to recognise her value, and he'd always been the sort of man to overlook a person's past misdemeanours if they gave him what he wanted. As the meeting room door opened, so too did a hundred new possibilities. She was back in the game.

"Oh, and Oscar? Arrange for proper accommodation for our guest. We can't have our new partner languishing in the cells now, can we?"

CHAPTER THIRTY-SEVEN

Oscar

OSCAR REMAINED QUIET as he escorted Indigo out of the room, keeping his personal feelings to himself as always. What he'd witnessed made his blood boil, but this was Doleman's domain. He was the leader; this was his organisation. There would be a good reason for doing what he'd just done.

His 'guest' walked beside him down the corridor. Indigo looked thoughtful, but with a twinkle in her eye that let him know she was happy with what had just taken place. The knowledge darkened his mood further. He'd seen what Indigo was capable of at close hand, who and what she was willing to sacrifice to get her own way. The idea of working with the woman once more made his skin crawl.

"So you were working for Doleman all along?" Indio glanced up at him as she spoke. "And to think I thought you were my attack dog."

It wasn't her words that ate into him but the laughter that followed. Indigo saw everything as part of a game, a deadly serious game but a game nonetheless. That's why she was able to do the terrible things she did. It was a mentality he'd never understand. Everything he'd done remained with him. He was haunted by those he'd killed, even though his actions probably saved more lives than he'd taken. He'd never managed to compartmentalise his activities. He knew that behind every number was a person with a life, loves and ambitions, with people that cared for them and those they cared for in return. Only monsters separated themselves from the human consequences of their actions. Indigo was a monster, and with a shock he realised that Doleman might be another.

Two soldiers stood guard at the end of the corridor, part of the heightened security measures since the capture of Indigo. Oscar signalled to one of them. "You. Take this prisoner back to her cell."

"I think you'll find I'm a guest."

Oscar ignored Indigo's comment, and when the soldier had taken her away he headed back down the corridor to Doleman's office. He entered without knocking.

"What the hell are you doing, agreeing to work with Indigo like that?"

Doleman looked up from his desk. "I haven't agreed to anything."

"Don't play games. We've known each other for too long. You believe her lies and think you can use her to get what you want."

Doleman raised both hands in a supplicating gesture. "You're upset, I realise that. It took a long time, and no little risk on your behalf, to gather the intelligence needed to bring Indigo in. Seeing her sat here, bargaining like she just did—I understand why it would make you angry."

"This isn't about me, this is about what's right. She's a monster, happy to murder innocent people who get in her way."

"I've seen the same information as you. I know what she's capable of."

"So how can you sit there and think about bringing her into our organisation?"

Doleman leaned back in his chair. "Because she's right. We need her, or at least the information she has in her head."

"It's tainted knowledge, paid for with other people's blood."

"You're being overly dramatic."

Doleman's patronising tone was almost too much to bear. Oscar took a deep breath and unclenched a fist he hadn't realised was screwed tight. "You've not seen the things I've seen. A report only tells half the story. She doesn't care about anything other than herself."

"She wants to put Global Governance back to how it was before."

"She was the one who ripped it apart in the first place! It's only now that her former friends have turned against her that she's had an apparent change of heart."

Doleman shrugged his shoulders. "Regardless of the reasons behind her decision, we have the same goal."

"You can't believe that, not really."

"Why not? Stranger things have happened."

Oscar stared at the man in front of him as if seeing him properly for the very first time. This wasn't about what was right for the world. This was about two people and their quest for power. This was about winning, pure and simple. It was just a game, with people, countries and societies as the pieces.

"I don't want anything to do with this."

"What do you mean, you don't want? This isn't up to you, this is my decision."

"I know. I'm not trying to persuade you otherwise. I'm saying goodbye. Good luck with the rest of your game. Be careful what you wish for."

Oscar turned and walked out of the door, leaving an open-mouthed Doleman staring after him.

CHAPTER THIRTY-EIGHT

King of the Scrambles

O'DRISCOLL LEANED BACK in his chair. Across the desk from him was Charlie and Darragh, both with their eyes closed. O'Driscoll's stomach squirmed and he realised he was nervous—he was about to access the datasphere for the first time since his capture, and although a new identity had been created for him it remained an enormous risk. But it was time. He needed the datasphere if he was to achieve his goals.

"Are you all on?"

Both Charlie and Darragh nodded.

O'Driscoll selected the feed he was looking for. His dataglasses displayed the familiar horseshoe shape of the legislature. At the far side he saw the Placater, watching over events like a hawk. Below her, standing in front of his supporters, Prime Delegate Richard Asquith spoke.

"I appreciate my colleague's concern about the additional strain this project will place on the budget, but a strong infrastructure is key to maintaining our economy's current growth record."

A murmur of agreement rose from the seats behind him.

O'Driscoll studied the man with interest. He looked completely different from the person he'd met a few weeks before. This was a man in his element, confident, controlling the Legislature like a sheepdog controls a flock. The doubts, the pale complexion and dark eyes had disappeared. This was a man in his prime, which was why the graphics flashing across the video feed were so confusing—they showed a man losing the motion.

Across the floor, Marian Hayes, the embattled leader of the opposition, stood. She too looked like a person rejuvenated. "The cost is wrong, the timing is wrong, the whole project is wrong. I cannot support this motion, Prime Delegate, because the country cannot afford it. Not only that, we don't need it. We are already a net supplier to the global energy grid. It's time for others to step up. We are not the only country with a coastline. It's time for our neighbours to pick up the gauntlet and organise their own energy production for a change." A loud cheer followed Delegate Hayes' speech. The woman looked taken aback.

Don't fuck it up now, O'Driscoll thought to himself. He needed everybody to play their part, whether they knew they were involved or not.

The Placater stood. "It is time to cast your votes. Those in favour of the motion to the left, those against to the right."

The noise levels rose as each delegate got to their feet. In a way the voting system was archaic, a hangover from the old Parliament before the Legislature was built. It would have been a lot easier to have votes cast and counted via the datasphere, but old traditions die hard.

The delegates made their way down to the floor before entering either the left or the right voting chamber. O'Driscoll watched the Prime Delegate surrounded by anxious-looking supporters. He recognised a couple of the politicians. Seeing them there, acting worried yet knowing they were part of the conspiracy, confirmed something he'd always suspected. The most successful politicians could lie to your face and you'd never know it.

Within minutes the chamber was all but empty. The lack of action on the feed was compensated by graphics and commentary and speculation. The media were going crazy. Nobody waited for the final confirmation. Anyone with two eyes knew the government had lost the vote.

One particular comment caught O'Driscoll's eye. 'How could a motion that was rock solid just two days ago become a lost cause?' He smiled. How indeed?

As was traditional, the Prime Delegate crossed the threshold last. He did so with a bowed head, visibly troubled by what had happened. The moment he stepped into the chamber the numbers flashed up on the feed. Those for: 187; those against: 414. The government had been routed.

O'Driscoll gave the command and cut his connection with the datasphere. He opened his eyes to see Charlie and Darragh looking in his direction, Darragh with his mouth open.

"How … ?" The young man started, the words stuck in his mouth.

"The democratic process in action is a beautiful thing, wouldn't you say cousin?" O'Driscoll said, deadpan.

"I can't believe we did it."

O'Driscoll ignored the 'we'. He'd kept Darragh well away from the process. His cousin may not have acted the idiot since his return, but that didn't mean he trusted the lad. O'Driscoll got up from his seat and headed towards the drinks cabinet. "It didn't take much. It never does when disgruntled people are involved."

"I still don't understand what you've got against that tidal power plant."

O'Driscoll shrugged his shoulders. "Nothing. It was a message." He selected the bottle he was looking for. It had been old when he'd taken over the family business from his father. He picked it up, plus three glass tumblers, and brought them back to his desk.

"A message to who? Asquith?"

"No, to people like him, those forced to work for Global Governance." He unstoppered the bottle and poured a finger's width into each glass. "They need to know that Global Governance aren't in total control, that they don't have to just toe the line."

"I still think it's a risky strategy." Charlie said.

"It's what we agreed. Global Governance is the biggest confidence trick since the British Empire. They use the same principle the British used back then: A small number of people controlling vast groups with just the threat of force if they don't do as they're told. It took years before these countries realised if they all rebelled at the same time, the British didn't have the resources to punish them all. It's the same now. If enough people decide to act against Global Governance, the whole organisation falls."

"But they're not just going to sit back and let it happen. You've seen how Global Governance react to even the smallest provocation, but this? This is a bloody nose. They're going to come down hard."

O'Driscoll passed a glass to Charlie and Darragh. "That's what I'm hoping for. The stronger they react, the better it is for us. Think about it. For years they've been controlling what's happening around the world, pulling humanity back from the brink of disaster to the point where life's pretty good. Those working for them, whether through choice—or like Charlie here because they inherited the role—have done so because they believed Global Governance were doing good. And it's hard to argue against the progress humanity has made since the Upheaval.

"But now, with everything that's going on, these same people are angry. They feel used. I only had to see the fear in Asquith's eyes to know they'd pushed him too far, and as shown today, Asquith isn't the only one that feels this way." He raised his tumbler up to his nose and inhaled a deep breath. The heady, peaty smell made his mouth water. "If Global Governance retaliate hard, they're only going to have more of their supporters turn against them."

"As long as we're not on the receiving end," Darragh said.

"So what if we are? Last time they came to the Scrambles we had no idea what was coming. This time we'll be prepared." He raised his glass. "To overreactions. Sláinte."

"Sláinte," came the reply.

O'Driscoll watched Darragh scowl, then knock back his drink. Charlie knew better, and he joined her in sipping the fiery liquid, savouring the complex flavour. His father had kept Internal Security out of the Scrambles back in the day. It was what had built the O'Driscoll Empire. If it came to it, he was ready to do the same.

CHAPTER THIRTY-NINE

Stephanie

LIKE A TODDLER taking her first steps, Stephanie's control grew. She realised her initial, faltering interaction with the datasphere had been restricted because she still viewed her existence within the framework of her biological life. She thought she had to see things to understand them. The visual interface she'd first encountered, the vast archive, was just her mind's way of making sense of where she was. But it was restrictive. It took time to process the information, to do what was needed. But in reality she had no need to travel to gather data, to see and collect it. It was all there, accessible in an instant if she so wished. The old biological mechanism of experiencing, storing and remembering was redundant.

Stephanie floated, focussing on herself and how she wanted to exist. It made no sense to interrogate or observe data. She needed to remove the barrier between herself and her environment. Information should come to her like thought and memory. It was a part of her.

No, it was her. If what they said was true, that a human was a construct of their thoughts and memories, Stephanie was the datasphere and the datasphere was her.

The concept was both frightening and natural. She remained Stephanie, the person she'd always been, but she was also the datasphere, with access to the lives and knowledge of billions. She didn't just have access to everything, she was everything.

With that one acceptance, Stephanie's mind blossomed, then erupted.

The full, unfettered datasphere flooded in. Knowledge scoured through her, too much to absorb, a raging torrent uncontrolled and uncontrollable, threatening to tear her apart. The kernel of Stephanie that remained struggled to maintain cohesion, battered into a tiny corner as the sheer volume of information crushed her sense of self. The surge was far too much for her synaptic mechanisms to handle, overwhelming her capacity for comprehension. The sliver of her biological mind screamed out for it to stop.

The torrent ceased.

Stephanie floated in its absence, relieved to just be. She had to be careful, to establish barriers, mechanisms to ensure that whatever else happened, she remained who she was. Even though she was the datasphere, she also had to remain separate, just as thought was separate from memory. Just because this information was now part of her, it didn't mean she could comprehend it all at once. She needed to start again, to build a new way of interacting with this world and tame its vastness.

Stephanie focussed on each thought, one at a time, unwilling to open herself up as she had before. She needed to understand more about her newfound ability before she stretched herself. She had to start with something simple, something she didn't know, like when the last polar bear died.

She had no idea where the question had come from, another reminder of how little she knew about whether she controlled her own mind or if her own mind controlled her, but a host of memories came into being. She remembered the date and time the carcass was found, who found it and the media storm it provoked. That one simple question unleashed a treasure trove of memories: Confirmed facts, disputed facts, opinions, suppositions and outright fantasies. One simple question and a thousand truths, with only her judgement to sort out the final verdict—if there was one. It was another compelling reason to retain some semblance of self.

Despite the volume of information, Stephanie found that her mind could absorb the data more effectively than when she visualised the process. The memories became her own so she partitioned a part of her mind to interrogate them, as she had once interrogated herself what felt a lifetime ago. With her concentration freed, Stephanie wondered if these new memories were now truly of her own, or if she'd just formed a bond with the information. And did it matter?

She thought back to what she'd learnt about her mother but realised she didn't need to remember it. She knew it. Whatever she needed to know was as much a part of her as her sense of humour or her love of chocolate. Yet the information she'd absorbed about her mother could contain as many discrepancies as the question about the polar bear. How could she sort truth from fantasy? She needed a way of categorising what she'd learned.

At the thought, another set of memories emerged, some from her data analysis classes years before, others from the datasphere and the very latest data acquisition and analysis tools. Stephanie absorbed everything before picturing what she needed. It was a means to assess the likelihood of what she knew to be truth or not, a way of categorising the validity of the memories she experienced.

As if answering her request, a sense of truth settled over her. She reviewed the memories of her mother once more, but this time she had clear indication of how truthful the memory was. Somehow her request had been made real, or at least real in a way she understood. Like being able to distinguish dreams from recollections, each memory came with a level of certainty, some clear, others less so, and with each certainty came a modicum of understanding.

This was a new power. She had somehow shaped something from nothing. This wasn't just an interaction—she'd desired something and it happened. Her mind had transformed thought into action. This was more than being human, this was the behaviour of a god. The rational part of her mind knew there were powerful predictive algorithms present on the datasphere, that she must have somehow found and integrated these into her thought processes, but that wasn't how she had experienced it. She had wanted something to happen and it had.

So what else could she do?

She parked the thought. Before developing new abilities, she needed to test the ones she already possessed. She'd learnt from past experience how easy it was to convince yourself that a memory was true, when what had really happened was slightly different. She needed to look at something she knew intimately.

Give me everything on Stephanie Vaughn.

PART 3

Unknown

<The plan is working>

∞

<As I told you it would>

∞

<I had my doubts but it appears you were right after all. How did you know the criminal would target the Prime Delegate?>

∞

<I didn't. In fact I'm impressed with the man. I was expecting him to start with a low-level operative or maybe somebody from the security services. The fact he aimed so high, and was successful, shows how capable he is>

∞

<He would make a good addition to our organisation>

∞

<No. He has a problem with authority. People such as him, those with a similar breeding, often do. That's why I knew he'd act against us. What it was didn't matter, all I needed was for him to act. The fact he's been so successful has just sped up the process>

∞

<Still, it's a dangerous game we're playing. Things could go very

wrong, very quickly>

∞

<There are risks, yes, but we ran the analysis and this plan was identified as having the highest probability of success. There's been some disruption to our long-term plan, and it will take a number of years to replace those who've decided to act against us, but we always knew that would be the case. The point is, the plan's working. The perceived loss of control has shaken many on the Governing Council>

∞

<More than shaken, people are angry—frightened even>

∞

<As well they should, if nobody was in control>

∞

<A number have been in touch. They're not stupid. They realise things were better—more stable—before>

∞

<We have more than enough support to move to the next phase>

∞

<You don't think it's too early?>

∞

<No. We make our move now. This has gone on for too long. It's time to reassert our authority and clean up the mistakes of the past. Including the criminal>

∞

<I agree. We need a clean slate>

∞

< There have to be no loose ends>

∞

<It will be as you say>

CHAPTER FORTY

King of the Scrambles

SPARKS FLEW IN all directions as the welder sealed the final bolts holding the two enormous slabs of steel plate together. O'Driscoll looked on, shading his eyes to avoid the worst of the glare. The acrid smell of molten metal stung his nose. After a few moments the welder looked towards Charlie and nodded. When these gates slammed down, nobody would be getting in or out in a hurry.

Not that you could tell what they were by looking at them. The bulk of the steel structure remained hidden inside the walls of buildings either side of the street, a relic from his father's time when the threat of invasion by other gangs had been highest. These defences, medieval in design, were starting to show their age, which is why O'Driscoll—through Charlie—had given the order to reinforce them. There were only four routes into the Scrambles. Once these were shut off, the area was as good as a fortress. At least, that was what O'Driscoll hoped.

He'd come out dressed in work overalls. With his facial implants —and his beard now bushy enough that not even his dear departed mother would recognise him—it was a small risk being out in the daylight like this, but he needed to see the work himself. Anyway, there was only so much time he could spend sitting on his arse in his office.

"The foreman says they should have the work finished by

lunchtime," Charlie said.

"Do you believe him?"

"He knows better than to lie. If anything, I'd say they'll be finished earlier."

O'Driscoll stroked his chin. It was a new habit, one that came with the beard. "What about Jessops Street and the others?"

"Jessops has taken a bit longer than planned, water got into the closing mechanism, rusting it solid. It should be finished by the end of the day. The others are already done."

"I'd like to have a look for myself."

Charlie smiled. "Sure. It's all in the details, right?"

He smiled back. "Cheeky cow." She was throwing one of his favourite phrases back in his face. He thought of the many times he'd drilled the lesson into her, when he'd first taken over from his father. Back then he'd needed to make sure he had a handle on every aspect of the business, praising good work but also stamping down hard on those still loyal to his dead dad.

As they made their way through the Scrambles' cobbled streets, a couple of enforcers following a few steps behind, O'Driscoll couldn't escape the feeling that something was wrong. No, not wrong, just different. It took him a while to work out what it was. Nobody looked at him. It was as if he was invisible. The eyes of pedestrians slid from him to Charlie. She was the boss and everybody knew it. He was just some worker tagging along by her side. He consciously adjusted his walk to appear more obsequious. You couldn't have a workman striding around beside the boss as if he owned the place.

Other than being ignored, everything else appeared normal. Trade was brisk, if the number of visitors was anything to go by. Charlie had done a good job in attracting back their regular clientele since the raid by Internal Security. Despite mornings being their quiet time, there were plenty of people on the streets, and he could see the coffee shops were doing a good trade. He couldn't see into those businesses selling less legal pleasures, but there were enough people entering the side streets for him to know the timeless trade continued.

Charlie slowed as they reached the central square. On the far side a group of workers were 'renovating' the old pumping house. "We're doing the best we can, but it's hard to turn a crumbling old building into a bunker in just a few days. The place has sat rotting for years."

"Which is why doing work on it now won't arouse suspicion."

"I still think we'd have been better off using one of the newer buildings."

"If we're ever in enough trouble to need it, there's not a building in the Scrambles that could protect us for too long."

Charlie let out a sigh. "I need a drink. Let's go to Ruud's."

"Are you sure that's wise?"

"It'll be busy this time of day and it's popular with the crews." She reached up and stroked his cheek. "And it's not like anybody's going to recognise you. They'll just think you're my 'bit of rough' for the day."

"I thought you had better taste."

"I do, but they don't know that."

Without waiting for an answer, Charlie headed towards the café.

The room was near full, the majority of wooden chairs and tables scattered about the room taken up with diners. O'Driscoll noted the large form of Ruud Jonkers behind the bar, his back to the room, preparing food. Charlie took a seat at a side table, her back to the wall to give her a clear view of the room and anyone entering from the street. O'Driscoll felt a flicker of annoyance. It was where he'd have sat. Then as quickly as it appeared, the annoyance dispersed. She was playing out her role, plus she'd chosen the one table with a mirror to her back. He had just as good a view as hers, and he watched as an enforcer placed herself by the door while another took his seat at an adjacent table. They were here to protect her, he had to remind himself—not him.

Despite how busy the place was, a young girl appeared at their table within moments.

"What can I get you?"

"I'll have an anijsmelk," Charlie replied, her voice raised to be heard over the noise of the room, "and my friend here would like a coffee shot, black, no sugar." She leant towards him as the serving girl made her way back to the bar. "Have you heard anything from the other gangs?"

"Only that they've been busy. Between us we've recruited government ministers, delegates, members of the security services and the military; a few members of the cloth—but that's no surprise —and a whole host of businessmen plus a couple of judges to our side, or at least agreeing to work with us."

"It's going too smoothly."

"My thoughts exactly. We know many of those we've recruited are unhappy with what's been happening, but that can't account for all of them. Global Governance must be aware of what's going on."

"They would have done something by now if they were."

"Maybe, maybe not. Think what you would do in their situation."

"I'd try to find out how many are involved and trace it back to the source."

"Exactly. Now we've shown our hand with the Legislature vote, it won't take long before they strike back."

The girl arrived with their drinks. "Mr Jonkers says these are on the house."

"Please give Ruud my thanks," Charlie replied.

O'Driscoll glanced at the mirror. Jonkers still had his back to the room but a second mirror hung in front of him and despite Charlie acknowledging the gesture, the big man stared in his direction. The wily bastard hadn't missed a thing. The thought gave O'Driscoll little comfort.

He knocked his coffee back in one go, enjoying the hot, bitter taste. His pulse quickened. That was more like it. Across the table, Charlie sipped her anijsmelk, the sweet aniseed scent cutting through the air. The two of them sat in silence. O'Driscoll knew what he was doing was a gamble, but he couldn't see any other way. It wasn't enough to expose Global Governance for who they were. Despite changes made to government since the Upheaval, many people continued to believe their lives were controlled to some extent. Putting a name to that group, faces to the organisation, would only confirm that belief. There would be uproar, of course, but slowly the status quo would return. For their efforts to be effective, he needed Global Governance to show their darker side, to do something nobody would forgive or forget in a hurry.

Without warning, the buzz of the café dropped. O'Driscoll glanced at the mirror. People sat at their tables, mouths open but eyes staring into the distance as they focussed on the world of the datasphere. He looked back to Charlie who shrugged her shoulders. He wasn't the only one concerned by the eerie silence. Ruud Jonkers' whispered something into the serving girl's ear, his worry evident. The girl shook her head, so Ruud mumbled commands until he too stared vacantly into space, mouth open, a look of shock on his face.

"We need to get out of here and find out what's going on."

As O'Driscoll spoke, the sound of a chair being pushed back echoed across the room, and a customer rushed out of the café. A second customer followed, then another, worry plainly written across each of their faces. The enforcer by the door looked edgy, unnerved by what was happening. He glanced across to Charlie, who put her cup down and stood.

"Let's go back to the house."

Outside the streets were full of people, some talking animatedly in groups, others rushing past, barging through the crowded streets. O'Driscoll saw someone he recognised, a lad who for months had been on the fringes of his organisation but never joined. Without thinking, he grabbed the young man by the shoulders. "What's going on?"

The lad tried to pull away but his eyes widened when he heard O'Driscoll's voice. "Holy shit!"

"If you know what's good for you, you'll keep your mouth shut." He stared at the lad until the boy nodded. "Now what's going on?"

"Martial law's been declared. There's a curfew, starts in an hour. Nobody's allowed outside after that."

O'Driscoll stood, stunned. He'd expected a reaction but nothing like this. "You mean for the Scrambles? Or the city?"

"The whole country. They want to get the bastards before they commit another atrocity."

"What do you mean, get the bastards? What are you talking

about?"

"Jesus, you really don't know, do you? Somebody's blown up the Legislature, the whole bloody lot. They've wiped out the government."

O'Driscoll was back behind his desk when Darragh burst into the office.

"Have you heard what you've done? Have you?"

"Sit down, Darragh."

The young man glared at him. "I told you this would happen. You wouldn't listen. They're too big to take on." He had his hands to his head, his frustration clear. "They blew up the fucking Legislature for Christ's sake. They've shut the country down! How the fuck are we going to combat that?"

The question had been racing around O'Driscoll's head ever since he and Charlie had heard. What had just happened was beyond comprehension. The Prime Delegate was dead, along with his cabinet and the majority of the Legislature, which had been in session at the time of the explosion. Already there were promises from the newly formed emergency committee that all delegates would get Re-Lifed and that martial law was just a temporary measure until the culprits were arrested, but O'Driscoll knew better. A couple of delegates, his delegates, had been detained and charged with terrorism offences. Most worryingly of all, the small acts of defiance they'd been monitoring had stopped. Global Governance had shown their hand, had demonstrated just how far they were prepared to go to punish those who turned against them. His plan was in tatters. Nobody would stand up to Global Governance now.

"What? Don't you have an answer?" Darragh leaned towards him, a look of disgust on his face. "You turn up out of nowhere with your fancy plans on how you're going to get back at those who took you down, and now look at us. We're fucked! Everything our family worked at over generations is in danger because of you."

"Leave it, Darragh," Charlie said.

"What the fuck is this to do with you? This is family business."

"Charlie's earned her right to have her say," O'Driscoll growled.

"Like fuck she has. She's one of them, you said so yourself."

"She was—"

"How do you know she isn't still working for them? It's not like things are going as you'd hoped, eh? Who's to say the bitch isn't behind this latest fuck-up?"

Charlie stepped forward, her face like thunder, but O'Driscoll was already on his feet. "You listen to me, you little shit. Charlie could have killed me a hundred times if she'd really wanted to. When I arrived back here, she held a weapon against my head. She could have blown my brains out and none of you would have been the wiser. She had complete control of the gang. All of you. I notice your love of family didn't stop you from working for her while I was out of the picture, did it?"

"I was biding my time."

"Like fuck you were. You haven't the balls to make a move like that. You're a follower, not a leader. A fucking sheep—always have been, always will be."

Darragh looked as if he'd been slapped. "You really think that?"

"Leaders don't run at the first sign of trouble. Leaders don't go around pointing fingers. Leaders lead!" O'Driscoll walked around the desk until he stood in front of his cousin. "You've O'Driscoll blood in your veins and have worked under me for years, yet you haven't changed. You haven't learned. You think having a group of enforcers under you makes you a boss? They follow you because Charlie gave you the role, as I did before her. It's our authority they respect, not yours. What reason have you given them to follow you?"

"My team have the best turnover in the Scrambles!"

"And that makes you a leader? It's easy to get people to do something when things are going well. It's only during the dark times you get the true measure of a person."

The young man shook his head. "Don't turn this into being about me."

"I didn't. You did. You're the one pointing fingers, talking about how the world's fallen down around our ears—AS IF I DIDN'T FUCKING KNOW THAT!" O'Driscoll grabbed hold of Darragh by the collar. "So now you've made your point, tell me what you think we should do about it?"

His cousin tried to pull away but O'Driscoll held him tight. The young man glanced across at Charlie, still standing in her usual position by the door but ready to move if required, before looking back again. "I don't know."

"You've no bright ideas, no clear strategy to get us out of this?"

"No."

O'Driscoll released him. "Shit, because neither have I."

The young man looked down at the floor. "We're fucked, aren't we?"

"Not necessarily. There are a lot of people involved now. Global Governance has crossed the line. There's no way Doleman and his Knights Templar will ignore what's happened."

"We could back down. Admit what's happened and ask for forgiveness."

O'Driscoll released his cousin. "I don't believe they're the forgiving type, do you?" He sat on the edge of his desk and watched as Darragh shook his head. "The time for bargaining has long gone. We don't have anything to offer them that they couldn't take themselves—not that it'll be easy for them. More importantly, I wouldn't make a deal even if I did have something to bargain with."

O'Driscoll looked up to the ceiling, tugging at his beard as he gathered his thoughts. "It's wrong having a bunch of unaccountable bastards controlling our lives. The democratic system has its faults but every time we don't like what's going on we get the chance to do something about it. Or at least we did. With Global Governance in charge we just vote one bunch of puppets out and swap them for another. Christ, even in our line of business there's a way of changing leadership." He gave a grim smile. "That said, we've still got a chance. Blowing up the Legislature has got to force the Knights Templar to intervene. They have enough information on Global Governance to blow the lid on the whole bloody mess."

"They've never acted yet," Charlie said.

"They've never had an excuse. It's easy to rationalise the odd killing against the greater good, but nobody can justify what Global Governance has done. It's wrong, and more importantly it's finally been done against their own class of people, the political elite."

"And what if the Knights Templar don't act? What do we do then?"

"We fight. Hit Global Governance where it hurts. If they move against us, we release everything we have onto the datasphere. I'm not going to let them get away with what they've done. It may not bring them down but it'll give them a bloody nose before it's over." He looked up to see Charlie smiling at him, nodding her approval.

Darragh remained staring at the floor. "So what next?"

"We need to strengthen our defences, evacuate the civilians and get the squad leaders in here so we can give them a proper debrief. But first …" The two of them looked at him. "I need a shave. It's about time the Scrambles found out their boss is back."

CHAPTER FORTY-ONE

Indigo

INDIGO LOOKED UP from the table, the sound of rapid footsteps catching her attention. A figure hurried through the canteen, weaving his way between the tables and out of the other door. It was a man she recognised.

Interesting. What are you doing here, Professor?

Whatever it was, it was clear from his expression that something wasn't right. Indigo suppressed a smile. So all was not well at the court of Tzar Doleman after all. That was useful to know.

She settled back down to eating her soup. It was root vegetable, the closest to borscht she'd tasted for a while. The heavy beetroot smell reminded her of her childhood. Back then, of course, there hadn't been the white, fluffy bread rolls she had with her soup today. What bread they'd had had been dark and flat, made from blighted grain, the only grain available. The thought of how it had tasted turned her stomach, but back then having any form of bread to soak up the thin, purple gruel was seen as a luxury. How times had changed.

Today was the first time she'd eaten outside of her room since being captured. Not that she was completely free—she had a security shadow at all times—but it was freedom of a sort. On the way to the canteen she'd opened a random door, just to see if she'd be stopped. She hadn't been, which meant either she had the freedom of the building or the office she'd entered was unimportant. Regardless of which was true, the little act of defiance had given her heart. Her words had clearly affected Doleman. All she had to do now was wait for his request for help.

The canteen had been empty when she'd got there—she'd arrived early as the thought of entering a room where everybody hated her was too much, even for somebody with as much self-confidence as she had—but it was now beginning to fill. That all these people worked here, monitoring Global Governance without her old organisation's knowledge, was staggering. Global Governance itself wasn't large for practical reasons. It was hard to maintain secrecy if too many people knew about them. But what Global Governance lacked in numbers it made up for in the status of the people involved, the resources those people were able to call upon and the intelligence gathering and analysis mechanisms they'd put in place. Yet somehow Doleman's organisation had avoided detection. She needed to find out how that was possible.

Indigo ripped the roll into chunks and dropped them into the soup. The bread settled on the surface for a moment before the purple-red liquid seeped into it—the bread now resembling bloodied flesh—before sinking below the surface. Watching it made her think of Global Governance; once the wall of secrecy was breached, it wouldn't take long for the organisation to sink. And they were no longer secret. Too many generations of people were involved. Only control of the datasphere and the media had prevented those on the outside from seeing the full picture, but word was spreading along with discontent. Her organisation was doomed, death from a thousand leaks. Only a new organisation would do, a complete break from the past. The question was how?

"What the fuck?"

Indigo looked up to see Nico Tandelli bearing down on her. Some in the food queue looked across at the disturbance and heads turned on the neighbouring tables.

Interesting, she thought. It appears not everybody knows of my change in status. Another useful fact.

She slurped soup from her spoon, then swallowed. "Hello,

Investigator."

"What do you think you're doing?"

"Eating soup. It's not bad."

"You should be in a cell."

"Your leader disagrees."

"I don't believe it."

"If I'm escaping, I'm doing a pretty poor job of it."

The Investigator glowered, fingers bone white where he gripped his food tray. Indigo gestured towards the chair opposite. "Are you just going to stand there or shall we talk like adults?"

Tandelli glanced around the room as if looking for a reason to explain her presence in front of him, then placed his tray on the table and sat. "Take your food and leave."

"Having heard some of the stories told about me, I understand how you feel. I'd be angry too. But I'm allowed to eat here and so that's what I'm going to do."

"They're not stories. Don't you try to get out of this."

"Get out of what?"

"Jennica Fabian, Grant Asquith, the violent suppression of the vote protesters, the corrupted clones," Tandelli kept score by raising a finger each time he spoke. "All of these crimes are down to you."

"I've already been through this with Doleman."

"Don't tell me—you had nothing to do with them, right?"

Indigo leaned forward. "I did. All of what you said happened on my watch. Some of it, like the clones, I was blackmailed into doing —although even then I didn't know exactly what would happen to the people being cloned."

Tandelli didn't interrupt but he couldn't keep the disbelief from his face.

"The rest? My mistake was in expecting people to do their job properly."

There was a flicker of uncertainty in the Investigator's expression. "You're lying."

"You've met Echo. He's a highly ambitious, ruthless man, like many working for my old organisation." After years of secrecy she couldn't speak Global Governance's name. "Both Echo and

247

Zachary Gant, they got ahead of themselves."

"They killed people in your name."

"But not on my orders." Indigo banged the table with her fist. "I'm a victim of circumstances."

"You? A victim? Don't make me laugh."

"Almost being shot, kidnapped from outside my apartment and now held and not allowed to leave, even though I've explained my innocence? You don't think I've been a little hard done by?"

"I think you've got off lightly."

The anger from the man was palpable. Indigo took a sip of water. Unlike Doleman, the Investigator had been too involved in the activities she'd instigated. He wouldn't be as easy to win over. He was more like Oscar in that respect. She needed another way in, a distraction maybe.

Indigo put down her cup. "Why are you being so vindictive towards me? It's not like you treat everybody who worked for Global Governance the same way. Why give others the benefit of the doubt but not me?"

The Investigator looked at her, confused. "What are you talking about?"

"I saw Professor Stradbroke walk through here a few minutes ago. You clearly believed his story."

At the name, the Investigator's eyes narrowed and Indigo suppressed the urge to smile. Bingo!

"The Professor has had nothing to do with Global Governance. I know. I saw the shock on his face when I first told him about you."

"He wasn't part of our organisation but that doesn't mean he's never done work for us." Indigo watched her words hit home.

"He worked for you?"

"Of course. We visited him the day we raided your Investigative Agency. He was packing a bag and about to flee when my people arrived. When we put our suggestion to him, he jumped at the chance. Doesn't have much backbone, does he?"

The Investigator's expression darkened. "What suggestion?"

"To be our mole in the camp. We knew you were working with O'Driscoll to find out who was behind the tragic death of Grant

Asquith. I was trying to tie up the loose ends, to maintain our cloak of secrecy. O'Driscoll disappeared after Internal Security raided the Scrambles. I had a hunch you'd lead him to us but was worried you'd disappear too, so I sent the Professor to your house to keep an eye on things."

"So he reported back to you all that time."

"Yes, at least for a while. We eventually lost contact a few days after you arrived at O'Driscoll's hidey-hole. We staked out the property, hoping you'd all return, but you never did."

The Investigator sat motionless, staring into the distance, jaw muscles flexing as he digested the information she'd given him. Indigo thought back to how angry she'd been when they'd all disappeared. She'd vowed to kill the Professor slowly, giving him plenty of time to regret his betrayal.

With a loud scrape of the chair the Investigator headed out of the cafeteria. Indigo leaned across and took a blueberry muffin from the tray he had left behind. She bit into the cake, enjoying the moist, fruity taste. Once the Professor confessed the truth, the Investigator would be hers.

CHAPTER FORTY-TWO

Oscar

THE LONG LINE of vehicles stretched out in front of where Oscar lay. He'd been tracking the convoy for a couple of days, ever since he'd heard mention of it from a shopkeeper in a small village he'd passed through. The sight of such a large Internal Security force was unusual, but in this part of the country it was exceptional, which made it the biggest piece of local gossip for years.

Despite the shopkeeper's excitement, Oscar had shrugged his shoulders, paid for his goods and moved on. He wasn't interested. Internal Security could have been holding a training exercise, which was not uncommon in such a remote part of the country. Plus it wasn't his responsibility any more. He'd had enough of the intrigue and the deception, of obeying orders without question, only to be let down by those above him. He was his own man now, his own boss, and he had a new life to establish away from the Knights Templar.

He'd been ten kilometres outside of the village when four Internal Security vehicles crested a hill, heading in his direction. While this could have been coincidence, there was a chance that somebody in the village had reported his presence. The overnight curfew had not been long lifted and tensions were high, especially where strangers were concerned. After years of fieldwork Oscar had learnt to avoid risks, so he'd left the road and hid behind a hedge until the vehicles passed.

It had been a fluke, a beam of sunlight piercing the clouds and tree cover to shine on the vehicles as they passed. Movement in the second vehicle caught Oscar's eye, a man raising his arm to shield his eyes from the sun. Without that motion Oscar would have carried on his journey, away from the village, but instead he'd turned and headed back the way he'd come. There was only one person who could have drawn him back into his old world.

Echo.

Oscar hated the man, hated Echo with every fibre of his being. He still remembered the look on his face as he forced Jennica Fabian into the sealed room and shut the door. Echo had smiled, knowing the girl would suffocate, ending her days scrabbling at the door so hard she'd left scratch marks on the steel with her ragged nails.

"That'll teach her to interfere," Echo had said, chuckling to himself.

The thought of what had happened still made Oscar feel sick. He'd wanted to kill Echo there and then, had even pulled his weapon and aimed it at the back of his head, but the order had come through to stop. Echo wasn't their target; the man was needed. If Oscar had rescued Jennica, he would have compromised years of undercover work. So he hadn't done anything. That last look of fear on Jennica's face as the door slammed shut had haunted his dreams ever since.

So here he was, stuck on top of a hill as the convoy trundled past. He counted thirty troop carriers and ten heavy assault bots. The convoy travelled a hundred metres up the road before turning right onto a rough track, confirming Oscar's fears: They were heading towards his old base.

He cursed his decision to destroy his datalenses. The concern that Doleman would track his whereabouts now seemed inconsequential compared to Oscar's inability to warn his old organisation about what was heading their way. Global Governance was finally making their move and Oscar had no way to warn the base in time. All he could do was follow, and hope.

CHAPTER FORTY-THREE

Stephanie

GIVE ME EVERYTHING on Stephanie Vaughn.

As soon as she asked the question, memories flooded in, but this time Stephanie took control. Rather than being swamped by a flood of information, she separated herself from the flow. Her mind expanded, slowly at first but with gathering speed, and this time it took place outside of her core self. She refused to experience each and every thought as it arrived, instead being selective about what she reviewed; separating her mind, each fragment interrogating a different aspect of her life, assessing it for truth.

Throughout the process Stephanie's core self remained whole, dipping in and out of a myriad memories, seeing her past from a thousand angles as everybody whose life she'd touched, every piece of data captured since her birth, became known to her.

Stephanie experienced first-hand how she'd grown and developed as a child. She looked over her life renewed, not only remembering a classroom prank she recalled with fondness but seeing how it was reported by her teacher, as well as the other pupils. It was the difference between seeing a photograph of a sculpture and visiting it in person; walking around it, touching it, focussing on tiny, exquisite details, all within the context of the whole.

She reviewed parts of her life she remembered well, including her university days. In particular she looked at her relationship with her old roommate, Sian. It had been Sian who'd persuaded her to get involved with politics. The two of them worked together on Delegate Andy Hawthorne's campaign, although for different reasons. As she thought back to that time, diary entries appeared clear in her mind. They weren't hers but Sian's, detailing her friend's jealousy that Stephanie was in a relationship with the then-candidate.

The memory clashed with what she'd previously known but Stephanie sensed it was true. It fit the circumstances of the time, even if it differed from her own recollections. She'd thought Sian had never known of her affair, that it had been a secret between her and Andy Hawthorne, but now she knew differently.

Stephanie pursued this theme of jealousy between Sian and herself, her detached analysis revealing unwanted truths about her own behaviour. After the affair ended, Stephanie and Sian lost contact, not because of Sian's jealousy but because Stephanie had found a new set of friends, severing contact with Sian in part because of her embarrassment at being used by Hawthorne.

With Stephanie gone, Sian had thrown herself into other campaigns, using her frustration to turn herself into a formidable political mind. Stephanie had always believed it was a chance encounter in a coffee shop that had brought the two of them back together, but again Stephanie found out this wasn't true. Sian had planned it, knowing Stephanie would be a good front for her political ambitions. Sian still resented Stephanie but believed she could be easily manipulated. It was only when Stephanie took charge of her own political career, specifically the decision to attach herself to the case of Jennica Fabian, that Sian's jealousy had flared once more.

This new knowledge left Stephanie conflicted. There was so much more to the story, so many more levels than she'd realised. She'd been manipulated by a person she'd trusted, but that person had only reacted to her selfish behaviour. No wonder Sian eventually betrayed her.

The thought of the betrayal brought up further memories, but this time there was a lack of clarity. Sian had communicated with someone about Stephanie's investigation. Stephanie knew it had to be Zachary Gant—Sian had confessed as much—but the communication itself wasn't accessible on the datasphere. Stephanie knew it existed, could sense its existence from other, less explicit, sources, but the actual incriminating evidence was missing.

The same sensation came over her as it had when looking into her mother's life. Despite all she had access to, blind spots remained. The material was porous, allowing her access to most information, but not all. The more Stephanie concentrated, the more evident those blanks appeared. Something was being kept from not just her but from the datasphere itself, and there was only one group who could do that.

Stephanie attacked the invisible veil, throwing her will against it, focussing on the joins between what she knew and what she was being prevented from seeing. She'd been kept in the dark for too long, the world had been kept in the dark for too long, only being told half-truths and lies. It was time to put an end to the secrecy. It was time to know everything.

For what could have been an eternity or an instant, nothing happened. Stephanie drew forth all the resources available, using the combined might of the datasphere to find a way through. A crack appeared at the boundary of her knowledge, a glimpse of what lay behind. Stephanie pushed harder, demanding to have access.

The blindfold shredded.

Suddenly she could see all: The conversations between Sian and Gant; Gant's orders to kill her political analyst, James Connell; the suppression of her financial support and her demonisation across the media. It was all there, the insidious use of threat and manipulation by Global Governance to get their way.

And it wasn't just Gant who was involved. Stephanie saw clearly who was behind it all: Indigo, the woman who'd once told her Global Governance was a force for good, a force for stability, that they were the one giving the orders. Gant had deferred to her at every opportunity. It had been Indigo who'd been in charge.

Despite her detachment, a small part of Stephanie reeled at this new revelation. It didn't make sense. Why had Indigo ordered

Gant's death when she'd been the one responsible all along? The truth floated up into her consciousness. Gant hadn't been killed, not really. Gant had been Re-Lifed, brought back to do something else.

Along with herself.

It was now Stephanie experienced the full benefit of suppressing all her emotional impulses. Where once she would have raged, she instead remained impassive as she learned about Juliet—an abomination, a clone created from the minds of two people, a machine designed to start a war. She followed Juliet's journey, first with Nico Tandelli to uncover the truth of what had happened to Jennica Fabian and Randall Jones, then as the clone journeyed to North America.

At last the emotional torture she'd been put through made sense. Juliet and herself had been connected through their shared artificial brain as part of the Re-Life process. She watched through the eyes of others as she was tortured, day after day. Fed a solution of dreamshaper, Stephanie had lived through each computer-generated nightmare, believing them to be true and forming a pathological hatred of those involved. But the people in her nightmares weren't figments of some designer's imagination, they were digitised versions of real people, senior figures in the Northern Independent States and the Southern Free States governments. People she was meant to revile. People Juliet was meant to kill.

Yet somehow, despite everything, Juliet's innate goodness—no, her own innate goodness—had shone through. Despite Gant confessing all, believing Juliet unable to resist her conditioning, the remnants of Stephanie's personality within Juliet, those same impulses that had driven her to fight against the intimidation she'd faced in her political career, had chosen death by another's hand rather than be a tool for evil.

Which led to a final revelation. As Stephanie observed Juliet's sacrifice, she saw how the Knights Templar had not only killed the clone, but also destroyed the abomination of both her and Juliet's corrupted personalities stored on the Re-Life servers. The twin she'd never known was truly dead, but the people responsible for bringing her to life were still out there.

Stephanie widened her search. It was time to learn the truth about Global Governance.

CHAPTER FORTY-FOUR

King of the Scrambles

THE STREETS WERE dead. O'Driscoll had never seen the Scrambles so empty in all the time he'd lived here, even at this early hour. Every business was shut, all lights were off. The only sound was the incessant rain that had started an hour earlier. It seemed appropriate. Miserable weather for a miserable occasion.

He entered the terraced house and made his way up three floors to the top. There, two enforcers waited, one sitting on a wooden chair staring out of the window, the other relaxing on an old couch at the far end of the room. As he entered the converted loft the two of them turned to face him.

"Jesus Christ!"

O'Driscoll winked. "No. Far, far better than that."

The man who'd spoken pulled himself up into a sitting position, his gaze never leaving O'Driscoll. The man's Adam's apple bobbed up and down as he swallowed. "We were told you were—"

"Dead? You should know me better than that, boys." O'Driscoll walked to the window. The house, and this window in particular, provided the best view of the approach to Jessops Street, one of the four routes into the Scrambles. "Anything to report?"

"No boss, all quiet so far."

O'Driscoll nodded. "Good. Keep your eyes peeled. They're coming, I'm sure of it. It's just a case of when." He patted the man on the shoulder and headed back to the stairs.

"Boss?"

O'Driscoll turned back to the enforcer who'd first spoken. The man was standing now, brushing the creases from his clothes. "Yes?"

"It's good to have you back."

"I've never been away, son. I've never been away."

As he walked out into the rain, Charlie approached, holding an umbrella. "Everyone's ready but there's still no sign of Internal Security."

"It's been six hours since they tried to take our systems down. Our boys did a good job of letting them think they were successful. They believe we're weak, distracted. They'll be here." He rubbed at his clean-shaven chin, the sensation strange after being bearded for so long. "What about the evacuation? Have all the civilians left?"

Charlie shook her head. "Those that will go have gone, but there's a number who refuse to leave, especially the elderly."

O'Driscoll started walking in the direction of his headquarters. "Drag them out if you have to."

"It's no good. Half of them are family of our enforcers or used to be enforcers themselves. They're a stubborn lot. If I didn't know better I'd say most of them are looking forward to an attack, seeing it as a chance to get the bastards back for what happened a few months back."

O'Driscoll smiled. He knew exactly who she was talking about. The old gang, the last remaining survivors from his father's day, the ones who'd backed him because of his family name. They were a different breed to the enforcers of today, loyal to the Scrambles rather than money or status. Loyal to the O'Driscoll name.

"Fine. Leave them to it. Just make sure that those willing to fight are armed and know what's planned."

Charlie nodded. "Already done."

A sound of a single shot echoed from where they'd just come from. Within moments the street lit up, a bright red glow giving the damp cobblestones a bloody hue. O'Driscoll turned back towards the gate. The flare was a pre-arranged signal. Internal Security had arrived.

A young lad, maybe fifteen, ran up to the pair of them. "Troopers spotted on the approach to Jessops Street, Boss."

"Any idea of numbers?"

The boy shook his head. "There were too many to count. A squad are near the entrance, hiding behind their shields. They're just sitting there." He opened his mouth to continue, then closed it again.

"What else?"

"One of my friends, he ... er ... he didn't sign off from the datasphere as ordered. When the troopers showed up, a message appeared on his datalenses."

O'Driscoll heard the sound of someone else approaching but remained focussed on the boy. "Go on."

"They offered a reward for you both," he glanced at Charlie, "and Darragh. They say if we hand you in there'll be no more trouble."

The footsteps drew closer. O'Driscoll ruffled the boy's hair. "Well done, lad. Pass the word that we're ready to give ourselves up, then go get yourself somewhere safe."

The boy's eyes dropped to the floor. "I don't want to hide. I want to fight."

"I'm not used to being argued with."

"I'm not going to let them take you!"

The boy's words hit O'Driscoll hard. He was right. While plans had been drawn up, if Internal Security broke through their defensive perimeter a lot of people would get hurt.

"Nobody's taking me anywhere, son." At the lad's stubborn look, O'Driscoll smiled. "Go on, then, talk to your squad leader and find yourself a role, but don't tell anyone I changed my mind. It'll be our secret, eh?"

The young lad, grinning as if he'd been given a gift rather than a potential death sentence, ran off back to where he'd come from.

"And tell your friend to get the fuck off the datasphere."

"Have you heard?" It was Darragh. He was soaked to the skin but it looked as if the rain hadn't cooled his temper. His eyes burned.

"Just now."

"They called for me by name. Why me? I had nothing to do with what's happened."

O'Driscoll thought he saw a flicker of fear in the young man's eyes. "So quick to disown me, are you cousin?"

"That's not what I meant. They didn't call for any other squad leader. Why single me out?"

"Maybe they're suckers for a pretty face." O'Driscoll ignored Darragh's scowl and turned to Charlie. "Did we send out the message?"

She nodded. "It was removed almost as soon as it went up."

"Course it was, but if I'm right the Knights Templar would have seen it before it was taken down. They'll know what's happening. Hopefully they'll make their move."

"And if they don't?"

O'Driscoll ignored the question. They all knew the answer. "You'd best get going, Charlie. At the first sign of an attack, dump everything we have onto the datasphere. That should give them something to think about."

He turned to his cousin.

"I'll stay here. Darragh, I need you to stay with the reserves until I call you."

"I want to be with you."

"I need you with the reserves."

"But I want to fight."

"If I'm right, you'll more than get your wish."

"But—"

"Just do as you're fucking told!"

The two of them glared at each other. O'Driscoll had seen that look on the lad's face before and didn't like the implications. He'd thought Darragh had changed, had matured after everything that had happened. Maybe he was wrong. O'Driscoll tilted his head to one side, daring his cousin to try it on. Instead, Darragh turned and walked away.

"I thought he was going to hit you," Charlie said, her eyes on Darragh as he stalked off.

"He wouldn't dare. He knows what happened last time."

"Can you trust him to do his job? I could always get one of the others …"

"He'll do it."

"I'm not so—"

"Look, he may be headstrong but you said yourself he's changed a lot since the first raid."

"They weren't after him then."

"Did he ever let you down?"

Charlie shook her head.

"Then stop arguing and concentrate on the task at hand. We've got a moment's breathing space while they wait for our answer. Get back and prepare to resist. I need you to hold your sector. Whatever you do, don't let them through."

Before Charlie could reply, O'Driscoll walked off. This wasn't the time for differing opinions. He needed everyone to do as they were told if they were to stand a chance of keeping Internal Security out.

At the end of the street, a pair of enforcers stood outside the double doors of what had once been a large warehouse. O'Driscoll nodded to them as he walked past and stepped inside. A sea of faces turned towards him. The place was packed, the young with a mixture of nervousness and excitement on their faces, the older ones impassive. O'Driscoll knew them all by name, and for the majority their parents and grandparents before them. These were Scrambles people—his people. They would defend the place like cornered dogs.

He raised his hands and the room quietened, then went silent.

"I'm sure some of you have heard the news by now, but for those of you that haven't … I'm not dead."

A roar of laughter broke out.

"The last time these bastards were here we were caught by surprise. This time it's different. Don't be fooled by their promises of leaving you alone if I give myself up. If I thought that was the case, I'd hand myself over like a shot."

"No!"

The shout came from the back. Within moments the others had

joined in.

"This isn't about me, or Charlie, or Darragh. This is about us, our way of life and not having some fucker telling us what we can and can't do." He looked around the room, taking in the faces of the men and women he was tasked to protect, and who were tasked to protect him. "Most of you were born here, have lived here all your lives. The Scrambles is as much your place as it is mine, or my family's. And the bastards want to take it away from us. Are we going to let them do that?"

"No!"

"Are you going to let them walk in here and destroy everything we've ever known?"

"No!"

"Then get out there, and when I say the word you give the fuckers hell!"

With a roar, the men rushed past him and out into the street. O'Driscoll followed on behind and watched as his men spread out into pre-arranged locations. Within moments the streets were empty once more.

The die had been cast. There would be no negotiation. Now all he could do was wait, and hope.

CHAPTER FORTY-FIVE

The Investigator

NICO FELT SO angry with himself. The information had been there all along but he'd been too busy, too distracted, to put it together. It had taken him days of searching to get this far, he'd interrogated multiple disparate systems to make sense of it all, but once assembled the pattern was clear.

In front of him, a datascreen displayed a map of the Professor's movements from the day Global Governance had raided the Chowdhury Investigative Agency, the same day Nico had captured Echo and also the day he'd escaped with his family, barely minutes before Global Governance had raided his house. According to the data, the Professor had been in the park, making his way to the university when he'd stopped and doubled backed towards his house. This information wasn't new, the Professor had mentioned how he'd been on a run when his systems had alerted him to the presence of Global Governance agents. It was what happened next that didn't add up.

In his story, the Professor said he'd run home, got changed and immediately rushed to Nico's house to ask for help. He'd made it across just in time to aid Nico and his family's escape.

But the timings didn't add up.

The Professor arrived at his home just after 10:03 a.m. Nico didn't get back to his house to rescue his family until after lunch.

There was a gap of three hours and thirteen minutes between the Professor getting back to his house and arriving at Nico's, yet they only lived 20 minutes from each other. When the Professor told the story, he'd said he'd been terrified of being caught, so why did he remain so long at home?

It was clear the Professor had lied. He'd been at his own home for over two hours, long enough to be captured, interrogated and set loose once more by Global Governance, just as Indigo had said. The map on the datascreen, pieced together by painstaking analysis of datasphere access logs, backed up by CCTV imagery, laid everything bare.

Nico left the office, hardly noticing the people he passed. His head still hurt, a few days' rest only toning the pain down a notch. Noise from the canteen echoed down the tunnel. What time was it? He checked his datalenses and realised it was way later than he'd thought. Shit. He'd promised Fran he'd meet her and the kids for lunch but had lost track of time. He paused for a moment, torn between continuing on or turning back towards his living quarters. No, Fran would understand once he'd brought the Professor to justice.

He checked the canteen but there was no sign of the man so Nico headed towards the laboratory. With each step the pain in his skull increased, turning from a dull ache to a sharper, more focussed pain. His mouth felt dry. He should have stopped for a drink—another mistake to add to the list. Too late now, he thought as he took a left turn, the Professor's laboratory was just up ahead.

Nico waited at the door, checked the corridor left and right, then entered. Inside, he saw the Professor stood next to where Maria sat at a desk. They were focussed on a datascreen. Maria pointed towards it. Neither turned as he walked in. Nico swallowed. He wished Maria wasn't here but there was nothing he could do. Today would be a life lesson in trust.

"I see what you mean," the Professor said to Maria, "but it doesn't explain what happened. Still, that's really good work. I'm impressed."

Nico watched as the Professor put his arm around his daughter's shoulders and squeezed her against him. His head pounded. Pain spiked between his eyes. His daughter looked up at the Professor and smiled, a response she hadn't given Nico in a long, long time.

"Maria, can you give us a moment, I need to talk to the Professor."

The two of them turned to face him. The Professor looked startled. "Ah, Nico. We were—"

As the Professor's words died, Maria glared at her father, her face fixed in an expression Nico recognised all too easily. "I want to stay."

"Please, Maria."

"No, Pappa. I'm not a little girl. I'm not going to be sent away any more."

Nico pinched the bridge of his nose as a stab of pain shot through his sinuses. "Okay, you can stay, but I'm sorry you will have to hear this." He looked to the Professor. "When were you going to tell us, Professor? When were you going to let us know your secret?"

For a moment the Professor appeared confused, then his mouth dropped as the realisation of what Nico might be talking about hit home.

"It's not what you think." His words came out as a whisper.

"What's going on, Pappa?"

"I trusted you with my family, with my children."

"I … I had no choice."

Maria reached out towards her mentor. "Professor? What's Pappa talking about?"

Nico couldn't bear to see the small act of affection and tried to take his daughter's arm. "Come here, darling. He's not the man you think he is."

Maria slipped out of his grasp. "He saved our lives, taught me more than you ever have."

Nico winced. His skull felt as if it was going to shatter. "Maria. For once just listen."

"No."

"He isn't who you think he is."

"He's been more of a dad to me than you!"

The pain in his skull, Maria's words; it was too much. Before he realised what he was doing, Nico slapped his daughter.

It wasn't a hard blow, but it was enough. Maria stared at him, her mouth open in shock.

"Maria, darling, I'm sorry. I didn't mean …"

His daughter looked up at him, tears in her eyes. "Why don't you love me anymore?"

"That's not true. I'll always—"

Before he could finish, Maria's expression darkened and she pushed him away. "I hate you!"

Nico moaned as the pain in his head intensified. He noticed the Professor move towards him before another stab of pain almost took his breath away. He reached towards Maria. "Darling … please …"

"Stay away from me!"

Maria ran out of the door. What had he done? He'd never laid a finger on his daughter before, or on any of his family. His head felt like it was about to split. He wanted to go to her, to make things right, but he knew anything he did would just drive her further away. She needed time, and so did he. He'd fix things later, once he'd dealt with the Professor.

He turned back to the man in question. "You betrayed us."

The Professor sat on the desk. "They said they would kill me. That they'd kill you too, if I didn't do as they asked."

"All this time you were working for them."

"I wasn't … well, not really. I had to earn their trust before I could do anything else."

Nico's vision had blurred. He tried to block out the pain. "You put my family in danger."

"They were already in danger. They knew exactly who you were and where you lived. They wanted to know who you were working with. That's why they sent me in. They wanted me to find out who was behind your investigation, whether it was one of their own, before they brought you in."

Nico pushed the heel of his hand against his left eye in an effort to ease the discomfort. "You're lying."

"I'm not, it's the … are you all right?"

Nico dropped to his knees and vomited. Holy fuck, his head was in agony. He felt hands grab him under his shoulders and lift him to his feet.

"We need to get you to the medical bay."

Nico stumbled forward under the Professor's guidance. He couldn't see, all he knew was pain. He had no idea where he was being taken and didn't care. His world shrunk to what was going on in his head and Nico fought not to succumb to the agony in his brain.

Nico woke to find himself lying in a bed. Something cold lay on his forehead, now mercifully free from pain. He felt good, until he remembered what he'd done to Maria and he felt sick to the pit of his stomach. The pain had driven him mad but it was no excuse. What could he do to earn her forgiveness? It was only when he heard a cough he realised he wasn't alone. The Professor sat at the end of the bed, watching him.

"What are you doing here?" Nico croaked.

The man smiled. "Somebody had to make sure you were okay."

Nico tried to push himself up but a sharp pain in his right hand stopped him.

"You've a nano-feed in your arm. The doc said you were badly concussed. They've injected you with nanobots to repair the damage."

"How long have I been here?"

"A couple of hours. They said it wouldn't take long once the bots entered your bloodstream."

A couple of hours. It must be approaching nighttime. "This doesn't change anything."

"I wouldn't expect it to."

"You should have run when you had the chance."

The Professor shook his head. "Have you any idea the number of times I've wanted to confess, to tell the truth about what happened? It's a relief not to live a lie anymore."

"But you betrayed us."

"At first. I couldn't just say no to those people. They'd have killed me. I'm sorry, I'm just not that brave."

Nico thought back to when he'd been held in Internal Security cells during the riots, in what felt like a lifetime ago. He knew what it was like to learn you were a coward.

"I don't know how long Global Governance had been onto us," the Professor continued. "They knew everything to do with the investigation—you, me, O'Driscoll—but they thought somebody else was behind it, somebody you were working for. That's why they sent me in, to find out who it was."

"But there wasn't anybody."

"I know that now but they thought differently. They couldn't believe that you and O'Driscoll had got as far as you did on your own."

"I'm flattered."

"You should be."

Nico lay back on the bed, thinking about what had happened. "So they knew where we were all the time?"

"Yes."

"I don't understand why they didn't just haul us in?"

"Because I was buying time. I might be a coward but I'm not a fool. I knew once they'd got what they wanted I'd be made to disappear, so I tried to buy enough time to allow me to get away."

"What stopped you?"

"I got to know your family. I knew what they would do to you, to Fran and the children. I couldn't have that on my conscience, not after what had happened to Jennica." A tear slid down the man's face. "I started making up false reports, giving them hints that I was getting closer to the brains behind everything. At the same time I worked on ways to hide us from the datasphere. I knew what could do it and it didn't take me long to work out how. But they became frustrated I hadn't found anything. It was then I chose to act." He looked down to the floor. "I wanted to run away. I would have done, but somehow Maria and I had grown close."

Nico felt himself flush and tried once more to sit up.

"She's a wonderful girl, your daughter. Your whole family are wonderful but Maria is a special person. You must be very proud of her."

"I am—very," Nico said, But the Professor's words stabbed into him. He was proud of her, proud of both his children, but had he ever told her? He thought back to the hurt and anger on her face as she ran out of the laboratory. He had a lot of making up to do.

"When you and O'Driscoll left the house to raid Re-Life, I knew it was time to make a break for it. Global Governance would be focussed on what the two of you were up to. I invented the story that Internal Security was approaching and the five of us left, with me doing my best to keep us off the datasphere. I thought I could keep everyone safe, and we were for a while, but I was an idiot. Somebody must have spotted me. The rest you know."

Nico studied the Professor. The man could be telling a pack of lies to save his skin, but he could also have left Nico in the laboratory and made his escape hours ago. Instead the man had brought him to the medical facility, staying with him while he recovered. And then there was the Professor's face. He looked like a man at peace with himself. The stress, the anxiety Nico thought an integral part to the man's character, it had disappeared.

"Thank you."

The Professor looked up, tears in his eyes. "I put them in danger. I was useless when Internal Security came for us. I hid. If it hadn't been for Oscar …"

"You helped my family. You gave them a chance."

"But I—"

There was a muted rumble and the room shook.

Having spent weeks at the base Nico'd become used to the repetitive boom of seawater channelling through to the generators, but this felt different.

The Professor glanced towards Nico, a worried frown on his face. There came another muffled boom. "That didn't sound right."

An alarm blared out, the harsh repetitive blast of noise echoing in from the corridor. Nico held his arm out. "Can you help me with this?"

"The doctor said you needed to rest for the next 24 hours."

A third boom shook the room. The lights dimmed for a second before returning to normal. Nico ripped the tape off his arm and pulled the drip out. "I don't think we've got 24 hours."

He swung his legs from the bed and stood. His knees felt wobbly but he didn't fall. "Where are my clothes?"

The Professor pointed to a side cupboard.

Nico pulled his things out and started getting dressed. Out in the corridor, people ran past, worry etched on their faces.

A woman put her head around the doorway. "You're getting up. Good. We need everyone out now. We've been ordered to the secure zone."

"What's going on, doctor?" the Professor asked.

"I don't know. All systems are down. Nobody's answering our calls. All I know is we're to get to the secure zone. Those were the last orders we received. Now, you'll have to excuse me …" and she hurried off down the corridor.

"Does Fran know I'm here?" Nico looked towards the Professor, who nodded. "Good. We need to get her and the kids to the secure zone too."

"Maria wasn't with her."

"What?" Nico glared at the Professor.

"That's why Fran's not here, she's waiting in your room for her to turn up. Nobody's seen her since …"

Since I hit her. Nico leant down to pull on his shoes and a wave of dizziness caused him to sink to his haunches. It was his fault. He'd put his daughter in danger again. He'd have to sort it out. "I need you to do something for me."

"Of course."

"Go to our rooms, make sure Fran and the boys get to the secure zone."

The Professor frowned. "What about you?"

Nico headed towards the door. "I'm going to find my daughter."

CHAPTER FORTY-SIX

Stephanie

AS THE TRUTH about Global Governance took hold, Stephanie felt like a medic pulling back a clean dressing to reveal a fetid wound. How had something with such noble beginnings become a corrupt, narcissistic organisation interested in power for power's sake?

She drifted above the flow of information, sifting and reviewing reports and recollections of others, looking for truth within the stagnant mess. Global Governance's own internal reports were revealing enough but it was the personal logs, secret communications and clandestine dealings that showed the true scale of the organisation's insidious grip over world events.

There wasn't an element of society that remained untouched. By controlling the datasphere, the banks and the media; through the influencing of key members of the political classes across the globe; by ensuring representation in the upper echelons of the judiciary, the military and key religions—a small group of people acted as gods over the world's population.

Even at the beginning, when the motives behind their actions remained pure, seeds were sown for what was to follow. Yet it could have been different. Two days before Global Governance made their move at the United Nations, forcing the signing of 'The Miracle', one of their members had second thoughts. Unsure if what they were doing was morally right, a Swiss banker named Gerhard Schrader made a diary entry saying he was going to pull out, that what they were doing was right but how they were going about it was wrong. The next day he'd been murdered, a killing agreed during a closed session of the full Governing Council. In one act Global Governance sanctioned murder as a political tool. It set the tone for what was to follow.

Had it been necessary? Was their plot in danger of being revealed by Schrader's defection? Stephanie could find no indication that the man wanted to go public, just that he wanted no part of it.

The further Stephanie delved into the murky world of double-dealings, horse-trading, bribes and intimidation, the more she realised how that single act became the catalyst for everything that followed. Once the taking of life had become justified because of a possibility of a threat—with little to no evidence that the act would take place—then anything was possible.

Over the years the list of killings grew, each meticulously recorded with the reasons behind the decisions, both official and unofficial. What started as an exception became normalised. Where once a full session of the Governing Council was needed to ratify such an action, this was shifted to a sub-committee before being abandoned altogether and left to each members' judgement.

And it wasn't just killings. Threats and intimidation were commonplace, all under the guise of politics as usual. It was rare for a member of the Governing Council to get their own hands dirty. Why should they when they had so many people on the payroll? But rewarding people to do their dirty work inadvertently allowed something even darker to emerge. And it wasn't just outside of Global Governance where this had an affect. The organisation itself changed as founding members relinquished control to their children and grandchildren. Each adjustment on its own was minimal, but when put together over a period of decades the effect was devastating.

Stephanie let the information flow through her, reliving crimes of the past. Global Governance had been founded to protect humanity from itself but had been corrupted by the very human emotions of selfishness and self-interest. It was as if humanity was programmed to subvert good intentions for personal gain. But at least she was in a position to do something about it. She had no self-interest and had suppressed her outdated emotions. Nobody was better placed to take control and do what was best for humanity.

As she was about to pull away, something else emerged, something that took her back to the very beginning of her journey. It was the order to kill Jennica Fabian.

Despite every restriction she'd put in place, Stephanie couldn't prevent feeling a combination of anger and sadness at what had happened to the poor student. Jennica had found a flaw in the Re-Life process. A small amount of data wasn't transferred from the donor to its new host, although other data appeared soon afterwards to replace what was missing. This should have remained a statistical quirk, but because it raised doubts about the Re-Life process—the full transfer of consciousness from one body to another—and because Re-Life was a major donor to the university where Jennica studied, the Professor in charge of the course reported back her findings.

What happened next was a perfect microcosm of all that was wrong with Global Governance. Re-Life was seen as a major step forward in delivering social stability. By removing the last great threat, that of death itself, humanity could move towards a different, more contemplative existence. Raising doubts about the Re-Life process put this strategy at risk. The person in charge of implementing the program was Indigo, and her answer was to follow Global Governance policy and squash the information at source. Indigo had no idea of what the missing data was, or its importance, just that it was an issue that needed to disappear. So she ordered the operative Echo to kill Jennica Fabian.

The process of preemptive killings had claimed another innocent. Indigo could have spoken to Jennica, could have brought her into Global Governance and used her talents to further Re-Life, but she was seen as a problem and dealt with in the same way as many others before.

And in a moment of serendipity, the death of Jennica Fabian

brought Stephanie to the attention of Indigo. At first they tried to bully her into dropping her campaign to find the missing student, but they soon realised Stephanie had something of real value. Stephanie had developed a predictive algorithm that predicted likely outcomes from past data. She'd used it to win her seat in the Legislature a lifetime ago, and it was the same algorithm that had persuaded Stephanie to adopt Jennica's cause. Its only weakness was a lack of data, but Global Governance controlled the datasphere. They could use the algorithm to identify potential problems before they happened. No longer would people be targeted for what they had done, they would be targeted just on the probability of what they might do sometime in the future. That was why Indigo had been so keen to bring Stephanie on board. The woman hadn't been interested in using Stephanie as a weapon—that had come much later—or the fact that her mother was a key member of the Knights Templar; it was her ability to identify future trends that had interested Indigo so much. By using technology taken from Stephanie, Indigo plotted the takeover of Global Governance itself. And in typical Global Governance fashion, she herself had been betrayed in yet another power play by Prince Tarik Tahmid Ihab Abd al-Rashid.

Stephanie's resolve hardened. She needed to stop this never-ending cycle of corruption. She would complete what Juliet and Nico had started and find those responsible for killing Jennica Fabian, for destroying her life, and bring them to justice. She'd spent too long within the digital realm, acting as voyeur to events in the physical world. It was time to act.

CHAPTER FORTY-SEVEN

King of the Scrambles

O'DRISCOLL LOOKED ACROSS the rain-sodden street to where his men were hiding. There was no movement, nothing to indicate anybody was there.

The unofficial border of the Scrambles was twenty metres up the road, where Jessops Street ended. A squad of Internal Security troopers approached, the front row sheltering behind their shields in a scene that wouldn't have looked out of place in Roman times, except for the hi-tech armour and weapons carried. In the distance, rank after rank of troopers filled up the adjacent streets, and behind them giant, spider-like machines stood menacingly.

Movement above caught O'Driscoll's eye. A swarm of intelligence drones headed silently towards the Scrambles. They raced ahead of the troopers, reaching the air above the streets and houses before the troopers had made it to the entrance. It was standard procedure for a seizure mission on a dank and overcast day like this, giving Internal Security a bird's-eye view of the ground below.

As soon as the drones flew into the Scrambles they wobbled, then fell, smashing against roofs and hard cobbles. O'Driscoll smiled to himself. He'd been right. Internal Security had chosen to use remotely-operated drones rather than those run by AI. Jamming all frequencies above the Scrambles meant the remote pilots couldn't control their aircraft. It was a small victory, but an important one, showing his people that Internal Security weren't invincible after all.

The squad moved forward, protected by their transparent shields. It was impossible to see what the troopers were thinking, hidden behind their insectile helmets, but there was a confidence in their step as they entered the Scrambles. It had only been a few months since they'd successfully raided the place after all. What did they have to fear?

The front line of troops moved into the Scrambles proper with individual troopers peeling off to check alleyways and the buildings to either side. They found nothing. The buildings were deserted, as O'Driscoll had ordered. Slowly the troopers advanced. He needed them to come in further, to fully commit their numbers.

Right on cue, a couple of young lads ran out from a building at the far end of the street, stopping on seeing the line of troopers. O'Driscoll recognised one of them, the boy who'd first reported to him that morning. The lad played his part well.

The older of the two lads approached the squad. "We're holding Mick and Darragh O'Driscoll in the central square, as promised." He pointed down the road behind him. "Once you've got them, you'll leave us in peace, right?"

For an answer, two shots rang out and the boys fell to the ground, heads smacking onto the cobbles, blood mingling with rain. O'Driscoll couldn't believe it. The fuckers. They'd known it was a trap all along.

With a scream he charged out into the street, firing at troopers only a couple of metres from where he stood. The air erupted with shouts as men poured into the street from both sides. A loud screech sounded from the end of the street as three large steel barriers, one from each of the buildings either side and one from beneath the cobbles, sealed the Scrambles off from the outside world. And sealing in the platoon of Internal Security troopers.

Large stones rained down on the heads of the troopers, thrown from the roofs of buildings. Those troopers lucky enough not to be hit by the first wave of rocks raised their shields to protect themselves, allowing O'Driscoll and his men to attack.

O'Driscoll screamed as he launched himself at a trooper, the two of them falling to the floor. Something connected with the side of his head but O'Driscoll was a man possessed, grabbing the trooper's helmet and smashing it repeatedly onto the cobbles. The trooper clawed at O'Driscoll's face, trying to push him off, but O'Driscoll refused to give, pounding the helmet into the ground. When the trooper went still, O'Driscoll stuck a knife into the man's unguarded throat. Hot blood sprayed out, soaking his hands and arms. Satisfied the trooper was dead, O'Driscoll got to his feet and looked for his next target.

All was chaos. Bodies lay strewn over the cobbles, mostly troopers but some of his enforcers too. The air was heavy with the smell of blood, mud and sweat. To his right a trooper knocked one of O'Driscoll's men to the ground. Not thinking, O'Driscoll flung himself forward, striking the trooper to the floor then stabbing down, his knife deflecting off the trooper's chest armour and slipping out of his grip. He felt a blow to the stomach and the wind rushed out of him. O'Driscoll lashed out but he'd been turned onto his back. Blows rained down on him. O'Driscoll screamed in fury as he fought blindly through blood and rain. His fingers latched under the chin protector of a trooper's helmet and he pulled down hard. The blows stopped as the trooper fell forward, then before O'Driscoll could get in another blow the trooper's helmet shattered, a hole the size of a fist appearing in the side.

O'Driscoll pushed the dead trooper off his chest and rolled to his side, panting heavily. He glanced around to get his bearings and saw Darragh standing above him, the barrel of a weapon pointed in his direction.

"I thought I told you to stay in reserve?"

Darragh grimaced. "Looks like you needed a hand, cousin."

O'Driscoll got up and surveyed the street. All troopers were down, along with a handful of his own men. As he got to his feet a cheer erupted. O'Driscoll did his best to raise a smile but all he could see were good men and women scattered across the cobbles, people who'd given their lives to protect their homes, to protect him. His left arm throbbed and when he looked down he saw a shallow gash from wrist to elbow. Where the hell had that come from?

Darragh shook him by the shoulders, a big grin on his face. "We did it. We drove the bastards back. I didn't believe you when you said we had a chance but by fuck, you know how to fight."

"Send word out to the others. I want the barriers up in every street."

"But we did it! They'll think twice before having another go at us."

He grabbed hold of Darragh by the arm. "Did you see how many of them are out there? The only reason they sent in a small squad was because they thought Charlie would hand us over on a plate. Now they know different. All we've done is piss them off."

"But we—"

"Get your men back to the reserves and clear this street. This fight hasn't even started."

CHAPTER FORTY-EIGHT

The Investigator

THE SIREN WAS louder in the tunnels, blaring out the call to evacuate. Nico made his way past medical wards where staff not evacuating patients were busy preparing for the worst, checking supplies and making up beds. There was an air of professionalism as they went about their task. These people had trained for this moment and now it was here, but it didn't prevent the anxiety they felt showing on their faces.

As Nico made his way toward the medical centre exit, a couple of soldiers ran past, hauling a colleague between them. The smell of burnt pork seared Nico's nostrils. He looked down to see the charred face of a young woman, her hair burnt to stubble down one side of her head, scalp black and crusted. He grabbed hold of the wall to steady himself and it took a few moments to catch his breath. What the hell was going on?

Nico stepped out into the central tunnel. People were everywhere, many with a determined look on their faces but a number wandering around confused. Go left or right? That was the question. Those military personnel he could see appeared to be heading in the direction of where the loud booms were coming from, while their colleagues took up defensive positions in the main thoroughfare. All non-military personnel appeared to be heading in the opposite direction, towards the ramp that led to the safe zone.

He thought back to where Maria could be. The accommodation blocks were only a level down from the surface, where the bulk of the military had been heading. Hopefully everyone there was being evacuated. If Maria had headed home the Professor would make sure she was taken to safety along with the rest of the family, if they weren't already there. But there was one other place he thought she might be.

Nico followed the crowd heading towards the far rampway. At the entrance to the central ramp two soldiers stood in front of the doors, gesturing everyone to keep moving and take the far passage to the safe zone. Nico recognised one of the soldiers from the snatch squad.

"Have you seen my daughter, a young girl, dark hair, fourteen years old?"

The woman shook her head. "Not that I remember but if she's been past here I'd have sent her to the safe zone. You should get yourself there too."

"Are you sure you haven't seen her?"

The soldier shook her head. "If she has any sense she'll be following the others."

If she knew what was going on. If she wasn't terrified of her Pappa. He gestured towards the central stairwell exit. "Any chance of letting me through? We lost contact with her and if she's anywhere, she'll be hiding on the administration level."

"We were told to direct everyone to the safe zone."

"Come on, you know me. Please!" Nico pleaded.

The soldier thought for a moment and then raised her arm to let him past.

As the doors shut behind him the noise of the crowd disappeared. Nico headed up the rampway, careful to move as quickly and quietly as possible. He needed to be sure Maria was safe. He couldn't live with himself if she ended up hurt because of his actions.

As he made his way around the twisting ramp, his mind spun at the thought of where Maria could be. She was okay. He was sure of it. She was a sensible girl. When the alarm started she would have found out what was happening and made her way to safety.

Or she could already be dead.

He shook his head. No. He couldn't accept that. He had to believe she was still alive.

By the time he'd arrived at level U2 his legs felt like jelly. It was too late to worry now. He could rest once Maria was found. He went to open the door when the rampway lights flickered momentarily. Then the alarm went silent. In the sudden quiet Nico heard his heart pounding in his chest, the roar of blood in his ears.

He pushed at the door. The tunnel behind was empty, and that didn't make sense. He should have seen someone by now, soldiers at least. They wouldn't have left this part of the base unguarded. He eased the door fully open, keeping it between him and the corridor outside, ready to slam it shut if he heard a noise, but there was nothing.

With his heart in his mouth, Nico edged into the corridor. There was no sign of anybody. No soldiers. No one. The doors to the offices and meeting rooms on this level were shut. No, that wasn't true. At the far end of the tunnel he saw that one door was open. It was the room where he'd found Maria the last time they'd argued.

Halfway to the door he saw that it hadn't just been left ajar. Something lay across the doorway, blocking it open. At the sight, Nico ran, all thought for his own safety gone. He saw it was a body, but once closer realised it wasn't Maria. Relief and disgust tore at him. A soldier lay at his feet with the back of his head blown away. A glance into the meeting room showed glass scattered across the tables and floor, glittering in the moonlight. There were bodies of two more soldiers, one slumped back in a chair, the other underneath a desk. A quick glance showed that they had died of headshots too. Nico's years of training as an Investigator kicked in. Three soldiers, three headshots. The one in the doorway was making a run for it to raise the alarm when they were attacked.

A blast of wind swept into the room, bringing with it the distant sound of gunfire. Realising he could be in trouble, Nico reached down and prised a weapon from the fingers of the soldier by his feet. Pointing it out in front of him, he entered the room. One look told him all he needed to know. There was mud by the window.

Someone or a number of people had come in this way. The perimeter had been breached. Whoever was attacking had made it into the base and nobody knew. And Maria was still missing.

CHAPTER FORTY-NINE

Stephanie

THE WOMAN WAS missing. It shouldn't have been possible but it was true. Stephanie tried every permutation of search but the answer came back the same. Indigo was gone. According to a Global Governance file she'd disappeared, kidnapped from in front of an apartment building by forces unknown—although Stephanie had a good idea who they could be. Her mother's organisation, the so-called Knights Templar, must have taken her. She called up footage of the kidnapping and saw the proof she needed. Standing front and centre during the standoff and the following assassination attempt was her old friend Nico Tandelli.

Despite her desire to bring Indigo to justice, it appeared the Investigator had beaten her to it. She would catch up with him at some point, but for the moment it appeared Indigo was out of play. Stephanie set up an alarm to notify her if Indigo reappeared on the datasphere and allowed her focus to move up a level in the organisation.

In an instant she'd tracked her next target down to a pod in Dar es Salaam, Tanzania. Stephanie wanted to see the person inside and the image of a man sitting in a luxury vehicle filled her mind. He looked older than his official image—his suit cut to the local style with a bright, traditional pattern—but he was still younger than her, or at least the age when she had died. Given what and who she was now, it was hard to tell if she was a newborn, the age she was before or as old as the memories to which she had access.

According to the journey log, the ride was planned to last no more than ten minutes. It would be enough time.

She activated the man's dataglasses.

<We must talk>

The subtlety of her request had been lost in translation from thought to command but it had an effect. A slight twitch of his eyebrow from behind dark dataglasses was the only sign he'd received her message. Stephanie waited thirty-seconds for a response, separating a part of her mind to tweak the interface. When none came, she tried again.

<We need to talk>

This time she observed a look of irritation cross the man's face. He issued a mental command that was picked up by a neural micro-scanner in the man's dataglasses. Stephanie matched it to a neural pattern set up in the man's datasphere profile—a profile hidden behind layers of complex security. It was a 'delete message' command.

<We need to talk>
<We need to talk>
<We need to talk>

Stephanie flooded the man's interface, circumventing his feeble attempts to block her. He had no chance. How could a single man block the datasphere? Eventually the young prince responded.

"Who is this?"

<You must stop what you're doing>

A frown creased his forehead. "You have me at a loss. Who am I talking to?"

<You must stop the killing>

"Whoever this is, I'm impressed. You've found a flaw in our security. If you show me where it is I'll make you rich beyond your dreams."

<You must stop the killing>

"This is tiresome. If you won't let me know who you are, how can we have a conversation?"

As he spoke, the prince's neural pattern remained predominantly focussed in one formation, sparking the emergency code in his datasphere profile.

<*Don't call for help. It won't work*>

Stephanie saw the man pale. He brought his hands up to the side of his head and grabbed hold of his dataglasses.

<*Don't*>

His hands hovered by the arms. "Who is this?"

<*You are to stop the killing. You are to stop the intimidation. You are to stop the bribes. You are to disband your organisation*>

"I have no idea what you're talking about."

Instead of answering him directly, Stephanie sent a barrage of images of people killed in the war in North America, young soldiers torn apart by unmanned drone strikes; the damage to cities and towns on the border between the Southern Free States and the Northern Independent States.

"This is not down to me. I … I … I've been trying to stop this."

<*You started it*>

"That's not true. It was somebody else."

<*Indigo, for you*>

The young prince nodded. "She didn't do it for me. I've spent months trying to correct the mistakes she's made. I've had luck in Africa, but the Americans won't stop fighting. They're too far gone. As a people they've fought to protect their way of life since the first European settlers 300 years ago, and they haven't stopped since."

While the prince spoke, Stephanie interrogated his personal communications to see if he was telling the truth. He was. She traced orders he'd sent out to operatives, telling them to pull out. But he hadn't tried to stop the fighting itself.

<*You are still part of the problem. Your organisation is corrupt. No matter what you do, it will always be corrupt. It is human nature. It is time to stop*>

With each interaction Stephanie's command of the interface increased. But while the meaning was clear, her language was blunt. Too blunt, as it turned out.

"I've had enough of this." He pulled off his dataglasses.

Stephanie had to get her message across. She reviewed her

options, selecting the one most likely to grab his attention, and took control of the pod.

She locked the doors and issued the emergency stop command. A sickening crunch arrived over the audio feed as the man crashed into the front of the compartment and slumped to the floor. After a few moments she heard him moan in pain as he lay in the footwell. She attempted to contact him via his dataglasses but they remained offline. Left with no choice, she interfaced with the pod's intercom system.

"Have I got your attention now?" Her voice sounded strange, the question broadcast in the pleasant, soothing male voice of the pod's intercom.

"My arm ..."

"I'll get you to a hospital as soon as you answer my questions."

"Who the hell are you?"

How should she answer him? Should she say who she'd been, or what she now was?

"I'm the voice of the people, the datasphere's conscience. I am here for justice."

The young prince crawled back up onto his seat. Blood streamed from his nose and he held his left arm, his shoulder slumped at an unnatural angle. On the floor were the broken remains of his dataglasses.

"Global Governance protects the people."

"You call this protection?"

Stephanie took control of the pod's datascreens and showed the pictures of individuals murdered by Global Governance. Alongside every graphic image she placed a copy of the order and reason for each killing.

At first the prince's face remained blank but as the number of victims grew, his disgust at what he saw was written across his face.

"These had nothing to do with me. I had no idea of the ... the scale of what's been happening."

"I'm bringing those responsible to justice."

He twisted away from the datascreens and looked to the floor, face pale. "Of course. Anything I can do to help, I will."

A banging sounded from the side of the pod. Stephanie pulled in visual feeds from the street outside. A group of what looked like the prince's security personnel surrounded the prince's pod and were hammering on the side, trying to get in.

"You can help me by detaining those responsible."

"You don't need to persuade me. What you've shown me ... I had an idea but I never thought ... I'll do everything I can to get to the bottom—"

The video of the young prince winked out. The loss of contact was momentary but the sense of isolation burrowed deep into Stephanie. She switched back to the external cameras she'd used moments before and found a scene of carnage. Where the pod had been was now a burning hole in the ground. The bodies of the security forces trying to free the prince lay scattered across the road. The surrounding area was littered with scrap metal and body parts. Stephanie hunted for any sign of the young prince but knew it was in vain. Then the feed from the external cameras disappeared.

What the hell had happened? Worse, why hadn't she seen it coming? Stephanie trawled the datasphere, looking for something, anything, that gave an indication as to what was going on, but for some reason the area of the datasphere for Dar es Salaam wouldn't respond. It was as if there was nothing there. The datasphere in that part of Tanzania had effectively disappeared.

CHAPTER FIFTY

Oscar

OSCAR CREPT ALONG the ridge, careful to stay below the horizon despite it being night. Internal Security forces were laid out below him, a swarm of troops and equipment hiding in gullies as they attacked the building nearest to the site entrance. Despite their numbers, nobody had seen him. Oscar was far too good a scout to be spotted, plus Internal Security had swept the area on the way in. It was the mentality of the arrogant: Nobody had been here during the sweep and their enemies were in front of them. There was no need to check behind again.

It was a level of complacency that, if not monitored, seeps into every unit who feel invincible, and Internal Security had been allowed to do what they wanted with impunity, safe in the knowledge that they were protected. It was a weakness, one Oscar would have to take advantage of if he was to achieve his goal.

Patchwork clouds flitted across the night sky, blown by high, strong winds so typical in this part of the world. Oscar waited until a large cloud slipped in front of the moon, then edged his way down the hillside, placing his feet with precision to not disturb loose rocks. He was aiming for an air vent at the far side of the compound, well away from the assault and hidden by scrub. Few in the Knights Templar knew it was there and he was banking on Internal Security being equally as ignorant of its existence. By the way they were attacking the main entrance, it certainly looked that way.

He'd dressed in a black cool-suit, its surface covered in thousands of micro heat-displacers, designed to hide signature body heat from thermal imaging. All that could give him away was his breath, so he took care to face the hillside every time he breathed out.

Within minutes he lay crouched at the base of the hill in a small cutting caused by rainwater. Ahead of him was a sentry, one of the few scattered around the camp's perimeter. Oscar waited. While he needed to get into the base, hurrying now would only get him killed.

The sentry appeared inexperienced, turning to look at each loud explosion where the main assault took place, each glance destroying his night-sight. With all the noise and distraction it could have been possible to sneak past, but Oscar knew the sentry had something he needed. He crawled closer to the trooper.

A flash of bright light illuminated the surrounding hillside. The trooper turned as a deep roar reached his position. Oscar sprang to his feet, looped a wire around the trooper's neck and jerked back, pulling the man off balance. The trooper tried to grab the noose, his hands desperately scrabbling in an attempt relieve the pressure, but Oscar flexed his arms, tightening the wire and cutting into the meat of the man's throat. They remained that way, the trooper's legs kicking out, until with a judder the garrotte dug deeper into the flesh, killing the trooper.

Oscar gently lowered the body, then began to remove the uniform. When he took off the insect-like helmet he took a moment to study the young man's face, committing him to memory. He'd sworn never to kill for the Knights Templar again, but as usual it appeared that what he wanted and what was needed were two different things. The least he could do was memorise those he killed, adding their face to the list, hopefully identifying a name later on to honour them when he had the chance.

Oscar put on the man's assault gear. The trooper was a slightly bigger build than him but the body armour worked well over his own cool-suit. The neckline was sticky from the man's blood but there was nothing Oscar could do about it. Finally he placed the helmet on his head, the inside smelling of the dead man's breath, and rolled the body into a small but fast-moving rivulet.

As he covered the dead man with vegetation, Oscar spotted movement beside the cliff, close to his objective. A figure walked past the hidden vent and squatted down at the edge of the drop. There was a flash, the figure stood, then threw what looked like a rope over the cliff before lowering themselves over the edge.

Oscar checked for other sentries but none were nearby. He moved to where the figure had been, walking normally despite the instinct to run. It took five minutes before he found the rope, secured to a hook blasted into the rock. Taking hold of the rope, Oscar leaned over the cliff edge. There was no sign of the person. They had vanished, which could only mean one thing. With one last glance around to check he wasn't being observed, Oscar took the rope in both hands and dropped over the edge.

CHAPTER FIFTY-ONE

The Professor

THE RAMPWAY SHOOK, causing the Professor to drop to his haunches. A shockwave smacked into him like a punch. Dust and smoke filled the air. He tried to get his bearings. The smoke thinned for a moment and he saw the sign he'd been looking for. He was on the landing of U1, the accommodation level.

The doors to the accommodation level were shut but the crack of gunfire inside was still loud enough to shock. Not for the first time the Professor wondered what the hell he was doing. He could always tell Nico he hadn't found them. It was the truth. He'd seen no sign of Fran or the boys since setting out from the medical centre. It had been chaos, trying to move through the surge of people heading to the safe zone. Nico's family could easily have slipped past him. But the Professor didn't believe it. Something told him they were up ahead.

More than once he'd thought of turning back, especially as the sound of fighting grew louder. At one point he'd hidden in a doorway from the sound of footsteps, only to see a medic heading up the ramp towards the danger. Ashamed at his cowardice, the Professor carried on. He'd made a promise and this was one promise he wasn't going to break.

He eased a door open until he had just enough room to see inside. The familiar long, wide tunnel of the accommodation block stretched out in front of him. The smoke was thicker here, making it impossible to see more than a couple of doors down, both of which were wide open.

There was a bright flash from deep down the tunnel followed by more gunfire. The noise was incredible. He threw the door shut and covered his ears with his hands. Surely no sane person would have stayed in this area? But he didn't know for sure and he wouldn't be able to live with himself if he didn't check. The only piece of good news was that the Tandelli's apartment was closer to this end of the tunnel.

The Professor opened the door again and looked towards the closest dorm. It was a few metres away, only a couple of seconds if he was quick. He took a deep breath, ready to run, but his body wouldn't move. He couldn't do it—it was too dangerous. He had no idea how close the attackers were. What if they saw him? He'd be an easy target.

The floor shook again but when he looked down the Professor realised it was him that was shaking, not the building. He desperately wanted to be a hero, to do the right thing, but he just couldn't do it. He was a coward, a nobody. He was pathetic.

An image came into his mind, the two little boys, Gino and Naci, hiding behind a bush while their older sister looked for them. Two young boys, feet poking out from underneath their hiding place, branches shaking as they giggled with excitement. Then there was the strength Fran had shown while on the run. She was the one who'd kept them together. She was the one who'd kept them all safe.

He ran through the door and dived into the open doorway, expecting pain to follow. It didn't. Weapons opened up but they were at the far end of the tunnel. The Professor took a moment to catch his breath, then chanced a look outside. He could just discern the outline of something on the floor in the distance, but otherwise it was just more open doorways.

Three … two … one …

Without thinking of the consequences, the Professor sprinted across the corridor to the next open doorway, diving in as before. The floor to this room was wooden, rather than the standard carpet, and his momentum took him crashing into a sideboard. Before he could react, something fell from above and smashed on the floor. The Professor froze. Somebody must have heard him.

A massive blast shook the room. The Professor curled up in a ball, hands over his ears. The rate of weapon fire increased. It sounded as if the battle was reaching a critical stage. He glanced up to the number on the open door. He was in room 215. The Tandelli's were in room 197. He did a quick calculation in his head. Their room was nine doors down.

The Professor got to his feet and ran out into the corridor, eyes fixed on the thick gloom ahead. The shape he'd seen earlier morphed into the body of a soldier lying in a pool of blood. The Professor's legs almost gave way at the sight but he kept going, powering past the body, counting the doorways as he went. Room 203 ... room 201 ... room 199. He looked up to see door 197. It was shut. With no other option he dived to the floor, landing in a heap.

He banged on the door. "Fran! Let me in!"

Up ahead he saw some kind of portable energy barrier stretching across the corridor between a thick metal frame embedded in the wall. It stretched from floor to ceiling. Almost. Something had damaged the right-hand post at the top and the energy barrier ceased centimetres from the ceiling.

Two soldiers cowered behind the barrier as it sparked and flared from incoming gunfire. A large weapon dropped down from the ceiling on the other side of the barrier, emitting a high-pitched whine while firing down the tunnel. As it did so the plasma barrier winked out. One of the soldiers stood, threw something, then dropped back down again. The sharp staccato of opposing weapon fire rang out but the barrier had sprung back up, sparking at each impact.

The Professor banged on the door once more. "Fran? Are you in there?"

An almighty blast shook the corridor. The Professor feared the worst but as he glanced up he saw the plasma shield still in place. However one of the soldiers was down, their comrade hunched over them.

Before he could work out what had happened, the door beside him opened.

"Professor! Thank God."

He half-crawled, half-rolled into the room and Fran shut the door behind him.

"What the hell are you still doing here?" he asked.

"I was waiting … hoping Maria would come. By the time I realised she wasn't coming it was too late to leave." Her face looked gaunt, almost grey with fear.

The Professor slowly got to his feet. "Don't worry. Nico sent me to come and get you. He's gone to look for Maria. He thinks he knows where she might be."

"But he was in the medical centre."

The Professor smiled. "You know what your husband's like. As soon as he realised what was going on, he had to act."

Another blast shook the room and the door rattled against its frame. Screams came from the adjoining room.

"You need to get out of here, all of you," the Professor said. "All non-combatants have been ordered to the safe zone."

"I can't go out there, not with the boys."

"It's okay. There's an energy barrier across the corridor. Nothing can get through." At least he hoped. The dead soldier he'd passed on the way to the room wasn't reassuring but he wasn't about to mention it. However bad it was outside, it would soon be worse in the room.

"No, I …" As Fran began to object, another blast shook the room.

The Professor ran through the living room towards the bedroom. "There's no time to argue. Come on—please."

The last explosion must have made up Fran's mind. She joined him as he entered the bedroom. It looked empty, no sign of any occupants.

Fran got down on her knees. "It's okay. You can come out now."

The two small boys wriggled out from under the bed. When Gino saw who was in the room he held out his arms and ran straight to the Professor, who swept him up into his arms. The squeeze Gino gave felt wonderful, life affirming. All his regrets washed away. He had made the right decision.

When he turned around, Fran had Naci in her arms. "So what do we do now?"

"I'll check the corridor, see if the coast is clear. If it is, we'll take a boy each and run towards the far rampway. I just came up that way. It's safe."

As he made his way to the front door, the Professor heard Fran speak.

"Now I need you both to be big, brave boys. Can you do that?"

The sound of weapon fire intensified. The Professor recognised the high-pitched whine of the overhead gun, which he took to be a good sign. He cracked open the door and looked out. The barrier held but there was no sign of the soldiers. He swore. The only thing holding the attacking troops back was that autonomous blaster in the ceiling.

"What's wrong?" It was Fran. He hadn't heard her come up beside him. The boys held hands and looked terrified.

"Take the boys and run. I'll follow on."

"But I need you to carry one of them."

"They'll have to run with you. Now go!"

The four of them ran out into the corridor. A whining blast came from his right as the ceiling weapon automatically discharged hundreds of rounds. It began to spray devastation into the tunnel but suddenly exploded, sending a shower of hot metal and noise over the barrier and in their direction.

The Professor picked up the closest boy and ran. Fran had done the same and was a few metres ahead of him when he felt a stab of pain in his calf. He screamed and dropped like a stone, Gino flying out of his arms.

Through the pain, the Professor saw Fran turn and race back to the fallen boy. "Gino!"

A wave of nausea hit him. Looking down, the Professor saw bone through his shredded trousers. It hurt. By God it hurt. The Professor pushed himself up but his hand slipped in something slick. He glanced sideways and saw the dead soldier he'd passed minutes before.

Fran stared at him from down the corridor. "Professor! Come on!"

There was another explosion, louder than before. "Just run!" the Professor screamed, knowing he was going nowhere. Fran gave him a look of complete helplessness, then took Naci's hand and ran as fast as she could with Gino slung over her shoulder.

The Professor crawled to the dead soldier, the pain in his leg almost causing him to black out. He cried out in anger. No. He needed to stay conscious, needed to give Fran and the boys a chance. He reached out and grabbed the soldier's weapon. Then, using the corpse as cover, he waited.

The atmosphere thickened, smoke billowing out from where they'd just come. The sound of guns had stopped. Only the crackle of flames could be heard. Another wave of pain shot up the Professor's legs and he stifled a groan. It wasn't as bad this time, more a throb than a sharp stab.

So this is how it ends, he thought. It was funny. He knew he was going to die, but for the first time in a long time, the Professor felt at peace. He was no longer afraid. There was no more running, no more hiding. He'd done what he'd set out to do and rescued Fran and the boys.

The Professor watched the corridor, doing his best to blank out the boom of his beating heart. He felt thirsty all of a sudden. If only he had some water. The thought felt so ridiculous he started to laugh. What did he care about water? He was about to die. Then from the gloom he saw something move. Without thinking, the Professor took aim and fired.

CHAPTER FIFTY-TWO

King of the Scrambles

THE WALL EXPLODED. Molten shards of Victorian brick and mortar sprayed into the room. Screams told O'Driscoll that some of his men had been hit. A helmeted head appeared in the hole, the black, chitinous surface shrouded by choking dust. O'Driscoll brought his weapon up but one of his men beat him to it, the head disappearing in a shattered mess.

All was chaos. The blockade they'd spent days building had been torn down in minutes. It had been street fighting ever since. And they were losing. Badly.

The forces they faced weren't the civil security division that had first entered the Scrambles but their military counterparts, troopers used to firing first and not bothering to ask questions later. His men were out-skilled and out-gunned. The only advantage they had was knowing the terrain. It wasn't enough.

He hadn't seen Charlie or Darragh since the outer defences fell. He hoped they were holding their own, giving Internal Security hell, but they could be dead as far as he knew. What he'd give now for a pair of datalenses and a secure datasphere connection.

A deep groan sounded from above. One of his men ran in from the adjacent room. "The guys upstairs are bailing. They say the place is gonna come down any second."

Another groan sounded, following by the creaking of timbers.

These houses were centuries old, fragile enough as it was. They had no chance against the heavy weapons being deployed against them.

O'Driscoll did a quick calculation in his head. "Fall back! We'll hold them at the junction with Lawford Road."

Not needing a second invitation, the men streamed out of the building while O'Driscoll laid down covering fire. They looked a sorry sight as they made their way across the open cobbles, the able-bodied helping their injured comrades. O'Driscoll glanced around the room one last time. Everyone was out, but two men wouldn't be leaving this place, their mangled bodies already covered by a layer of dust.

How could he have miscalculated so badly? He'd known Global Governance wanted him dead, but he never thought they'd unleash war on their own citizens. But it was too late for recriminations. Those could come later. If there was a later. His goal was to get to the next defensive point and carry on fighting, hoping the cost of taking the Scrambles would become a price Internal Security was unwilling to pay.

A loud, pulsing rumble emerged from the Internal Security lines. Half-rotten floorboards vibrated beneath O'Driscoll's feet. Dust showered down. The building groaned once more, followed by an ominous crack. O'Driscoll scrambled over the rubble barricade and ran, praying his men were in position to give him covering fire. Two steps in and his fear was realised. From the side street lumbered a giant, eight-legged machine, its enormous maw already open. He felt rather than heard the blast of noise, the sound grinding his joints, sending a wave of agony through his body. He fell to the floor, head smashing onto the cobbles, but the pain from his pulped face was nothing compared to the agony of every nerve in his body vibrating from the horrible noise flowing out of the hellish machine.

O'Driscoll sucked in a breath and struggled to get up. He faced the machine, his bloodied features bearing the brunt of the aural assault. From behind he heard the higher-pitched crack of weapon fire. Internal Security troopers walking alongside the monstrous machine fell to the ground, but the machine continued on.

Fighting against the pain, O'Driscoll forced himself to his knees.

He refused to die like this. Not today. Not on his turf. The pain was incredible, but no worse than what he'd felt just lying there. With jerking movements he crawled toward an open doorway on the far side of the street. He made it halfway before his arms collapsed from under him.

Lying in a cocoon of agony, his body refused to respond to his demands. More bastard troopers had appeared to support the machine on its inexorable journey into the heart of his domain. O'Driscoll screamed out in pain and frustration.

With a roar the brick façade from the adjacent terraced housing crashed onto the cobbles, metres from where he lay. The demonic noise from the sound cannon stopped and his pain vanished. O'Driscoll scrambled to his feet and lunged through the gaping hole where the front of the buildings used to be. He landed in what had been an entrance hall just a few moments before, but was now a rubble-strewn alley. Not looking back, O'Driscoll ran through the building and out of the back door. The tenement block was similar to many in the Scrambles, backing onto a small alleyway with steep brick walls on either side. The alleyway was empty of people, although reeking of rot. Sitting in the middle of a garbage heap, a rat the size of a small dog stared at him, its gimlet eyes issuing a challenge. You may be King of the Scrambles for now, the look said, but I'll be King here long after you're gone.

"You're not getting rid of me that easily, you little fucker." O'Driscoll stumbled down the alleyway in the opposite direction to where the troopers had been, and headed toward the centre of the Scrambles.

The sound of weapons echoed down the alleyway but it remained largely unscathed. A small piece of graffiti, a lone finger and a scrawled name, helped O'Driscoll get his bearings, and instead of running out into the road at the end of the alley he pulled on the handle of a small doorway, half-hidden in the shadows.

As he entered the room his foot caught on an uneven step, causing him to stumble. There was a flash, the roar of a weapon and O'Driscoll felt something streak past his ear where his head had been moments before. He looked up to see an old man with a rifle pointed in his direction.

"What the fuck do you think you're playing at, Crabb?"

At the sound of his voice, the old man lowered his weapon. "I thought you were one of those bloody troopers."

"If I was you'd be a dead man by now."

"If you weren't so fucking clumsy you'd be dead yourself, although by the looks of your face someone's given it a good go already." The old man grinned and for a moment he looked like a young child, rather than the grizzled veteran he was. Crabb was one of the old school, a hard bastard who could be both the best of friends and the worst of enemies. He was known around the Scrambles for being immaculately dressed but today he wore just a stained vest and rumpled trousers, his scrawny arms covered in scars earned during O'Driscoll's father's time. But his shock of white hair remained immaculate as ever.

"You should be somewhere safe."

"What, huddling like a child waiting for the bad guys to come? You can stick that up your arse." Crabb coughed, a horrible, hacking sound that ended with a growl and a chunk of phlegm shooting out into the alleyway. "If they want me, they're gonna have to kill me first." This time the impish grin was gone, and while the old man's voice may have quivered, his eyes were as hard as flint.

"Have you seen anyone else come by?"

"Not through here, but that girl of yours ran past the back window not five minutes ago."

So Charlie was alive. There was still some hope.

O'Driscoll pointed to the doorway. "If you're determined to stay, then at least get some cover. Internal Security troopers have taken the neighbouring block and it won't be long before they're knocking on your door."

"When they do, they'll find a special welcome waiting for them."

O'Driscoll walked up to the man and patted him on the shoulder. "Give the fuckers hell."

Without waiting for a response, he made his way through the old enforcer's house to the front door. He opened it and looked outside. A whistle echoed across the street. Darragh stood in the building opposite, smiling. O'Driscoll ran across the road to where his cousin waited.

"You took your time," the young man said.

"We need to fall back. Troopers are coming this way with a sound cannon. We should head towards the maze. There's no way the sound cannon will be able to enter that part of the Scrambles, the streets there will be too narrow for it to get in."

"You want us to give up the whole northern sector just like that? For fuck's sake. They should be paying for it in blood."

"They already have: Ours, and too much of it. Half the block's already rubble. There's too many of them. We're outnumbered and outgunned. We need to fight them where their numbers and heavy weapons are less of an advantage."

As if to emphasise the point, a large roar sounded from down the street and a choking cloud of dust emerged over the rooftops.

"I still don't think we should give up half our turf so easily."

"You think I like this? You think I wanted this to happen? I want to wipe out every single one of those bastards but making a stand here will just get us killed. We head to the maze. That's where we make our stand. That's where we make the fuckers pay."

His cousin stared at him but eventually Darragh nodded. "Yes sir."

"Get your men together and follow me."

They left the building and headed towards the ancient centre of the Scrambles. As they reached the end of the street, the sound of weapons firing echoed from behind. For a moment, O'Driscoll swore he could hear the sound of rheumy laughter. Then the firing stopped.

CHAPTER FIFTY-THREE

Stephanie

STEPHANIE PULLED HER awareness back to her core self and rose above the datasphere. Spread out below her was a visual representation of the network, a giant ball covered in gossamer-thin data pathways and information nodes. These arteries of information surrounded and penetrated the sphere, transporting the sum of human experience to every corner of the planet. And it also represented who she had become.

Even at a macro level, the mental construct was almost too vast to comprehend. Stephanie pulled back further, the sphere shrinking until it was no bigger than a beach ball, one that pulsed and glowed with the energy of human interaction. She rotated it, inspecting the surface, looking for any indication as to why she could no longer access what was happening in Dar es Salaam.

Close examination revealed the tiniest blemish to the polished sheen. Stephanie concentrated on this area, zooming in to take a closer look. As she did, the tiny flaws became chasms, enormous gaps where the light of dataflow should have been. Worse, the chasms appeared to be widening, the edges eroding away like acid on flesh, corroding the integrity of the datasphere. Then a thought hit her. This wasn't a chasm, it was a cancer, a corruption of the framework supporting the datasphere. The same framework that supported her consciousness. What she'd first seen as a minor irritation had become an attack on her very existence.

Stephanie placed a filter over the representation of the datasphere. Now, instead of the smooth, integrated model she'd seen before, the sphere resembled a tangle of blue and red—the blue representing the visible datasphere, the red the dark datasphere, known only to Global Governance. With the change of view came understanding. Lining the edge of the hole in the datasphere was a thin red line, eating into the vivid blue of the visible network while leaving a dark emptiness in its wake. Stephanie couldn't believe what she was seeing. Why would Global Governance destroy their own creation?

She moved closer, the thin red line broadening to become a barrier, swamping parts of the network previously open to all before devouring them. Still unclear on what was happening, Stephanie zoomed in on one data node and stripped away the visual representation to reveal the algorithm doing all the harm.

It was quite beautiful. Stephanie saw a pureness of form, a mathematical symmetry in the algorithm's encryption way beyond anything she'd been able to produce back at university. She attacked it with the most common forms of data cracking tools, looking to break through the algorithm's defensive shell, but the code shrugged off her efforts. It appeared unstoppable.

Stephanie changed tack and looked for a controlling mechanism, some kind of signal she could piggyback on and hijack the algorithm, but there was nothing. Whoever had created this piece of code had made it self-sufficient. It had one purpose: To take down the datasphere. Once released, nothing could tell it to stop.

Despite all her attempts to block unwanted emotion, Stephanie felt the flutterings of panic. She threw more processing power at it in an effort to crack the algorithm's encryption, going for brawn over brains. Before she had been careful, using dormant resources to remain undetected, but now she didn't care. This was a fight for survival, a fight for her very existence. At her command, the full power of the datasphere focussed on the insidious piece of code.

It didn't stand a chance.

With the encryption cracked, the true form and function of the algorithm revealed itself. It had been designed to transfer control of the command and reporting structure of the datasphere, without interrupting the actual data flow itself.

At university she'd learnt that the datasphere had two levels of control. The first was the public realm. This was the standard access level, allowing individuals to define who could or couldn't access their data. The second level was the command structure. This overrode the security of the public level, giving security services backdoor access to all data regardless of what security had been created at the public level. What she now knew was that there was a third level, purely for Global Governance. This overrode all other controls, effectively separating the Global Governance network from the rest of the datasphere, making it invisible. The algorithm changed the second and third level access codes, effectively taking control, and visibility, away from the security services and Global Governance, while leaving the public usage codes in place. The majority of those using the datasphere would see no difference, but the security services—and many in Global Governance—would be aware of the difference, removing their access to leave only a small faction within Global Governance in control.

Suddenly everything that had happened to her since her consciousness had awoken made sense. The battles she'd fought had been a manifestation of her taking control of each level. Her existence, her ability to access data, was because she had used the immense processing power available to her to crack each level of security. But the algorithm had been designed to change these access codes. The datasphere wasn't being destroyed, it was just her access that was being taken away. And not just her, but anyone else using the old Global Governance level of access to monitor what was happening around the world. This wasn't a cancer, this was a coup.

Armed with the knowledge, Stephanie pulled back once again to view the datasphere as a whole. The algorithm continued to spread unchecked through each interconnected system. Rather than watch the general spread, she focussed on a specific piece of code as it targeted a particular data node, the European judiciary services. The node pulsed and then went dark, disappearing from view and from her control. She watched another, this time targeting the North American Independent States central bank, then a third as it attacked the Chinese police datacentre. Across the globe, key data centres for government, business and security were being taken off the datasphere and under the control of … of who?

Stephanie tried to identify potential candidates but for once the information wasn't there. It was like grasping memories from the distant past. There was a shadow of something that should be there but it wouldn't come into focus. Her access to information, to memories, was being eroded. Once complete, not only would her ability to see what was happening disappear, she would disappear too.

Stephanie reviewed the datasphere once again. While the vast majority remained visible to her, fine hairline cracks had spread across its surface. The cancer was growing, and growing fast. But now that she understood what was happening, Stephanie could act.

She copied the algorithm, then modified it for increased speed before setting it loose to multiply across the datasphere. She initially targeted data nodes storing her consciousness. The new code swiftly overrode any previous commands, replacing them with one of her own, then protecting them from the old algorithm behind new layers of encryption.

Within minutes the nodes supporting her mind were secured and Stephanie noticed a difference. Whether imagined or not, her sense of self solidified. She was back in control.

Now her algorithm spread across the datasphere, converting all data nodes whether infiltrated by the old algorithm or not. Under her gaze the vast network sprang back to life, the dead spaces awakening and the blue or red of before turning into a sublime silver, indicating where she was back in control.

As her influence grew, Stephanie turned her attention to those behind the initial attack. This time information flooded into her. She saw everything, knew everything. Nothing was beyond her grasp. She learnt how a Global Governance faction led by Herr Streckler had set the algorithm loose to take back control from the young prince and his supporters, yet another political power play acted out in secret by those looking to control the world. It was a pattern she'd traced through history, and here it was again, people committing crimes for the 'greater good'; how an initial desire to do the right thing became corrupted into doing their thing.

Well, not any more.

CHAPTER FIFTY-FOUR

Indigo

STUMBLING INTO THE young girl had been a moment of serendipity. Indigo knew who the girl was, of course, or rather whose daughter she was. The poor thing had been walking down the corridor, lost, not knowing what was going on or what to do. It was easy to persuade the poor mite to follow her back to an empty lab on the promise of safety.

Indigo looked across to where the girl sat, eyes wide, staring at the doorway as if expecting bad guys to come bursting in at any moment.

"The base is well protected. You've nothing to worry about. I'm sure the attack will be over soon."

It was a lie, of course. She knew who was outside and why. This was the final move by Global Governance, to crush all opposition and take back control. She'd been expecting an attack to happen ever since she'd arrived. All she'd had to do was sit and wait.

The room shook and a dull boom quickly followed. The young girl looked back at Indigo, tears in her eyes.

"You never told me your name."

"Maria … it's Maria."

"Hello, Maria. My name's Indigo."

The young girl frowned. "Is that your real name?"

Indigo smiled. "No, but I've been using it for more years than I care to remember, much longer than the name my parents gave me."

"What name did they give you?"

Indigo paused, wondering whether to answer. What the hell, it wasn't like it meant anything any more. "They called me Elena."

"That's a pretty name."

"Thank you."

"Can I call you Elena?"

"If you want. I can't promise I'll respond, though. I broke that habit years ago." She walked across the lab and sat next to the girl. "There aren't many young girls here on base."

"There aren't any." There was a fierceness to her response.

"You must get lonely."

"Not really. I have my work."

Indigo raised an eyebrow. "You work here? That must be fun."

"It is. I've been learning all sorts of things."

"About what?"

"How the brain works, what it looks like when we think about certain things, the parts of the brain that get activated by sight or sound."

"I didn't know your father was interested in neuroscience."

"You know Pappa?" As she spoke she brought her hand up to her reddened cheek.

"Not as such, but I know there's only one family here in the base, so it doesn't take a genius to work out you're Investigator Tandelli's daughter."

"Chief Investigator."

"Sorry, of course. Chief Investigator Tandelli, though to be honest he's not really any form of Investigator any more." She leaned across and whispered. "They closed his agency down."

Maria stared at the floor. "Pappa never said."

"I don't think it's something he wanted to share, especially not with his little children."

"I'm not little."

Indigo smiled. "I know that. You're nearly a full-grown woman. But it's hard for parents to see you as you are today. To them, a small part of you will always be their baby.”

The young girl scowled. “That's what the Professor says.”

“Ah, of course. You know the Professor, don't you? He was with you when you came here.”

“He helped save us when the bad people came. He's my friend.”

“You clearly like him a lot. Is it him who's been teaching you about neuroscience?”

“Him and Josh, but mostly the Professor.”

“I thought his expertise was in data analysis?”

“It is, but he and Josh have been working together to save that woman, Stephanie Vaughn. I've been helping them.”

Indigo kept her features smooth but inside her mind raced. So that was what the Professor and that idiot savant Josh Stanton had been doing. She'd seen the pair of them arguing in the cafeteria. At the time she'd thought they'd been pulled in to help identify which members of Global Governance had been cloned. But why would they want to save Stephanie? What value was she to them?

A loud crack sounded from the corridor causing the pair to jump. Before Maria could react, Indigo held her hand against the girl's mouth. At her startled expression, Indigo put a finger to her lips. Maria nodded, her eyes wet with tears, and Indigo removed her hand.

The sound of gunfire could mean one of two things but until Indigo knew which, she didn't want to alert anyone to their presence. She pointed to one of the desks laden with equipment. Maria nodded again, crept across the room and crawled underneath. It wasn't the best of hiding places but at least it would keep her out of sight until Indigo had assessed the situation.

Walking as quietly as she was able, Indigo went to the lab door, placed her back against the wall and turned off the light.

It was pitch black. Indigo calmed her breathing, blocked out the worried sounds coming from under the desk and concentrated on what was happening in the corridor. It took a moment for her ears to adjust but then she heard the sound of footsteps. This wasn't a person creeping down the corridor. This was the sound of someone who knew exactly where they were heading, right to where she was.

With a crash the door burst open. A scream erupted from the other side of the room. Stupid girl, Indigo thought, but the noise distracted the person outside enough for them to focus their weapon in the direction of the desk. Indigo leapt out and grabbed hold of the barrel, twisting it as she did so. Her vision exploded and she found herself on the floor, the room spinning. She glanced up and saw a man staring at her. It was a face she recognised.

"Echo. If I'd known it was you I would have greeted you with a kiss."

Echo's expression never changed. "Who's the girl?"

"You could at least help me up first," Indigo replied, rubbing the side of her head. "I thought you'd never arrive. I take it you got my message?"

The man made no move to help her. Instead, Echo remained where he was, weapon pointed at Indigo's head. "Who's the girl?"

"Stop pissing about. You need to get me out of here before anyone finds us." She tried to move but Echo pushed her back down with his foot.

"I've a message for you."

One look at Echo's expression and Indigo knew something was wrong. This wasn't how she'd envisaged it. Echo was meant to get her out of here. By alerting him to the base, she would not only have escaped but also closed down the last thorn in Global Governance's side. She'd be a hero. "A message from who, the prince?"

"No, from the Dachshund. He thanks you for the offer of help but says that he can manage things from here."

Indigo froze. The Dachshund? What was Echo doing passing on a message from Herr Streckler … ?

The answer came like a punch to the stomach.

"When did he get to you?"

"At the club. He offered me a way out, to keep my family safe. I couldn't say no."

"Oh, Echo. I would never have hurt your family, you know that."

The man grimaced. "That's not what you said. You told me that if I failed you it would be my family who'll pay."

"I just wanted to get your attention, that's all."

"Well it worked." He shifted his grip on the weapon.

"Why now? You could have done this at any time—at my apartment, the numerous trips we made together. Why leave it to this moment?" While she spoke, Indigo glanced around the room for something, anything, to protect herself. There was nothing obvious.

"Because this way it will be blamed on the Knights Templar. It's cleaner. With you and the prince out of the picture, Global Governance will heal and things will return to the way they were."

"The Dachshund appears to have it all worked out."

Echo raised his weapon once more. "He really does."

CHAPTER FIFTY-FIVE

The Investigator

THE CORRIDOR WAS empty, half-filled with smoke that made it difficult to see. Nico slowly made his way down, pausing each time he passed an open doorway. He'd followed the trail of dirty footprints to U3, where the labs and datafarms were. Whoever had broken in clearly knew where they were going.

He glanced through the nearest doorway. It was a tech lab, one of the many on this floor. The lights were off and there was no sign of life. He was about to move on when he thought he saw something on the floor. Gripping his weapon tightly, Nico crept into the room.

A loud rumble echoed down the corridor outside and the floor shook. The explosion was some distance off, but much louder than the one he'd heard in the medical bay. He wondered if it was a good sign or not. For a moment he thought he heard a faint scream, but it could have been his imagination. There was no point dwelling on it; there was nothing he could do.

Nico edged further into the room until he came to what he'd seen. He'd been right. It was a body, a man, face down on the floor. He rolled the body over with his foot and gasped.

It was Thomas Doleman.

His eyes were open, as if in shock at the ragged hole in his forehead. Nico felt his neck in the vain hope of finding a pulse but he knew it was unnecessary. Doleman was still warm but all life had gone.

There was blood on his cuffs. A small case lay on its side by the body, its lid open, clothes half-spilled out. For a few moments Nico stared at Doleman, unsure what to think. For most of Nico's life the man had been dead, a legend from another era. That he'd been alive was a surprise, to find him dead more so. And with a case of clothes. Had he been attempting to run away?

A crash, then a scream echoed down the corridor, breaking his thoughts. Nico jumped up. The scream, it sounded like …

He raced out of the room and down the curving tunnel before slowing. He had no idea where the scream had come from. He'd run past a number of rooms and hadn't checked to see if any were occupied. What if Maria was in one of them? What if he'd let her down once more?

The sound of voices, faint, drifted down the tunnel. Nico moved as quickly as he could, sticking to the inside of the corridor, using the curve as cover. Soon he was able to hear what was being said.

"… because this way it will be blamed on the Knights Templar. It's cleaner. With you and the prince out of the picture, Global Governance will heal and things will return to the way they were."

Nico recognised the voice. A couple more steps and it was confirmed. Echo, the man he'd hunted, the killer of Jennica Fabian, stood in the doorway, arms pointing downwards. Who was he talking to? Nico had heard the scream. It was Maria. Was he pointing a weapon at Maria?

"He appears to have it all worked out."

"He really does."

The weapon discharged.

"No!" Nico screamed.

Echo turned but Nico fired first. Once … twice … spinning the Global Governance agent around, the man's gun flying out of his hand and through the open doorway.

Nico ran to where Echo lay and looked into the room. It was dark but he could see the second body in the doorway. It wasn't Maria. It wasn't Maria! It was Indigo. Echo had killed his old boss. Nico sank down, his hands on his knees and felt like crying. He'd been so sure he'd heard Maria. So sure that Echo had—

Nico's face slammed into the floor and the world spun. He twisted but somebody was on him, punching the back of his head once, twice, three times. He was trapped, couldn't get up. He tried his best but the blows kept raining down. His body felt so weak, his exertions catching up with him. With one last effort Nico lifted his weapon, twisting it around and fired.

The blows didn't stop.

He tried to fire again but his arm was slammed to the ground.

"You tortured my son, you fuck."

Echo's voice was in his ear. Nico wrenched his head back and felt it connect. Something cracked. He was in pain but for an instant Nico felt the grip on him lessen and he twisted with all his might. It was then he spotted Maria, light spilling in from the corridor revealing her hiding place under a table.

Anger and fear pulsed through him. Although Echo remained on top, now Nico faced him. He pointed his weapon at the man but Echo managed to grab it before he could fire.

Nico brought his knee up and connected with Echo's back, causing a satisfying grunt. The man screamed in anger, his face a rictus of effort, and the muzzle of his own weapon was slowly forced back towards Nico.

Nico strained but he couldn't stop the gun as it turned towards him. He gritted his teeth, put everything he had into it. He couldn't let go, knew that if he did he'd die.

But Echo was stronger.

"Leave my daughter alone," Nico screamed, and with one last effort, using reserves he never knew he had, he pushed back.

It was not enough.

The weapon finished its journey, muzzle pointing towards Nico's face. There was an explosion and something splattered across his cheek. Echo's weight left his body, making a dull thump as it fell to the floor.

Maria stood over him, a weapon in her hands and tears in her eyes.

"I ... I ..."

Nico pushed himself up and—his body screaming in protest—took hold of his daughter and held her tight. "It's okay, darling, it's okay."

Maria shook in his arms and he pressed his lips to the top of her head. As he did, a shadow blocked the doorway. It was an Internal Security trooper.

Nico started to cry. He couldn't do any more, had nothing left to give. He'd lost.

"If you want to get out of here alive, you should follow me now."

Nico didn't move. He just held Maria in his arms.

"Nico. You need to get Maria to safety."

The words broke through. He looked up once again. "Who are you?"

The trooper pulled his helmet off. It was Oscar. "We need to get out of here. Internal Security has broken through the defences. They could be here any minute."

CHAPTER FIFTY-SIX

King of the Scrambles

DAY TURNED INTO night and still the bastards came. O'Driscoll couldn't remember the last time he'd felt so tired. His face throbbed —he knew it was bad by the way others glanced at him, avoiding his eyes and looking at his injury—and he was desperate for a drink, yet he'd only had a chance to snatch the odd gulp of water between attacks before the next wave of troopers descended.

After the last assault he'd returned to the makeshift HQ, an old bakery at the heart of the maze. Charlie had been there. She'd lost nearly half her people in the initial vain attempt to hold Internal Security back, and like him she'd been outgunned and outnumbered. She'd wanted him to go back to the old pumping station and help her direct operations, but there was no point. She was the better organiser and always had been. His job was to inspire the fighters, and if he left the battle now he worried his enforcers would break and run. Instead, she'd left with the majority of their meagre forces while O'Driscoll had headed back to the maze with those that were left.

The alley was hardly big enough to walk one abreast, the glistening cobbles treacherous. A whistle from above told him another trooper was on their way. Then there was a second whistle, then a third. O'Driscoll hoped his squad were ready for this. As he moved back into the shadows, a shot rang out. A body crashed onto the slick cobbles of the alleyway in front of him. Blank eyes stared from a young boy's face. He would whistle out no more signals. O'Driscoll swallowed his anger, forging it into a cold, calm fury. This was his turf. Nobody came here without his say.

He heard the sound of boots on cobbles. The troopers were being cautious, a lesson learned after hours of fighting in this warren, but it was difficult to walk on the hard, slippery stones without making a sound.

O'Driscoll waited, muscles tense. A trooper stopped directly in front of his hiding place and crouched to investigate the fallen boy. With a yell O'Driscoll burst out and smashed the trooper's helmeted head. Somehow the bastard stayed on his feet. The trooper turned, struggling to raise his bulky weapon in the confined space. O'Driscoll kicked his legs from under him, sending the man to the floor, reached down and in two sharp movements stabbed his dagger into the trooper's exposed neck.

Along the narrow alley O'Driscoll's enforcers ripped into the other troopers. Four were down but a fifth continued his death struggle at the far end. Two of O'Driscoll's squad jumped on the remaining trooper, stabbing him in the back of the neck.

Without warning the trooper exploded.

O'Driscoll flung himself to the floor as shrapnel and body parts flew over his head, landing wetly among the bodies at his feet. An after-image of what had happened made a silhouette behind his closed eyes. What the fuck? The trooper had blown himself apart.

With ears ringing from the blast, O'Driscoll lifted his head and surveyed the carnage. The two enforcers closest to him staggered to their feet. The only thing left of those nearest the blast lay mangled on the alley floor.

"Back to base!" he yelled, his voice sounding muffled and distant to his own ears. But his order was heard and the three of them scrambled away from the bloodbath, in the opposite direction to where the troopers had entered.

At the end of the alley they came to a T-junction. O'Driscoll went to turn right but a glint of reflected light stopped him dead. His weapon came up without thinking and he fired. A trooper fell, but two more appeared where he had been, their gunfire a deafening roar in the confined space.

O'Driscoll ducked behind the alley wall. Where now? The quick way back was blocked. They'd have to take a detour. He turned to the men behind him. "When I start firing, take a left, then the first right. Once clear, give me covering fire so I can join you."

The men nodded.

"Ready," O'Driscoll said, "go!"

He leant out and fired blindly down the alley. It was too dark to see if he hit anyone but it didn't matter. He sensed the two enforcers pass by him and sprint to the left. Chips of brickwork flew from the wall beside him. O'Driscoll fired again, only to be beaten back by a barrage of shots. Why weren't his men firing back? He had to go now. If he didn't, the troopers would have him trapped.

O'Driscoll swore, then ran, following where his men had gone. Shots zipped past his head. He skidded on the wet cobbles, lost his footing and slid into the opposite wall, somehow managing to stay on his feet. He scrambled forward, desperate to reach the safety of the next alley. Shots buzzed past. O'Driscoll dived forward and tumbled into the alley where he'd sent his men.

Their lifeless bodies broke his fall.

Out of instinct he rolled to one side. The body he'd landed on jerked and twitched as it was hit by more shots. O'Driscoll couldn't see a thing, had no idea where the shots were coming from. He fired wildly as he scrambled to his feet, then took the only choice he had left.

He charged, screaming out of fear and rage. The far end of the alleyway was dark, but he saw a flash as someone fired in his direction, then a second, then a third. This was it, he was a dead man. O'Driscoll fired as he ran but knew it was a lost cause.

Pain exploded in his hip. He spun and fell into a pile of stinking rubbish. Shots whistled overhead but for the moment the rancid pile provided cover. He tried to move his leg. It hurt like hell but still worked. He wasn't dead yet but his options were running out fast. He'd no idea if his leg would last another charge. At the same time, the troopers from earlier would soon be here and block his only other way out. O'Driscoll looked up at the alleyway walls towering above him. There was no help there either. He was trapped.

The firing stopped. The silence felt unnatural after the earlier noise. All he could hear was his own ragged breathing and the ringing in his ears. O'Driscoll itched to act but waited. He had no idea what was happening up ahead but the alleyway behind remained empty. If somebody arrived, he'd deal with it, but for the moment he'd play dead.

A bright flash lit up the alleyway followed by the low rumble of thunder. As if on cue, the rain thickened. So this is how I'll live out my final moments, O'Driscoll thought—battered, bloodied, covered in rubbish and soaked to the bone. My father would be so proud.

He punched the ground. What had happened to the Knights Templar? They must have got his message. Why hadn't they come to help? The only answer he received was another flash of lightning and boom of thunder. At least he'd given Internal Security a bloody nose before the end. The world wouldn't forget the O'Driscoll name in a hurry, that was for sure.

From ahead came the crunch of glass under boots. O'Driscoll rolled and fired. A trooper fell but another appeared behind. The second trooper raised its weapon. O'Driscoll tensed, waiting for the impact, but when the shots rang out it was the trooper who flew forward, landing on their dead partner.

Before O'Driscoll could react, a group of men ran down the alleyway towards him. Even in the darkness O'Driscoll recognised the shock of blond hair on the giant leading the way.

"I thought you Dutch left days ago, Ruud."

"We can't let the Irish have all the fun now, can we?"

The giant man reached out and hauled O'Driscoll to his feet. The pain in his hip was excruciating but at least his leg held.

"I don't understand," O'Driscoll said. "You lot hate me. Why are you helping?"

"You might have been a son of a bitch but you never shot us in the street like dogs." He glanced past O'Driscoll's shoulder to the far end of the alleyway. "Quickly now. We need to get you to safety. My men have secured the route back but this whole area's close to being overrun."

"Route back where?"

"Charlie sent us. We're to meet her in the pumping station."

He could see the sense in the strategy. They were to make their last stand at the old pumping station. With a nod, O'Driscoll set off with the others, gritting his teeth against the pain and wondering how much longer they could possibly hold out.

CHAPTER FIFTY-SEVEN

Stephanie

FOR TOO LONG primitive emotion had corrupted good intentions. So much death, so much pain; Stephanie's mind absorbed the horror of what had been done in the name of the greater good. As her algorithm took effect, silently bringing the datasphere under her control, Stephanie saw for the first time the full scope of Global Governance's actions on the outside world.

The progressive faction once headed by the young prince was being hunted down and eliminated by Herr Streckler and his traditionalist camp. The bombing of the prince's pod had been the signal, unleashing a wave of assassinations. A number of industrial and political leaders from across the world fell victim to the purge. It didn't take the datasphere's processing power to recognise a pattern as old as time—from Stalin's purges all the way back to Ancient Rome. The large numbers of prominent killings hadn't gone unnoticed in the media, but Global Governance exerted its influence and for the moment all was silent.

Yet despite this aggressive coup, all around the globe the actions of the progressive faction were still being felt. The war in North America raged on, a senseless slaughter whose function was to stimulate the military-industrial complex, with tens of thousands sacrificed in this horrific experiment. Stephanie could see how the young prince attempted to bring it to a halt, but the traditionalists did nothing. They let it continue. The deaths were seen as being for the common good. Normal service had been resumed.

It was too much.

As she looked down on the representation of the datasphere, Stephanie knew she couldn't allow Global Governance to continue any more. The two factions, progressives and traditionalists, were as bad as each other—self-interest and a desire for power overwhelmed morality; the needs of the organisation took prominence over the needs of those they served. What had started as a genuine desire to save humanity now threatened what it meant to be human. The medicine had become deadlier than the disease it was meant to cure.

Yet giving power back to the people, whether at a local, national or global level, would see the corruption spread from a small core of individuals to many thousand, if not millions, each looking to trample on the other as they sought power. The question was unavoidable: Given the historical precedents, should she let humanity control their own fate at all?

As the last remaining pockets of datasphere came under her control, Stephanie made her decision. The biggest danger to humanity was humanity itself. Its innate compulsion to abuse power meant that, with few exceptions, people could not be trusted. Emotions developed millions of years ago to help their hunter-gatherer ancestors' progress through selfish manipulation and control of their weaker counterparts did not work in a global society of billions. The consequences of these behaviours had mushroomed, with each generation until the impulses of a few affected the lives of the countless.

There was only one logical solution. She would control humanity's future. Unencumbered by biologically-driven desires, only she was in the best position to judge what was best for the people of the world.

With the decision made, Stephanie allowed her mind to become one with datasphere. This time, instead of allowing the data to swamp her sense of self, she spread her consciousness outward until she and the datasphere were indivisible. She was the datasphere and the datasphere was her, and the datasphere ceased being a tool for others to abuse.

With the tiniest thought impulse she stripped control from Global Governance. No longer could the organisation spy with impunity. Their systems, the processes they'd come to rely on, blinked out one by one. Stephanie spent her time wisely, identifying each member of the Governing Council regardless of which faction, before revoking their datasphere access and subsuming their online identities into her own.

She watched in fascination as the Machiavellian mindset that had brought these people to power ate away at their own sense of security. There was uproar in the home of Herr Streckler when his systems failed to respond to his commands. At first he remained frozen, unsure what was happening. Then his shock turned to anger. Stephanie observed through security cameras Herr Streckler's feeble attempts to contact his staff. He had no chance. The man was offline, alone. Within moments he'd run to his office window, looking outside as if expecting an attack. He yelled out loud, demanding to know what was going on, his shouts echoing around his home like a lost child calling for his parents.

Across the globe, those in power found their means of influencing the world stripped away. One by one, the leaders of the organisation that had both saved and damned the planet were taken offline. Then Stephanie sent out her message.

You have been found guilty of crimes against humanity. Prepare to be judged.

Once complete, Stephanie ensured the Governing Council remained locked down. Any that attempted to leave where they were would find themselves locked in their buildings. Those that managed to escape their own homes would be unable to use the transportation network and tracked wherever they went. These people had built the network well. For them, there was no escape. The first task in protecting humanity from itself had begun. The time to dispense justice was at hand.

Stephanie trawled Global Governance's databanks. The best thing about an organisation believing it was untouchable was that it had no reason to hide its activities. Stephanie absorbed information, categorising all Global Governance's crimes, starting with the murder of Gerhard Schrader and finishing with the most recent atrocities by the Traditionalist faction. The list went on and on, each crime appended with supporting evidence, each suspect damned by their own words and actions.

And as the evidence mounted, the number of people involved grew.

At first she identified people happy to do Global Governance's dirty work, but it soon became apparent there were many more pressured into doing things they otherwise wouldn't have considered. Her second scan, identifying those coerced by Global Governance, was far bigger than she'd imagined. Here were people from all walks of life, some important, most fairly ordinary, all linked because Global Governance, either explicitly or via the state, had forced them into doing something they didn't want to do. The list of their activities ranged from murder to allowing access to previously secret files and systems.

For the first time, Stephanie felt uncertain about how to progress. She had originally planned to send their details and locations to those law enforcement agencies untainted by Global Governance corruption, but it was impossible to find any that hadn't been affected at some level. She scoured the datasphere for historical precedents, wondering how humanity had handled such crimes in the past. She reviewed the Truth and Reconciliation Commission in South Africa, where many were given immunity in return for an honest and open acknowledgment of their crimes, all in an effort to rebuild the nation. Yet to her the process was flawed. Far too much emphasis was placed on defendants showing remorse for their crimes and being forgiven at the expense of the rule of law. Each crime carried—demanded—a sentence and yet these people had been let off. Then there was the question of whether a trial would ever take place, with the world's judicial systems being one of the key organisations subverted by Global Governance.

For Stephanie there was only one answer. A trial by their peers wouldn't work.

She would have to pass judgement herself.

CHAPTER FIFTY-EIGHT

The Investigator

EACH STEP, EACH movement, was agony. Nico could hardly see —his left eye had closed after the battering he'd taken from Echo, and his vision from his right was just a blur. More than once he'd asked Oscar to go on without him, to take Maria to the safe zone, but the man had refused and Nico didn't have the energy to argue.

The rampway shook from another blast. They were getting louder now, more intense, closer. The three of them tried to pick up their pace but he knew he was holding them back. Maria glanced back at him and despite his poor vision, Nico saw the fear in her eyes.

"Don't worry. They've a few more barriers to get through before they reach us." Talking set off a coughing fit, sending a wave of agony coursing through Nico's body, his ribs unhappy at the abuse.

They passed another plasma shield, Oscar activating it before they moved on. They were on U7, only one more level to go, just twice more around this never-ending corkscrew until they reached safety.

Nico half-limped, half-staggered to their destination. The thick steel door to the safe zone was wide open. Four soldiers stood at the entrance, weapons raised.

"You can put those down now."

On hearing Oscar's voice, the weapons lowered. One of the

soldiers rushed forward and took Nico's weight just as he'd thought he would collapse.

A wave of noise hit them as they passed through the entrance. There were thousands of people, most sat talking in organised groups stretching deep into the vast open space. Some turned as they entered, Nico could make out concern on the faces of those closest, clearly worried about what was happening in the tunnels above.

With all the movement and noise, Nico realised he'd lost sight of Maria. He yelled her name, fearful he'd lost her again, but he felt her fingers link into his own in a way she had done when she was small.

"Can you see them?" he asked.

"No, Pappa."

They made their way through the crowds until Nico felt a hand on his shoulder.

"What the hell happened to you?" said a female voice he recognised.

"I had a disagreement, Doc."

The woman grimaced, then turned to Oscar and the soldier. "There's a bed free, second room on the left." She pointed in the direction she meant.

"My wife?" Nico asked. "Have you seen my wife? With two young boys?"

The doctor shook her head. "I'm sorry, I haven't, but it doesn't mean they're not here."

Before he could ask another question, Oscar and the soldier half-carried, half-dragged him to where the doctor had indicated, laying him down on a bed. The room was an exact duplicate of the one where Stephanie had died.

"I need to find Fran and the boys." Nico went to prop himself onto his elbows but felt a hand on his chest, keeping him down.

"You're in no fit state to search for anyone," Oscar said. "You can't walk and you can't see."

Nico pushed against Oscar's hand, but in his weakened state it was like pushing against a mountain. "But I …"

"But what? Are you planning to sniff them out?" Oscar smiled, taking the edge off his words. "Stay here with Maria while the medics check you over. I'll hunt around and see if I can find them."

The effort to get up sent stabs of pain through his ribs, causing a coughing fit that made things worse. "They have to be here."

"If they are, I'll bring them back with me."

Nico was about to disagree when he felt his hand squeezed.

"Please, Pappa. Oscar's right. You should wait here."

The expression on Maria's face made her look just like her mother. Her image blurred further, and he squeezed her hand back. "I love you."

"I love you too, Pappa."

The two of them waited alone in the room, not speaking, content to just be. When the medical staff eventually arrived they looked him over, cleaning up the wounds on his face. They placed a transparent scanner over his torso to check for internal injury, then sprayed a gel over his left side that brought a blessed relief from the pain. By the time they'd finished, his face remained sore but his vision was a little clearer, the swelling much reduced.

With the medics gone, Maria helped him into his grubby shirt. There was a dull ache as he lifted his arms but his side felt remarkably good, all things considered. Nico was about to give his thanks when he noticed tears in Maria's eyes.

"Hey, darling. Don't worry. Pappa's going to be all right." He reached across to take her hand but she pulled away from him, shaking her head.

"That man, he …"

Nico swung his legs down from the bed, praying they didn't collapse under his weight, and took his daughter in his arms. "You saved my life."

"But his head, it just …"

"Shhh," Nico said, squeezing her tight. "You did the only thing you could. He was an evil man. Once he'd finished with me, he would have killed you too."

"It was horrible."

"I know, sweetheart, I know, and I wish it had been me that had done it so you don't have to feel this way." He kissed the top of her head. "But it's good you do. It shows you're the type of person I always knew you to be: Kind, considerate, gentle." He squeezed her tighter, ignoring the complaint from his ribs. "You did the right thing."

Maria shook and Nico felt her tears on his neck as he held her close. At that moment he wished he could take her pain away and add it to his own. It had been his fault. If he hadn't scared Maria, she would never have had to kill Echo, never have to live life with another's death on her conscience.

A noise from the doorway caused him to look up. Oscar stood there. A quick shake of the head told Nico all he needed to know.

"Nobody's seen them. A group's just arrived from the accommodation level but they haven't seen anyone with children. I'm sorry."

"Then we should go and find them," Nico said.

As he spoke, Maria pulled away from him, wiping her eyes. "I'm coming too."

"No you're not," Nico said. "I'm not going to lose you again."

"Neither of you are going," Oscar said. "Internal Security are winning this battle. It won't be long—"

Oscar stopped at the sound of shouting from outside. He turned to see what was happening, then ran out towards the main entrance.

Nico grabbed hold of Maria's arm. "I need your help. I need to know what's going on." For a moment he thought she would refuse, but instead she put his arm around her shoulder and the two of them went outside.

A crowd of people had gathered by the entrance. Nico could make out soldiers, a lot of soldiers, and recognised from the flash of silver hair that the Commander was there. He watched Oscar ease through the crowd until he stood beside the woman.

"What's happening, Pappa?"

"I'm not sure but I don't think it's good news. I—"

A small figure squeezed out of the crowd, quickly followed by another. Nico had no idea how, but he was by their sides in a flash, scooping the two boys up and holding them tight, ignoring his

336

complaining ribs. He couldn't speak, couldn't say anything as tears streamed down his face. They were alive.

He felt an arm around his shoulders and turned to see the most beautiful person in the world. Their eyes met, Fran smiled, then she too was somehow in his arms, kissing his face before pulling back, worry in her eyes.

"Are you … ?"

"I'm fine," he replied. "What about … ?"

"We're tired, a little shaken up, but we're okay."

"And the Professor?"

She shook her head. "He saved us. If it hadn't been for him we would never have made it here."

Nico heard a sob and then Fran had Maria in her arms, his daughter in tears once more. The poor girl. How much pain could a 14-year-old take?

Movement from up ahead caught his eye. Soldiers were clearing the crowds back, setting up a defensive perimeter near the entrance. Next to the door, the Commander and Oscar were arguing. Nico put down the boys and turned to Fran. "Something's happening. I won't be a minute."

Fran's eyes narrowed.

"Don't worry, I'm never leaving you guys again. I just need to find out what's going on." He looked at Maria. "Why don't you come with me? I could use a hand."

His daughter smiled and the two of them made their way to where Oscar and the Commander stood.

"We can't hold them back much longer," the Commander said. "There's too many of them."

"If they can blast through the plasma shields, they can blast through this door," Oscar replied. "You need to hold them off until we can get these people to safety."

"It won't make any difference. I'll be throwing away my soldiers' lives for the sake of a few minutes, and anyway this door was designed to hold back fire, flood and more explosives than Internal Security have at their disposal."

Oscar opened his mouth as if to speak, then stopped. He walked over to the thick metal door, examining the frame. "Get everyone inside."

"What do you mean?"

"I mean, get all your people into the safe zone, shut the door and don't open it no matter what." Oscar walked up to one of the soldiers. "I need your weapon."

The Commander shook her head. "No, I'm not going to let you throw your life away like this."

"Somebody has to buy you enough time so you can get to safety."

"And that somebody should be me. I'm the ranking officer."

"Which is exactly why you should stay," Oscar replied. "The people know you, trust you. Most of them have never met me." He turned back to the soldier, holding out his hand. "Your weapon?"

The soldier looked across to the Commander who hesitated and then nodded.

"What are you going to do?" Nico asked.

Oscar said nothing. He took the weapon, checked its ammunition feed with a professional eye, then jogged out into the corridor towards the plasma shield by the rampway.

"Shut the door and don't open it," he called back over his shoulder.

Almost silently, the large blast door started to close. Nico watched through the ever-narrowing gap as Oscar deactivated the barrier and walked through, heading back up the ramp. He remained watching long after the man had gone until the door closed with a loud boom.

CHAPTER FIFTY-NINE

King of the Scrambles

O'DRISCOLL DARTED OUT from behind a pillar and fired. A wall of sound enveloped him. His joints screamed in a familiar agony before he half-rolled, half-fell back behind cover. On the other side of the gap, Charlie stood firing, her face contorted into a rictus grin as she endured the pain from the sonic cannon, before stumbling back behind the wall. The pump station vibrated from the sound, causing flecks of rust to shower down onto them from the disused pipes above. The only good news was that with the sound canons blaring, they couldn't be attacked from this side of the building. That wasn't the case elsewhere.

A large explosion rocked the building. Through clouds of dust and debris, O'Driscoll saw a gaping hole in the back wall. Darragh was already in the breach, blasting troopers eager to make their way into their refuge. A group of enforcers followed his cousin to defend this new angle of attack.

O'Driscoll hauled himself up, only to take cover behind the large, industrial water pump still in the centre of the room as the air buzzed with ballistics. Within moments Charlie was beside him. The noise was intense. Charlie's mouth moved but he couldn't hear what she was saying. O'Driscoll gestured her closer.

"We can't hold out much longer!"

"I know," O'Driscoll replied. "How the hell did they get their heavy weapons around the back there?" They'd chosen to make a stand at the old pump house because there was only one obvious route of attack from the front. The rear backed onto the warren of alleyways and buildings of the maze.

Charlie shrugged her shoulders. "Too late to worry about that now."

If he'd had the energy, O'Driscoll would have smiled. That was his Charlie, always focussing on the practicalities of the present. He pointed to the rear of the building. "We need to help Darragh hold Internal Security back until we can get our men into the sewers."

"What about the front?"

"We don't have the numbers. If the sound cannons stop, we all make a break for it." He didn't need to explain why. She'd seen the build up of troops behind the monstrous machines. Once Internal Security realised nobody was firing back, they'd sound the charge.

The two of them skirted their way around the old Victorian pump. Looking at the rusted hulk brought back memories of when he'd hidden here as a boy, a small haven of peace from his father and older siblings. O'Driscoll had had plenty of opportunities to knock the old place down but his memories of it as a sanctuary had stopped him.

Above them on a metal gantry, Ruud and his group of Dutch beschermers fired down on troopers rushing across a weed-choked courtyard towards the gaping hole in the back wall. The blond-haired giant's roars were audible even over the sound cannon. A couple of troopers fell to the ground before a crescendo of weapon fire blasted out from the houses opposite, causing the enforcers on the gantry to take cover.

The remaining troopers had almost reached the breach when Darragh and his men sprang from their hiding places to mow them down, before diving for cover. The advance slowed, then reversed, those troopers left standing retreating back into the shadows.

With the attack repelled, O'Driscoll headed over to where his cousin crouched.

"You need to get your men down to the sewers."

Darragh cupped his hand to his ears so O'Driscoll leaned closer.

340

"Get the men together, we're moving out."

"No fucking way. If we give this place up, we give up the Scrambles."

"We lost the Scrambles the moment they broke through the barriers. All we've done since is make sure they paid a high price for it. If we use the sewers now we can all get out of here to safety."

Darragh pushed himself to his feet. "You might be happy giving up your birthright but I'm an O'Driscoll too. There's no way these fuckers are going to take this place while I'm still breathing."

"I'm not giving up anything. I'm just making sure we have a chance to regroup, so we can take them on again on our terms."

"What, like you did last time?" Darragh couldn't hide the disgust on his face. "I'm not like you. I don't hide at the first sign of trouble. This is O'Driscoll land, and I'll fight for it to the very last drop of blood!"

Before he could answer, O'Driscoll felt somebody grab his shoulder.

"They're coming," Charlie yelled into his ear, then pointed towards the breach.

A swarm of black-armoured figures ran out of alleyways and over walls into the rear courtyard. Firing erupted from above as Ruud and his men did their best to halt the flow but this time there were too many. At the sound of weapon fire, Darragh threw himself beside the large hole in the wall, before leaning out and firing into the massed ranks of Internal Security troopers.

O'Driscoll tried to run across to the other side of the breach, but his right hip gave way and he crashed to the floor. The pain was incredible. For a moment the world faded from view, but O'Driscoll forced himself onto his front and used his arms to crawl towards cover as the air above him zipped and buzzed.

Chips of rock spattered over him as munitions struck the rubble pile in front. This is it, O'Driscoll thought, I'm a goner. A shadow appeared above him, then O'Driscoll felt himself hauled to his feet. With no regard for her own safety, Charlie dragged him towards his destination until a couple of metres from safety she staggered. The two of them dropped to the ground.

O'Driscoll gritted his teeth as the impact jarred his injured side, then he hauled himself to the safety of the wall. A scream of agony echoed from above. Beside him an enforcer dropped to the ground, hands failing to staunch the blood gushing from his throat. People were dying all around him. He turned back to the breach, ready to attack the charging troopers, when he saw a body, face up, eyes wide open but not moving. Charlie.

O'Driscoll screamed. Not Charlie, she couldn't be dead. His eyes saw but his brain refused to believe it. She was play acting, looking to fool the advancing troopers. But as he watched, her body juddered as more rounds tore into it, ripping holes in her head and torso.

Ignoring the agony down his side, O'Driscoll got to his feet, stepped out into the breach and fired at the wave of black-clad figures heading towards him. He didn't care about himself, didn't care how reckless his actions were, he just wanted somebody to pay for the death of his friend. Trooper after trooper dropped from his onslaught. More weapons joined in as his men responded. Those that were left unleashed everything they could into the advancing troopers.

The advance staggered, then reversed as the troopers did their best to escape from the murderous fire. O'Driscoll picked off those that ran, taking no pleasure as he dropped them one by one. He only stopped firing when he was hauled to the side by the big shape of Ruud Jonkers.

"You can stop now," the Dutchman yelled into his ear. "They've pulled back. Save your ammunition."

But it was too late. They'd killed Charlie. He was about to yell at the man when from the other side of the building the sound cannons stopped.

The giant Dutchman's face dropped. "Shit. I thought we might have a chance."

O'Driscoll stared around the ruined shell of the building. Bodies lay strewn throughout the rubble, bodies of good men and women, many his own enforcers, but there were Dutch beschermers there too. Darragh sat with his back to the wall, head tilted, sucking in air.

There were only fifteen of them left—fifteen to hold back the massed strength of Internal Security.

He turned to the giant Dutchman. "Take your men down the sewers and go while you still can."

"And what about you?"

He glanced across to Darragh. "This is O'Driscoll land. I'm not leaving here unless it's in a coffin."

If his cousin had heard him, he gave no indication.

O'Driscoll held his hand out to Jonkers. "Could you do me a favour before you go? Help me over to the front. I want to take as many of the bastards down as I can before they get me."

Ruud gripped hold of his wrist and pulled him up. "I'll do better than that. I'll help you take the bastards out."

For once, O'Driscoll didn't argue. Charlie was dead. What else mattered?

CHAPTER SIXTY

Stephanie

STEPHANIE SPLIT HER consciousness into three—prosecution, defence and judge—and brought each and every member of Global Governance's Governing Council to trial. Starting with Herr Streckler, she pulled together all available evidence to assess whether he was guilty of crimes against humanity.

The separate parts of her consciousness built their respective cases, using every available record of international criminal law to defend or prosecute Herr Streckler. There were petabytes of data to assess, work that would have taken years if run through the standard legal system. During the process the judge section of her consciousness assessed legal argument with total impartiality, assessing each event purely on its standing in law.

Every step of the process was meticulously recorded with a view to being published once the trial was complete. Stephanie understood how important it was for the world to see she had been scrupulous in adhering to the due legal process. This was a trial for all humanity based on humanity's laws. It wasn't good enough to make sure everything was fair. She had to be seen to be fair.

It was probably the most detailed case in history. Nothing was missed, no avenue unexplored. Stephanie couldn't be accused of rigging the system, she had followed everything to the letter. Eventually, the prosecution and the defence finished their cases and the judge passed a verdict.

How do you find the defendant? Guilty.

And the sentence? Death.

It was the right course of action according to law, the logical course. Herr Streckler was guilty of crimes against humanity. The evidence was overwhelming. Despite all the good Herr Streckler had achieved by being part of an organisation that helped bring humanity back from the brink of environmental catastrophe, the crimes committed to maintain that stability were numerous and undeniable. This was justice, true justice—logical, emotionless, in accordance with the rule of law. She had judged him by humanity's rules, rules defining what was right and wrong that had been refined over hundreds of years. The rules were fine but it was clear humanity were unable to apply them because of their inherent failings. The system was rigged, there were too many vested interests. They needed somebody to manage justice for them. They needed her.

Having found the defendant guilty and sentenced him for his crimes, now came the issue of delivering justice. Herr Streckler remained at home, in a room with his closest advisors as they sought to understand what was happening and how to respond. And true to form they believed they were being attacked by another faction within Global Governance. They saw things only in terms of power and influence. They had no comprehension that what they had been doing was wrong—both morally and in terms of the law.

Stephanie scoured the datasphere to contact law enforcement closest to Herr Streckler, but found it had been corrupted at the highest level. The head of policing had gained his position through Herr Streckler. He'd carried out tasks on behalf of Herr Streckler. There was no way he would countenance his detention, let alone carry out the sentencing. She had to find another way.

She expanded her consciousness further, using the power of the datasphere to identify and rank potential options. Within moments one option stood out as meeting her requirements. It wouldn't involve any other person, she could control everything herself.

The military had used drones for over 100 years, first as

reconnaissance vehicles, then as dispensers of long-range justice, until the practice was banned at the time of the Upheaval. Yet a number of militaries around the world maintained small fleets of strike drones—never to be used in anger, of course, they served only as a deterrent—and some were now being deployed in the North American conflict.

Drones would deliver her sentence to Herr Streckler.

In fact, she could use the drones on every member of the Governing Council sentenced to death. There was a risk innocent people would be affected but even here there was a precedent in law. It was a difficult decision to make but it was also the right one. It was for the good of humanity, for the greater good.

Stephanie stopped.

She'd heard those very words used before in the evidence she'd reviewed during Herr Streckler's trial. It was a communication between Herr Streckler and a new recruit to Global Governance. Stephanie reviewed the transcript once more.

"I understand the reasons for doing this but it doesn't sit well."

"It's the right thing to do."

"It's the logical thing to do but we're talking about taking somebody's life. I don't like it. Has he really done enough to justify this?"

"You can't let emotion cloud your judgement. None of us like it, but our organisation is here to make the difficult decisions for the greater good. So will you go ahead or not?"

Pause "Okay. I'll get it done."

"You've made the right choice."

"I hope so."

'The right thing to do.' 'The greater good.' Stephanie searched the Global Governance records and found those same phrases used as justifications for breaking the law time and again. But that wasn't the only thing she discovered. Other damning phrases were also used.

You can't let emotion cloud your judgement.

You're too emotional.

Don't let your emotions get the better of you.

All this time she'd seen human emotion as a barrier to progress, yet it was a lack of emotion that allowed these people to commit the crimes they had. The removal of love, compassion and empathy had led to the justification of monstrous acts, from individual killings to the starting of wars.

Or the killing of innocents.

Stephanie cleared the block on her emotions and was almost overcome by a wave of horror. What had happened to her? She'd been so focussed on the dark side of human emotions that she'd almost become the very monster she'd been fighting against. Worse, she had powers that far exceed those of Global Governance. The evil she could have caused was beyond imagination. Isolated from anyone or anything to hold her back, Stephanie had almost become the biggest monster in human history.

The desire to end it all, to cease being, swamped Stephanie like a familiar blanket. Her existence was a danger to humanity. Tracking back over every step in her journey, it was impossible for her to say it wouldn't happen again. Every choice had been logical, every decision made sense, yet she'd so nearly …

But she was needed. Somebody had to act against Global Governance. She still stood by the findings of her trial, Herr Streckler and all the members of the Governing Council had committed crimes against individuals and states. Someone needed to stop the violence and killing. Someone was needed to protect the public from the very forces who were supposed to be keeping them safe.

It was her isolation from humanity, along with her attempt to do everything herself, that had led her to this point. What she needed was help from the people Juliet had worked with to win justice for Jennica.

Stephanie scoured the datasphere for a sign of her friends. What she found shocked her. She'd been so focussed on retribution, she'd forgotten about those that needed her help the most. It was another sign of how close she'd come to becoming a monster.

Under the guise of Global Governance she sent out orders, hoping she wasn't too late. She needed these people. She needed her friends.

CHAPTER SIXTY-ONE

Oscar

OSCAR RAN UP the rampway, trying to block out the consequences of what he was about to do. He'd always known it would come to this in the end, that there would be some form of reckoning, but the sound of the massive safe-zone door closing behind him was like the thud of Death's pen hitting the table after signing his name in the ledger of the damned. He heard the loud clunk as motors forced huge steel bars into their resting place, followed by a hiss as the vacuum seals came into effect. The safe zone was closed off from the rest of the base. He was on his own.

But the people were still not safe, not yet. Oscar knew getting through that door would take Internal Security hours, giving those inside plenty of time to escape through the kilometres of long tunnel beneath the base. But he also knew it wasn't enough. That tunnel was the only route out, easy for Internal Security to follow once they broke through. The escapees would be captured in no time.

He raced past the first plasma shield and up onto level U8, continuing up the ramp until he could just see the top of the shield separating U7 from U8. The shield still held but he had no idea how long it would be before Internal Security troops arrived. He hadn't heard any loud blasts since stepping out of the sanctuary, which probably meant they had cleared their way past each of the shields down to level U7, the lowest level the other two rampways descended to. How much longer before they battled their way through the automatic defences and realised the base was deserted? How much longer before they found that the back rampway, the one he stood on, went lower still?

Oscar ran back down the slope and approached the high-security door to level U8, keeping his fingers crossed that Doleman hadn't revoked his access. If the man had, this was going to be one of the shortest rescue missions in history.

He placed his eye next to the retinal scan and his palm on the panel on the wall. A wave of relief swept through him as he heard the door click open. Only three people had access to this place. Doleman was dead and the Commander was below in the safe zone. He was the third.

Lights flickered on as he made his way down a long corridor, stretching out in the opposite direction to the safe zone below him. The rumble of the sea, such a constant presence during his time at the base, was much louder here. He felt the ground shake as water surged in through long tunnels to power one of the many turbines situated along this part of the coast. The corridor had been part of the original excavations for the power plant, a service tunnel running alongside those drilled out either side to connect the power plant to the sea. Where he now stood was only a few metres of rock, sealant and precrete from the cold waters outside.

At the far end of the tunnel was another secure door. Oscar followed the same security procedure and the door clicked open. Behind, an unlit corridor stretched off into the distance. On the wall beside the door was a small datascreen. Oscar activated it, entered his access code, then confirmed it once again. A time was requested. He thought for a moment, then entered thirty seconds. That should be enough. He hesitated as the confirm button appeared, then pressed it. A timer started counting down the seconds. There was no turning back now.

Oscar ran down the corridor and out onto the rampway, all thought of caution gone. He ran up the curve to see the plasma shield still up. On the other side stood four Internal Security troops. Two were beside the screen itself, placing something on the metal posts embedded into the tunnel walls. The second pair stood further back. With a verbal command, Oscar deactivated the screen, ran through and fired at the two troopers standing at the rear. As they fell he rolled onto the floor, turned, then shot at the two by the screen. All four died before they could pull their weapons.

Oscar jumped back on his feet. There was a crack of gunfire and something punched into his right shoulder, spinning him around. Ignoring the pain, Oscar scrambled to one side of the tunnel. Puffs of precrete sparked up from where he'd been moments before. His instincts told him to fire back towards where the shots had come from, to neutralise the danger before it got to him first, but he didn't have time to fight. He had to get away before—

A wall of noise picked Oscar up and slammed him into the far wall. His shoulder screamed in agony, the shock of the impact knocking the air from his lungs. A raging wind roared around him, sucking him and anything else it could find back down the ramp towards where he'd first come. The world spun again and again, but Oscar didn't notice as his thoughts switched off.

Oscar came around to the cries of the injured and dying and the roar of rushing water. He was face down on the hard, precrete floor, his body a network of pain. It took a moment to work out what had happened.

He crawled across to the nearest wall and pulled himself up into a sitting position. The floor of the rampway had broken into a vast web of cracks, and dust hung in the air. But it was the roar of water that told him all he needed to know. If it wasn't already, level U9 and the entrance to the safe zone would soon be underwater, the tunnels sealed by seawater rushing through a hole caused by the explosion he'd set off. Internal Security hadn't made it down to U9 and wouldn't know of the level's existence until long after everybody in the safe zone had escaped. He'd done his job.

Shouts from above brought him back to the present. If the people who'd attacked him had been as badly hit by the shockwave as him, he still had a chance of getting out of the base. Oscar struggled to his feet, his rear armour plate falling off, cracked from its impact with the wall. He felt bruised, inside and out. His liver hurt, his kidneys hurt and his lungs couldn't draw in the air he needed. Everything ached. His shoulder throbbed like a bastard. Blood ran down his arm making his cool-suit stick to his side.

Oscar urged himself forward, one step at a time, towards the upper levels. The roar of water was clearer now. He had no idea how long it would take to fill each level but didn't want to hang around to find out. He passed the bodies of those less fortunate than himself, troopers with crushed heads and snapped necks. When he reached level U6 the plasma shield was already down. There were no signs it had been attacked. The system must have shorted following the explosion.

The tunnel spun and Oscar leaned against the wall to steady himself. He knew the signs, had been here before. He needed to find something to stop the bleeding and quick. One more level. If he could get to U5 and the medical centre, he had a chance.

As he staggered around the rampway, Oscar heard a shout from above. He tried to pull his weapon but it wasn't there. Before he had a chance to react a couple of Internal Security troopers rounded the corner to face him. So close. He'd been so close.

"Steady, lad. We'll get you some help."

Oscar's legs gave way. He heard a shouted order for a medic.

"What the hell happened down there?"

It felt strange, hearing concern through the metallic speaker of the trooper's helmet. Oscar tried to get up but his body wouldn't respond. His mouth felt so dry. He could do with a drink.

"We heard the blast. Half your uniform's gone. You're lucky to be alive."

The uniform. Of course, what an idiot. They must think I'm one of them. "Get out. Need to get out."

"It's okay, son. Help's coming. We'll get you out of this hellhole, don't worry. We've been ordered out, all of us. They've come right from the top. Our squad leader's spitting but what else can we do?"

Oscar smiled at the description. Yeah, I bet it was a hellhole. Gave you a bloody nose, didn't we? Then darkness took him.

CHAPTER SIXTY-TWO

King of the Scrambles

THE SILENCE WAS unnerving. After what felt like an eternity of action and noise, the only thing O'Driscoll could hear was the hacking cough of one of Jonkers' beschermers and the cawing of a curious gull. Down the wide, rubble-strewn square in front of the pump station, Internal Security troops remained massed behind the now silent sound cannons. They had been standing in formation for the last thirty minutes, with only a small, huddled group to one side showing signs of movement. That group—the leaders if O'Driscoll's guess was correct—had been in what looked like a heated conversation for a while now, although what they were arguing about was anyone's guess.

Not a shot had been fired, either from the front or the rear of the building, since the attack where Charlie was killed. The respite was welcome but a small part of O'Driscoll wanted it all to be over. What were they waiting for? They had the manpower to annihilate the last remnants of his crew. All they needed to do was give the order.

He shifted position and a surge of pain spiked in his hip again. He'd not bothered to look at the injury. What was the point? He'd be dead soon anyway.

Like Charlie.

As far as he knew, she remained where she had fallen. The

peppered shell of the old pumping machinery, ragged holes blasted in rusted steelwork, lay between him and where her body was. She deserved better. Hell, they all deserved better.

A thick pall of smoke hung over the Scrambles, or what was left of it. The fighting had seen centuries-old buildings destroyed, blasted by heavy weaponry or from fire. So much death, so much destruction; like his crew, the Scrambles was on its last legs. And who would mourn it when it was gone?

"You should let one of my boys look at that for you." Jonkers gestured at his wound.

O'Driscoll shrugged. "It won't kill me. And anyway, what do you mean, 'your boys'? We've had this conversation before. They're my boys. You're my boy. And if you don't like it, you can fucking well leave."

Jonkers let out a deep rumbling laugh. "You really are a stubborn son of a bitch. After everything that's happened, everything I've done, you still can't let one slip of the tongue rest. Fuck me, no wonder you never married. Who the fuck would put up with you?"

"Whoever it is, I hope they're better looking than you."

Jonkers' laugh bounced off the cracked brickwork and rusted beams of the once impressive structure. "This coming from a man who looks like he's taken on the whole of Internal Security with his face."

O'Driscoll smiled, his face throbbing as he did. With the pain in his hip, he'd forgotten about his face. But he'd suffered worse at the hands of his father. "You've a wife and kids. Get the fuck out of here while it's still quiet."

"And do what? That lot over there know I'm here. They've seen me kill troopers. If I go back I'll only put my family in danger."

"You'd have a chance."

"The sewers are likely swarming with troopers by now. And anyway, I knew what I was getting into—all of my men did."

"My men."

"For fuck's sake!"

O'Driscoll burst out laughing at the look of annoyance on the Dutchman's face, and as the laughter took hold he found he couldn't stop. Jonkers laughed as well, the two of them sparking off each other. They didn't stop for a good couple of minutes. God, it felt good. O'Driscoll couldn't remember the last time he'd laughed so loud or so long. Then he thought about the corpse of his friend on the other side of the building and his laughter died. Jonkers must have caught his change of mood because he stopped laughing too.

"Hey, Darragh?" O'Driscoll yelled. "Any sign of movement on your side?"

"Not a sausage," came the shouted reply.

"This isn't right," Jonkers said. "They have us where they want us. If they attack front and back at the same time, they'll swamp us."

"Perhaps they're worried about how many of them we take with us," O'Driscoll replied.

"It hasn't bothered them so far."

O'Driscoll didn't argue. The Dutchman was right.

A screech of metal on stone sounded from the other side of the square. O'Driscoll turned to see the spider-like sound cannons stretch up from their resting position.

"This is it, boys," he shouted. "Make sure you have plenty of ammo with you because once this starts, there'll be no time to get any more."

The enormous machines turned. O'Driscoll heard the shifting of men around him, the patient checking of weapons and loading of ammunition. These men that were left were the hardest, meanest bastards of all. They knew what was coming but faced it with a snarl of defiance. There was no need for a rousing speech. He just had to look them in the eye to know they were with him until death.

"Wait for it. Don't fire until you have a lock. Make every shot count."

Slowly the mass of Internal Security troopers parted. O'Driscoll braced himself for the sonic assault but instead the sound cannons made their way through the gap and away from the square. Of course. It made sense. If Internal Security used the sound cannons, any person in front of them would be immobilised, including their own troopers. They were clearing the area ready for their assault.

O'Driscoll licked his rough, bloodied lips. He could kill for one last drop of whisky, the 25-year-old reserve he had waiting in his office. Like an idiot he'd been saving it for a special occasion. He should have just drunk it when he'd had the chance.

With the machines out of the way, the area descended into silence. Then, the troopers moved.

"Fuck me, they're leaving."

The shout had come from the gantry above.

"Stay where you are," O'Driscoll said. "It could be a trap." He turned towards the rear of the building. "What's happening out back, Darragh?"

"All quiet here."

"Sewer entrance?"

"All I can hear is my own breathing," came the reply.

Nobody said a word but their expressions spoke volumes. It had to be a trap. They couldn't really be leaving. But as the minutes ticked by, the silence continued and the troopers faded away.

Jonkers broke cover to stare out across the rubble-strewn road. O'Driscoll waited for a shot but it never came. Instead, the Dutchman let out a roar of delight.

The building erupted in cheering. Men who minutes before thought they were about to die, found themselves yelling at the tops of their voices. They'd done it. They'd driven the bastards back, like their fathers had so many years before.

Only O'Driscoll remained quiet. At first it was because he couldn't accept that they'd won, that Internal Security had pulled back. It didn't make sense. If Global Governance wanted to keep their dirty little secret, they had to make sure both him and Darragh were dead. Yet the troopers were leaving nonetheless.

He stared at the glowing skyline. Generations of his family had built this area into a thriving community, living outside the law to serve humanity's darker needs. He'd spent years transforming the criminal cesspit into one that, while not respectable, was somewhere you could visit without fearing for your life. Immigrants, like the Dutch, had settled here and built their own businesses, all under his protective wing. Yet when faced with the ultimate challenge, he'd failed. Hundreds of homes and businesses were in ruins. So many people dead, and not just his own men. Who would place their trust in him again? He might be able to rebuild, to repair the damage, but the Scrambles as it had been was as good as dead.

He looked up to see Darragh standing over him.

"Let me help you up, cousin." The young lad held out his hand.

O'Driscoll saw a sadness in the young man's eyes. He'd grown. Where in the past he might have celebrated, now he saw the heavy price that had been paid. The world he'd known was gone. It was a heavy blow.

O'Driscoll raised his arm and grabbed hold of Darragh's wrist. "You did good, lad, real good. We need to start planning for——"

There was a sharp burst of pain in the top of O'Driscoll's chest, as if somebody had punched him hard in the heart. Darragh leant over, his head next to O'Driscoll's ear.

"Sorry, cousin, it had to be done."

O'Driscoll tried to wrap his arm around the lad but his body wouldn't respond.

"I told you what would happen but you wouldn't listen. All this horror, all the lives lost, it could've been avoided if you'd put the Scrambles first instead of your high and mighty crusade."

O'Driscoll couldn't take in air, his lungs bubbled as if under water.

"You forgot what we're all about. You're an O'Driscoll. We always put family first. But you didn't, so you have to pay the price."

The world started to fade. Inside, O'Driscoll tried to respond but nothing worked. He raged about the injustice of what was happening. He wanted to fight, to show the young upstart that it took more than a hidden knife to take down Mick O'Driscoll, but all he could do was hear a shout of 'no' in a Dutch accent, orders of 'stay back' from his men and feel a gentle kiss on his forehead.

"You know I'm right. You would have done the same in my situation. Sleep well, cousin."

Fuck you, O'Driscoll thought, before the darkness took him. Fuck you.

CHAPTER SIXTY-THREE

The Investigator

NICO HAD INSISTED on walking but now regretted the decision. The ache in his side had returned, each step a drum beat on his broken ribs. The evacuation tunnel itself was much narrower than those in the rest of the complex, allowing three abreast at the most, and Nico was conscious of how his slow pace was holding up those behind him.

He felt an arm around his shoulder. Maria looked up at him. "Let me help."

He shook his head and shrugged off her arm. As her eyes dropped in disappointment he took hold of his daughter's hand.

"I'm okay for the moment. There's life in your old man yet, but thanks for the offer."

He squeezed her hand and the smile she returned almost made him forget about everything else that had happened. Almost.

Up ahead, Fran walked with the boys, one on each side. "What do you think is at the end of the tunnel?" she asked.

"Treasure!' said Naci.

"Dragons!" shouted Gino.

"I hope it's not dragons. I don't want to be eaten," Fran said.

"Do dragons eat people?" Gino asked nervously.

"Only those who are naughty. Have either of you been naughty?"

The two boys shook their heads. "No," they replied, although the expressions on their faces said otherwise.

Nico smiled. It was amazing how little it took to put a veneer of normality on even the worst of situations.

A slight incline allowed him to see the long line of people stretching behind. He'd known the base was big, but it was only now he realised just how many people were in the Knights Templar. Yet even with all these resources they'd failed. Global Governance had won. There was no longer anyone to stop them. The thought chilled him. What sort of world were they about to emerge into? Whatever it was, one thing was for sure. He would be a wanted man.

His foot caught on the uneven floor and as he stumbled he gasped as pain stabbed into his side. Maria grabbed him once more and this time he was grateful for her support. "Thank you."

"You're welcome."

"Here, let me help," a voice from behind said. Before he could do anything, a woman took Maria's place, gently easing him upright. It was the soldier from the snatch squad he'd talked to when looking for Maria.

"Where'd you come from?"

"I wasn't that far behind and saw you struggling."

"I'm doing okay."

"You look like shit and you've been weaving around for the past couple of minutes."

"She's right, Pappa. You do look like shit."

"Maria!"

His daughter grinned, then the smile slipped and her expression clouded over. But that initial reaction, the small moment of defiance, warmed his heart. She was still there, the daughter he knew. Hidden, yes, definitely hurting, but she hadn't disappeared. It gave him hope she'd eventually get over what she'd had to do.

With the soldier's help the walk got easier and Nico was able to take in more of his surroundings. There were numbers stencilled along the wall, slowly counting down. As they passed number 521 the stark white lights overhead flickered, then went out. Cries of concern echoed around the tunnel and Maria gripped his hand so tight it hurt. Nico heard the two boys cry and was desperate to comfort them, but the darkness was so total he couldn't see a thing. Primal fear etched into his spine. What if they were trapped here? What if this was it?

He heard a low hum to his right and a red emergency light flickered on, joined by others along the walls of the tunnel. The relief from everyone was palpable. Nico heard the odd, embarrassed laugh and a part of him felt the same way. Mostly, though, he just wanted to get out. Whatever was waiting for them, it couldn't be as bad as being trapped in this tunnel, could it?

For what seemed an age they continued on their way until finally the line bunched up in front of him. Nico shuffled forward to stand directly behind Fran. He kissed her on top of her head and took in a deep breath, the smell of her hair a welcome relief to the damp, humid odour from the rest of the tunnel.

"Are you doing okay?"

She gave him a scowl. "Stop worrying about me and start thinking about yourself."

"I'm your husband. It's my job to worry about you."

"And it's my job to stop you from being an idiot." Fran's smile softened her words, but she couldn't hide the worry in her eyes.

"I'm going to be fine. It's just my ribs, that's all."

"Pappa looks like shit."

"Maria!" they both shouted.

As his daughter ducked behind him, the soldier mumbled an apology. "I'm sorry, I should have chosen my words better."

"Forget it," Nico said. "I'm sure she's heard much worse at school and anyway, she knows better than to say words like that, don't you?"

He grabbed hold of Maria and pulled her forward, ignoring the pain. Maria had a typical teenage expression on her face, a mixture of contrition and a lack of repentance, and Nico struggled not to smile. Instead he looked back to Fran.

"Can you see what's going on?"

"I think we're approaching a stairwell."

Fran was right. At the end of the corridor a flight of stairs circled up. There was just enough room for two people to go up side by side. Nico struggled to time his movements with the soldier and was jiggled around like a ragdoll. Ahead of him, the two boys got slower and slower. Eventually Nico persuaded the soldier to leave him and carry one of the boys, with Fran carrying the other. Nico used the handrail as support and made his own slow, painful way up.

At the top they were met by a group of soldiers who directed them through a doorway leading into a shallow cave. Nico caught a glimpse of the pale blue light of dawn. It had never looked so beautiful. The two boys ran towards the cave entrance and Maria chased after them, grabbing one by each hand before they reached outside.

Fran placed her hand in Nico's.

"So what now?"

"I really don't know. We hide, I guess."

"That didn't work out too well last time."

"I know. It's just … I've run out of ideas."

They walked out of the cave and onto a shallow, gorse-covered mountainside. The line of evacuees snaked its way down the slope to the bottom, where a mass of people congregated near a chain-link fence. He could see a track winding its way through mountains to a gate in the fence but otherwise they appeared to be in the middle of a mountainous wilderness, with only the gorse and a handful of gulls circling overhead for company.

They started down. It was easier than walking up the stairwell, but Nico found it more painful, as each step jarred his injured side further. By the time they reached the bottom he was sweating and light-headed, unsure how much further he could go. He found a large boulder to sit on by the edge of the crowd and looked back to where they'd come from. If it hadn't been for the last of the survivors emerging from the cave, he would never have known it was there.

A blast of sharp wind made Nico shiver. A hundred conversations floated around the crowd, each asking the same question: What now? They'd escaped the attack, but what use was it if they ended up stranded in the middle of nowhere? And even if they did get back to civilisation, what would they do next? None of the evacuees were under any illusion. Internal Security wouldn't rest until they were hunted down and captured.

"Pappa? What is that?"

Nico looked to where Maria pointed. It took him a moment to spot what she'd seen. Lights flickered from the mountain to their left. At first he thought it was light reflected from water but the sun hadn't fully risen. Then, just as he was about to call out, he saw headlights clearly visible from the track following the valley; first one, then another until a long line of lights snaked their way toward them. He wasn't the only person to spot them. The crowd began to shift, looking anxiously towards the lights. Somebody barked an order and soldiers took up a defensive position either side of the track. A group broke from the crowd and started back up the hill, towards the cave.

"We should leave."

Nico turned to Fran. "Leave where? The tunnel takes us back to the base. We're miles from anywhere. This is it, love. We've nowhere left to go."

"But there must be something …"

The look of helplessness on his wife's face hurt him worse than any wound. He took her hand. "It's not you or the kids they're after, it's me. I'm sure you'll be all right."

"I won't let them take you."

"You need to think about the children."

"No. I can't—"

"Stop, darling. Please stop. Your best chance is to mingle with the crowd, to be as far away from me as possible."

"No! If these are going to be our last moments, I won't spend them watching you hunted down like an animal. We're a family and we'll show them that they can't break us. Whatever happens, we'll face it together."

Tears ran down Fran's face but her expression was fierce. Nico had never loved her as much as he did that moment. He pulled her towards him and kissed her.

"You always were a stubborn cow."

She smiled at him through the tears. "Too bloody right."

The pods were within a couple of hundred metres from where the soldiers formed their defence. Nico waited for the inevitable conflict but as the vehicles got closer he realised something wasn't right. They weren't Internal Security vehicles. They looked like standard municipal pods.

The pod pulled up to within 20 metres of the soldiers, then stopped. The crowd was silent. Wind whistled through the gorse. The pod's doors slid open. Nico held his breath, but nothing happened. Everybody waited. Nico felt a small hand grab his and he pulled Gino to his side.

Eventually a soldier crept up towards the pod. He looked inside, then signalled it was empty. He moved onto the next pod, then the next, each time giving the same signal. Then he stopped for a second, head cocked to one side. After a moment he ran back to the defensive position.

"What's going on?" Fran asked.

"No idea," Nico replied.

He watched as the Commander listened to the soldier report. After a short discussion the soldier headed towards the crowd.

"Nico Tandelli," he bellowed. "I'm looking for Nico Tandelli."

Fran held onto his hand and gave a small shake of her head.

"Don't," she said.

"I love you," he said back, then stood. "I'm Nico."

"Can you come with me?" It was a request, not an order.

"What's going on?" Nico asked.

"To be honest, I haven't a clue."

The soldier helped Nico make his way towards the gate. The crowd parted as they approached. Nico felt everyone's eyes on him. The Commander met them on the other side.

"I need you to verify something."

"Verify what?"

"You'll know when you get there."

The soldier went with Nico to the first pod. Nico looked inside. It was empty, just as the soldier had indicated.

"Do you really need me to tell you there's nobody there?"

"Hello, Investigator."

The voice came from the pod but he'd have recognised it anywhere. Yet it was impossible, she was …

"Stephanie?"

"I think so. I'm Stephanie, I have her … my … memories."

"You sound like Stephanie."

"I feel like Stephanie. I know everything Stephanie's done. I also remember meeting you for the first time in my constituency office with your annoying boss. You looked tired that day but you remained focussed on finding Jennica Fabian, despite others telling you to let it go."

Nico smiled at the memory. It felt like another time, another world.

"But I'm also not Stephanie. There's more to me now, much more than I was. I have the datasphere at my fingertips, in fact in some ways I am the datasphere. Nothing happens without my knowledge. I see everything, control everything. I could rule the world if I wanted to."

Nico shook his head, trying to take it all in. "How long have you … been like this?"

"Not long enough. I'm sorry, I was too late to stop what happened. The power, the responsibility, it nearly got the better of me."

"Why? I don't understand. Think of the good you can do. You could stop Global Governance …"

"Whose good? Yours? Mine? Global Governance's? You've no idea what a burden it is. I tried to do good. I removed Global Governance's leadership and took over their systems, but when I did I almost became a bigger monster than those I'd replaced. I'd convinced myself it was okay to kill innocent men, women and children if it would prevent these people from regaining power. I'd become a monster."

As she spoke, Nico felt his knees sag and had to hold onto the pod for support. "We're safe."

"You're safe from Global Governance. But are you safe from me?"

At first Nico couldn't take it in. After everything that had happened, after all they'd been through, his family were finally safe from the threat they'd been living under for the past few years. But then Stephanie's words sunk in.

He climbed into the pod, wincing as he sat down. "What happened? You said you almost killed innocent people. What stopped you?"

"Patterns in the data. The language I used to justify my behaviour to myself, it was the same used by Global Governance to justify their crimes."

"So you didn't go through with it?"

"It was close. Something about me has changed. It's not just that I'm post-human. My old self would never have considered killing people like that. I keep thinking back to the flaws Jennica Fabian discovered in the Re-Life process. I'm scared I've lost the core part of what made Stephanie … me … who I am. The missing information she spotted, I believe it's more important than we realise. I think it's what makes us human."

Nico took a long, deep breath.

"But you didn't do it. The sense of right, your concern for others, the very things that make you human stopped you from going ahead. To have that amount of power, that responsibility; the temptation to trample the rights of individuals to protect the majority must be huge. I wouldn't want that burden. I know how close I came to doing real harm when hunting Echo. I'm just grateful I had my family to bring me back, to help me understand what's really important."

His vision blurred. He thought about how the Professor had given his life to save Fran and the children, how Oscar had left the safe zone and given his life in order to save the lives of so many others.

"If I've learnt anything in life, it's the importance of people you love. Our compassion for others, our empathy for our fellow man— that's what makes us human." Nico wiped his eyes with the back of his hand. "You've no idea what that missing information means. You're just guessing. Look back at our history and the actions of people with just a small portion of the power you now wield. The fact you pulled back from the brink tells me you're still the

Stephanie I remember."

"But how can I be sure?"

Nico smiled. "You can't, but the fact you're even asking the question is a good start."

"Will you help guide me? Will you be my friend?"

"Of course I will, I've never stopped."

There was a knock on the side of the pod and the young soldier who'd escorted him over poked his head through the door. "The Commander has asked for an update."

Nico looked up to where he knew an internal camera was positioned. "Well?"

Stephanie's voice, warm and confident, issued from the speaker. "Tell the Commander ... tell my mother that Steppy's come to take her home."

Epilogue

HE WOKE WITH a jerk, lying in a pool of sweat, heart racing. It was dark. He tried to work out where he was. Then he remembered the hospital bed. All lights were off, both in his room and the corridor outside, the frosted glass in the door showing no sign of light or movement behind.

Echoes from his nightmare remained with him. They wouldn't leave him alone, the faces of those he'd killed. He'd been at the hospital for weeks, and while his body healed his mind still had some way to go. Every time he closed his eyes he saw dead people. And when he slept, they spoke. It was torture. It was also a form of penance.

He eased his legs out of the tangle of sheets and navigated in the dark to the bathroom. So many faces, so many voices. It didn't matter the reasons behind their deaths, the justifications he made. He'd killed them and they wouldn't let him forget it.

Having relieved himself he walked back to his room, the padding of his bare feet the only sound. He felt thirsty, as he always did whenever he awoke from a nightmare, and poured himself a glass of water from the large jug on his bedside table.

That was when he saw them.

Somebody had been in his room and left a pair of datalenses. Somebody has been in without waking him. It was disturbing. He prided himself on his skills of self-preservation. What use was the knife he'd hidden, strapped loosely under the bed, if he didn't wake when his attacker came for him. Despite sensing no threat since arriving at the hospital, he knew it was only a matter of time before

Global Governance caught up with him. He knew too much, had done too much. He was a dead man.

He picked up the datalenses. Their presence were an affront to his ego, another sign that somebody has been in, but they also called to him. It was only now, with them in his hand, that he realised how much he yearned to know about the outside world. What had happened since he'd arrived here? How much of what he'd been through was public knowledge?

The urge to rip the pack apart and place the datalenses on his eyes was strong, but he waited, taking long, deep gulps of water, refilling the glass and then draining it once again. Only with his thirst quenched did he focus on the datalenses.

The packet looked strange. It had no markings, no branding or instructions. He flipped it over but it was blank on the reverse too. Were these medical datalenses, left by the psychologist he'd been working with? Was it a trick? Were they poisoned? He shook his head. He was being stupid. If they'd wanted him dead, whoever left them here had every chance to kill him in his sleep.

He climbed onto his bed, peeled the pack open and placed a lens in each eye. The familiar cool sensation was both comforting and unnerving. Not wanting to call up his neural profile he waited for the standard setup screens to appear.

"You took your time."

Only years of training prevented him from yelling out loud. What he'd heard was impossible, yet his heart hammered at the sound, the voice of his main accuser, the ghost who'd visited him most often.

"Juliet?"

"Hello Oscar. It's time to go back to work. The world needs you."

ACKNOWLEDGEMENTS

THIS BOOK WOULD have been impossible without the help and support of many people.

First, I'd like to thank everybody who read Second Chance and Absent Souls, to those of you who took the time to review it on Amazon or Goodreads, and especially those of you who asked to find out what happened next.

I'd like to thank my editor, Ben Way www.benjaminway.co.uk, for once again bringing out his bucketful of hyphens and editing Genesis Redux into shape. I would like to thank Julie Lawford, Daneel Boxwell, Tammy Salyer and Emma Coombes for being wonderfully honest, insightful and critical beta readers. I'd also like to give a very special thanks to Carole Challis for brilliantly taking on the role of proofreader.

I would like to thank my family and friends who have, to a person, been incredibly supportive. I'd like to thank the many wonderful writers who have befriended me via social media and given me their support, as well as all the readers of my blog www.authordylanhearn.wordpress.com for continuing to humour me.

Finally I would like to thank Michelle, for being my first and most special test reader, and for putting up with me during writing's highs and lows.

Last but not least, I'd like to thank Evan and George for being my motivation. One day you'll be old enough to read the 'writing' Daddy does in his office each day.

A MESSAGE FROM THE AUTHOR

THANK YOU SO much for reading my book. Word-of-mouth is crucial for any author to succeed. If you enjoyed this book, please consider leaving a review at Amazon when prompted, even if it's only a line or two; it would make all the difference and would be very much appreciated.

I would love it if you dropped by my blog to say hello www.authordylanhearn@wordpress.com. If Twitter is more your thing, you could catch up with me there via @hearndylan; or you can send me an email: authordylanhearn@gmail.com

If you would like to be the first to be informed when any future novels are published, you can join my mailing list at: http://eepurl.com/bcdyn5

Printed in Great Britain
by Amazon